Books by Kate Pearce

The House of Pleasure Series

SIMPLY SEXUAL

SIMPLY SINFUL

SIMPLY SHAMELESS

SIMPLY WICKED

SIMPLY INSATIABLE

SIMPLY FORBIDDEN

SIMPLY CARNAL

SIMPLY VORACIOUS

SIMPLY SCANDALOUS

Single Titles

RAW DESIRE

Anthologies

SOME LIKE IT ROUGH

LORDS OF PASSION

Published by Kensington Publishing Corporation

SIMPLY
SCANDALOUS

KATE PEARCE

APHRODISIA

KENSINGTON PUBLISHING CORP.

www.kensingtonbooks.com

APHRODISIA BOOKS are published by

Kensington Publishing Corp.
119 West 40th Street
New York, NY 10018

All Kensington titles, imprints, and distributed lines are available at special quantity discounts for bulk purchases for sales promotion, premiums, fund-raising, educational or institutional use.

Special book excerpts or customized printings can also be created to fit specific needs. For details, write or phone the office of the Kensington Special Sales Manager: Kensington Publishing Corp., 119 West 40th Street, New York, NY 10018. Attn. Special Sales Department. Phone: 1-800-221-2647.

Aphrodisia and the A logo Reg. U.S. Pat. & TM Off.

ISBN-13: 978-0-7582-6947-8
ISBN-10: 0-7582-6947-1

First Kensington Trade Paperback Printing: January 2013
10 9 8 7 6 5 4 3 2 1

Printed in the United States of America

*Thank you to everyone who has loved
the House of Pleasure series as much as I have.
I hope you enjoy this book, and will follow me into
a new establishment called The Sinners Club next year.*

For anyone interested in the history behind Ambrose's life, I would recommend reading Gretchen Holbrook Gerzina's book *Black London.*

1

London, 1827

"Surely you are exaggerating, Emily." Richard Ross studied his sister's indignant expression. "Paul St. Clare is heir to a dukedom."

Emily raised her chin. "And Lucky is my dearest friend. Do you think she would lie to me?"

Richard put his half-empty bowl of hot chocolate down on the kitchen table. It was early in the morning and most of the staff at the pleasure house had already gone home. If one discounted Madame Durand, the cook, and Ambrose, the manager, he and Emily had the kitchen almost to themselves.

"But think of the scandal!"

Emily sniffed. "The higher the rank of the individuals involved, the less of a scandal there seems to be. Think of the Duke of Devonshire. His domestic arrangements were highly unorthodox. It is *because* Paul is heir to a duke that the *ton* will look the other way and pretend that he and Lucky have a perfectly respectable marriage." Emily put her elbows on the table and rested her chin on her hand. "In truth, their marriage is respectable. It's not as if Constantine Delinsky has moved in with them."

"He maintains lodgings on the same street, but he practically lives in their house. Everyone knows that he shares Paul St. Clare's bed. Doesn't your friend Lucky object?"

Emily grinned at him. "Are you shocked, brother of mine? I never thought you were so straitlaced. What if I told you it was far more complicated than that?"

"What do you mean?"

"Constantine shares Lucky's bed too."

Richard just stopped himself from gaping like a fool. "He beds them both?"

"They all bed each other."

Richard shook his head. "I would never have thought it of Lady Lucinda. She seemed like such a nice, quiet, well-behaved young lady."

"Unlike me, you mean."

"You are sitting in the kitchen of a notorious pleasure house at three o'clock in the morning," Richard pointed out. "That hardly helps your reputation."

Behind Richard, Ambrose cleared his throat. "Miss Ross is not allowed upstairs, Mr. Ross. Madame Helene was very insistent about that."

"More's the pity," Emily groused. "I'm practically on the shelf. Why shouldn't I have some fun?"

"Because our revered father wishes you to marry well and be happy. You know that."

Emily glanced at Ambrose, who kept his gaze fixed steadily on Richard. "And what if I refuse to marry well and marry where my heart is?"

"That is something you will have to take up with our father." Emily's face fell and Richard felt compelled to continue. "But as his own second marriage was scarcely an orthodox one, perhaps he will be more willing to listen to you than most parents."

"I doubt it. He thinks I need the stabilizing influence of a wealthy, titled man. What he doesn't understand is that most of those men view me with great suspicion because of *his* decidedly odd marriage to Helene."

"Would you like me to mention it to him?" Richard asked.

Emily smiled. "I don't want to add to the friction between you two. I've already told him how I feel, but he chooses not to believe me." She sighed. "Eventually he'll have to face the facts. I'm three and twenty. All I can hope is that I'm not too old to marry before he listens to me."

Richard reached across and took her hand. "I'm sorry, Em."

"It's not your fault. And I truly am happy that after his disastrous relationship with our mother, Father has Helene in his life."

"You don't know that."

She raised her candid gaze to his face. "That he is happy?"

"Our mother was scarcely any happier than our father, and she blamed him for that."

"You weren't there. You were away at school and then at university. Despite what Mother told you, she brought most of her unhappiness on herself."

Richard carefully released Emily's hand. "We'll never agree about that, will we? Perhaps we should talk about something else. Isn't it time you were going home?"

Ambrose got to his feet. "I'll call for your carriage and find your maid, Miss Ross."

Emily shot Ambrose a glare. "I asked you to call me Emily."

"And I've explained several times why that would be inappropriate."

Richard stared, entranced, as his sister and the manager of the pleasure house continued to glower at each other. Had he missed something very obvious? Was his sister in love with the dark-skinned ex-slave and pickpocket Christian Delornay had saved from the streets?

Ambrose bowed. "I'll fetch your maid."

Emily turned away, but not before Richard had seen the hurt in her dark brown eyes. He waited until Ambrose had most uncharacteristically slammed the kitchen door before turning to his sister.

"Is Ambrose the reason why you spend so much time here? I thought you were just avoiding your social obligations."

"What on earth does it have to do with you?"

Well used to the ways of his stubborn sibling, Richard didn't take offense at her combative tone.

"I'm your brother and I care about your happiness." He hesitated. "Have you told anyone how you feel?"

She hunched her shoulder at him. "If you mean have I told Ambrose, I have. He told me to stop behaving like a spoiled little girl and find a proper husband."

"*Ambrose* did?"

"That's what he meant, although he put it in a far more conciliatory way."

"Perhaps he had a point," Richard said quietly.

"Because he's too *different*? Because his skin is too *dark*?"

"Emily . . ."

"You are as bad as he is. I don't care about those things, so why should anyone else?"

"You are still very young and . . ."

Emily spun around to face him. "I am old enough to know what I want!"

"And what about what Ambrose wants? Is he to have no say in this?"

Emily opened her mouth to reply and then closed it again as Ambrose reentered the room with her maid.

"I'll see you to your carriage, Miss Ross," Ambrose murmured, his face a smiling mask that mirrored Emily's.

"Thank you, Ambrose. Good night, Richard."

Emily hurried out before Richard could even attempt to kiss her good-bye. He sat back down with a soft oath and stared at the kitchen door. He didn't like being at odds with Emily, but he wasn't sure how to make amends without offending her further. If she asked for his help to intercede with their father, or even with Ambrose, he would do so willingly, but he was past the age when he thought to force his opinions on anyone. He'd wait to be asked and in the meantime, keep his own counsel.

Ambrose came back into the kitchen rather slowly, his expression distracted. He directed his gaze at Richard with a visible effort.

"Is there anything else I can help you with, Mr. Ross?"

"You can start by calling me Richard."

Ambrose half smiled. "And risk the wrath of your sister? If you don't mind, I'll continue to call you Mr. Ross. She would never forgive me if I made an exception for you and not for her."

"My sister is a very determined woman."

"I know that, sir. But she is still young."

"For God's sake, don't tell her that." Richard shuddered.

Ambrose sighed. "It's too late. I already have." He picked up Emily's empty cup and took it over to the sink. "Are you staying the night, Mr. Ross?"

Aware that Ambrose had deliberately changed the subject, Richard rose to his feet. "I'll just take a stroll through the pleasure house, and then I'll probably turn in."

"Excellent, sir. I did ask one of the maids to ready your bedroom on the off chance that you would be staying."

"You are a marvel, Ambrose. Thank you."

"I am certainly a first-class servant."

Richard paused at the door. Was there a hint of bitterness in Ambrose's words? "You are far more than that. Christian sees you as more of a brother to him than I am."

Ambrose's smile was sweet. "I doubt that. Blood, after all, *is* thicker than water."

Richard wasn't so sure, but he didn't feel up to discussing the interesting family dynamics of the Delornay-Ross clan at this point of the evening. He nodded a farewell to Ambrose and started up the stairs to the main levels of the pleasure house.

There weren't many guests in the larger of the salons, and those guests were mostly naked and writhing in a tangle of bodies on the pile of scarlet silk cushions. Richard recognized a Member of Parliament, an archbishop, and a prominent social hostess energetically fucking each other while the woman's husband watched and commented from the nearest couch.

He managed to avoid gazing directly at any of them, and made his way to the buffet table where he poured himself a glass of excellent red wine. There was no sign of his half brother Christian Delornay or his delicious wife, Elizabeth. Richard knew they would be somewhere on the premises making sure everything was running smoothly. Christian was eager to prove he could manage the pleasure house his mother had founded as well, if not better, than she had.

Richard sipped at his wine and sighed. At least Christian *had* a purpose. All Richard was supposed to do was wait for his father to die so that he could assume his titles. It seemed a ridiculous waste of his life. Sometimes he dreaded the thought of shouldering the enormous responsibilities that went with it. He almost wished he were back in France avoiding Napoléon's soldiers and saving forgotten souls. Life seemed sweeter when all he had were his wits and strength to protect him. . . .

None of his family had any idea what he'd been doing in France. His father thought he'd stayed there to avoid coming home. In the beginning, that had played a part in Richard's decision, but the real thrill had been the dangerous and deadly work he performed for the government. And that couldn't be spoken of in polite society. So his family continued to think he was a boring, brainless, *ungrateful* drone.

He drained his glass and refilled it, his attention caught by an influx of new people at the door. A young man of medium height dressed in the latest fashion was laughing up at one of his companions. Something about the joy on the man's face reminded Richard of a woman he'd once known—a woman he'd foolishly loved to distraction. . . .

He stiffened as the little group came toward him, aware that they were all speaking French and that he knew at least two of them from his previous activities on the Continent.

"Ah, Mr. Ross. Good evening to you."

Richard bowed in response to the cheerful greeting from the tall, blond-haired peer. "Good evening, Lord Keyes, gentlemen."

"Not taking advantage of the facilities, eh, Ross?" Lord Keyes nudged his arm and Richard almost tipped red wine everywhere. "No lovely ladies to tempt you tonight, or do you like to watch, eh, eh?"

Richard smiled politely and stepped away from Lord Keyes. He'd already noticed that despite his outward display of drunkenness, Lord Keyes's blue gaze was as sharp as ever. Only a fool would underestimate him.

Many had.

"Actually, my lord, I was just considering retiring."

"You're spent then, are you?"

"Indeed. Have you just arrived?"

"Aye, we've been to the theater." Lord Keyes put an arm around the shoulders of the slight, dark-haired man. "I was just introducing my young friend here to the pleasures of London."

The man stuck out his hand. "I'm Jack Lennox, Mr. Ross. It is a pleasure to meet you."

As he shook the proffered hand, Richard found himself studying the perfection of Jack Lennox's features. He looked as if he had stepped out of a painting, or a young lady's dreams. His likeness to the deceased Violet LeNy was quite extraordinary.

"Is it your first trip to London, sir?" Richard asked.

"No, Mr. Ross, I was born here; but I must confess I haven't been back since well before the war."

Richard smiled. "You will perhaps forgive me for remarking that your command of French is that of a native."

"I'm aware that it makes my claim to be English sound rather suspicious, especially since the recent conflict." Mr. Lennox's grin was meant to be disarming, but Richard wasn't quite swayed. The mere fact that Keyes had deliberately introduced Lennox to him meant something was afoot. "Perhaps the more I speak English, the more convincing I will become."

"I'm sure of it, sir. Are you planning on making your home here in England?"

"I would like to, but, naturally, there are various plans that need to be put in place before I can achieve my aim." Mr. Lennox shrugged. "I heard that you spent many years in France yourself, Mr. Ross."

"I suppose Lord Keyes told you that."

"Among others. It seems we have several acquaintances in common."

"Indeed." Richard studied Mr. Lennox. "Is that why you instigated this conversation?"

"*Instigated*, Mr. Ross?" Lennox raised his eyebrows. "You make my motives sound rather suspect. Perhaps I merely wished to exchange pleasantries with a man who spoke French as well as I do."

"You came in with Lord Keyes and Sir Adam Fisher, who both speak excellent French. Are they not up to your high standards?"

"No, I fear they are not."

Richard met the other man's vivid blue eyes. "What do you want, Mr. Lennox?"

"To talk to you?"

"We are talking." Richard glanced over his companion's shoulder and saw that the other men had moved on to other more salacious pursuits involving the hasty removal of their clothes. "Do you not wish to join your friends?"

"Only if you wish to come with me."

"I thought you wanted to talk."

"We're in a pleasure house. I assume you can talk and fornicate at the same time?"

"Not if I intend to make any sense."

Jack Lennox laughed out loud. "You are a man after my own heart, Mr. Ross. Perhaps we might just share a glass of wine together before we adjourn for the night?"

Richard studied the other man's amused expression. Despite the openness of his manner, there was something dangerous lurking at the back of Mr. Lennox's eyes, something ruthless that demanded to be recognized. Richard had met his own kind too many times before to be fooled. For the first time in a long while, he felt a lick of excitement curl through his gut.

"Of course, Mr. Lennox. Would you like to join me at the far end of the salon, where I hope we shall remain relatively undisturbed?"

He led the way past the piles of writhing bodies to the quieter end of the salon where several chairs were grouped around small tables. He took a chair that allowed him to see the rest of the room and waited to see which seat Jack Lennox would pick. Lennox sat directly opposite him, half-blocking Richard's view, a brave move that Richard could only admire.

"Now, Mr. Lennox. What can I do for you?" Richard signaled for one of the waiters and asked for some brandy to be brought to them.

"It is a delicate matter, Mr. Ross. One I am not quite sure how to approach."

"Are you under the impression that I can somehow help advance your career? If that is so, you are quite mistaken. Lord Keyes is the man for that kind of thing. He already holds an important position in the government and is connected with all the best families."

"Lord Keyes has already offered to help me, Mr. Ross." Jack Lennox thanked the waiter for the brandy and then turned his intent gaze back to Richard. "The matter I wish to speak to you about is a more personal one."

"Yet you hardly know me, sir."

"Which presents me with some difficulties, I know. But this request is not entirely on my behalf." Jack Lennox hesitated. "I am charged to deliver a message to Madame Helene Delornay. I understood from Lord Keyes that you have some connection with her."

"I might have." Richard sipped his brandy and wondered exactly what Keyes had told Lennox. "But since you are in her house of pleasure, why not simply ask to meet Madame Helene herself?"

"I understood that she no longer runs this establishment."

"She still looks in occasionally. Why did you not attempt to speak to her son, Christian? He is in charge now."

"Because I am not sure if the message I bring will be welcome to Madame Helene." Lennox's smile was roguishly charming. "I hoped you might act as a—how do you say it? A go-between."

"That is certainly the correct phrase, but I'm not sure if I like the idea at all. Why should I offer myself up for such a potentially hazardous duty?"

Jack Lennox sat forward, one hand clenched on his knee, and lowered his voice.

"My grandmother knew Madame Helene when she was a

young woman. I believe they shared some terrible experiences during the revolution. I'm unsure if Madame Helene would wish to revive those memories. I hoped you might intercede with her, or her son, on my behalf."

Richard studied the other man. He'd always considered himself an excellent judge of character. There was a sincerity behind Lennox's words that couldn't be denied. Instinct also told Richard there was far more to the story. Did he want to become involved, or did he wish Jack Lennox and his grandmother to the devil?

"Why didn't your grandmother just write a letter to Madame Helene?"

"Because she is reluctant to commit anything to paper. She is extremely suspicious. After surviving the twists and turns of a revolution, I can understand her fears, although it makes my task more complicated."

"I can see that." Richard let his gaze linger on Jack Lennox's perfect face. If the man did stay in London and was accepted by the *ton,* the ladies were going to swoon over him in droves. "Is there somewhere I can reach you when I have made my decision?"

Disappointment flashed in Jack Lennox's eyes, but he quickly masked it. "Of course. I'm staying at 33 Curzon Street. Do you know it?"

"The Harcourt family house?"

"My grandmother knew the previous viscount before the revolution. They remained friends until he died. The Harcourt family is in the country, so we are not disturbing anyone too greatly."

"Then I will contact you there." Richard rose and held out his hand. "It was a pleasure to meet you, Mr. Lennox. Do you intend to stay and sample the delights of the pleasure house before you retire? I think Lord Keyes and his party are still rather occupied."

Jack shook his hand and then glanced around at the orgy going on behind them. "I heard there was more on offer here than that. Is it true?"

Richard smiled. "Indeed. What do you prefer? Madame boasts she caters to every sexual taste known to man or woman."

"Or both?" Jack held his gaze. "I am not averse to sharing my bed with either sex."

Richard gently disengaged his hand from Jack's grip. "Then take yourself up the stairs to the second level and ask Marie-Claude to help you discover what you desire."

"You will not come with me? Perhaps we could find a willing woman to share."

"Alas, I am rather tired, but thank you for the offer. Good night, Mr. Lennox."

"Good night, Mr. Ross."

For a moment Richard wondered what it would be like to share a bed with a man who reminded him so strongly of Violet. Would he feel desire for him? Richard squashed that thought and turned toward the door. It wasn't the first time he'd been propositioned by a man at the pleasure house, but it was certainly the first time he'd stopped to think about it.

Perhaps his association with the Delornay family was starting to erode his morals. Richard smiled as he unlocked the door that led into the servants' stairwell and headed toward the private quarters at the rear of the house. Not that his morals had been particularly strong to start with. Surviving in a war-damaged country had taught him that right and wrong were more fluid concepts than he had ever imagined.

A fire had been lit in his bedchamber and his bed was warm from the hot bricks Ambrose had directed be placed at the foot. Richard sighed as he took off his black coat and started on the buttons of his waistcoat. In the morning he would talk to Lord Keyes, and then depending on the result of that interview, he might approach Christian with Jack Lennox's request.

Richard pictured the young man and found himself smiling. Such arrogance and *such* determination wrapped in a beautiful exterior package. Had Lennox gone home, or had he succumbed to the lure of the pleasure house and found himself another man to play with? Richard stripped off his underthings and lay in bed, his hand automatically cupping his cock and balls. His last thought as he drifted off to sleep was a startling image of Lennox, Violet, and himself naked and writhing on the silken covers of his bed. . . .

2

"I'm not sure what you want me to tell you, Ross."

Richard concealed his impatience behind a slight smile and studied Lord Keyes, who sat opposite him in the warmth of the secretary's office at the Sinners' Club. It was always the best place to find Lord Keyes, who barely visited his official lodgings. Richard suspected Keyes had a more private set of rooms on the top floor of the club where he plotted his nefarious schemes. Despite the advanced hour, the paneled room was still quite dark and smelled strongly of the Spanish cigarillos Keyes enjoyed.

"I would have thought it was quite obvious. You deliberately introduced Jack Lennox to me last night. He even confirmed that. Why?"

Lord Keyes stretched out his long legs and propped his booted feet up on the grate.

"Why must you assume I have a disreputable purpose for everything I do? Perhaps I just thought the man needed a few French-speaking friends to see him through his debut in polite society."

"Mr. Lennox told me that he had a message for Madame Helene. Is that what interests you?"

Keyes gave Richard his most charming smile. They were of a similar age and had been through school and university together, although Richard would never claim Keyes as a close friend. They were more like competitors.

"I'd forgotten that when you get the bit between your teeth there is very little that will shake you off course, is there? Why would I be interested in anything Mr. Lennox has to say to a notorious madame?"

Richard put his glass down on the table with a decided click. "If you persist in answering every one of my questions with one of your own, I shall assume you don't wish to know the outcome of Mr. Lennox's meeting with my stepmother." He started to rise. "I'll wish you good day."

Keyes put out a restraining hand. "Devil take it, Ross, don't be so impatient." He paused until Richard sat back down. "I *am* interested in what passes between Mr. Lennox and Madame Helene."

"Why?"

"Because Madame Helene is a fascinating woman who has contacts all over Europe."

"You believe she is a spy?"

Keyes laughed. "On the contrary. She has always provided our government with excellent information. I'm more interested in what Mr. Lennox has to say to her."

"You believe *he* is a spy."

"I'm not sure. The affecting tale he spun me was quite convincing, but you know I tend to err on the side of caution."

"So you want me to befriend him, introduce him to Madame Helene, and glean all the information I can without him realizing it."

"That's about the sum of it."

"And why would I want to do that?"

Keyes raised his eyebrows. "For your King and country?"

Richard grimaced. "Haven't you anything better to offer me than that?"

"Well, you don't exactly need money or a title, or even gainful employment. Why not consider this as something to keep you occupied?"

Richard met Keyes's all-too-knowing gaze. "Is that why you continue to dabble in such matters?"

"Touché, my friend. We are both in the same situation, aren't we? Waiting for our esteemed fathers to die, living precariously on our expectations."

Richard sighed. "All right, you've made your point. I'll help you. Now, what else can you tell me about Jack Lennox?"

Keyes lit another cigarillo and Richard waited while he inhaled and then puffed out a perfect smoke ring. "He has a brother named Vincent and a mother."

"Have they accompanied him to London?"

"I believe they have." Keyes hesitated. "I'm not sure if that really is his mother, but I've been told that the brother is almost identical in looks. They might even be twins."

"You haven't met him?"

"Not the brother, no."

"Anything else?"

"Nothing that I am at liberty to disclose to you at this point."

"Even though you've asked for my help," Richard muttered. "Typical." He rose to his feet and this time Keyes didn't try and stop him. "I'll be in touch."

"Thank you."

Richard looked down at his sometimes friend, sometimes adversary. "If she allows it, you have no objection to Lennox speaking to Madame Helene, do you?"

"None at all, although I would ask that you insist on being present at the meeting."

"I thought the grandmother wished to talk about the gory days of the revolution."

"That might be so, but I'd still like you to be there."

Richard inclined his head the barest inch. "I'll do my best."

"I know you will, otherwise I wouldn't have asked for your help."

On that positive note of approval, Richard decided it was time to leave. He abandoned Keyes in his comfortable spot by the fire and ventured back into the more social areas of the club. There were very few members present at this early hour, but Richard saw a couple of his cronies and went to sit with them.

Compared to most London clubs, the membership of the Sinners' was small, but there was a reason for that. Other clubs picked their members by their social pedigree and politics. The Sinners' Club picked its members from those who had served their country in less obvious and more dangerous ways. Class was less of an issue. Honor and bravery were valued above all.

After arriving back in London, Richard had decided not to join his father's club and had eventually been invited to join the Sinners', where he felt quite at home. One never knew if one was sitting next to a duke's son or a clerk from a bank—but one did know that these men would defend their friends and their country to the death.

"Good morning, Ross." Sir Adam Fisher hailed him and Richard took the seat opposite him. "Been in to see our lord and master, then?"

"If you mean Keyes, he's no longer any master of mine. In fact, at this precise moment, I wish him to the devil."

Adam Fisher grinned. "We've all felt like that at some point in our dealings with Keyes. In truth, I think he's more in danger of being throttled by a member of his own sovereign nation than any other."

"That's because he is a devious bastard."

"Who has saved many lives," Adam said quietly. "Including yours."

Richard sighed. "Which is why I always turn up like a well-trained dog whenever he whistles."

"You do not wish to help us with Lennox?"

"It seems I have no choice. What did you think of him?"

"Of Lennox? He seemed very charming but rather dangerous to me."

"That was my impression too. Have you met his brother or his mother?"

"I haven't had that pleasure, but I have convinced my mother to leave her cards at the Harcourt residence, so perhaps Mrs. Lennox will visit in return."

Richard poured himself a cup of coffee from the silver pot on the table. The bitter, slightly burned taste suited his mood perfectly.

"Adam, did Keyes tell you anything else about the Lennox family, or the reason why they have returned to England?"

"Unfortunately not. He just asked me to befriend young Jack and keep him informed of his movements and acquaintances." Adam tapped Richard's arm. "You know how close-mouthed Keyes can be when he wants to be."

"Closemouthed? That man could teach an oyster his trade," Richard muttered, then finished his coffee. "I have to go and speak to Christian at the pleasure house."

"Perhaps I might see you here later?" Adam asked. "I've invited Jack Lennox as my guest for the evening."

"If Christian reacts favorably to my request, I might well join you."

"Excellent."

Richard nodded to the other gentlemen clustered around the fire and went to collect his hat and gloves. It wasn't that far from the club to the pleasure house, so he decided to risk the frostiness of the air and walk. It also gave him the opportunity to gather his thoughts ahead of meeting his half brother, who but for a twist of fate would have been heir to all that Richard stood to inherit.

Not that Christian ever made anything of it. He seemed quite happy running the pleasure house, supervising his step-children, and, no doubt, making love to his beautiful wife, Elizabeth, on every possible occasion. Richard tried to remember that Christian's life hadn't always been so happy. He'd hardly known his mother for the first eighteen years of his life, and the discovery that she owned a notorious brothel had seriously threatened their relationship.

Richard crossed the street, avoiding the filth gathered in pools on the uneven surface of the pitted road. Because of their respective mothers, he and Christian both had difficult relationships with their father, Philip. That common bond had united them and set all other jealousies aside. Richard still wasn't sure how he felt about Philip, but at least they were trying to get along.

The stuccoed white walls of the pleasure house appeared ahead of him, and Richard took the steps down to the basement and went through to the warm and welcoming kitchen. Seamus Kelly was eating porridge at the table flanked by Elizabeth, who was talking intently to him and pointing at something in an open book.

Richard cleared his throat. "Good morning, Mrs. Delornay, Seamus. Is Christian on the premises?"

Elizabeth smiled at him and he couldn't help but smile back. She was as daintily built as a china doll, but Richard knew that fragility was an illusion.

"Elizabeth, please. We are almost related. Christian is in his office." She hesitated. "Do you wish to speak to me as well? I'm just finishing Seamus's reading lesson."

"No, I won't disturb you. My business is with Christian. I'm sure he'll tell you all about it later."

Richard nodded and went on up the stairs to the first floor that housed the main offices. He knocked on the door of Christian's and waited to be asked to enter.

His half brother had blond hair like his mother and hazel eyes the same color as Richard's and their shared father's. Christian smiled when he saw Richard and waved him to a chair.

"Good morning, Richard. Is everything well with our father?"

Richard took the seat and crossed his legs. "Why do you always assume I come here to talk about our esteemed father?"

Christian raised his eyebrows. "Because you usually do." He sat on the front of his desk. "Is it Emily, then?"

"No, although I did wonder if you have noticed how attracted she is to Ambrose."

"I did notice that." Christian sighed. "Ambrose won't talk about it, and I'm loathe to force his confidence. I think he's hoping it is just a silly infatuation and that Emily will soon forget all about him."

"If that is his hope, he might be disappointed. As our father proved, the Ross family is very stubborn when they are in love."

"I hadn't thought about that," Christian admitted. "And I don't think Ambrose is quite as unaffected as he claims." He contemplated the toe of his boot for a moment and then looked up. "So if it isn't about the family, what else can I do for you?"

"It is rather a complex matter, but I hope you will hear me out."

Christian sat up. "Don't tell me you have become embroiled in a scandal?"

"You'd enjoy that, wouldn't you?"

"Well, your life is remarkably staid and boring."

"I come here to the pleasure house." Richard scowled at

Christian. "That's hardly boring, and I have duties and respon-sibilities. . . ."

Christian waved an airy hand. "I'm sure you do, but you hardly qualify as a rake."

"And I wouldn't wish to be one."

Richard took a moment to gather his temper. Christian de-lighted in baiting him. Sometimes he yearned to tell his skepti-cal elder brother exactly how dangerously he'd once lived his life, but he was still bound by his loyalty to his country.

"If we might return to the topic at hand? I made the ac-quaintance of a man named Jack Lennox last night."

"Here?"

"Indeed. He wished to speak to your mother."

"Then why did he approach you and not me?" Christian asked. "How did he even know that you had a connection to my mother?"

"I believe that information was given to him by an acquain-tance of mine."

"An acquaintance I hope you will drop."

Richard found himself smiling. "I appreciate how you strive to protect my reputation, but I fear it is too late. Several people know that we are connected."

"What did this Lennox character want with my mother?"

"He wished to give her a message from his grandmother in France."

"And?"

"He was unsure if your mother would wish to hear from an old acquaintance who had suffered through the years of the revolution with her. He thought she might not wish to reawaken such harsh memories."

Christian sat back. "Then he doesn't know my mother very well. She is the strongest woman I have ever met—apart from Elizabeth." He paused. "Although she does not talk of those days very much."

At Richard's puzzled look, Christian continued, "Her whole family was imprisoned in the Bastille. She watched them all being taken away to the guillotine."

"How horrifying for her."

"That's not the worst of it." Christian held his gaze. "Her father sold her to the guards to save her life. I suspect she would have preferred to die with her loved ones." He swallowed hard. "God knows how she survived such treatment, but she did."

"Then perhaps she might not want to speak to Lennox after all."

"I don't know. The only thing I can do is ask her. She is currently at Knowles House with Philip. I'll go and see her tonight."

"If you think it wise." Richard hesitated. "I hardly know Lennox. I'd hate to upset Helene over this."

"You know her well enough to understand that my mother would rather make up her own mind than have any of us dare to make the decision for her. I'll ask her and she'll decide. Come and see me tomorrow and I'll give you her answer."

Richard rose. "Thank you, Christian. I appreciate it."

His half brother considered him, his head angled to one side. "If you hardly know Lennox, why are you even bothering yourself with him?"

Richard shrugged. "A favor for an old friend?"

Christian smiled. "Did I mention that I'd heard some rumors about you recently?"

"About me?"

"Yes, that perhaps your past was more exciting than we had been led to believe."

Richard kept his expression benign. "Would you object if I brought Lennox and his twin brother to the pleasure house as guests?"

"Not at all. The more the merrier. Are you hoping to make Lennox more than just a passing acquaintance?"

"I don't bed men, Christian."

"Is that so?" Christian stood and retreated behind his desk. "That's not quite what I've heard."

Ignoring Christian's soft laughter, Richard forced himself not to respond and turned toward the door.

It was true that when in France, Richard had seduced anyone he'd been told to, but how would Christian have discovered that? Mentally Richard forced the issue to one side. As manager of the pleasure house, Christian was privy to a thousand indiscretions and secrets, and however he might tease Richard, he would never betray his confidences.

Richard contemplated his options. Should he meet up with Adam Fisher and Jack Lennox at the Sinners' Club or spend a quiet evening at home in his lodgings? He didn't want to be present when Christian spoke to Helene, so he intended to avoid the Knowles town house at all costs.

Christian's words about his dull existence echoed in his mind. An evening with a book in front of the fire suddenly seemed unappealing. He'd go home, change into his evening attire, and meet Adam and the mysterious Jack Lennox at the Sinners' Club.

"Ambrose?"

Ambrose looked up from his newspaper to see his employer entering the kitchen, and went to stand. "Mr. Delornay."

Christian waved him back to his seat and helped himself to the pot of coffee at Ambrose's elbow.

"I've just been talking to Richard, and he intends to bring a couple of guests with him to the pleasure house—a Mr. Jack Lennox and his twin brother."

"I met Mr. Lennox last night. He came in with Lord Keyes. He seemed quite amiable."

"And his tastes?"

Ambrose regarded Christian carefully. "His sexual tastes?"

"Naturally, I don't care what the man eats."

"He found the main floor too dull. I sent him to Marie-Claude on the second level. You will have to ask her how he fared up there." Ambrose sipped his own coffee. "Why are you so interested in Mr. Lennox?"

Christian's smile was deceptively sweet. "Because Richard is."

"You think your brother is enamored?"

"Don't look so surprised, Ambrose. You of all men know that a person's sexual tastes can be quite complicated."

"But Mr. Ross is . . ."

"Not quite what he seems." Christian lowered his voice. "I've heard that my esteemed brother was involved in some extremely secret missions in France during the war."

"And who told you that?"

"One of his companions blurted it out last week while I was watching him being fucked."

"It seems rather unlikely."

"That someone would share something like that with me, or that dear, safe, boring Richard could be involved in anything at all?" Christian put his cup down on the table. "It did occur to me that the information had been given to me deliberately, but then for what purpose? I have nothing to do with Richard's life."

"Except that Richard wants you to allow the Lennox twins into the pleasure house. To be quite honest, in my experience, anyone who arrives with Lord Keyes is likely to be mixed up in something dangerous."

"And Keyes is a friend of Richard's," Christian said. "It might even be more complicated than that. Richard wants me to introduce Jack Lennox to my mother."

"And at one time your mother was involved in a lot of dangerous activities in France."

"She still is." Christian groaned. "Which is why I'd like you to help me keep an eye on the Lennox brothers."

"I'll do that." Ambrose picked up his newspaper. "Is there anything else?"

"There is one more thing." Christian hesitated. "Is Emily bothering you?"

Ambrose slowly lowered the paper and stared at Christian. "Of course not."

"Are you sure? Because if she was *bothering* you, I could ask her not to come here."

"It would seem unfair for her to be the only member of the family who is excluded from the pleasure house," Ambrose said carefully.

"But as she cannot go upstairs, she spends her whole time in the kitchen with you."

Ambrose met Christian's gaze. "And you'd rather she didn't? Am I not considered fit company for her?"

"That isn't what I meant and you know it. She is my half sister, but you are my best friend. I don't wish to see you hurt."

"Why would I be hurt?"

"Because you care for her."

A spark of anger ignited low in Ambrose's gut. "Certainly I care for her. I've known her for years. She is like part of my family."

Christian reached across and patted his hand. "There is no need to be so defensive. I'm not trying to pry. I just want you to know that if you wish to talk about anything, I am more than willing to listen."

Ambrose dropped his gaze to their hands, noticing the contrast between the whiteness of his employer's skin and the darkness of his own. "There is nothing to talk about. Your family has my complete loyalty. You know I would do nothing to disgrace you or yours."

Christian sighed. "I never thought you would, but I'm here

if you need me, and so is Elizabeth. She is very fond of you, you know." After a final squeeze of Ambrose's hand, Christian stood up and left the kitchen, leaving Ambrose staring at the floor.

Was it really so obvious that he cared for Emily Ross? He'd tried so hard to suppress his feelings, to force them down, to treat her as he treated the rest of the Delornay-Ross family. Or was it that Emily's recent impatience with him had finally drawn the attention of her brothers? That was more likely the case. Emily had never been good at concealing her emotions.

Ambrose opened the newspaper and stared unseeingly at the print. She claimed that she loved him, and that she would never love another man. But how could he believe her? She was the daughter of a peer of the realm and he was . . . God, he didn't even know what or who he was. Only that he was so far below her that the idea of her actually returning his secret passion was ridiculous.

He closed the paper and began to fold it carefully into a neat square. Despite the confusion of his feelings, he didn't want Christian to stop Emily coming to the kitchen. He lived for the sight of her. He groaned. And how pitiful was that? He was pining like some love-struck swain from a bad play.

Ambrose looked up at the closed kitchen door. He would have to find a way to extricate himself from this situation without hurting Emily or losing his friendship with Christian. Unfortunately, he just couldn't think of a single way to do it without destroying something—probably himself.

3

Richard paused at the door into the members' dining room and let his narrowed gaze travel across the assembled diners. The lighting was low and not helped by the dark wainscoting and thick curtains. He finally spotted Adam near the window and made his way through the closely packed tables to his friend's side.

"Good evening, gentlemen." Richard bowed. "May I join you?"

Jack Lennox looked up at him and smiled. "Mr. Ross! What a delightful surprise. Mr. Fisher said that you might drop by."

Richard pulled out a chair and sat down. "Your brother hasn't accompanied you out this evening, Mr. Lennox?"

"Alas, Vincent is still suffering from the indignities of our sea voyage." Jack winced. "He is not a good sailor."

"I can only sympathize," Adam replied. "I don't travel very well myself. Even the motion of a carriage makes me nauseous."

Richard shuddered. "Yes, I remember that about you now,

my friend. I hope never to have to travel in your company again."

All the men laughed, and Jack poured Richard a glass of red wine that already stood open on the table. Richard realized he was beginning to wonder about the mythical twin brother no one had actually seen. The dinner menu at the club tended to be rather limited, but Richard didn't mind. He'd rather eat a good steak and kidney pie than some of the more fanciful creations his father's chef put on the table.

"May I ask how the Sinners' Club acquired such an interesting name?" Jack Lennox inquired as he finished his first glass of wine.

Richard and Adam exchanged glances; then Richard smiled. "I'm not quite sure. I believe it was Lord Keyes's father's idea. He was one of the founding members of the club, and Keyes is the current membership secretary."

"I wonder if I would stand a chance of gaining membership?" Jack mused. "I have certainly sinned. How is membership decided?"

"On an individual basis by a committee, I believe," Richard said. "You need two established members to put your name forward for consideration."

Adam smiled at Richard. "I'm sure that if you wished to apply, we would be more than willing to support your application, Mr. Lennox."

"That would be very kind of you." Jack nodded to them both. "I will certainly consider it."

The three of them sat back as the waiter delivered their food, and the succulent smell of roast beef and steak and kidney pudding rose from their plates.

"Ah." Jack Lennox inhaled slowly. "I've missed this."

"A plate of roast beef?" Richard inquired. "I thought the French believe English cuisine to be fit only for dogs."

Jack Lennox met his gaze, a challenge flashing in his blue eyes. "But I *am* English, Mr. Ross."

Richard refused to look away. "Oh, yes, that's right. I had quite forgotten."

He returned his attention to his plate, listening to Adam talk about the weather and the appalling state of the roof on his father's country house—innocuous subjects that would lull most men into a false sense of security. Adam had always been good at that. His unremarkable features allowed him the ability to change his appearance at will and play any character. The mild-mannered English squire was, of course, his specialty, and he was playing that role to the hilt for Jack Lennox.

After their plates were removed, Adam stood and bowed. "Will you excuse me for a minute, gentlemen? I must speak to Lord Brookstone about the bill he is proposing to take before the House next month."

Richard filled his glass with some of the excellent port that Keyes insisted be kept at the club, and eyed his fellow diner. Jack Lennox wore a dark blue coat that brought out the blue in his eyes, and a black waistcoat and trousers. Although his attire wasn't particularly fashionable, it fitted him like a glove. Briefly, Richard wondered who his tailor was.

"I assume you don't have an answer for me yet, Mr. Ross?"

Richard raised his gaze from Jack Lennox's waistcoat to find Jack staring expectantly at him.

"Not yet, Mr. Lennox. These things take time."

"I know that." He sipped at his port. "I must say that the pleasure house proved worthy of its reputation."

"I'm glad to hear it. I'll pass on your compliments to Mr. Delornay."

"Who is your half brother, I understand."

"That is correct."

"You have the same father, Lord Philip Knowles."

"Also correct." Richard paused. "Have you been research-ing my family tree, Mr. Lennox? It certainly is an interesting one, but I cannot see why you bothered."

Jack shrugged; the gesture far more French than English. "I am interested in you, Mr. Ross, and it pays to be careful."

"And why do I interest you?"

"Because you seem quite different from the rest of your family; far more—how do you say it? Conventional."

There it was again, the assumption that he was a boring, dull man. Richard sat forward. "All families have their black sheep, Mr. Lennox."

"But you are whiter than white."

"You don't know me well enough to make that assump-tion."

His companion inclined his head a bare inch. "That is true, sir, but I doubt I am mistaken. I'm considered an excellent judge of character. Please excuse me while I visit the necessary."

The smile he gave Richard was almost pitying. Richard watched him walk through to the back of the club and re-mained in his seat, fuming. Lennox didn't know him at all! No one in London did apart from a select few members of the Sin-ners' Club. How juvenile was it that Richard wanted to run after Jack Lennox and tell him just how dangerous and uncon-ventional he really was? Something about the man unsettled him. Richard wasn't sure if it was his resemblance to Violet or his brazen effrontery.

He realized that he needed to use the necessary himself and followed Jack Lennox's path to the facilities at the back of the house. There was no sign of his dining companion as he com-pleted his business, readjusted his clothing, and turned back to-ward the comforting low hum of conversation in the dining room.

Just as he reached the end of the quiet corridor that connected to the deserted hallway, someone stepped in front of him.

"Did you come after me to prove a point, Mr. Ross?" Jack Lennox inquired.

"No, I came to take a piss." Richard glared at his nemesis. "I have nothing to prove to you." He tried to push past, but for a slender shorter man, Jack Lennox held his ground pretty well.

"Are you sure about that? You seem a little angry."

Richard shoved Lennox back against the wall and held him there with one arm across his throat.

"I'm not angry, Lennox." He deliberately licked his lips. "What is it you really want from me? Are you that desperate for a man that you think to goad me into touching you?"

Lennox slowly exhaled. "As it seems to have worked, then yes."

Richard simply stared into the other man's eyes as a forbidden lick of pure lust flowered in his loins. He wanted to slide his hand between their two bodies and see if Lennox spoke the truth, if he was aroused, or even half-aroused, as Richard knew his own cock already was.

"I don't let men fuck me."

"Ever?"

A few salacious memories danced behind Richard's eyes and he struggled to concentrate. On occasion, Violet had liked having more than one man in her bed, and it had seemed a shame to waste the opportunity to explore another facet of his sexuality.

Jack groaned and Richard realized that he had slowly allowed his whole body to rest against Jack's. There was no doubt that Jack was aroused. Richard could feel the heat of his cock pulsing through the fabric of his trousers.

Without releasing his grip on Jack's throat, Richard carefully brought his mouth down toward the other man's. He reveled in hearing the hitch in Jack's breathing and inhaled the heady scent of the port they'd both shared. He flicked out his tongue and traced the seam of Jack's lips. The kick of Jack's cock against his was unexpectedly stimulating. He forced himself to step back.

"Good night, Mr. Lennox."

Jack opened his eyes wide. "Leaving so soon, Mr. Ross?"

"I haven't finished my dinner yet."

"I'm sure I could satisfy any appetite you have."

Richard smiled. "I'm sure you could, but perhaps I prefer something less invigorating. I wouldn't want to upset my delicate digestion."

To his surprise, Jack Lennox grinned at him. "You prefer one of your oh-so-dull English puddings, perhaps?"

Richard found himself smiling back. There was something about the way Jack Lennox took rejection that impressed him. "Indeed. Will you join me? Adam will be wondering if we have deserted him."

As he followed Jack back to the dining room, Richard heard a slight noise behind him. When he looked back over his shoulder, he saw Lord Keyes standing in the doorway of his office, his expression amused. Richard kept walking. He had no intention of adding to Keyes's enjoyment by acknowledging him or asking the other man exactly what he had seen.

Emily read the letter again and still couldn't make much sense of it. Why would an old employee of the family wish to speak to her and not to her father? The note also suggested that their meeting should be private as it concerned her late mother. Emily paused to consider the badly written signature scrawled at the bottom of the letter and squinted hard at it.

"Oh, my."

She held the letter closer to the light and read it again. "Thomas Smith, Esquire." Gentleman? If it was the man she was thinking of, he certainly hadn't styled himself that way before. In truth, he'd been a gardener at her parents' country estate. She tried to picture him but could only remember a dark-haired, thickset man with a strong country accent.

She shivered and put the letter down. Should she meet him? What could he possibly have to say to her that he didn't wish her father to hear? Her father never spoke of her mother, and she'd learned long ago not to ask questions. She sighed. Curiosity had always been her besetting sin, but she wasn't quite stupid enough to agree to meet the man without someone accompanying her.

Would her maid be enough protection? In her mind, Thomas Smith had always seemed rather large and threatening, but she had just been a child. Emily folded the letter and put it in her reticule. Perhaps she could ask Seamus Kelly from the pleasure house to accompany her, or maybe Ambrose would come.

Ambrose was avoiding her, and it was all her own fault. She'd tried to push him into a declaration of love, and like most men, he'd retreated in the opposite direction with all the speed and desperation of a runaway horse. Perhaps by asking for his help with the mysterious letter writer, she could put things right between them again.

She rose to her feet and headed for the door. Helene and her father had retired to his study to speak to Christian, who had arrived unexpectedly just after dinner. It would be a simple matter for her to slip out of the house and go and find Ambrose—if he wanted to be found.

She hated the fact that she was even second-guessing herself in this manner. Where had her courage gone? She'd always loved visiting the pleasure house, sitting with Ambrose in the kitchen, watching as he managed the staff with such calm competency. She couldn't remember when her shy admiration for him had turned to love. She refused to let *anyone*, even Ambrose, tell her that she was mistaken in her own feelings.

When she reached the bottom of the stairs, she paused. There was no one in the hallway or the drawing room and the light still shone under the door of her father's study. It was easy enough for Emily to find her maid and escape through the back entrance of the house. She reckoned she could return before her parents even noticed she had gone. Helene's other less respectable residence was not that far away, and Emily was used to walking there.

As she walked, she considered what she would say to Ambrose, how she would present him with a smiling face and calm demeanor to rival his own. He would have no cause to describe her as a spoiled child denied a special treat ever again.

With that thought firmly in mind, she descended into the basement of the pleasure house, her maid trailing uncomplainingly behind her. To her delight, Ambrose was sitting at the kitchen table eating his dinner and reading from a book propped up against a tankard of ale. Before he noticed her, she had the opportunity to study his graceful figure, the quiet strength of his features, and the sense of calm that always surrounded him. How could she not think him beautiful?

"Miss Ross." He stood up hastily, wiping his mouth with his napkin. "I wasn't expecting you this evening."

She forced a smile. "Please don't mind me. Carry on with your dinner. I'll just sit quietly until you are ready to talk to me."

A wary light entered his dark brown eyes. "You wish to talk to me?"

"Yes. Is that not possible?" She hurried on. Had she ruined everything between them with her impulsive nature? "There is a personal matter I wish to ask your opinion on."

He looked even more dubious than he had before she'd tried to explain. Emily sighed. "Ambrose, it's about a letter I received."

"A love letter?"

"Of course not. No man has ever sent me one of those." She sat down opposite Ambrose and extracted the letter from her reticule. "Here, you can read it for yourself."

He took the letter with all the reluctance of a man offered a poisoned chalice and started to read. After a short while he looked up at her.

"Do you know this man?"

"I believe I do. There was a gardener at our old family home called Thomas Smith. I remember him because my mother liked to consult with him about the rose garden, which was a particular passion of hers."

"But why would he suddenly want to talk to you after all these years, and without the permission of your father?"

"Even back then it was fairly obvious that my parents didn't have a very good relationship. In truth, my mother probably spent more time talking to Thomas Smith about her roses than she did conversing with my father. Perhaps Mr. Smith was aware of that and decided he would rather not have any contact with my father."

"I assume you wish to meet with him?"

"You know me so well." She smiled and for a precious moment, he smiled back. "But I don't wish to meet him alone. I was hoping that either you or Seamus Kelly might accompany me."

He pushed the letter back across the table as if worried that their fingers might touch. "When do you wish to meet him?"

"Well, I will have to write back and arrange a time and a place. I was thinking about meeting him in one of the parks during the day. Do you think that is a good idea?"

"If you are accompanied by Seamus or myself, yes."

Emily let out a relieved breath. "Then shall I let you know the date?"

"That would be most helpful. I doubt the man means you

any harm. He might just have had a sentimental wish to see his favorite employer's daughter again. Is he an elderly man?"

"No, he was quite young. About my mother's age, I think, when I knew him."

"Did you not like him?"

"Why would you think that?"

"Because you just shivered."

Emily laughed. "I have no idea why. I hardly remember the man at all. He was one of the gardeners. I only saw him when he consulted with my mother."

Ambrose's gaze remained watchful, but he nodded and sat back. "Is there anything else I can help you with today, or can I find someone to escort you home?"

Emily's smile faded. "Are you so eager to be rid of me, then?"

Ambrose looked distinctly uncomfortable. "Unfortunately, I am not able to sit here with you in the kitchen all night. Your brother is out, and Elizabeth is with her children, so I am in charge of the pleasure house."

Emily stood in a rush, smoothing down the skirts of her gown with a hand that shook. "Then I would not wish to keep you from such important duties."

"Miss Ross, I . . ."

She pushed her chair back with such unnecessary force that it screeched against the flagstone floor. "I understand that you do not return my regard, Ambrose, but I at least thought we could remain friends."

He stood, too, and studied her across the expanse of the table that separated them. "I do not wish to quarrel with you, Miss Ross."

"Of course, you don't." She sighed. "And here I am again, embarrassing you with my stupid, childish behavior."

He turned away. She was aware that her cheeks were flushed

and that she was biting down so hard on her lower lip that she would soon draw blood.

"I'll find your maid, Miss Ross."

Emily remained beside the table, her fists clenched and her whole being focused on not embarrassing herself with a humiliating flood of tears. She hated to cry and Ambrose knew it. Was that why he had turned away? Did he hate the thought that she might expect him to comfort her?

With sudden resolve, she drew on her gloves and headed for the kitchen door, which connected to the servants' dining hall, where she knew her maid would be waiting for her. She had barely passed through the door before she cannoned into Ambrose, who was coming back the other way.

As she stumbled against him, he instinctively reached out and held her close, wrapping his arm around her and pulling her into the curve of his body. Emily couldn't help but lean against him, her senses suddenly alive and her knees weak.

"Ambrose . . ." she breathed.

His mouth brushed her ear and she shuddered, turning her face until her lips met his.

With a groan, he kissed her and she kissed him back, opening her mouth to him without a qualm, letting her tongue dance a shy dance with his.

He drew her even closer, one hand closing on her hip, the other around the back of her neck. She didn't object to his touch, even the urgent press of his cock against her stomach. It felt like she was coming home. She tried to wiggle even closer.

With a low sound, Ambrose wrenched his mouth away from hers. "I can't be a friend to you anymore, Miss Ross. Can't you see that it is killing me?"

Even as she understood his words and reached for him again, he pushed her away until her back met the wall. She held his gaze, tried to put everything she felt in her eyes and saw the answering passion in his. Behind him the door to the servants' hall opened and she saw her maid smiling at her.

"Are you ready to go, miss?"

Emily took a deep breath. "Yes, I believe I am."

Even though she walked away from Ambrose with her head held high, her mind was in total disarray.

4

Emily adjusted the angle of her parasol to deflect the sun and continued to walk toward the banks of the Serpentine. Despite the sunlight, there was a sharp breeze blowing across the water that made all the little toy boats speed up, their white sails frantically bobbing up and down as their small owners chased them along the shoreline.

For some reason, Ambrose had decided that both he and Seamus should accompany her to meet Thomas Smith. The tall and beefy figure of Seamus Kelly dressed in his best livery walked just behind her. Ambrose wasn't visible, although Emily knew he was there. She scanned the benches that faced the water, and her gaze settled on a lone figure waiting on the farthest seat.

Despite Seamus's reassuring bulk behind her, she suddenly felt quite nervous. Perhaps she should have spoken to Richard before she embarked on her expedition to meet Mr. Smith. Richard might have clearer memories of the gardener than she had.

"Is everything all right, miss?"

Seamus's soft Irish accent intruded on her scattered thoughts and she turned toward him.

"I'm fine, Seamus. I think I see Mr. Smith over there." She pointed at the farthest bench and started walking again.

The man stood as she approached, and she realized he was still much taller than she was. In his prime, she reckoned he might have rivaled Seamus for size and strength. She remembered hearing a vague rumor that he had been the local boxing champion. He was no longer so hard muscled and had run to fat, his hair gray under the hat he swept off at her approach.

"Why, Miss Ross, I would've recognized you anywhere. You are the very spit of your mother."

"Mr. Smith." Emily curtsied and took a seat at the far end of the bench.

"Do you remember me, then, lass?"

"A little, sir. I remember that my mother considered you an expert on roses."

He gave an odd laugh. "Your mother considered me an expert at many things."

Emily kept her smile firmly in place. "I'm sure she did."

"Did she ever tell you about me?"

Emily blinked. "Tell me what?"

He sighed. "I'll wager she didn't. Your father wouldn't have allowed it, and she was too frightened of his wrath to disobey him." He fiddled with the brim of his hat before replacing it on his head. "She asked me to give you something."

"My mother did?"

"Aye." He slid his hand inside his greatcoat and brought out a wooden box. "I've been out of the country for several years. I promised her I would wait until you were grown up before I delivered her gift to you."

He put the box down on the seat between them, and Emily studied the battered wooden carvings.

"It's a little battle weary because I've carried it with me all these years."

Emily considered him. "Do you know what is in there?"

He smiled. "Aye." Abruptly he rose and touched his hat again. "Good-bye, Miss Ross. If you should wish to speak to me, I'll be at the Angel Inn, Islington on the Great North Road."

"Thank you, Mr. Smith."

He stared at her for another long moment before nodding to Seamus and striding away toward the entrance of the park. Emily remained on the bench gazing at the box.

"Do you want me to open it for you, miss, or shall we wait for Mr. Ambrose? I see him coming down the path now."

"Let's wait for him, then," Emily murmured. Seamus turned to welcome Ambrose and told him briefly what had happened.

"Are you quite well, Miss Ross?"

Emily started and looked straight into Ambrose's concerned brown eyes. "I'm . . ."

From the moment she'd heard Mr. Smith's voice, a series of confused memories had surfaced in her head. Her mother crying, Mr. Smith shouting, her father . . . She swayed and raised an unsteady hand to cover her mouth.

"Miss *Ross!*" Ambrose grabbed her upper arm and squeezed hard enough to make her jump. "Are you quite well? Are you sure that you want me to open the box, or shall we leave?"

She managed to breathe again and nodded. "We should look first, shouldn't we?"

Ambrose moved away from her again and carefully undid the tarnished gold clasps on the side of the box. Emily craned forward to look as a pile of letters bound with a faded blue ribbon was revealed.

"Is there anything else?" she whispered.

Ambrose gingerly lifted out the letters. "There appears to be a book underneath. Do you want me to open it?"

Emily sat back. "I know what it is. My mother always kept a journal. We couldn't find them when we packed away her things. I always wondered what had happened to them all."

"And now we know." Ambrose carefully put everything back in the box and secured the clasps. "Do you wish to keep this 'gift,' or shall I have it sent back to Mr. Smith at his current abode?"

Emily reached for the box and held it close. "I'll not be sending it back quite yet."

"Are you sure, Miss Ross?"

"Quite sure, Ambrose." Emily regained her composure and smiled at him. "Thank you for your help, and thank you, too, Seamus."

As they walked back toward Knowles House, Emily pondered the sudden appearance of Thomas Smith in her life. Why did she suddenly feel so vulnerable? He hadn't done anything to frighten her; in fact, he'd been courteous and respectful. But she had a strange sense that he would not allow himself to be ignored.

"Miss Ross? I need to get back to the pleasure house. Seamus will escort you the rest of the way," Ambrose said.

Emily paused at the corner of the busy street to focus on Ambrose, who looked as worried as she felt.

"Thank you," she responded involuntarily, and left him standing there, his expression grim, his gaze fixed on the box she clasped to her chest like a lover.

"You'll be pleased to hear that my mother will meet with your friend Mr. Lennox," Christian said.

Richard nodded. "That is very gracious of her, although as I've already mentioned, he is scarcely my friend." Even as he spoke, an image of Jack Lennox's smiling mouth tantalized his senses, making a mockery of his dismissive words.

Richard was seated in Christian's office at the pleasure house, toasting his wet boots against the grate of the fire. The curtains were drawn against the night. Beyond the door, he sensed that the pleasure house had already come to life.

"There is no shame in being attracted to a man, Richard," Christian observed mildly. "From what Marie-Claude told me about Jack Lennox's first visit here, he is quite willing to bed anyone."

Richard lifted his gaze to Christian's. "I am not attracted to Jack Lennox. There are other reasons why I seek out his companionship."

"Really." Christian didn't look away, and Richard found himself glaring at his half brother. "Did Philip ever tell you that my mother and I share a remarkable ability to understand people's sexual desires, even ones that they might not even be aware of?"

"As if my father would ever tell me anything like that."

"You don't discuss your sexual partners?"

"Of course not! For your information, Christian, in polite society such matters are not discussed quite so openly as they are in the Delornay household."

Christian grinned. "It's a shame. You should ask Philip about his experiences here, Richard. I'm sure you would find them most enlightening."

With some effort, Richard controlled his temper. "We are not here to talk about me or our father. Did your mother suggest a time when it would be convenient for her to see Jack Lennox?"

"Yes, she said you should bring him to Knowles House tomorrow night for dinner." Christian stood up. "And she said you should invite his brother and mother to join us as well."

"Us?"

"You can hardly expect me to miss this, can you?"

Richard rose too. "I suppose that would be too much to ask. I'll take myself off to Harcourt House and relay the invitation to the Lennox family."

"There's no need. My mother intends to send them a note this evening."

"Then I might as well go home to my lodgings." Richard sighed.

"Why leave? There's plenty of fun to be had here at the pleasure house." Christian paused at the door. "I heard that the Lennox twins are causing quite a stir on the second floor this evening."

"They are both here?"

"Indeed."

"Then this is an excellent opportunity for me to pass on your mother's invitation in person."

"I'm sure Jack Lennox will be suitably grateful."

Richard narrowed his eyes. "Christian . . ."

His half brother laughed and walked down the hallway. "I have guests to entertain and a wife to pleasure. I will leave you to the enjoyment of your own particular sins."

Richard couldn't deny that the thought of Jack Lennox being in the pleasure house did give him pause. He firmly reminded himself that it was only because Jack reminded him so much of Violet. He followed Christian's path down the hall and up to the main reception rooms on the second floor. To his surprise, the rooms were already quite crowded and there was a sense of heightened sexual awareness in the air.

As he neared the center of the room, he understood why. A troupe of Oriental acrobats, accompanied by an unfamiliar wailing stringed instrument and a steady drumbeat, was performing a sensual dance involving males and females who were almost naked and entwined in various complicated sexual positions. He counted four men and four women, but where one began and the other ended, he wasn't quite so sure. The sinuous grace of the participants made each movement a delight to watch and set off a low hum of sexual excitement in his loins.

One of the women arched backward, her long black hair pooling at Richard's feet. She met his gaze upside down, her dark eyes wide with lust or fabricated lust, and licked her lips. The man supporting her weight was fucking her hard, his thrusts making the woman's small breasts quiver with every jolt.

Richard started as her outstretched hand gripped on to his hip and she tried to draw him closer into the writhing mass of bodies. Across the room, Richard caught the amused gaze of Jack Lennox and found he couldn't look away. The woman tugged at the front of his trousers. Blindly, he undid them and pushed down his underthings, gripped his shaft around the base, and fed it into her warm and waiting mouth.

His groan wasn't just for her skill, but for the fact that Jack Lennox was still watching. Even as he climaxed, Richard couldn't tear his gaze away from Jack's, or stop his cock from starting to fill out again. He remembered to thank the woman and pressed a coin into her hand before hastily buttoning up his trousers and heading across the room to where he'd last seen Lennox.

But where had Jack gone? Richard hastily scanned the crowds and noticed a dark-haired man moving toward the more private rooms that lined the long hallway between the two main salons. He had to follow him and sort out this matter once and for all, convince Jack Lennox that he had nothing to offer him but memories of a dead woman.

But was that really all he wanted? Richard paused in his headlong flight. Was it possible that he wanted Jack Lennox just for himself? Richard shook his head and carried on. He needed Jack to trust him, and if that meant he had to pretend to go along with the other man's obvious sexual interest, he would do his duty. How had Keyes put it? For his King and country.

Richard quickened his pace, moving swiftly past anyone

who blocked his way, his gaze intent on his prey, who seemed oblivious to Richard's pursuit, but who was probably quite aware of it. Almost at the end of the corridor, Richard caught up with Lennox and touched his shoulder.

"Are you going to run away from me all night?" Lennox swung around and Richard went still. "What the devil! You're not Jack Lennox."

Bright blue eyes glared at him. "I'm Vincent Lennox. Who in God's name are you?"

"You know damn well who I am."

Cold fury removed Richard's ability to speak. He kicked open the nearest door and shoved the still-protesting Vincent Lennox inside.

"Your brother knows me rather well, 'Vincent.' Did he tell you to engage my interest? Has that been his intent all along, to lead me back to you?"

"I have no idea what you are talking about, sir. I don't even know your name."

"You bloody little liar."

Lennox made a lunge for the door, but Richard blocked the way.

"Let me go, sir. What do you want from me?" Vincent gasped.

Richard yanked open his trousers. "The same thing your brother offered me: the opportunity for a fuck."

"You cannot mean to . . ."

"I'll do whatever I damned well like." Richard paused, one hand on his already erect cock. "Unless you want to tell me the truth?"

"There is nothing to tell you, sir!"

"Then lie down and take it like the man you insist you are."

Richard advanced and Lennox kept moving backward until he came up against the side of the bed. His color was high and his breathing harsh. He held up his hand. "Mr. Ross, Richard, I . . ."

"So you do at least know my name, *Mr.* Lennox?"

For the first time in his life, Richard was beyond listening, of being careful, of being the *sensible* one. Rage and shock and disbelief consumed him, and he was enjoying the feel of it roaring through his veins. With all his strength, he spun Lennox around until his face was buried in the covers of the bed and his arse was at a nice angle that begged to be fucked.

Keeping one heavy hand in the small of Lennox's back, Richard reached into the drawer beside the bed and found a bottle of oil. He'd almost like to plunge into Lennox's arse dry, but even he wasn't that much of a bastard. He slathered oil around his already wet cock and then onto his fingers.

He pulled down Lennox's trousers to expose the smooth muscled globes of his buttocks and plunged his oiled finger deep in the other man's arse. He quickly added a second and then a third, widening the passage for his cock, making the body on the bed as wet and needy as he was.

And then he was easing his cock deep inside the tight passage, groaning with each thrust until he was balls deep, his whole body covering the prone form of "Vincent Lennox."

Richard bit down on Lennox's ear and heard him whimper. He shifted his weight, allowing one of his arms to wrap low around Lennox's hips and delve lower.

"I suppose you want me to play with your cock." His fingers settled over the swollen wet folds until he found what he sought. "A shame it is so small." He pinched the nub of flesh between his forefinger and thumb, and then rubbed back and forth. "Perhaps I can make it bigger for you, all swollen and sensitive like mine, all ready to explode."

"Richard." The muffled word was more like a cry than his actual name.

"You always liked things a little differently, didn't you? Or did you consider the sacrifice of your body a fair exchange for avoiding telling the truth?" He increased his pace, thrusting in and out until he could only hear the smack of flesh on flesh, of his own animalistic grunts. "Will you come for me, then? Will you take your pleasure from me?"

He squeezed hard and as Lennox screamed, he felt the answering throb in his cock as he spilled his seed deep and then lay still, collapsed over the other shuddering body.

After a few long moments, he eased his cock free, rolled away, and flipped Lennox over onto his back. Furious blue eyes stared up at him.

"If you are going to pretend to be a man, Violet, you really need to grow a better cock."

Violet stared up into the angry face of Richard Ross and considered the changes that time had wrought. It was almost ten years since she'd last seen him, and he looked rather different. His face had filled out, the lines of exhaustion and lack of nourishment eased by his new safe existence. Bitterness filled her and she shoved at his chest.

"Get off me." He didn't budge an inch, and she fought to free her hands. "You are a vile seducer!"

"It's too late for that, Violet. You didn't even try to stop me."

"That doesn't mean I enjoyed being mauled." She lowered her eyelashes. "And mayhap I was pretending so that you'd get it over with and get off me."

"You were so wet I could've stuffed all four of my fingers in you."

"Then why didn't you?" she snapped.

His expression hardened. "If you choose to dress like a man, I'll fuck you like a man."

Violet fought to control her panicked breathing. Jack had been wrong when he'd insisted her former lover was no longer a threat. Richard might look soft, but beneath the surface, he was the same cold, calculating bastard he had always been. She should remember that.

"There are reasons why I must dress like this."

He raised one eyebrow. "Because you are supposed to be dead?" His grip on her shoulder tightened. "Because you damn well *lied* to me?"

"It's not that simple, Richard, and it isn't all about you."

"Of course not. Why in God's name would you care about my feelings? I was just available for you to fuck, wasn't I?"

Violet stared up at him, heard the hurt behind his words, and for a moment she yearned to reach out, to stroke his cheek and tell him that he'd meant more to her than that, much more. But, of course, she couldn't. She had to protect her family, and what Richard thought of her was irrelevant.

"In truth, you fuck very well." She deliberately relaxed back against the pillows and stopped resisting him. He shifted his weight over her, and she felt the hard press of his half-aroused cock pulse against her stomach.

He pushed away, his arms extended, his hands now planted on either side of her shoulders. "I'm not sure if I want to fuck a corpse."

"You just did."

"No, I fucked Vincent Lennox because I couldn't find his twin."

He levered himself completely off her and strode over to a low table that contained a bowl of water and soap. Violet watched him warily, one eye on the door. Could she dress and escape before he reached her? Considering his anger and his earlier speed and strength, she doubted it. The scent of lavender soap drifted toward her, mingling with the smell of the sweat and seed he'd left on her skin. She remembered the lavender fields of France, of the two of them finding joy even in such perilous circumstances. God, her arse was sore where he'd pounded into her, but she'd take him again if he wanted her . . . let him take her hard and fast and . . .

She started to sit up and he glanced back at her.

"Don't even think of leaving, Violet. I'm not done with you yet."

He walked back to the bed and threw a washcloth at her. "Clean yourself."

She met his impatient gaze. "You don't want me wet?"

He swallowed hard. "I want to get to the bottom of this mystery."

"As opposed to my bottom." Violet couldn't resist. She carefully rubbed the cloth between her thighs, aware that he was watching her and that she wanted to keep cleaning herself until she climaxed right in front of him.

Richard gave a bark of laughter. "Now I see why Jack Lennox reminded me so much of you. Neither of you has any bloody sense." He turned toward her again. "Is he truly your brother?"

"Yes, he's my twin." At least she could tell him the truth about that.

"You never mentioned him."

"I didn't know he existed until fairly recently."

"How convenient for you."

Violet put down the washcloth and pulled up her underthings and breeches, wincing slightly.

Richard frowned. "I hurt you, didn't I?"

She met his gaze. "As you pointed out, you did nothing that I didn't encourage or enjoy."

He sighed. "I lost my temper. That doesn't excuse what I did, but—"

Violet held up her hand. "I forgive you." She edged toward the side of the bed. "Now, this has been very nice, but I have to find Jack. There is something I have to do for him."

"Are you trying to pretend that Jack didn't engineer this entire event and order you to lead me here?"

"No, he didn't!"

He slowly shook his head. "You lie so well I'm almost tempted to believe you. But why else would your brother deliberately lead *me* on a sexual dance and then not deliver the goods?" He considered her for a long moment. "Although I suppose he might consider he fulfilled his purpose by delivering you to me. Was that the plan all along?"

Violet raised her chin. "I wasn't expecting to see you here tonight."

"I don't believe you."

She stalked toward him. "I don't care what you believe. I'm going to find Jack!"

As she tried to get by him, he pushed her back into the room and escaped through the door. Seconds later, she heard the key turn in the lock. Even though she knew it would do no good, she banged on the solid door panels until her fists hurt. Would Jack have deceived her like that? It wouldn't be the first time. Eventually she gave up and started searching the room for a suitable weapon.

Richard leaned against the locked door and struggled to master his breathing. He should have realized that Jack Lennox's elusive twin was none other than his long-lost love, Violet. Her likeness to Jack was indisputable. But he'd not known her as Lennox. But he'd not really known her at all, had he? They'd been thrust together into a series of dangerous missions where they'd satisfied their natural urges with fierce lovemaking to remind them that they were still alive.

That was all.

Nothing else.

Then why did he feel as if his whole world had been rocked to its foundations? She'd taken the joy from his life and turned him into the dull man his family joked about. Richard briefly closed his eyes. He was still furious at Violet's deception, but deep down, not surprised. If anyone could escape death, it would be his feisty first love.

Richard headed back down the corridor to the larger of the public salons. The Oriental acrobats had dispersed, and there was no one performing in the room apart from the huffing and puffing of the regular guests. There was also no sign of Jack Lennox, and Richard *dearly* wanted to see him.

He waved at Marie-Claude and went back along the hall to the second and smaller salon, where a group of chairs faced a small stage. The room was in half darkness and silent, apart from the lascivious sound of a man sucking another man's cock. Richard halted and stared at the stage where Jack Lennox stood, his breeches open, a tall blond man kneeling between his legs.

The man wore a leather mask that covered his whole head and almost all his face. There was a chain attached to the thick collar around his neck with one of the footmen holding it. The rest of the man's body was a mass of intricate leather straps that wrapped around his hips and tightly caged his cock and balls. His arse was plugged with a leather dildo with a curly tail on the end that brushed against his buttocks as he sucked.

Richard sighed and leaned against the wall. He refused to disrupt the "performance." Hopefully Lennox would be so befuddled by lust that forcing him to do Richard's will would be easy.

Jack's lowered gaze reached Richard's and he smiled. Richard smiled back, imagining his hands around Jack's throat squeezing the life out of him. Jack groaned and his hips lifted as if he was pushing his cock deeper into the man's mouth. Richard felt an answering twitch in his own shaft and remembered how Violet felt, the tightness of her arse, the slap of his flesh against her buttocks . . .

Jack shouted out and climaxed to polite applause from the

audience. The blond man sat back on his haunches and the footman patted him on the head and offered him a sweetmeat. As soon as Jack walked away, another willing candidate took his place.

Jack sauntered over to Richard, buttoning his trousers.

"Do you want a turn? He makes an excellent dog, doesn't he? I'll stay and watch."

Richard palmed his knife and placed the blade against Jack's throat.

Jack blinked. "I didn't realize you were the jealous type. I didn't threaten *you* with a knife when that woman sucked your cock."

"This isn't about your cock," Richard murmured, marveling yet again that Lennox had remained alive for so long. "Come with me."

"I will if you put that knife away."

"Then you will have to be disappointed." Richard pressed the tip of the knife against Jack's skin until a thin trickle of blood appeared. "Move."

He grabbed Jack's arm and maneuvered him to the locked room, turned the key, and shoved his nemesis through the door. A flash of movement caught Richard's eye as Violet tried to brain her brother with a candlestick. Jack only narrowly avoided her blow as he lurched to one side.

Richard relocked the door and pocketed the key as the brother and sister shouted at each other in guttural French. Eventually they faced Richard and went quiet. He studied their faces, marveling at both their likeness and their differences.

"The first thing I want to know is, do you still wish to speak to Madame Helene, or was that simply a ploy to gain my attention?" Richard asked.

Jack glanced at Violet and then at Richard. "That was a genuine request. Our grandmother did know Madame in her youth."

Richard inclined his head. "Then Madame will see you to-morrow night at Knowles House for dinner."

"Thank you." Jack hesitated. "Considering everything else, that is most gracious of you."

"Considering that you *failed to mention* that your twin was an old, supposedly dead lover of mine," Richard glared at Jack, "you should be on your knees thanking me."

Jack licked his lips. "I'm quite happy to get on my knees for you."

"Oh, for God's sake, you can stop that act right now," Richard said.

"What act?" Jack glanced at Violet. "Tell him I'm speaking the truth."

"As if I'd believe anything that came out of her mouth," Richard muttered. He suddenly felt weary of their lies, of the very sight of them. "Shall we adjourn this discussion until tomorrow night?"

"You don't intend to kill us, then?" Jack said.

"You are not amusing, Jack, and your sister is officially already dead."

"Then if you don't intend to dispose of our lifeless bodies, we shall take ourselves off." Jack held out his hand to Violet. "Come on, love."

She didn't take his hand and he shrugged and started for the door. Richard waited as Violet slowly followed Jack and then hesitated right in front of him.

"I didn't know that you would be here tonight." She glared at Jack's departing back. "My brother didn't mention it."

Richard held her gaze. "As I said, why should I believe *you?*"

Her skin flushed. "I did know that you were connected to the pleasure house, and I *did* want to speak to you, but—"

Richard placed two fingers over her mouth. "And I don't want to speak to you. I need to think on this."

In truth, he wanted to take her back to bed, strip her naked, and fuck her until she begged him to stop. And if he did that, she'd have won. He couldn't allow himself to be led by his prick again. He wasn't the young man who had fallen in love with a stranger. Her supposed death had changed him too profoundly for her return to mean *nothing*.

He slowly removed his hand from her trembling mouth. "Good night, Vincent."

"Richard, I . . ."

He turned and walked away, knowing that if he didn't, he'd never be free of her again.

5

Violet refolded her cravat and pinned it neatly in place. "There, I think I look quite respectable."

They had gathered in Violet's bedroom at Harcourt House to await their carriage to the Delornay-Ross household. Sylvia, Violet's "mother," came forward to inspect Violet, her blond head angled to the side.

"Hmmm . . . you look like a very pretty man, *Violette*. Not as pretty as your brother, though."

"We all know that my brother should have been born a girl. Some say he fights like one too."

From his seat by the fire, Jack looked up. "Are you still angry with me, sister dear?"

"Of course, I am." Violet allowed Sylvia to help her into her tightly fitting blue coat. "You put me in an extremely difficult situation."

Jack got up and stretched. "So difficult that you immediately fucked each other? I'm not a fool, Violet. I could smell him all over you."

"It wasn't like that. He was . . . very angry with me."

Jack swung around, all the humor drained from his face. "Did he hurt you?"

"No, but he wasn't exactly a tender and considerate lover." Violet sighed. "But who can blame him? It's not often that a woman you thought you saw die comes back from beyond the grave."

Jack grinned at her. "I almost wish I'd seen his face when he spun you around and found out it wasn't me."

Violet shivered. "It wasn't very pleasant." And it wasn't just anger she'd seen on Richard's face. There had been far deeper emotions there, too; emotions she feared had mirrored her own visceral reaction to him.

"I wish I could return to being a woman and just forget this stupid masquerade," Violet muttered.

Sylvia shook her head. "You cannot do that. There is too much at stake. Your very life may depend on it."

"She's right, Violet," Jack added as he checked the arrangement of his cravat in the mirror. "You need to remain incognito until we find out exactly who is trying to blacken our characters and have us killed."

"I'm just tired of it all, Jack. I want to stop running."

Jack walked up to Violet and took her by the shoulders. "I told you, if everything goes well, we should be able to make our home here in England and live out the rest of our lives in peace."

"And if it doesn't go well?"

"Then we'll be dead and beyond worrying about anything at all."

Violet cupped his cheek. "You are incorrigible."

His smile was sweet. "I know." He placed his hand over hers. "If you don't want to see Richard Ross again, you don't have to attend this dinner. If he inquires, I'll explain *exactly* why you are absent."

"You will not." Violet searched her brother's face. "I have no wish to avoid him at all."

"After what he did to you?"

"He did what you had primed him to do, and he did offer me a way out before he took me."

"I find that hard to believe." Jack looked skeptical.

"He asked me to tell him the truth." Violet grimaced. "I pretended not to understand him. He was quite clear about what the consequences would be if I chose not to answer him."

"So you let him fuck you."

Violet raised her chin. "It seemed the less dangerous option."

Jack put on his gloves. "He could have made it *far* more dangerous. He could've beaten you to death."

"But he didn't." Violet felt herself blushing as she relived the moments when Richard Ross had been inside her, his fingers on her clit, his cock pounding her arse. . . . "Even in a towering rage he was remarkably considerate."

"And you like a *considerate* man, don't you?" Jack handed over her gloves and cloak. "Let's be off, then. I'm quite anxious to meet Madame Helene. Aren't you?"

He offered his arm to Sylvia and they walked out of the bedchamber ahead of Violet. With a sigh, Violet followed. She was tired of being Vincent Lennox. She wanted to look as charming as Sylvia in her pink satin evening gown with blond lace.

But Jack was right. Violet put on her hat and pulled on her gloves. If they didn't sort out this mess, the next garment Violet would be wearing would probably be a shroud.

"Do sit down, Richard dear," Helene murmured. "You are causing a draught."

Richard paused in his pacing to stare at his stepmother, who was sitting at her ease in the drawing room of Knowles House. She looked as beautiful as ever and far too relaxed for Richard's liking. Philip sat opposite her, and Emily and Christian shared the loveseat.

Emily still looked rather distracted. When Richard had arrived, he'd intended to sit beside her and find out what was wrong. Unfortunately, Christian had taken the seat beside Emily and remained there ever since.

"Oh, *Maman*, leave Richard be. Can't you see how anxiously he awaits our guests?" Christian asked. "One might think they held a very special place in his heart."

Richard glared at Christian. "Don't you have a business to run?"

Christian smiled. "I've left my wife and Ambrose in charge tonight. I hardly think I need worry."

"More's the pity," Richard grumbled. He could only hope that Christian would become bored of baiting him and leave, but even he doubted that would happen.

The doors into the drawing room opened, and the butler came in and bowed.

"My lord, may I present Mrs. Sylvia Lennox, Mr. Jack Lennox, and Mr. Vincent Lennox."

Helene and Philip rose and advanced toward their guests, leaving Richard with plenty of time to view the new arrivals before he had to step forward and greet them. The twins were dressed identically in dark blue coats, black trousers, and silver-gray waistcoats. Both of them were smiling at their hosts and seemed incredibly at ease.

"Well, well, well," Christian murmured in Richard's ear, making him jump. "I do believe I am smitten. There really are *two* of them. I wonder if they ever share their lovers?"

Richard tried to move away, but Christian followed him. "Maybe you should ask Jack if he would consider it, Richard."

"I will do no such thing."

Christian's smile held more than a hint of wickedness. "Why not? I've fucked twins before and it is quite enjoyable."

"You are a degenerate."

"And you are the heir to a title, and thus above such things, I suppose?"

Richard ignored Christian and stepped forward, his hand outstretched to shake Jack's.

"A pleasure to see you again, Mr. Lennox."

He turned to Violet and shook her hand too. "A pleasure."

Jack touched his sleeve. "Indeed, Mr. Ross. May I introduce you to my mother?"

It took Richard but a moment to decide that whoever Sylvia Lennox was, she definitely wasn't related to the twins. She looked far too young to be their mother. Perhaps she had agreed to give them her name in return for some favor he had yet to discover. Lord Keyes might be able to help him with that. In fact, Richard was looking forward to meeting Keyes again. He had the distinct feeling that he had been deliberately given this assignment, and that his old adversary already knew damn well who Vincent Lennox really was.

"Mr. Ross, I have heard so much about you." Mrs. Lennox smiled charmingly at him, and he bent to kiss her gloved hand.

"And yet I have heard almost nothing about you," he countered lightly. "How can that be when your beauty demands attention?"

She laughed, her brown eyes dancing up at him. "One's children rarely recognize one's attributes, do they?"

"Not having any children myself, I cannot argue the point."

Beside Richard, Violet cleared her throat. "*Maman,* I believe Lord Knowles is waiting to take you in to dinner."

Mrs. Lennox looked around. "Oh, so he is."

Richard bowed. "We shall speak more after dinner."

"Indeed, we shall."

Richard watched as Mrs. Lennox walked across to Philip and he held out his arm to her.

"Your mother is very beautiful," Richard said.

"Yes, she is." Violet sighed. "As is yours."

"Helene isn't my mother."

Violet glanced up at him. "I'm sorry. I didn't realize. Have I offended you?"

"Helene is Christian's mother. They are quite alike. We only share the same father." He nodded at Emily, who was talking to Jack. "Emily is my full sister and I have two other half sisters who are both married."

"Your family sounds almost as complicated as mine."

"Most families are. Your mother, for example, seems rather young."

"As does Madame Helene."

Richard glanced down at Violet's composed face. She betrayed no hint of concern at his questions. A reluctant admiration twisted his gut. She had always been calm in the face of adversity.

Richard gestured toward the door, and he and Violet followed the others into the smaller of the two dining rooms, which seated the eight of them in perfect comfort. Jack took a seat next to Emily and managed to bring a smile to her face, for which Richard was grateful. Was Emily still pining over Ambrose? It seemed likely. Richard wondered what else could have happened to make her look so preoccupied.

The servers brought in the first course, and Richard turned to Violet with a determined smile.

"Are you looking forward to your first London Season, Mr. Lennox?"

Richard waited until Philip closed the doors before taking his seat. Emily had remained with the charming Mrs. Lennox in the drawing room, and everyone else had adjourned to Philip's study. Philip sat behind his desk and Christian perched on the side of it. Richard had taken a seat next to Helene by the fire so that he could study the Lennox twins, who sat opposite his stepmother.

Helene nodded at Jack. "I understand your grandmother believes she knows me."

Despite her conversational tone, Richard noticed that Helene's hands were twisted tightly together in her lap.

"Yes, madame," Jack answered. "She was held in the Bastille for a while. I understand she met you there."

"It is possible, I suppose." Helene shrugged. "There were many people who came and went."

Jack hesitated. "My grandmother was brought in to . . . service the guards' needs."

Helene raised her eyebrows. "You mean she was a whore like me."

Philip cleared his throat. "You were scarcely that, my dear."

"Yes, I was a whore, Philip. There is no point in denying it." Helene sighed. "What was your grandmother's name?"

"Jeanne."

"And what did she look like?"

Jack looked down at his clasped hands. "She said you might remember her because you saved her from being badly burned. Her face and her hands were still scarred, which is why she was cast out of the Bastille." His expression twisted. "I suppose after her disfigurement she was no longer of interest to the guards. She always believed her expulsion kept her alive."

"That is true, not many women in our circumstances lived very long." Helene drew in a quick breath. "I do remember a Jeanne. She was a lot older than me and, unfortunately, very popular with the guards."

"My grandmother also said to tell you that your friendship made each day bearable, and that she has never forgotten your indomitable spirit."

"Oh . . ." Helene brought her hand up to cover her mouth.

"Helene!" With a soft exclamation, Philip came out from behind his desk and rushed to his wife's side. When Richard realized Helene was crying, he shot to his feet and offered his chair to his father.

Philip sat down, wrapped an arm around his wife, and held her close. He offered her his handkerchief, which she took and used to dab at her eyes.

"I'm sorry, madame," Jack said softly. "I didn't mean to upset you."

"I am not upset." Helene raised her head and looked at Jack. "I am glad you told me about your grandmother. I am delighted that she survived. Does she ever visit England?"

Jack glanced at Vincent. "I don't think so, madame. She is rather a recluse. That is why she asked us to convey her message to you instead."

"And I am unlikely to visit France. I am too afraid." Helene dried her eyes and sat up straight. "Would she allow me to write to her?"

"Of course, madame."

"Then that is what I shall do." Helene handed Philip back his handkerchief and smiled into his eyes. "Thank you."

Philip touched her cheek. "I love you, Helene."

"And I love you too."

Richard saw Christian grimace at such an open declaration of love and wondered if his own face bore the same expression. Neither of them was entirely comfortable with the obvious passion that burned between their respective parents.

Still holding Philip's hand, Helene turned back to the twins. "You must visit me here later in the week. I will have a letter ready for you to send to your grandmother."

"It will be our pleasure to deliver it, madame." Jack bowed and then looked at his twin. "It will also be a pleasure to converse with you further, won't it, Vincent?"

"Indeed."

Violet's voice was lighter and softer than Jack's. From the corner of his eye, Richard noticed that Christian had sat forward and was staring intently at the two brothers. Inwardly, Richard groaned. Christian was far too experienced not to notice that the younger Lennox twin was not quite what he seemed.

Philip and Helene stood and everyone else followed suit. Helene walked across to Jack, kissed his cheek and then Vincent's.

"Thank you for coming to find me. I appreciate it."

"Thank you for having the courage to meet us, madame, although after what our grandmother told us about you, we weren't surprised."

Helene laughed and patted his cheek. "I see her spirit in you both."

Philip shook Jack's hand. "Shall we return to the drawing room? Your mother must be wondering where the devil we are."

Christian waited until everyone but Richard had preceded him from the room and then turned to his half brother.

"This makes it even more interesting, doesn't it?"

"What does?"

"That Vincent Lennox isn't quite the man he claims to be."

Richard moved toward the door. "Really? I hadn't noticed."

Christian smoothly barred his way. "Which begs the question, which Lennox *did* you fuck at the pleasure house?"

Richard just stared at Christian. "Perhaps I had them both."

"And, yet again, I underestimated you, my dear brother." Christian stepped out of the way.

"Perhaps you did."

Emily opened the door into her bedchamber and stepped inside. The long evening of avoiding Richard's inquiring looks and remembering to be polite to the Lennox family had given her a headache, and she never had headaches. She considered them a ridiculous female weakness. Thank goodness, Jack Lennox had proved an amusing companion and had kept her entertained during dinner. Like most gentlemen of her acquaintance, he'd barely expected her to do anything except laugh at his gallantries and utter one-word answers whenever he required them.

With another furtive glance at her door, she hurried to her chest of drawers and drew out the box Thomas Smith had given her in the park. She'd already started reading the letters, which were not addressed to anyone but were obviously meant for a lover. Emily had a sinking feeling that the lover was not her father, but another man entirely. But why had Thomas Smith kept the letters? Had he acted as some kind of go-between?

She took out the pile of letters and put them in order from the first tentative note to the last impassioned plea for the lover to take her away from the horror of her marriage, of her children. . . . Emily stared at the last of the letters, the one that had shaken her so badly. In the world of the *ton*, it was not uncommon for a married woman to take a lover after she had fulfilled her duty to her husband and provided him with an heir. But this affair, this affair of her mother's, appeared to have started before her marriage and continued almost until her death.

Emily put the pile of letters down and stared at them. It certainly explained why Philip had been such an unwelcome visitor in his own home, and why he had stayed away. Had Philip lied and never actually relinquished Helene? Was that why Anne had taken her own lover? Her mother was dead, and she could hardly ask her father such an indelicate question. He would surely want to know why she wanted answers after all these years, and she was reluctant to disclose her recent reacquaintance with Mr. Smith.

Emily put the letters aside and took her mother's diary out of the box. She suspected that many of the answers to her questions lay within the pages of the thick journal. A hint of her mother's stale perfume wafted up from the book and something tugged at Emily's memory, making the task of opening the book too painful. She dropped it back into the box and tossed the letters on top.

It seemed her courage had deserted her again, just as it had after Ambrose had kissed her so passionately and stepped away. She put the box back into her dresser and rang for her maid. Mayhap she would try to read the book again tomorrow.

6

―――――――

"I hope you don't mind us coming around to the kitchen."

Ambrose put on the pine table the bottles of wine he had just collected from the cellar and studied the two men who had entered through the back door of the pleasure house. It was just after ten o'clock, and he was mentally checking through his plans for the evening's entertainment and anticipating the arrival of the guests. He had seen the two men before, but not in such close quarters. In truth, they were a remarkably handsome pair. Ambrose reckoned they would be much appreciated by the other members of the pleasure house—especially if they liked to fuck together.

"It's Mr. Ambrose, isn't it?" The first man advanced with his hand held out. "I'm Jack Lennox, and this is my brother, Vincent."

Ambrose shook the proffered hand. "It is just Ambrose. I remember Mr. Delornay mentioning you, Mr. Lennox. Welcome back to the pleasure house."

Jack Lennox smiled. "Even in such an unorthodox fashion? I expect most of your guests come through the front door."

"They do." Ambrose gestured for the men to join him at the table. "Usually only members of the family use this entrance."

"Miss Ross told me that if I wanted to know anything about the pleasure house, you were the man to ask. So I decided to come straight to the source," Jack said.

"Miss Ross is very kind, but Mr. Christian Delornay is the owner of the house, and he is far more knowledgeable than I will ever be."

"And far less approachable." Jack winked. "I met him last night at Madame Helene's house. He seems to delight in causing as much controversy as I do."

"Impossible," his brother muttered. "You are the master of that."

Jack nodded at his brother. "Thank you."

"It wasn't a compliment. If it wasn't for you, we wouldn't be in our current predicament."

Ambrose concentrated his attention on the soft-spoken twin. If he was correct, Vincent Lennox was no man. As he considered their involvement with both the usually staid Richard Ross and the enigmatic Lord Keyes, his interest in the couple deepened.

"Was there something in particular you wished me to help you with?" Ambrose inquired.

Jack put his elbows on the table and settled himself in his seat. "We were wondering about payment."

"For your sexual services?"

Jack laughed. "God, no! I meant how much it will cost us to have a temporary membership here." He glanced at his twin. "We're not that plump in the pocket at the moment."

"There is no charge."

"Are you sure?"

Ambrose shrugged. "Mr. Ross asked Mr. Delornay if you could be added to the guest list. Mr. Ross is part of the family; therefore, there is nothing to pay."

"That seems rather generous."

There was a note of skepticism in Jack Lennox's voice that made Ambrose reevaluate his first opinion that the man lived off his charm and good looks.

"If you and your twin decide to participate in the sexual games here, I'm sure Mr. Delornay will consider you to have paid your dues."

Jack met his amused gaze. "Do you participate, Ambrose?"

"Indeed, I do, Mr. Lennox."

"And what do you prefer?"

"In terms of sex?" Ambrose held Jack's gaze. "I am willing to try anything at least once."

Jack's smile was slow and heated. "A man after my own heart."

"Scarcely that, sir. We do not trade in the finer emotions of love here, merely the physical ones." He'd been repeating that truth to himself every time he thought of the feel of Emily Ross kissing him.

Vincent Lennox nudged his brother. "If you have finished trying to disconcert Ambrose, Jack, perhaps we should go upstairs." He hesitated. "Is Mr. Ross here tonight?"

Ambrose studied her carefully. "I believe he is expected later this evening. Do you wish me to tell him that you are here?"

"If you would." Vincent smiled at him. "Thank you."

The back door opened again, and a gust of wind blew Emily Ross and the tall form of Seamus Kelly inside in a rush. Ambrose got to his feet and tried to school his features into his usual welcoming smile. Despite all his vows, he'd kissed Emily Ross. What was worse was that he still wanted to kiss her, to taste her, to have her underneath him screaming his name as she climaxed. . . .

"Good evening, Miss Ross."

"Ambrose." Her smile was almost as guarded as his. Did she regret what she'd said, what he'd done? He could hardly ask her now with the Lennox twins watching them. And then there was that puzzling matter of the man from her past. . . .

"Miss Ross!" Jack Lennox rose to his feet and bowed, as did his brother. "What an unexpected pleasure. I was just talking about you to Ambrose."

Emily took a seat at the table, her face becomingly flushed, her brown hair caught up in ringlets that framed her strong features. Ambrose loved her face, had watched her mature, had seen the intelligence and courage blossom in her eyes, and for years had wanted her to look at him alone.

She took off her gloves and laid them on the table. "I've just returned from the most boring musical evening I have ever attended. None of the young ladies who performed were more than averagely talented, and even if they were, they were too busy simpering at all the men to pay attention to their music."

"You don't believe in flirting, Miss Ross?" Jack Lennox asked, his blue eyes dancing, his attention completely focused on Emily. Ambrose felt his smile slip. Did Jack Lennox have to be so charming to everyone?

"I fear I've had my fill of it, Mr. Lennox." Emily pulled a face her chaperone would not have approved of. "I'd much prefer to have an honest conversation with a man about what I want and what I expect from him."

"An admirable wish, Miss Ross, but one that I suspect would frighten off all but the most timid of suitors."

"Exactly." Emily glared at Jack as if he was personally responsible for the failings of the entire male race. "Most men are afraid of an intelligent woman and terrified of being caught in some ridiculous marital trap."

For some reason, Ambrose felt compelled to divert Emily's attention away from Jack. "I appreciate your intelligence, Miss Ross. I always have."

Emily stared at him, a combative gleam in her eye. "But you are still afraid of me, aren't you?"

"I . . ." Ambrose swallowed back the rest of his words. "This isn't the appropriate time to discuss my many short-comings." He rose to his feet. "Would you like me to escort you upstairs, gentlemen? I have to attend to my duties."

He didn't dare look at Emily. He knew she'd be thinking him a coward, and perhaps she was right. He *was* afraid to deal with his feelings for her, but not for the reasons she thought. Why admit to wanting something that he could never have?

Vincent Lennox rose, too, and bowed to Emily. "A pleasure, Miss Ross. Are you coming upstairs too?"

"I am not permitted upstairs," Emily said. "My family thinks I am too young and impressionable to see such sights."

"And you agree with them?" Jack asked, and Ambrose wanted to curse.

"No, I don't."

Emily scowled at Ambrose, who walked toward the kitchen door and held it invitingly open. Unfortunately, only one of the Lennox twins took the bait, and it wasn't the one he wanted. Jack remained seated at the table opposite Emily.

"Mr. Lennox?" Ambrose asked, and Jack looked over his shoulder. "Are you coming?"

"I'll be there in a moment. Please don't wait for me."

Ambrose could do nothing but bow and escort the more malleable of the Lennox twins up the stairs to the first level of salons. His desire to escape back to the kitchen was immediately thwarted by the appearance of Elizabeth Delornay asking him to assist her in the room of desires. With a sigh, he followed his employer and could only hope that Jack Lennox quickly left Emily alone for the more salacious delights of the pleasure house.

Emily watched Ambrose leave and let her determined smile slip.

"Does Ambrose not approve of you, Miss Ross?"

She looked up at Jack Lennox, who was watching her attentively.

"Ambrose definitely doesn't want me in his kitchen."

"Ah." Jack nodded. "I did wonder about that."

"What do you mean?"

"I'm not stupid, Miss Ross. There is obviously something between you and Ambrose. His whole demeanor altered when you arrived."

"It did?"

Jack smiled at her. "Of course, it did. How could he resist you? I've only just met you and I'm quite smitten."

Emily scowled at him. "Don't try and dally with me, Mr. Lennox."

"Why not?" He raised his eyebrows. "Don't you think it is time Ambrose saw you as a desirable woman rather than the family member who comes to annoy him in the kitchen of the pleasure house?"

Emily studied Jack Lennox. "What exactly are you proposing?"

"I'm supposed to be doing the Season with my mother and brother, and I'm determined to keep the matchmaking mothers away from me. What if we pretended to form an attachment to each other?"

Emily considered his words. "No one would believe a man as attractive as you would be interested in me."

"Miss Ross, you're not thinking clearly. I'm an impoverished man with great charm, beauty, and wit, and you are an heiress." He sat back and spread his arms wide. "Some might say it was a match made in heaven."

"And you don't care if the gossips call you a fortune hunter?"

"Why should I care? It's not as if I really intend to marry you, is it?"

Emily bit down on her lip. "I'll help you with the society mothers, but only if you will help me with Ambrose."

"I'm quite happy to assist you with winning Ambrose." His smile was devilish. "But I think we will have to be a little more direct than dancing too many times together or slipping off to wander around the family grounds. I doubt Ambrose will play by society rules. Are you willing to risk your reputation?"

Emily met his wicked blue gaze. "Yes, for Ambrose, I believe that I am."

Violet took up a position in the main salon that allowed her to see everyone who entered through the main doors. She'd almost been relieved when Jack stayed to talk to Emily Ross. It gave her more time to find Richard without Jack's interference. She loved her brother dearly, but he did have an annoying habit of upping the stakes and tempting the Fates. She shuddered to think what he had been like as a boy. His antics must have terrified their grandmother. It was surprising he had survived to adulthood unscathed.

She sipped at a glass of wine and tried to ignore the sexual frolics happening around her. She had no desire to join in and expose her lack of manly equipment—although, if she gave them pleasure, her sex probably wouldn't matter to the majority of the guests.

Just after she replenished her glass of wine for the third time, Richard strolled into the salon, his hands behind his back, his posture upright and commanding. He wore a brown coat that brought out the gold in his hazel eyes—eyes that were staring directly at her. She inclined her head an inch and he walked toward her, his expression bland, his mouth a firm, unsmiling line. When had he stopped smiling so readily? She had a horrible feeling that if she asked him directly, he would either dismiss the question or, even worse, blame her.

"Mr. Lennox."

"Mr. Ross." Violet indicated the empty chair beside her. "Will you join me?"

He sat down, his keen gaze still scanning the room. "Where is your wastrel of a brother?"

"I believe he was talking to Ambrose in the kitchen."

"Not to Ambrose. I just saw him heading into the room of desires."

Violet waved a vague hand. She knew what older brothers were like, and she had no desire to get Emily Ross or Jack into trouble. "Then he is probably here somewhere. Why, did you want him for something?"

"Would you be jealous if I did?"

Violet blinked. "I wouldn't. Jack can be very persuasive when he wants to be. If he wants you, he'll be the first one to let you know."

"I noticed that," Richard said drily. "He is charm personified."

Violet felt an unexpected surge of anger. "Like me, he has lived on his wits and very little else. We are not all blessed with your good fortune, Mr. Ross."

Richard sat back in his chair and regarded her. "You sound quite bitter, *Mr.* Lennox. Is that why you have come back into my life? To take from me the things you think I don't deserve?"

Violet drew an unsteady breath. "I'm not quite that small-minded or vindictive."

"You want money, then, instead?"

She rose to her feet and stared down at him. "I *wanted* to have a reasonable conversation with you, Mr. Ross, but that seems to be impossible. I'll wish you good night."

He reached out and locked his fingers around her wrist. "Sit down."

"Don't tell me what to do."

Without thinking, she tossed the remains of the glass of wine she held right in his face. His sudden intake of breath was wonderfully satisfying, as was the sight of the red wine dripping down his chin and onto his white shirt. He didn't, however, release her; instead, he tightened his grip as he rose.

"Now you'll have to come with me while I change."

"Let me go, Mr. Ross." Violet looked desperately around for Jack, but as usual, he was nowhere to be seen. "You have no right to manhandle me like this."

He jerked her even closer, his mouth close to her ear. "Do you want me to put an end to this masquerade, pick you up over my shoulder and take you out of here? Or will you come quietly?"

The menace behind Richard's quietly spoken words sunk in and Violet nodded. She couldn't afford to be exposed as a woman yet, and Richard probably knew it.

"Come on, then."

Still holding on to her, he turned in the opposite direction to the one she had anticipated and pulled her along with him. At the very end of the hallway, he stopped, withdrew a key, and unlocked the plain door. Violet found herself on the narrow servants' stairs, Richard urging her upward, with a hand in the small of her back.

She lost track of how many levels and staircases they traversed, until Richard drew to a halt beside another more ornate door and pushed her inside. A fire burned in the grate, and the large four-poster bed was turned down to display white linen sheets.

"Where are we?" Violet asked as she rubbed unobtrusively at her wrist.

"My bedchamber." Richard glanced at her over his shoulder as he stripped off his coat.

"You live here at the pleasure house?"

"No, I have other lodgings. This is just for convenience."

He took off his waistcoat and started on his stained cravat

and shirt. Violet stayed by the fireplace, where she could still see the door. It was the second time he'd taken her into a room against her will and she didn't want to be locked in again.

"What did you wish to talk about, Violet?"

He loosened his trousers and pulled his shirt over his head. For a moment, she was too distracted by the sight of his muscled chest and flat stomach to remember what she wanted to say. By the time she found her voice, he'd emerged from the shirt, his hair ruffled and his gaze fixed firmly on hers.

"I wanted to explain why we had sought you out."

He balled the fabric up and threw the shirt on the floor. "So you did come looking for me, after all."

"And for Madame Helene. It was just by chance that you were related to her."

His faint smile died. "Chance. You can't help but lie every time you open your beautiful mouth, can you?"

Violet held her ground. "As far as I understand it, the relationship between Madame Helene and your father isn't widely known. You certainly didn't mention it when I first met you."

He walked over to the basin and jug of water, and poured some water into the bowl. "I didn't mention it because it wasn't something I wanted to believe had happened." He splashed water over his face and torso, seemingly oblivious to the cold. "In truth, I bolted to France to avoid having to deal with it at all."

Cautiously, Violet took a seat and stared up at Richard's dripping wet chest. "I can understand that your father taking up with a notorious madame might have upset you."

"It didn't upset me. I was absolutely furious with him."

He grabbed a drying cloth and rubbed vigorously at his face and damp hair. She sat forward as he walked across the large room to a chest of drawers and extracted another shirt. Before putting it on, he came toward her and she tensed.

All he did was lay the shirt over the back of the chair nearest the fire to warm and stare down at it. The firelight dappled his skin, making him look like an ancient statue cast forever in stone. Violet realized he was as unlikely to elaborate about his feelings as she was to take him completely into her confidence. She decided her best course of action was to forge ahead and hope that he'd at least listen.

"When Jack told me that you were connected to Madame Helene, I knew we would most likely meet. I told him about our . . . relationship. I had to."

"And Jack, being Jack, was quite happy to exploit every opportunity you gave him. Did he tell you to seduce me again?"

"I didn't seduce you the first time."

Richard just raised his eyebrows and waited, one hand grasping the back of the chair.

Violet regarded him coldly. "I believe it was a mutual decision."

"If that is how you choose to remember it, who am I to argue with a lady?" His smile was both sardonic and dismissive, and stirred her simmering temper. "And if we are discussing the past and things not shared between us, why didn't you mention that you had a twin brother?"

"I didn't know he was still alive."

"Perhaps you found him loitering in the underworld when you died and brought him back with you?"

Violet clenched her fists so hard that her fingernails dug into her flesh. She would not allow him to distract her from the truth. It was little enough to give him, but it was all she had.

"During the aftermath of the revolution, our parents went their separate ways. My father took Jack, and I was left with my mother. We only met again about three years ago at our grandmother's house."

"The grandmother who knew Helene during the revolution."

"Yes." Violet flicked an irritated glance up at Richard's bare skin. "Aren't you going to put your shirt on?"

He rubbed a leisurely hand over his muscled chest and his nipple hardened. "You used to enjoy the sight of me displaying far more skin than this."

Violet met his gaze. "That was a long time ago."

He shrugged. "You seemed to enjoy me fucking your arse the other night as well."

"Can we get back to the reason for my being here?" Violet snapped.

"In my bedchamber?"

She ignored him and took a steadying breath. "As I was saying, Jack turned up at our grandmother's house barely alive."

"Now that doesn't surprise me at all. I've been wanting to strangle him since I met him," Richard muttered.

Violet fought a sudden urge to smile. "After talking to each other at length, we realized we had both been working for the good of the true France, as had our parents."

"What a surprise."

Violet glared at Richard. "Do you wish to listen to what I have to say or not?"

He sighed. "I suppose I should at least hear you out." He took the seat opposite her, still shirtless, and sat forward. "Please, carry on."

"Things have . . . changed in France. Reviving the monarchy is not such a popular cause anymore. We were no longer sure that the people we worked for were trustworthy. Recent events have proved that beyond a doubt. We decided it was time to abandon our ties with France and find a safe haven in which to live out the rest of our lives."

"And you decided on England. France's oldest enemy."

"Our father was English. We have a right to live here."

"Jack told me that you were born here."

"That is true."

"You have proof of this?"

Violet hesitated. "No, all our documents were lost with our

parents. But Lord Keyes assured Jack that such records could be found and authenticated."

Richard sat back, his face in the half-shadows, his fingers drumming on the arm of his chair. "So you just wish to settle down and live in peace."

"Yes." Violet put all the sincerity she could into her answer. She was weary of the subterfuge; she desperately wanted to escape before she was killed.

He stood up so suddenly that she shrank back in her seat. His hands came up to grab the wings of her chair, caging her in.

"Do you think I am stupid, Violet? No one walks away from a spymaster and gets to live happily ever after."

"You did."

His laugh was humorless. "Why do you think I still associate with Lord Keyes? Do you think I *like* him?"

"Are you suggesting that you are still spying for your country?"

He stared at her for a long moment; then his face relaxed into a smile that didn't relieve her suspicions at all. "Your imagination runs away with you, Violet. Unlike you, I was never a spy in the first place. Lord Keyes asked me to help you and Jack assimilate into society. And as you have just told me that you wish to live in England, you must admit that his request makes perfect sense."

He didn't move back and his gaze dropped to her waistcoat. "But why must you be disguised as a man?"

"Because you are right. There are certain people who did not wish Jack and I to leave France."

"Alive?"

She fought to control her surprise at his quick leap to the correct conclusion. He leaned forward and stroked his finger along the line of her forehead. "Don't frown. It doesn't become you. You believe you will be safer in England?"

"Yes." She shivered as his finger trailed down her nose and traced her upper lip.

"So what do you require from me if it isn't money?" he asked softly.

Your protection? For a moment she thought she'd said the words out loud, but he continued to stare at her and she realized he was waiting for her to speak. Her courage failed and she smiled at him in return.

"Exactly what Lord Keyes asked of you: your help in establishing us in society. I wanted to make sure that you would not betray us." He went still and she held her breath as his gaze hardened. She hurried on. "It will be difficult for Jack to claim our father's title and lands. He will need all the assistance he can get."

"And I am to provide that assistance."

"If you are so inclined, sir. With you, Lord Keyes, and Madame Helene on our side, I believe we can establish ourselves quite credibly."

"And what do I get in return?"

"You don't wish to help us?"

His mouth twisted. "You haven't changed at all. You still answer my questions with questions of your own. What of Mrs. Lennox?"

"My mother?"

"If that woman is your mother, I'll eat my hat."

Violet let out her breath. "Sylvia is also in need of help. We agreed to aid each other."

"She is another poor spy?"

"No, she is my father's second wife. He died about three years ago."

"How convenient for you all."

Violet shivered as she recalled Jack's version of what had happened to their father and how he'd barely escaped with his life trying to save the older man's wife.

"I am *not* lying."

He cupped her chin. "As if I could ever tell the difference between your lies and your truth. I'm not sure even you know. When we first met, I thought you an innocent."

"I was." She jerked away from his touch. "I still know what is true."

His mouth descended and caught hers, nipping at her lower lip until she let him in and he deepened the kiss. She moaned as his tongue tangled with hers, making her arch helplessly toward him. He ripped his mouth away, but he didn't retreat.

"This is true, your response to me. It always has been."

The male satisfaction in his voice as he dove in for another kiss made her recoil.

"How do you know that? If I am such an accomplished liar, how do you know I don't lie about this?"

He pulled back, his expression lethal, one hand attacking the buttons of her trousers until he cupped her wet, needy sex.

"You can't fake this, Violet." He plunged one finger deep inside her. "You're wet for me." His tongue slid into her mouth, mimicking the thrust and retreat of his finger.

She couldn't escape him, could only drown in the complex emotions he aroused in her and surrender to the determination of his kiss and the rhythm of his probing finger. He grabbed her hand and pressed it against the front of his trousers.

"I cannot lie about this either. I want you."

Her fingers curled around the throbbing heat of his shaft and he groaned.

"If this is the truth, Richard," Violet whispered, "it is just lust, and it means *nothing.*"

"Nothing?" He withdrew his finger from the heat of her core and sucked it into his mouth. "Lust is more than nothing. It is the most basic need a human has, the need to copulate."

"Don't you mean to procreate?"

"You're a man, now, Violet, and I'll fuck you like one. There is no need to worry about us procreating."

She shoved at his chest, but he didn't move an inch. "And what if I don't want to fuck you?"

"We've already established that you want me." His stare was pointed. "But do you want me enough to play by my rules?"

She stared at him, her mind trying to recover from the haze of desire and work out what he was trying to say.

"Are you suggesting I trade my body in exchange for your help?"

"I hadn't thought of it in quite those terms, but I'm quite willing to go along with it."

"But you'll only fuck me like a man."

He nodded, his gaze drifting down to her still-open trousers. She wanted to cross her legs to placate the ache there but knew he'd enjoy it too much.

"You'll not betray Jack either?"

"Much as it pains me to say it, no, I will not betray Jack."

"Then if this is the only way I can persuade you to help us, I will agree to your terms."

Richard's smile was slow in coming. "Thank you."

Violet glared at him. "You haven't changed at all, have you?"

He straightened, one hand on the buttons of his trousers. "Oh, I've changed. I'm no longer prepared to take your word for something." He pulled down his trousers to display the thick length of his cock. "This time I'd like a little something on account before you run off and use me for a fool."

Richard held his breath as Violet considered him and slowly licked her lips.

"You wish me to suck your cock?"

"What do you think?" He cupped his balls and stroked his thumb along the base of his shaft. He was already wet and more than ready for her.

"You would force me?"

Briefly, Richard closed his eyes. Violet looked far too innocent to be sitting there contemplating his cock. She had such a talent for eluding him, for making him feel like a complete bastard. "How can you ask that? Didn't we just make a bargain?"

"And you want to seal it with my mouth around your cock?"

His shaft twitched at that salacious image. "You were the one who suggested the arrangement in the first place."

"Only because you . . ." She sighed. "You are impossible. All I wanted was to talk to you and explain my position."

"And you have done so."

She raised her chin. "And my *position* is on my knees servicing you?"

"Yes, I believe it is."

Her gaze measured the length of his cock; then she got down from her seat and onto the floor in front of him. His heart rate sped up and his crown grew even wetter.

"In the humor I am in now, I might just bite it off."

He wrapped one hand around her neck and drew her close. "If you try it, I'll strangle you."

"So much for truth," she muttered, then leaned forward and drew his shaft deep into her mouth and down her throat.

Richard groaned as she started to suck him hard, his hand clamped around the back of her head, his hips joining the pulsing rhythm of her mouth. He knew it wouldn't take long. He'd been primed to have her all night, ready for whatever she would give him, desperate for the touch and taste of her.

He closed his eyes as she used her teeth on his flesh, drawing his whole length in and out of her mouth until he could stand it no longer and he climaxed with a hoarse shout. She released his cock and rested her forehead briefly against his thigh, her chest heaving as hard as his.

With a growl, he dropped to his knees and took her mouth, slid his hand inside her still-open trousers, and pumped all four fingers inside her in a quick and greedy pattern that had her tightening and coming all over his hand, squeezing his fingers and coming again.

Before she'd finished climaxing, he withdrew his hand, picked her up, and dumped her back in her seat. She looked up at him, her face flushed with lust, her blue eyes wild with need.

He slowly closed his trousers over his rapidly recovering cock. Had Violet told him anything that was true tonight? Some of the things had *sounded* sincere and others not at all. All he knew was that he had barely scratched the surface of what was going on with the Lennox twins. His instincts told him something was very wrong, but he had no idea where, or from whom, the threat came from.

Now at least he had a way to connect with her, and to keep her safe. He studied his lover's deceptively beautiful face. And whatever she claimed about wanting to live quietly, she needed to be kept safe. Despite her display of bravado, something was obviously very wrong to have sent her fleeing to England and into the arms of the one man on earth guaranteed to hate her.

Richard put on his fire-warmed shirt and the rest of his clothes. When he was suitably dressed, he turned back to Violet, who had managed to straighten her own clothes quite well.

"Your brother will be wondering where you are."

"I suppose he will."

"I'm surprised he didn't come after us."

She shrugged. "He knows I can take care of myself."

"If he thinks that, he is a fool."

She walked to the door. "He probably assumed I was with you. He wouldn't be worried."

"And why is that? Am I no longer seen as a threat?"

She opened the door and half turned back toward him. "I told him you would never harm me."

The quiet confidence of her tone annoyed him far more than he had anticipated. "Why, because I am too meek and mild?"

She raised her eyebrows. "No, because you know your own strength, and despite everything you say, or perhaps because of it, you would never hurt a woman."

"I've hurt women; I've even killed them. You know that."

"But not me."

"There's still time." He took a deliberate step toward her, but she didn't flinch away.

"Richard, if you restrained yourself from killing me when you found out I was still alive, you are very unlikely to hurt me now."

"Are you saying I've missed my chance?" He shot her a furious glare. "You don't know that."

She smiled. "Good night, Mr. Ross."

And she was gone before he could call her back and . . . and what? Demand a chance to kill her? Richard sighed and followed her down the hall. She had no idea how to get out of the more private side of the pleasure house, so she would have to bear his company for a little longer until he could set her free.

7

*I have kept him out of my bed for months
now, and he is both angry and suspicious. I
cannot bear his touch, my love, but I will have to
endure it unless all our plans are to fail. At least
if I persuade him to bring me back to his country
estate, I can be near you in spirit when he
completes his loathsome marital duties. . . .*

Emily slowly put the letter down and stared at the cramped
script. Her mother had tried to avoid her marriage bed with an
increasingly annoyed Philip because she already had a lover.
Her timid, sickly mother had been far more devious than Emily
could ever have imagined. What had possessed her to marry
Philip when her heart was obviously elsewhere?

She reached into the wooden keepsake box, took out her
mother's diary, and leafed through the pages. There was nothing written on the day the letter had been composed. Emily had
noticed that her mother tended to do either one or the other:
pour her heart out into her journal or to her lover. It didn't

make any sense. From what she knew of her parents, they had been betrothed before her father was sent to India. Her mother, Anne, had often complained that she hadn't enjoyed a proper Season in London because she was already engaged and the expense was considered unnecessary.

So when had she met this other man? Emily contemplated the letter. Unfortunately, there were no addresses on the correspondence. After her parents died, Anne was brought up with Philip's family, which meant that her paramour had to have been encountered at the Ross family country estate.

Could she think of a pretext to go and visit her old home? Since her father's elevation to the peerage, they had moved to the much larger Knowles estate and leased their old home to distant cousins. It wasn't that far out of London. All she needed was for someone to accompany her.

There was a knock on her door and her maid came in. "Miss Ross, there are two gentlemen awaiting you in the drawing room with Mr. Richard."

"Thank you, Jess." Emily smoothed down her green skirts and patted ineffectually at her hair. "I'll be down in a moment."

She tidied the box and locked the contents away in her clothes chest. It was past time to bring the matter to Richard's attention, although she was dreading it. He had a stubborn affection for their late mother, which she suspected merely supplied him with fuel for his disagreements with his father.

As she descended the stairs, she wondered who else had come to call. She thought she'd managed to discourage all but the most determined of suitors from visiting her at home. The three men stood up when she entered, and Richard came across to kiss her cheek.

"Emily, my dear, you've already met Mr. Jack and Mr. Vincent Lennox."

Jack winked at her as he gravely kissed her hand. "Miss Ross, what a pleasure."

Emily tried not to smile at him and turned to accept the more conventional greeting from Jack's slighter, quieter twin. She gestured for them to sit, and Richard rang for some tea.

"I'm sorry that Madame Helene is not here to receive you today."

Jack shrugged, the gesture very French. "We came to see you, Miss Ross. Who else?" He glanced over at Richard, who didn't look quite so amused. "We have been invited to a ball by Lord Keyes's mother. I was hoping that you might be prevailed upon to save me a dance."

"As was I, Miss Ross," Vincent added.

"I would be delighted to dance with both of you." Emily smiled. "I believe the ball is to be held on Friday next."

"Indeed," Richard said. "And you can always call on me if you need a partner, Emily, you know that."

"And I so often lack for partners these days, don't I?" Emily kept her smile firmly in place. "One might almost think that I had deliberately driven them all away."

She noticed Vincent Lennox hastily conceal a smile. Jack leaned forward, his blue gaze fixed on her.

"I cannot believe that, Miss Ross. If the fools do not choose to dance with you, my brother and I will be only too delighted to exploit their inexplicable blunder."

"You'll dance with her twice, Lennox, that's quite enough," Richard interrupted. "Any more will give rise to just the sort of speculation and scandal my sister strives to avoid."

Jack continued to smile at Emily, and she sat there and pretended to bask in his blatant, if quite false, admiration. It was remarkably invigorating to be the object of such intense interest. If only Ambrose, the true object of her affections, were there to see it.

Richard cleared his throat as the tea was brought in. "Do you wish to pour, Emily?"

"Certainly."

She distributed the tea in its dainty cups to her guests and picked up her own cup. Richard drank the scalding brew in two quick swallows as if anxious to be done with it. The Lennox twins displayed much better manners. After a short while, she noticed Richard glance at the clock.

"Do you have another appointment, Richard, or am I just boring you?"

He put his cup down with a distracted air. "I'm sorry, Emily, that was very rude of me."

"I was hoping to speak to you before you left." Emily held his gaze so that he could see both her sincerity and her determination to make him stay.

"Of course."

Jack stood, swiftly followed by his brother. "Then we will be on our way. We look forward to seeing you at the ball, if not before. Do you enjoy a walk in the park, Miss Ross? If so, I would be delighted to accompany you one afternoon when it is fine."

"I would enjoy that *immensely*," Emily said, aware that Richard was now scowling at the Lennoxes. "Perhaps I might send you a note. I understand that you are staying at Harcourt House."

"We are." Jack pressed a hand to his heart. "We await your commands with great anticipation."

Richard waited until the Lennox twins finished their effusive good-byes, then shut the door firmly behind them.

"Don't get any ideas about Jack Lennox being in love with you, Emily. That man doesn't have a sincere bone in his body."

Emily pretended to sigh. "Every man meets his match at some point, Richard. Perhaps Jack Lennox is ready to be caught by an exceptional woman like me."

Richard's expression was not encouraging. "He is a rapscallion and probably a fortune hunter as well. I'd tell you to keep away from him entirely, but I know if I did that, you'd be announcing you were marrying him next week."

Emily patted the seat next to her and Richard joined her. "I don't want to talk about Jack Lennox."

"Then what is troubling you, sister?"

As briefly as she could, Emily told Richard about her meeting with Thomas Smith and the box of letters he'd given her.

Richard went still. "Did you meet with this man alone?"

"No, I took Seamus Kelly and Ambrose with me."

"You told Ambrose about this matter before discussing it with me?"

Emily touched his hand. "I hoped to spare you. I knew you would find it difficult to hear anything about our parents' relationship."

He went still under her hands. "Are you suggesting there was something in those letters that might offend me?"

"I think you should read them for yourself."

He removed her hand from his. "I'd much rather you just told me the worst of it."

She met his gaze. "Are you sure? There is a rather long tradition of the bringer of bad news bearing the brunt of the receiver's displeasure."

His smile was both warm and encouraging. "I'd never blame you for the mess our father created. Tell me."

Emily took a deep breath. "That's just the point. It appears from the letters that Mother was the one who had a lover, not Father."

He actually went pale and then shook his head. "I cannot believe that. She was too sick, too frail, too . . . *pure* to do such a thing." He rose to his feet and started pacing the hearth rug.

Emily decided it was best to just keep going. "According to her letters, she had the same lover before our father returned from India right up until just before her death."

Richard stopped pacing and faced her, his expression now unreadable. "And who was he?"

"I don't know. She never addresses him by name, and we don't have his letters to her." Emily looked down at her joined hands. "I'm sorry, Richard. It must be something of a shock for you."

"He must have caused this," Richard said quietly.

"Who?"

"Our father. *He* was the one who made her life miserable; she told us so."

"But perhaps that wasn't true?" Emily whispered. "Perhaps she sought to make excuses for her own behavior?"

Richard turned away from her, one hand raised in instinctive denial. "I can't believe that."

Of course, you can't. Even as she thought it, Emily realized she would never say it to her distraught brother. He hadn't lived at home all year as she had. He'd only seen their mother when he'd come back from school. She'd done her best to win him from his father.

"Where is this Thomas Smith character hiding himself?"

"He isn't hiding. He is residing at a perfectly respectable London inn at the Angel Islington."

"I'll seek him there, then."

Emily rose to her feet and blocked his path. "You will not do so alone. He asked to see me, not you. You don't even know what he looks like."

"I can ask Ambrose."

Emily stamped her foot. "You will do no such thing! Firstly, you will read the letters and Mother's journal yourself, and then we will go and meet with Mr. Smith *together.*"

The cold fury died on her brother's face, making him look more like himself. He let out his breath.

"All right, Emily. You deserve to be there as much as I do.

Give me the letters to read, and if I agree with your conclusions, we will visit Mr. Smith together."

Ambrose walked through the main salon in the direction of the buffet table, intent on checking the condition of the food. The pleasure house prided itself on offering the best food and drink in London, and it was Ambrose's task to ensure that reputation continued.

It was also his task to make sure that any leftover food was distributed to the staff and to the poor of London, a job he found far more satisfying than watching the rich gorge themselves. He deliberately sought out orphanages and slums stuffed full with ever-growing families. It made him feel less ashamed of his pampered and protected existence.

A shriek of laughter to his left made him look up just in time to catch a half-naked woman in his arms who was being pursued by a man. The woman clung to him, still laughing back at the man who came to a stop and grinned down at her.

"Come here, my beauty!" There was the hint of an American accent to the man's speech.

"No, I won't!"

The protest was uttered in such a way as to be meaningless. Ambrose started to set the masked woman on her feet and step away.

"Ma'am."

The woman gasped and stared right at him.

"Is that blackamoor's face scaring you, my love? Is he being impudent?"

The man shoved at Ambrose's shoulder. "Cast your gaze down, slave, don't you dare to presume to look at her."

Ambrose continued to stare at the mottled red features of the American.

"We do not have slaves in England. I am a free man who may look at any woman he pleases."

"Damn your impudence!" The man raised his arm and Ambrose caught his wrist in a hard grip.

"Please don't cause a scene, sir."

"I'll cause any damn scene I like, *boy*. Where's the manager of this place?"

Ambrose smiled. "I'm the manager, sir." He nodded to Seamus Kelly and his brother, Patrick, who had appeared behind the American. "Please remove this gentleman from the establishment and make sure that he is barred from the premises for life."

Ambrose ignored both the man's blustering and his continued crude insults as to the color of Ambrose's skin as he was led away. Instead, he turned to the woman who remained standing beside him.

"I apologize for the disruption, ma'am. Perhaps you might find someone else to enjoy your evening with?"

Her hand moved to her mouth. "He should not have spoken to you like that, as if you were . . . not even human."

Ambrose half smiled. "In America, I am not considered human. He cannot help what he has been taught to believe."

"That is very generous of you."

He didn't feel quite so generous beneath the surface. Years of learning to control his temper had made him able to present a calm face to the world.

He bowed to the woman. "I hope that you can still enjoy the rest of your visit here. Is there any particular room where I can escort you?" She still didn't move, and Ambrose hesitated. "Ma'am, would you like me to call someone for you?"

She grabbed his arm. "What is your name?"

"It is Ambrose."

Her grip tightened so quickly that he winced.

"Oh, my God." She swallowed hard. "Don't you remember me? I'm Lady Mary Kendrick."

Ambrose stared into the blue eyes of the masked woman and couldn't look away.

"Lady *Mary?*"

She nodded vigorously. "Yes, you were my mother's page boy. We all doted on you, and you suddenly disappeared. I cried for a whole week." She glanced around the salon. "How on earth did you end up here?"

"It is a long story, my lady." Ambrose bowed. "One that I'm sure will not interest you, although I am delighted to see you in such good health." He tried to ease out of her grasp, but she still clung to his sleeve. "My lady?"

"Is there somewhere we might sit and talk? Somewhere quieter, perhaps?"

Inwardly, Ambrose sighed. "Are you sure you want to do that, my lady?"

She raised her chin in her old autocratic manner. "I am absolutely sure."

"Then please follow me."

He stopped one of the footmen and asked him to tell Marie-Claude that he would be unavailable for the next hour, then walked with Lady Mary through to one of the vacant bedchambers at the rear of the house. It was cold in the room, and Ambrose went at once to the fire and lit the kindling before attending to some of the candles.

Lady Mary took off her mask and stood in front of the gilded mirror, her blue eyes focused on Ambrose, who slowly got to his feet.

"Have I changed much?" she asked softly.

Ambrose studied her dark curling hair, tall figure, and striking features. "You have certainly grown into your beauty."

She lifted one shoulder. "I am a little tall."

He smiled. "Not for the right man."

"You have grown into a handsome man yourself."

"Thank you."

She gestured at the chairs that sat on either side of the fireplace. "Can we sit down?"

"If you wish, my lady."

Ambrose waited until she settled herself into her chair and then took the one opposite. "I didn't know you frequented this place."

"I haven't been here before. I came with Lady Cooper and her American guests." She shivered. "I think I drank rather too much wine."

Ambrose smiled. "No harm was done. I suspect our American friend will complain to Lady Cooper about his treatment and try and have me dismissed."

She sat forward. "I will not allow it! I will tell Lady Cooper how badly he behaved toward you. We are very close." She hesitated. "It's not widely known yet, but I'm going to marry her brother."

"Congratulations, my lady. I hear Lord Thomas Cooper has an assured career ahead of him in politics."

She grimaced. "So I understand. Who would ever have thought I'd become a great political hostess?"

Ambrose found himself smiling. "I'm not surprised. You always got what you wanted when you were a child."

"Not everything." She paused. "I remember wanting to marry you quite desperately at one point."

"When you were eight and I was twelve."

"That's right." She sighed. "I was desperately in love with you and then . . ."

"And then what?"

"I told Mother and she laughed at me."

"That wasn't kind of her."

"But she wasn't very kind, was she?" Lady Mary met his gaze. "And she was rather possessive of you."

"As she was of her favorite lapdog."

"No, it was more than that." Lady Mary's color rose. "I saw you once, leaving her bedchamber early one morning."

Ambrose smiled but said nothing and waited for her to continue. If she had suspicions as to the nature of his relationship with her mother, he was certainly not going to encourage them.

"She took you to her bed, didn't she?"

"I can hardly answer that, can I?"

She grimaced. "I suppose not. It took me years to work out why you left so suddenly, but that was it, wasn't it? Mother grew tired of you and sent you away to our country estate."

Ambrose felt a knot of pain grow in his stomach. "Is that what she told you?"

"That's what she told everyone. But when we went down to Fairleigh Hall that summer, you weren't there. She said you must have run off, and that she wanted nothing more to do with you."

Ambrose contemplated Lady Mary's earnest face. Was it worth spoiling her mother's version of the truth with his reality? Part of him wanted to shout it at her, to share the savage beating he'd received at the hands of Lord Kendrick, and the way he'd been tossed into the gutter like a piece of useless rubbish.

"Ambrose?"

"I have worked here for the last ten years and I consider it my home now." He took a deep, steadying breath. "I could not have stayed with your family. There was no position available for me there."

"I'm sure Father could have found you something. He was always very fond of you."

"I will always be grateful to your family for sheltering me during my childhood years." He couldn't help but reach across and take Lady Mary's hand. "You were especially kind to me. I will never forget that. If you ever need my help, you know where to find me now."

"That sounds very final." She squeezed his fingers. "I suppose you don't want me to tell my mother and siblings that I've found you."

"I think it would be best if this secret remained between us, don't you? I don't want to rake up old hurts."

She released his hand and sat back. "I suppose not. Did you know that my father died last year, and Dominic is now the fourth earl?"

"I did read about your father's death, my lady. I offer you my belated condolences."

"He died on the hunting field, which would have pleased him greatly." Lady Mary swiped at the corner of her eye. "I miss him tremendously."

"I'm sorry, my lady," Ambrose murmured. His own reaction to the earl's death had been far more joyful. The man had been a tyrant who had beaten his wife and terrorized his servants.

"Well, there's nothing to be done about that. Despite his youth, Dominic is proving most satisfactory as the new earl."

"I'm sure he is. He was always a levelheaded boy."

"Apart from when he got into scrapes with you."

Ambrose smiled at the bittersweet memories her words evoked. Dominic had usually been the instigator of their escapades, but it had always been Ambrose who was punished. He glanced up as the clock on the mantelpiece struck the half hour.

"My lady, it has been such a pleasure to talk to you, but I fear I must get back to work."

Lady Mary stood up in a rush, pushing the puffed sleeve of her low-cut bodice back onto her shoulder again.

"Of course, I didn't mean to distract you from your duties."

"You didn't, my lady." Ambrose blew out most of the candles and walked toward the door.

"What exactly are your duties here, Ambrose?"

He looked back over his shoulder as she closed the distance between them. She was so tall that she was almost at his eye level.

"I mainly manage the staff."

She was so close that he could smell her flowery perfume and her natural warm scent. "You don't get involved with the guests?"

He held her gaze. "Only if I am required to do so."

"Oh." She stared at his mouth for a long moment before leaning in and placing a slow kiss on his lips.

He forced himself neither to respond nor to recoil, but to remain exactly where he was. He couldn't prevent the skip in his heartbeat or the burst of heat in his groin.

"Good night, Ambrose." She breathed the words against his lips. "Thank you for saving me from that boor."

"Good night, my lady," he replied, and opened the door wide, allowing her to float past him, her smile secretive, her eyes amused.

He let her go and stayed leaning against the door until he could decide how he felt about such an unexpected encounter with his past. Would she insist on pursuing their acquaintance, and if so, how did that make him feel? Part of him wanted her gone again, the other was eager to see if he could bend a member of the mighty Kendrick family to his will, to take her as her mother had taken him, to leave her brokenhearted as he had been left, bleeding in the gutter . . .

With a curse, Ambrose slammed the bedroom door and headed back to the second floor. What in God's name was wrong with him? There was work waiting, and he intended to push all other considerations from his mind.

8

"When were you going to tell me that Vincent Lennox was a woman, Keyes?"

Richard slammed the door of Keyes's office shut behind him and marched toward the man behind the desk.

"I needed to tell you that?" Keyes looked mildly offended and not at all put out, which only served to annoy Richard more.

Richard sat down and poured himself a large glass of brandy from the decanter on Keyes's desk. "You also failed to mention that I knew her rather well in France."

"Is that so?" Keyes topped up his own glass and swallowed slowly. "Coincidence is a strange beast, isn't it?"

"I don't believe in coincidence at the best of times, and when you are involved, I don't believe in it at all!"

"I speak the truth, Ross. I can't say that I wasn't delighted to find out you already had a connection with the Lennox family, but it wasn't intentional."

"I knew her only as Violet LeNy." Richard studied Keyes. "Was their father really a Lennox?"

"As far as I can tell, he was. I told Jack I would help him establish their identity."

"Why?"

"So that he would trust me."

"Do you really want them to stay in England?"

"I don't care what happens to them as long as I get the information I require."

"Which is what?"

Keyes steepled his fingers and stared down at them. "I'm not sure yet. Jack Lennox suggested that he and his sister had been made scapegoats for a series of events that happened in France. I think he might have a point."

"But why would someone want to implicate the Lennox twins in anything?"

"That's the question I cannot answer."

"Do you think they might be in danger?"

Keyes glared at him. "Don't be obtuse, man. Why else would I have asked you to keep an eye on them?"

"And why else would Violet be masquerading as a man?" Richard murmured to himself. "They are not exactly in hiding, though."

"I don't want them to go to ground. I want them alive and visible."

"You mean you want to use them as bait for something bigger."

"Exactly." Keyes raised his glass in a mock salute and then finished his brandy in one swallow.

"But why is the British government interested in the survival of two French Royalist spies?" Richard narrowed his gaze. "Do they still have important information?"

"As I said, I can't decide." Keyes sighed. "It's just that the story Jack Lennox told me was remarkably similar to a couple of others I've heard recently. And, as you said, I don't believe in coincidences."

"Then your concerns must have something to do with the security of *this* nation rather than the French. You no longer dabble in the fate of common spies." Richard rose and put his glass down on the desk. "I'll keep them under close surveillance."

Keyes winked. "Very close, I hear. Which one did you fuck in the pleasure house, or was it both of them?"

"Wouldn't you like to know?" Richard smiled. "What a shame that I don't kiss and tell."

"I don't care which one you fuck as long as you do what needs to be done."

"You can rely on me."

The humor vanished from Keyes's expression. "I damn well hope so."

Richard paused at the door. "As bad as that, Keyes?"

"Just keep them safe until I can question them further or the matter resolves itself."

Richard nodded and left the office, his mind in a whirl of conjecture. It seemed that Violet was right to be afraid. The thought of someone trying to kill her made Richard feel quite murderous himself. He was the only one who had the right to wring her neck.

He walked back to his lodgings and let his valet divest him of his coat, hat, and gloves. An hour reading and replying to his correspondence would calm his thoughts and give him some much-needed objectivity that he seemed to be lacking at the moment. Violet had always done that to him—made him act like an impetuous fool.

His gaze fell on the box of letters Emily had given him and he picked them up. He should read them. Emily would be waiting to hear from him. But did he really want to find out that his much-loved mother had deceived his father and her children? With all that was going on in his life with Violet, he wasn't sure if he could stomach another betrayal. He put down the box and turned back to his desk. He'd look at them later.

As Jack made himself agreeable to an aging duchess, Violet stood slightly to his left and concealed a yawn behind her gloved hand. They were at a small, informal evening party hosted by Adam Fisher's mother, and were being introduced to all the people who could smooth their path into English society.

Violet wondered again why Lord Keyes was being so helpful. In truth, when she and Jack had first decided on their wild plan to come to England, she had half expected to be immediately incarcerated or hung as spies. But something about their outlandish claims must have interested the enigmatic Keyes, and their lives were saved. But for how long was anyone's guess. She knew that if their story were discredited, they would be left to endure their, no doubt, grisly fate.

She wandered over to the windows and wished she could take off her coat. Even though she appreciated the freedom wearing breeches gave her, she disliked the numerous layers of fabric swathed around her neck and upper body. It was all too damn hot.

A slight disturbance at the door made her turn to see Emily and Richard Ross being greeted by their hostess. Emily looked deliciously cool in a blue satin shoulder-revealing gown and Richard his usual elegant self. He dressed with the quiet confidence he had displayed even in his youth. She was the only person who had ever been able to raise his temper then, and it seemed that nothing had changed.

Jack immediately walked over to Emily Ross and kissed her hand before leading her over to the refreshments in the conservatory. Richard said something as Jack led his sister away, and even though Violet wasn't close enough to hear the actual words, she guessed their intent from Richard's grim expression.

She would have to warn Jack not to meddle with Miss Ross; but for some reason, he seemed rather fascinated by her.

"Good evening, Mr. Lennox."

Violet smiled up at Richard. "Mr. Ross."

"Are you enjoying yourself?"

"Mrs. Fisher is very kind and she has quite taken to my mother. I hope they will become friends."

"Do you miss that?"

"Having friends?"

He smiled and the grave beauty of it struck her anew. "Female friends."

"Yes, men are so uninteresting."

"I can't help but agree with you." He hesitated. "Will you walk with me to see the library? It has some interesting medieval manuscripts saved from a monastery fire in it."

"Are you going to shout at me again, or lock me in?"

He placed his gloved hand over his heart. "I'll try not to."

"Then that would be delightful."

Richard touched Adam Fisher's arm as they went past him. "I'm taking Lennox to see your library."

"Absolutely. Take your time." Adam nodded at Violet. "I'll make sure your mother is well taken care of."

"I'll wager he will, the old letch," Richard murmured to Violet. "Despite his benign exterior, that man is lethal with women of any age."

Violet chuckled. "Well, then he has probably met his match. Sylvia is no fool."

"Ah, that's right, she was married to your father, wasn't she?"

Violet refused to take offense. "Indeed, and my father was a very charming trickster and not to be relied on at all."

"Not an ideal parent."

"No, I'm glad my mother took me away from him, or I might have turned out like Jack."

104 / *Kate Pearce*

It was his turn to smile. He opened a set of double doors and bowed. "Here we are."

She walked ahead of him into a large room filled with bookshelves and the indefinable smell of pen, paper, and ink. Violet slowly inhaled.

"I have always dreamed of owning a library like this. I understand there is one at Lennox Park. I hope I get to see it one day."

"I'm sure you will."

Richard placed one of the candelabra beside a large reading plinth and turned to bring down a massive leather-bound book. He carefully untied the ribbons that bound the great manuscript and opened it.

"Oh, my goodness." Violet breathed as the candlelight caught the vibrant colors and gold enamel of the illuminated letters. "They look as if they were painted yesterday."

She came across to peer over Richard's shoulder and he immediately made room for her.

"Adam said that they found the books when they dug up part of the old cloister at their country house."

"Their house must have been built on the ruins of one of the monastic foundations that disappeared after the Reformation."

"I assume you are right, seeing as the house is called Melton Abbey."

Violet traced the beautiful penmanship with one careful finger. "It could take a monk months just to finish one of these letters. Just imagine how long it took to manage a whole book."

She looked up and found that Richard was staring down at her, a concentrated expression on his face. She found she couldn't look away.

"Violet," he murmured, before bending his head and kissing her so sweetly her knees buckled. She kissed him back, her hand sliding into his hair to keep him close.

He groaned and wrapped an arm around her hips, bringing

her completely against him. Oh, God, she couldn't resist him when he was like this, so urgent, so tender, so . . .

His fingers slid between her legs and started rubbing her sex in time to the long, slow thrusts of his tongue. She whimpered and he drew one of her legs over his hip, opening her farther to his touch. She grabbed at his hand and tried to push it inside her trousers.

"Ah, God, yes," he breathed into her mouth, his fingers easily working her buttons until he could uncover her most needy flesh. "I want my mouth on you."

She didn't resist as he brought her down to the floor and pushed down her trousers and underthings to display her mound. His mouth descended, licking at her already swollen clit, parting her lower lips and delving into the heat and wetness with his tongue until she writhed against him. He slid two fingers inside her and pushed them in and out until she could hear the slick sound and smell her own arousal.

His thumb probed her arse, steadily pushing deep until she was trapped between the delights of his mouth and his fingers, a cage of intense delights she didn't want to escape. He added another finger, pumping into her until she climaxed, her tight passage gripping on to him with an enduring strength that begged—no, demanded more.

He didn't stop touching her, exacting another climax from her before he finally raised his head and kissed her mouth, letting her taste her own need.

"Violet, why are you here?" he murmured between kisses.

"With you on the floor?"

"No, here in England. Who do you fear? If you tell me, I can help you. I swear it."

Violet wrenched her mouth away and tried to roll away from him. He stopped her with one heavy thigh across her hips.

"What are you doing?"

"I'm getting as far away from you as I can," she hissed.

"Because I made you come?"

"No! Because you did it to make me talk to you."

He moved off her and lay on his back, one arm braced beneath his head. "That's true, but I enjoyed every second of it." He sighed. "I want to help you, Violet. But between you and Lord Keyes, I feel as if I'm floundering around in the dark."

"I cannot tell you anything." Violet fought to control the trembling in both her voice and her fingers as she struggled to refasten her trousers.

"Why not?"

"Because you don't trust me."

"And do I have reason to trust you?" His hazel eyes snapped fire. "I thought I'd caused your death! I *mourned* you."

"I know." She swallowed hard. "You probably won't believe me, but I was just following orders. I was told you had to accept that I was dead, that it was the only way you would leave me alone."

"Who told you that?"

"My superiors."

"And you believed them?"

Violet dropped her gaze and concentrated on the final button of her trousers. "You told me that you loved me, that you would never leave me."

She closed her eyes as silence stretched between them, not sure what she wanted him to say, dreading he'd either agree with her or worse, laugh.

"I mourned you, Violet. I thought I would never recover from your loss."

The pain in his voice made her flinch.

"But I did recover and moved on just as you did." He paused. "Although you never promised to stay with me forever, did you? Perhaps I should have listened to you more carefully."

"I couldn't promise you what was not in my power to deliver."

"Because you always knew you were just using me to further your 'great cause.' "

"No!" She dropped back down onto one knee and stared at him. "I never expected to come to care for you."

"How inconvenient for you."

"I never meant to hurt you either," she whispered.

"As I said, I recovered. Don't waste your pity or your tears on me, my dear."

The click of the library door opening had Violet coming abruptly to her feet. Jack closed the door behind him and studied her.

"You really should lock the door, my twin. Anyone could have walked in."

She met his amused gaze and saw beneath it his very real concern for her.

"We weren't doing anything."

"Then why is Mr. Ross lying on the floor?" Jack strolled over to the desk and stared down at Richard. "Did you hit him with that enormous book?"

"No, I . . ." Violet realized she was far closer to tears than she had expected and brought her hand to her mouth.

Jack patted her shoulder. "Why don't you go back to the drawing room and leave Mr. Ross to me?"

For once, she didn't argue, and without daring to look at Richard, she ran for the door, closing it quietly behind her. Why should he trust her at all? She'd forfeited every right to his regard forever.

Richard let out his breath as Violet abandoned him to the tender mercies of her brother. The ache in his unsatisfied cock matched the ache in his heart. Not that hearts could hurt, but it was the only explanation for the hollow sensation in his chest that Violet's words had left him with. She'd seduced him as ordered; then she'd left him *as ordered,* making him feel like the guilty party.

Damn her for making him feel like this. He pushed one hand down onto the floor and started to get up, only to have Jack kick his elbow out from under him, sending him crashing back down.

"What the devil are you doing, Lennox?"

Jack shoved him onto his back, one strong hand wrapped around Richard's throat, his knee on his chest. All traces of his amicable expression disappeared, leaving only cold anger.

"I don't like seeing my sister cry."

"She's crying because she feels guilty about faking her own death. That is hardly my fault."

"You're a fool." Jack's grip tightened. "She did that for you."

"I'll be damned if that is true. She did it for her puppet master."

"You misunderstand. They wanted her to stay with you, to see if she could entrap you into marrying her. Violet refused. *She* was the one who insisted on ending things and set you free."

Richard stared up into Jack's intense face, his thoughts in a whirl. "I don't believe you. You weren't there."

"I worked for the same masters. I know what they planned."

"You are her brother. Of course you would defend her."

Jack reached down and cupped Richard's still-erect cock and balls, and squeezed hard. "And you lust after her like a stallion in heat. What drives your decision making, Mr. Ross? Your cock or your brain?"

Jack jerked Richard's cock and within seconds, Richard was climaxing, his back arching off the ground as his seed soaked into his underthings. With a roar of rage, he shoved at Jack, but the other man didn't release his stranglehold on Richard's throat.

"Oh, dear. I made you come."

"You *bastard.*"

"Would you like me to lick you clean, or would you prefer me to call my sister? Although I doubt she would oblige you." Jack started to unbutton Richard's trousers. "At least your trousers are black and will not show the stain too badly."

He let go of Richard's neck and shoved his hand lower, pushing aside Richard's soaked underthings. Although Richard tried to buck him off, Jack's knee remained firmly planted on his chest. Jack bent so close that his breath fanned Richard's cock, which jerked in response.

"Ah, you smell divine."

"I don't." Richard grabbed for Jack's hand and then moaned as Jack's tongue licked a long, sultry line along his shaft, pausing at the crown to circle and probe his still-wet slit. "Oh, God, don't . . ."

Jack continued to lick him until Richard felt his cock stirring and found the strength to finally shove him away.

"Stop it."

Jack sat back and smiled. "I think I'm done now anyway."

Before Richard realized his intent, Jack pressed his mouth to Richard's and ran his tongue along the seam of his lips, giving him a taste of himself.

"Now that I have taken care of you on behalf of my sister, who will give me relief?" Jack asked.

Richard rose to his feet and set about rearranging his clothing. "I'm sure you'll find someone."

Jack sighed. "But obviously not you. How selfish, Mr. Ross."

"I owe you nothing. You should have made your demands clear before you touched me."

Jack glanced down at his trousers and smoothed a hand over the bulge of his cock. Richard couldn't help but look and notice how large a bulge it was.

"I'll remember that next time, Mr. Ross. I didn't realize you regarded fucking as a business proposition."

"We didn't fuck."

"But I'd like to fuck you, Mr. Ross—properly, I mean—my cock buried deep in your arse, my hand wrapped around your shaft while I make you beg for release."

"Even though you know I'm involved with your sister?" Richard was proud of the level tone of his voice. If Jack Lennox could discuss his shocking sexual desires without a qualm, Richard would do so too.

Jack shrugged. "I'm willing to share if she is." He headed for the door. "Are you coming back to the drawing room?"

"In my own time," Richard replied, his mind too busy considering Jack's casual statement and the carnal images it evoked. Had Violet and Jack shared lovers before? If he asked Jack, he'd probably tell him, but he wouldn't ask. He didn't dare.

9

"I'm tired of waiting for Richard to come and talk to me about the letters my mother wrote," Emily said. "I can't decide if he is refusing to believe that she was anything less than a saint or is just too busy to read them. He has been behaving quite oddly recently."

Ambrose poured her another cup of tea but said nothing. In her need to discuss the letters, Emily had been reduced to seeking him out again at the pleasure house. She glanced at him over the brim of her cup. In truth, he seemed as distracted as her brother and just as unwilling to discuss the matter.

"Mr. Ross does seem to be behaving rather oddly. I suspect it is because of those Lennox twins."

There was a note of reserve in Ambrose's voice that made Emily study him more closely.

"They seem rather nice to me. In fact, Jack Lennox has made a point of seeking me out at various events and offering his companionship. It is quite refreshing to meet a man who doesn't treat me like a dressed-up doll and who respects my opinions."

Ambrose made a sound that could only be described as a

snort. "Jack Lennox is a rake. You should keep away from him."

"Whatever makes you say that?" Emily asked. "He has never made an improper advance toward me."

"Of course, he hasn't."

Emily opened her eyes wide. "Because I am not the sort of woman that would interest a rake, am I?"

"That's not what I meant. Jack Lennox knows that your brother and father would not stand for any nonsense."

Emily pretended to look doubtful. "I hadn't noticed that he was afraid of anything. In truth, that's why I like him. He seems so different from all the other men I have met."

"That's because he is a dangerous adventurer."

"You sound just like Richard." She laughed, but Ambrose didn't even smile back at her. "And yet, Richard seems quite happy to spend all his time with Vincent Lennox. I don't understand him at all."

"I believe your brother might have met Vincent in France when he was younger."

"Oh! That might explain his interest, then." Emily paused. "I was beginning to think he was . . ." She waved her hand in a vague gesture.

"Was what?"

Emily shrugged. "Developing an interest in his own sex—not that I object to that at all."

Ambrose looked amused. "I'm glad to hear it."

"You bed both men and women, don't you?"

"Yes."

"Do you bed them because you like it or because Christian told you to?"

Ambrose looked down at his linked hands on the table. "I owe my life to Mr. Delornay. I would've done anything he asked me."

"Then you didn't feel as if you had a choice?"

He met her gaze and she suddenly felt rather warm. "Oh, no, I had a choice. Mr. Delornay told me I could remain behind the scenes or I could join in. He never made me feel obliged to sell myself. He knew that would be abhorrent to me."

"Because you were born a slave?"

"Yes, and it wasn't as if I hadn't had sex before I came to live here. The technique was quite familiar to me."

"Is that how you see it, then? As a matter of physical technique?"

"At the pleasure house? Of course." He sat back. "It is hardly about love, is it?"

She took a deep breath. "Haven't you ever wanted it to be about love, though?"

His smile was guarded. "There are many different types of love, Miss Ross. One can hardly be lucky enough to have them all."

"Why ever not?"

"Ambrose? Are you there?"

Emily looked up to see Christian coming into the kitchen, a letter in his hand. At that moment, she wished him to the devil. Ambrose rose to his feet.

"Yes, Mr. Delornay?"

Christian noticed Emily and nodded at her. "Here again, Emily? We should set you to work."

"I wish you would," she snapped.

Christian stared at her for a long moment before turning back to Ambrose. "Did I interrupt something?"

"Not at all, sir," Ambrose said, and Emily's irritation grew. "I think Miss Ross was just leaving."

"No, I wasn't."

Both men were staring at her now, and she scowled back. "Don't mind me."

Christian opened the letter. "I had the most extraordinary letter today from a Lady Mary Kendrick."

"Ah," Ambrose said. "I wondered if she would try and contact me again."

"She writes to assure me that you are not to blame for the behavior of a recent American guest. That if I even *think* of dismissing you from your position, she will use her considerable influence to have you reinstated."

Christian handed the letter to Ambrose. "Go ahead, read her robust defense of you. What did you do to make her your advocate?"

"Not what you think, sir." Ambrose kept his gaze fixed on the letter and ignored Emily. "She is an old acquaintance of mine."

"You must have performed *most* handsomely if she has never forgotten you."

Ambrose handed the letter back to Christian. "I've never, she isn't . . ."

Christian winked at Emily, who stared mutely back at him. "It's all right, Ambrose. Whatever you did has paid off magnificently. I suspect she'll be back soon to give you her thanks in person."

Christian bent to kiss the top of Emily's head and then exited the kitchen, leaving Ambrose standing by the table. Emily slowly rose and began to yank on her gloves with unnecessary force.

"I really do have to go now. As Richard doesn't seem to want to be involved, I was thinking of attempting to see Mr. Smith again. I hoped you might accompany me, but I'm sure you will be too busy with *other* things."

"Miss Ross, Mr. Delornay was just being his usual amusing self. There is nothing for you to worry about."

"I'm not worried about anything, Ambrose." She forced a laugh. "After all, you've made it very clear that I have no claim on you. I just find it interesting that you are prepared to fawn around one titled lady and yet insist that I am too good for you."

"Please, don't be like this." Ambrose took a step toward her, his hand outstretched. "I'll come with you to meet Mr. Smith, just . . ."

Emily walked right past him and then turned at the door to offer him her best smile. "Oh, no, don't worry about me, Ambrose. I'll ask Mr. Jack Lennox to accompany me instead."

Violet waited until Jack was seated beside the fire with a glass of brandy before she went and sat opposite him. Sylvia had retired for the afternoon with a headache, although Violet suspected she simply wanted to finish reading the latest gothic novel in the peace and quiet of her bedchamber.

"Jack, I need to talk to you."

"What is it?" Jack put down his glass. "Did Richard Ross decide he prefers me, after all?"

"That isn't amusing."

"No? I think it is. The poor man doesn't know what to make of me at all. He can't decide if he is attracted to me because I resemble you or if he is just attracted to me. You'd think with all his connections with the pleasure house, he'd be more aware of what he wants."

"You don't really want him," Violet said. "You're just being annoying."

"Or mayhap I want to make you jealous, to make you admit that you still care for him?"

"What good will that do? I lied to him. He will never forgive me."

"I don't agree."

"Then perhaps you will agree with what I propose." Violet held his gaze. "I want to tell Richard why we are really here."

Jack's ready smile disappeared. "Are you mad? You just said he will never forgive you."

"But we need someone to trust."

"And you trust *him?*"

"I trust him more than I trust Lord Keyes."

"There is that." Jack shoved a hand through his black hair. "Keyes smiles so convincingly, but his eyes are cold."

Violet shivered. "I can see him washing his hands and leaving us to our fate without a backward glance."

Jack leaned forward, his hands clasped between his knees. "But Richard followed Mr. Brown's orders just as well as Keyes did. He has no reason to doubt where the man's loyalties lie. Why do you think he would even listen to your claims?"

"Because I *know* Richard, and I detected a certain distance between him and Lord Keyes. I don't think he trusts Keyes any more than we do."

"Then he is a wise man," Jack muttered. "I suppose if you do tell him, it can't make anything worse, can it?"

Violet tried to smile. "Knowing our luck, I wouldn't place a wager on it."

"Then tell him what you think he needs to know." Jack sighed. "If he doesn't believe us, and goes running back to Mr. Brown, at least it will all be over soon. I'm getting rather tired of all this playacting and inaction, and I'm sure you are desperate to get out of those breeches."

Violet reached for his hand. "Thank you, Jack."

"You are welcome, my love." His grin returned. "When are you seeing the esteemed Mr. Ross next?"

"I'm supposed to be riding with him in the park this afternoon. Why?"

"Oh, because he is likely to be rather out of patience with me."

Violet paused in the act of rising. "What did you do? Did you quarrel? He looked quite unharmed when he returned to the party last night."

"I merely told him not to make you cry."

"And?"

"And inadvertently helped him out with the small problem you left him with—although, in truth, the problem was quite large."

"Jack, what are you saying?"

"He was hard and I gave him relief."

"You did what?" Violet gripped the back of the chair. "He *let* you?"

"He didn't have much choice, my dear. I was holding him down by the throat at the time."

"*Jack.*"

"Incidentally, he almost inquired as to whether we often bedded the same person. I told him he should clarify that issue with you."

"You did not!" Violet struggled for words. "Surely he did not mean, did not imagine that I, that you, that we would . . ."

Jack waved airily at her. "Don't worry, I didn't commit you to anything." He chuckled. "It was rather amusing to see his face, though."

Violet stalked toward the door. "You are a devil."

"I know."

"And one day you will get your comeuppance and I shall laugh!"

But he was the only one laughing as Violet slammed the door behind her and stormed up the stairs to change.

By the time she was due to meet Richard in the park, her indignation and confusion had still not abated. What on earth must Richard think of her? It would be a miracle if he even condescended to keep their appointment. And what if he did turn up? What did that mean? That he wanted to bed both of them? It was hardly a subject she wanted to introduce into their conversation.

Violet mounted her bay gelding and concentrated on navigating the skittish horse through the busy streets of central

London. The iron railings of the park came into view along with a thin sliver of sunshine that illuminated the grassy lawns and the few brave souls who had chosen to promenade along the walkways.

Watching the ladies shivering in their finery made Violet glad for once of her thick wool coat, hat, and long boots. She studied the other horsemen but couldn't see Richard. Nodding to her new acquaintances, she made her way down the graveled path to one of the fountains where she had agreed to meet Richard. Her horse shied at a falling leaf, and she brought her attention back to controlling him until he settled down.

By the time she looked up, the area around the fountain was almost deserted, apart from a group of gardeners who were working on one of the flowerbeds. The faint sound of hoofbeats on the gravel behind her made her look over her shoulder. In the distance, she spied a man on horseback, one hand raised as if trying to catch her attention.

Just as she went to respond, a shadow loomed up at her. She jerked back, but not before a glancing blow from a shovel knocked her half out of the saddle. As she scrabbled to right herself on her already panicking horse, a second strike dislodged her completely and she started to fall to the ground. Her breath was knocked out of her and she stared up into the face of an unknown man, a metal spade raised above his head.

A shout from behind her made the man pause and mutter an obscenity. He spat, lowered the spade, and delivered a casual kick into her ribs that had her curling up in agony.

When she opened her eyes again, Richard knelt by her side.

"Are you all right? What happened? Did they try and rob you?"

Her shoulder was throbbing alongside her ribs and she couldn't seem to draw in enough breath to answer him.

"Mr. *Lennox!*"

With a curse, Richard bent down and picked Violet up before striding toward the nearest park bench and laying her carefully on it. Her face was as pale as her cravat. He held his breath as her eyes finally fluttered open again.

"Knocked . . . the wind . . . out of me," she managed to wheeze.

He touched her face and then gripped her hand. "Of course. Take your time."

While Violet concentrated on her breathing, he waited, watching as waves of shock shuddered through her body.

"Can you help me get home?" she whispered. "I don't know what happened to my horse."

"I've already sent my groom for a hackney. He can take care of our horses as well."

"Thank you."

His gaze swept over her. "Where are you hurt?"

"My shoulder and my ribs." She winced. "But I don't think anything is broken."

"We'll see what the doctor has to say about that."

He suspected he sounded angry, but the sight of her falling from her horse, of that *rogue* standing over her with his weapon raised, had almost stopped his heart. "I assume you didn't plan this?"

"Not this time." She squeezed his hand. "I swear it."

"It's all right. This isn't exactly your style. I seem to remember that last time I watched you die, you were shot cleanly through the heart. There was rather a lot of blood."

"Pig's blood," she whispered. "I had it concealed beneath my shirt."

"Ah, that's how you did it. I've been meaning to ask you about that."

His anxious gaze scanned the entrance to the park as he absentmindedly rubbed his thumb against the back of her gloved hand. He saw a hackney approaching and waved to attract the driver's attention.

"Barrow's here with the hackney. Let me carry you into the cab."

"No, I'd look weak and we're still on display. Can you just help me walk?"

For a moment, when all he wanted to do was sweep her into his arms and hold her close, her bravery and resolution confounded him. With his help, she levered herself into a sitting position and stared determinedly at the hackney. Richard braced his arm around her waist and brought her upright. Her fingers dug into his coat sleeve like a bird of prey's.

"Are you sure about this?"

She bit down on her lip, her eyes half-closed. "Yes, and if anyone asks, tell them I fell from my horse or something."

"Don't worry about that now," Richard said. "Let's get you home."

In the hackney, he ignored her protests and sat beside her, one arm locked around her waist, absorbing as many of the bumps in the road as he could. She didn't lean fully against him, and he sensed how carefully she was holding herself through her panting breaths and rigid posture.

When they pulled up, he released her and got down first to pay the driver and alert his manservant.

"This isn't my house," Violet said.

"It's mine." Richard took a swift glance along the street and, seeing no one, picked Violet up and carried her directly into his lodgings. "I've already told the doctor to come here."

He took her through the open doors into his bedroom and laid her on the bed before lighting the fire. "I'll find you some warm blankets."

"What will your doctor think?"

He turned at the door to study her and noticed her face was beginning to display a collection of bruises that rivaled a prize-fighter.

"He is the physician for the Delornay family. I suspect he is used to keeping secrets."

"Thank you," she whispered.

He frowned as she brought an unsteady hand to her head. He didn't like seeing her so defeated. He wanted her defying him at every turn, standing toe-to-toe with him and arguing her case.

"Mr. Ross? The doctor should be here soon." Richard turned to find his manservant behind him. "I've warmed some blankets, and I have a hot brick to put on the poor young gentleman's feet."

"Thank you, March." Richard moved aside to let March through the doorway and watched while his servant spoke quietly to Violet and covered her with the quilts. While he waited, he tried to imagine what would have happened if he'd arrived just a few minutes later. Would he have found Violet dead on the ground, her head smashed in, her beautiful eyes forever darkened? The thought made him want to puke.

A knock at the door had March moving past him to admit the doctor. He was much younger than Richard had anticipated, and very well-spoken.

"Good afternoon, Mr. Ross. I'm Dr. Bailey. How may I assist you?"

The doctor's brisk manner helped to restore at least the appearance of calm to Richard. He ushered Dr. Bailey into the bedroom and closed the door behind him.

"Firstly, this matter requires your complete discretion."

"You may have that." Dr. Bailey nodded. "I owe your stepmother my life." His gaze moved toward Violet. "What happened?"

"She was set upon in the park."

Dr. Bailey halted by the bed. "Did you say, 'she'?"

"Indeed, which is why we require your discretion."

The doctor held Violet's wrist, took out his pocket watch, and went silent.

"Well, your pulse is certainly raised. Were you injured?"

"The man hit me on the left shoulder with his shovel and I fell off my horse."

Her voice was a little faint, but at least she was speaking again. Richard forced himself to take a seat by the fire and not hover over Violet like an anxious parent.

"Ah, we need to remove your clothes."

Richard started up again. "I'll help with that."

Easing her out of her tightly fitting coat was a slow process, which obviously caused Violet great pain. By the time they were down to her shirt, sweat beaded her brow and she looked as if she might swoon again.

"Unbutton her breeches, please, Mr. Ross, so that we can take off her shirt."

Dr. Bailey whistled as Violet's shoulders emerged from the shirt. Richard noticed her breasts were bandaged flat against her rib cage, but Dr. Bailey seemed oblivious.

"He certainly marked you." The doctor traced the rapidly swelling bruise that curved up her arm and across her back. Violet grimaced as he carefully manipulated her shoulder and arm. "But from the look of you, I don't think anything is broken."

"That's good," Violet managed. "I turned away as he hit me, which probably put off his aim."

"Indeed, although I should imagine you are in considerable pain."

"Of course, she is," Richard snapped.

Dr. Bailey's gaze flicked to Richard. "And we will make sure she is relieved of that pain as soon as we have discovered the full extent of her injuries." He returned his attention to Violet. "Your face is bruised from the fall, but the cuts look superficial. Do you hurt anywhere else?"

"He kicked me here." Violet placed her hand over her lower right rib cage. Her breath hissed out as Dr. Bailey probed her side, and Richard tensed.

"Again, I don't think it is broken, merely bruised. You were lucky."

"If Mr. Ross hadn't appeared, I believe my attacker intended to finish me off with his shovel." Violet shivered, and Dr. Bailey patted her bare shoulder, making Richard want to growl a warning.

"You'll be sore for a week or two, but then you should start to feel better. I'd keep your ribs bound as you have them now. That will help." He stood and went to fetch his medical bag. "I'll leave you some laudanum for the pain. Use it wisely and sparingly."

"Thank you," Violet whispered. She sank back against the pillows and closed her eyes.

Richard ushered the doctor into his sitting room, where March was hovering with a tray of drinks.

"How much do I owe you for the visit, Dr. Bailey?" Richard asked as he offered the physician a drink, which was politely refused.

"Nothing, sir. I am far too indebted to the Delornay family to ever ask for payment for my services."

"I'm not quite a Delornay." Richard sipped his own brandy.

"Close enough." Dr. Bailey smiled, and Richard marveled anew at how young he was. He put on his hat and cloak. "I'll come back and visit the patient in a day or two. Don't hesitate to call me if you see any signs of fever or internal swelling."

"I will do so, Dr. Bailey. Thank you again." Richard shook hands with the man and watched as March escorted him out.

He drank all his brandy and then started on another glass until his hands stopped shaking and anger began to replace fear. It was obvious that someone had decided to dispose of Violet, but who? Was it the unknown adversaries Keyes had hinted at, or was it Keyes himself now that his protégés were no longer important?

"March, Mr. Lennox will be staying here, at least for the night. I need you to take a message to his mother and brother at Harcourt House."

"Yes, sir. Do you want your dinner first, sir?"

Richard sat down. "I think that would be an excellent idea. It might be a long night."

10

Violet slowly opened her eyes and allowed her gaze to wander around the still-unfamiliar bedchamber. It was night and the curtains were drawn. A fire burned in the grate, and a single candle illuminated the figure slumped in a chair by the fire. Richard was asleep, his long elegant frame at rest, his face as peaceful as an angel's. A book dangled precariously from his fingers and as Violet watched, the book fell and woke the sleeper with a start.

His hazel gaze flew to the bed and met hers.

"Are you all right, Violet?"

"I am quite well, sir. I wish you would allow me to return to Harcourt House and let you have your bed back."

"March has made me quite comfortable." Richard stretched, his open-necked shirt white in the firelight. "We've already discussed this. It is better for you to be here. Even Jack agrees with me about that."

Violet sat up against her pillows, ignoring the stab of pain in her shoulder. "But I've been here for over a week. Hasn't anyone noticed that I've been absent from society?"

Richard came over to sit on the side of the bed. "Your mother said that several people have asked after you. She told them you are somewhat sickly and catch every passing cold and malady."

"I am rarely sick!"

"True, but Vincent Lennox is." He reached for her hand. "How are you really feeling?"

She looked up into his face. "A little sore and rather frightened." She shivered. "I didn't expect to be attacked out in the open like that. I'm just glad you arrived when you did."

"So am I." He brought her hand to his lips and kissed it. "Seeing you die once was quite enough for me."

Briefly, Violet closed her eyes. "There is something I want to tell you."

"What is it?"

He didn't relinquish his warm clasp on her hand, and she gained courage from that.

"I wanted you to know exactly why we came to England."

He bit down on the tender skin at the base of her thumb and she wanted to moan. "I thought you came for social advancement and to stake your claim on the Lennox family estate."

"There is that, but there was another reason too."

"Mmm?"

It was hard to concentrate when his lips were moving over her skin. "Over the last few years almost everyone we worked with who was involved in the Royalist resistance against Napoléon has disappeared or died in mysterious circumstances."

"Including your father."

"That's right. When Jack and I realized we were the only two people left, we decided it was time to abandon France. Our grandmother agreed."

"But it seems that trouble has followed you across the Channel." Richard raised his eyes to hers. "What did you think to find here that would help you?"

"Friends, allies . . ." Violet shrugged and then wished she hadn't. "And some kind of proof against the English spymaster we think is responsible for so many deaths."

"An *Englishman?*"

"During the war, the person we all reported to was an Englishman."

Richard sat back. "You are suggesting your spymaster is attempting to kill you all? For what reason?"

"Because we know who he is, and what he's done." Violet held Richard's disbelieving gaze. "There were discrepancies in the financial accounts, of the treasures stolen or lost . . . of people killed for money rather than for political reasons."

"You suspect *Mr. Brown* is responsible for all this?"

"I know it is hard for you to believe, but—"

Richard held up his hand. "Wait. You came to England suspecting this? Why didn't you run in the opposite direction?"

"Because he is a very powerful man, and Jack and I are tired of running. We want to *live.*"

Richard held her gaze and the silence lengthened. "I find this quite difficult to believe."

"I knew you would, and as you have pointed out on many occasions, you have no reason to trust me at all."

"Apart from the fact that someone tried to kill you last week and I don't think it was a crime of passion or because they objected to the cut of your coat."

Violet exhaled. "Then you believe me?"

"Lord Keyes told me he had heard other rumors about a traitor in our own ranks. It would explain why he is so interested in you and your twin."

"And why he let us parade around in society where Mr. Brown could see us."

"Did you know he intended to do that?"

"We assumed that was the price for keeping us alive."

His hand curled into a fist. "I'm going to kill Keyes when I find him."

"You haven't seen him recently?"

"Not since the day before your 'accident.' "

Violet bit her lip. "Do you think he might have been involved?"

"It's possible, I suppose, but I got the impression that he was after someone much bigger than you. Your Mr. Brown would obviously fit the bill. I believe he is a peer of the realm."

"Perhaps they are waiting for me to show myself again so that they can finish me off." Violet sighed. "You did warn Jack to be careful, didn't you?"

"Of course." Richard patted her hand. "If I can't find Keyes, there are other men in the government I can talk to about this matter."

"Do not put yourself into danger on my account. What if this acquaintance of yours inadvertently told Mr. Brown he was under suspicion?"

"Oh, that won't happen. The man I am thinking of is very discreet."

"But you will be careful, won't you?"

He smiled into her eyes. "Of course. I'm no fool, love."

She gently disengaged her hand from his. "Don't call me that."

He opened his mouth to speak, then seemed to think better of it and got off the bed. "I'll ask March to bring you a hot drink to help you sleep before he leaves for the night, and then I'll retire to my sleeping quarters."

Violet watched him walk toward the door. "Richard?"

He looked back over his shoulder. "Yes?"

"Thank you for believing me."

His smile was wry. "Don't thank me yet, my dear. You know me, I like to check all the facts before I commit myself to anything."

For some reason, she felt like crying. Why wouldn't he just believe her? But she knew the answer. She'd taught him to suspect everyone.

"You will be careful, though, won't you?"

"Naturally. Good night, Violet. Sleep well."

She turned on her side and breathed in the scent of the linens that still smelled of Richard. At least she'd told him the truth. Not quite all of it, but enough. What he did with that information was entirely up to him. Like Jack, she was at a point where she simply wanted the masquerade to end.

Richard found himself pacing the hearth rug, unable to settle, and stared into the fire. "I'm going out, March. Will you remain here and watch over our guest until I return?"

"If you wish, sir, but it is rather late. Would it not be better to wait until the morning?"

"The man I intend to visit suffers from ill health and rarely sleeps. He'll probably enjoy the interruption."

Richard put on his coat and hat, and picked up his gloves. He also took his walking cane, which concealed a rather fine rapier within it highly suitable for dispatching the undesirables of London. He didn't bother to call a hackney, as his destination was only two streets away through a well-lit part of the city.

When he reached the narrow town house, he knocked on the front door and waited patiently until he heard labored footsteps approaching. Several locks and bolts screeched back; then he was face-to-face with one of the oldest men he had ever met.

"Good evening, Mr. Daniels."

The butler peered intently at him through his thick spectacles. "And who might you be?"

Richard leaned closer and raised his voice. "It is Richard Ross. Is Lord Denley at home?"

"Oh, it's yourself is it, then?" The butler's Irish accent was almost as dense as the glass in his spectacles. "The master is still awake. I'm sure he'll be glad to see you, my boy."

Richard went into the hallway, divested himself of his outer garments, and handed them to Mr. Daniels, who staggered under the weight.

"Go on up, my boy, give him a nice surprise."

Richard trod carefully up the worn stair runner and headed for the large chamber at the front of the house where Lord Denley tended to hold court. He knocked softly on the door and was rewarded by a shouted, "Come in, you deaf old man! Why are you bothering to knock at all when you can't hear my reply?"

Richard grinned as he pushed open the door and went inside. Lord Denley sat with his back to the door, a book in one hand and a glass of something in the other.

"Good evening, my lord."

Lord Denley turned and his face broke into a smile. He held out his hand. "Well, I'll be damned! Richard Ross. How are you, my friend?"

Richard came around the back of the chair until he faced his old mentor and shook his hand. Time had been kind to Lord Denley. He looked barely older than Richard, and yet he was at least twice his age.

"How long have you been back in England?"

Richard sat down. "I'm embarrassed to tell you that I've been here for quite a while. I should have visited you sooner."

"It is of no matter, you are here now." Lord Denley studied him intently. "Are you in trouble?"

Richard smiled. "How like you to understand that I would still come to you if that was the case."

"You still haven't made things up with your father, then?"

"Actually, I have. We get along quite well these days." Even as he said the words, Richard realized they were true. As long as he and Philip avoided talking about his mother, they were fine.

"I'm glad to hear it. Every son needs his father."

"At times you were more of a father to me than he ever was, and I thank you for that."

Lord Denley shrugged. "I did what I could, but I knew you would eventually reconcile."

"So you kept telling me, although I hardly believed you."

Lord Denley's smile died. "Life plays some very peculiar tricks on us sometimes, doesn't it?" His hand smoothed over the rug that covered his crippled legs. "I'm glad to see you, Richard, and more than willing to help you in whatever limited way I can."

"I'll wager you still have your ways of finding out information. You were the best spymaster the English ever put in France."

"You flatter me. I did my part just as you did."

"I dabbled and thought of it as something of a game. *Until Violet died.* You almost gave up your life for your country."

"I did what needed to be done. The question is, what can I do for you now?"

Richard studied the calm face of his mentor and considered exactly how to broach such a delicate subject.

"I swear that I will keep your confidences, Richard. Have I ever let you down before?"

"No, never." Richard slowly let out his breath. "Lord Keyes told me he had heard rumors that one of our former spymasters in France had not behaved with honor."

"I don't think any of them behaved terribly well. There was a war going on, you know."

"I understand that; God, I was part of it, but this is more serious." He raised his gaze to Lord Denley's. "This man is so concerned about maintaining his reputation that he is still attempting to eliminate anyone who might have evidence against him."

"That is a different matter." Lord Denley sighed. "And I will confess that I have heard a similar rumor. Do you have any idea whom it might refer to?"

"I've heard the name 'Mr. Brown' mentioned. Does it mean anything to you?" Richard asked.

Lord Denley went still. "It means quite a lot to me. If the rumors are true, we are all in terrible trouble."

"Can you tell me who it is?"

"Not yet." Richard went to speak and Lord Denley held up his hand. "If I tell you my suspicions, you will go off like a half-cocked pistol and I can't have that. I must be certain of the facts."

"How quickly can you be sure?"

"Why the urgency, Richard? You of all men know that diplomacy and espionage take a long time to come to fruition."

Richard sat forward. "Because someone I care about was almost killed last week. Someone *Mr. Brown* wants silenced."

"Then this is a personal matter for you as well as a national one." Lord Denley nodded. "I will do my best to help you as quickly as possible."

"Thank you." Richard smiled at his mentor. "And have you any idea where Lord Keyes is?"

"Keyes? Why, do you think he is involved in this?"

"I'm certain he is involved. He was the one who got me tangled up in this matter in the first place."

"Do you suspect him?"

"I'm not sure." Richard rose from his seat. "I'd just like to speak to him."

"You never got on very well, did you?" Lord Denley chuckled. "Too alike, I fear."

"Probably," Richard acknowledged. "If you see him, tell him I wish to speak to him."

"I will, and I'll get straight on that other matter." Lord Denley held out his hand. "Good night, Richard, and thank you for calling on me. I'll do my best for you, I swear it."

"Jack!" Violet hissed. "You scared me! What time is it?" She clutched the bed covers to her chest and slowly sat up as her twin set a single candle by the bed.

"It's past one in the morning. Why, were you asleep?" He glanced around the shadowed bedchamber. "And where is Mr. Ross?"

"He doesn't sleep with me."

"That's not what I meant. I saw him leaving about ten minutes ago."

Violet stiffened. "He told me he was going to bed."

"Then he lied, my dear. Perhaps he's off visiting his latest mistress." Jack settled himself on the bed beside her and took her hand. "How are you, by the way?"

"I'm feeling a lot better and getting rather tired of being confined in this small space." Violet eyed the billowing curtains. "Did you come through the window?"

Jack got up and slid the sash window down. "I didn't think March would let me in at this late hour and I wanted to talk to you."

Violet scowled at him. "About what?"

"What Richard is up to, for one? I followed him, you know, and he went to a house about two streets east of here. It wasn't a house I recognized, but I will find out who lives there."

"I told him about Mr. Brown. He said he had an acquaintance in the government who might be able to help us. Perhaps he went out to see this man."

"Or he went running straight to Mr. Brown himself. Did he give you any idea if he knew what was going on?"

"No." Violet sighed and sank back onto her pillows. "I think he wanted to believe me, though."

"That's because he is still in love with you."

Violet met his gaze. "No, he is not. He never was."

Jack squeezed her hand. "You can say the words, love, but I see the truth in your eyes and in his. You are kindred souls."

"Then perhaps we will meet again in heaven." Violet pulled her hand away. "Go away, Jack. I'm tired."

"And frustrated, I'll wager, if he's not sharing your bed." He considered her for a long moment. "What would you say to a night of unbridled passion at the pleasure house?"

"Not with you."

"No, with Richard Ross."

"As I said, he doesn't want me."

"He wants you. He's fucked you."

"But only . . ." Violet glared at her twin. "He treats me like a man."

"Ah, hence your frustration." His smile was devilish. "Which is why you might wish to consider attending the pleasure house on Tuesday evening. The second level is closed off to the majority of the guests, and those who choose to . . . express themselves differently are given free rein."

"What do you mean?"

Jack shrugged. "Men who prefer to dress as women do so, and women who wish to be men find the partners they desire. You could attend as a woman." He bent and kissed her cheek. "Just a suggestion, my dear. Richard could hardly refuse you then."

He slid off the bed and blew her an airy kiss. "I'll find out who Richard is visiting and let you know as soon as I can. Good night, my love."

Violet waved him away and then lay sleepless staring up at the plasterwork on the ceiling until she heard the faint sounds of Richard returning and March relinquishing his post watching over her.

Despite everything, she still wanted Richard, wanted to be

free of her confinement and free of fear. He was still the only person apart from Jack she trusted to keep her safe. She swallowed hard. Making love to Richard wouldn't solve anything, but it might be her last opportunity to try and show him how she felt before her assassin completed his task. Because Jack was right, damn him. She still loved Richard and she probably always would.

11

Emily glanced up at Jack Lennox as he held the door open for her. He wore a long black coat and brown trousers that fitted him to perfection. His waistcoat was also black with silver buttons.

"It is very kind of you to accompany me, Mr. Lennox. I do hope I'm not taking you away from your mother or your poor, sick brother. How is he, by the way?"

"Progressing nicely, Miss Ross. I expect him to be back on his feet in the next day or two. And my mother is visiting Lady Fisher, so she is very happily occupied." His smile was dazzling. "I am quite at your disposal and, I confess, quite intrigued by your request for my company."

Emily sighed. "I know I shouldn't have asked you, but Richard seems to have disappeared and Ambrose . . ."

"I heard that Ambrose had rediscovered his childhood sweetheart. Is that why you are annoyed with him?"

"I'm not annoyed. I just don't understand how he insists I am too far above him to love, and yet seems to find plenty of time to moon around this Lady Mary person."

Jack checked the street and then guided Emily across. "It's quite simple, Miss Ross. Ambrose is rediscovering a part of his life he thought lost."

"Lady Mary is part of the family who discarded him like dirt in the gutter. How can he not see that?"

"As far as I understand it, she was still a child when he left. He probably doesn't associate her with that part of his life at all."

"And what am I supposed to do? Stand by and watch him fall in love with her?"

Jack patted her gloved hand. "He won't do that. He is in love with you."

"He has a strange way of showing it, then," Emily huffed.

"He is a man, Miss Ross. None of us is very good at understanding what a woman wants."

"Apart from you." Emily cast him a sidelong glance. "You are a rake of the first order."

"Indeed, I am." He hailed a hackney. "But I'm hardly trustworthy. I think we're far enough away from your house to start our journey without being seen. Where exactly is our destination?"

"The Angel Inn at Islington."

Jack gave the driver the information and handed Emily into the hackney.

"What do you require of me, Miss Ross? Am I to remain hidden, or do you want me with you?"

"I want you with me." Emily shivered. "The man I am to meet frightens me a little."

"Then I promise I will remain close." Jack patted his pocket. "I have my pistol and my dagger ready to use if you are in any danger."

"Thank you," Emily said.

"You are more than welcome, Miss Ross."

Emily stared out of the grimy window until they reached their destination and Jack handed her down. Despite his pleasant exterior, Emily didn't doubt that Jack Lennox could defend himself and her. The Angel looked to be a prosperous place with a busy trade.

"Miss Ross, where did you arrange to meet Mr. Smith?"

"In one of the private parlors." She looked up at Jack. "Do you think you could inquire for me?"

"Of course."

She followed Jack inside and waited while he conversed with one of the servants, who pointed them in the direction of the back of the inn and promised to fetch Mr. Smith. In the morning light, the parlor smelled of coffee and steamed cabbage and had a vaguely disused air. Emily found it impossible to sit down, so she stood in front of the fire and pretended to warm her hands.

The door opened and Jack stood up, blocking her view.

"Miss Ross?"

The familiar, rough tones of Mr. Smith reached her and she stepped forward.

"Good morning, Mr. Smith. Thank you so much for agreeing to see me again." She glanced at Jack. "This is my friend, Mr. Lennox, who agreed to accompany me today."

"Sir." Mr. Smith nodded at Jack, who resumed his seat by the wall. Emily sat by the fire and Mr. Smith took the chair opposite hers. "Now, how may I help you, Miss Ross?"

"The letters and the journal that my mother left in your care . . ." She hesitated. "Thank you for sharing them with me. They were most enlightening. Were there any more of them? The journal seems to end rather abruptly."

"There are no more letters, Miss Ross. I burned the rest of them on her instructions."

"The ones she received from . . . from her lover."

"Aye."

"What about her diary?"

He smiled and she noticed he had several missing teeth. "I

knew you'd turn out to be a sharp one. I still have one more of those."

Emily waited, but he simply kept staring at her expectantly. She glanced at Jack, who was listening, a frown on his face.

"Is there something you require from Miss Ross in order for her to see the journal?" Jack asked.

Mr. Smith turned to Jack. "Well, you see, sir, it isn't quite as simple as just *giving* it to her."

"Why not?"

"Because I believe there might be several, shall I say, *interested* parties who might want to read what's in that journal? And I am a poor man, Mr. Lennox."

"So you want money for it?"

Emily gasped. "Why? Who would want to read the scribblings of a dead woman?"

Mr. Smith met her gaze. His eyes were a very dark brown and full of a deep hatred that chilled her to the bone. "Lord Philip Knowles, for one."

"My father?" Emily shook her head. "Why would you want him to know about this?"

"Oh, he already knows what he did, don't worry about that." He chuckled. "I wonder how much he will pay to reclaim that journal so that he can destroy it once and for all?" He nodded at Jack. "And don't think I'm stupid enough to have the journal here with me. It is well hidden."

He returned his attention to Emily. "Your mother knew Lord Knowles would search for any evidence of her infidelity on her death, so she sent everything to me."

"And why *did* she send everything to you, Mr. Smith?" Emily stood and stared at her adversary. "What exactly was your part in this?"

His smile widened. "Haven't you guessed yet? I thought you might remember me. I'm the man your mother was in love with for all those years." He bowed to them both. "I've no more time for you now. I'll give you a week to think over what I've said and to work out how much you are prepared to offer me to save your father from public humiliation on a grand scale."

Jack sprang to his feet, but Mr. Smith was quicker and he was out of the door before either of them could stop him. Emily went to give chase, but Jack caught her arm.

"There's no point, Miss Ross. He probably doesn't have the journal with him, and he's too dangerous for you to tackle alone."

"But . . ."

His grip tightened. "We will use the time he gave us to defeat his schemes." She tried to pull away from him, but he held firm. "Miss Ross, I promise you that we will not let him get away with this."

"I cannot allow him to blacken my father's name!"

Jack drew her back to the chairs by the fire and made her sit down. "With all due respect, Miss Ross, your father is married to one of the most notorious women in London. I doubt the revelation that his first wife had a lover will raise more than a ripple of interest. You'd probably do best to lay this matter at his feet and allow him to deal with Mr. Smith as he wishes."

Emily stared at Jack. She couldn't bear to reveal the fears that corded her throat, making her want to scream. Jack had no idea what other secrets she feared were in the remaining journal.

"Will you take me home, Mr. Lennox? Or, better still, will you help me find Richard?"

Richard wasn't quite sure how he'd ended up in Lady Fisher's drawing room with a cup of tea balanced on his knee, while Vincent and his mother chatted merrily away to their hosts. Violet had been so desperate to get out of Richard's lodgings that she'd threatened to jump out of the window. To his dismay, she'd looked quite capable of carrying out her threat.

Richard had decided to take her out to call on the Fishers, thinking they would at least be safe there. Adam was also in attendance and knew what had happened to Violet, so he was also on his guard. There was still no sign of Keyes, which was beginning to annoy Richard, and he'd had no word from Lord Denley either.

His gaze slid to the clock on the mantelpiece, but Violet seemed in no hurry to leave. Richard resigned himself to a long visit and sat back in his seat, sipping his tea. The sound of approaching voices had him sitting up again as the butler opened the door.

"Miss Emily Ross and Mr. Jack Lennox, my lady."

Lady Fisher rose to greet her new guests, who both seemed a little out of sorts. Richard narrowed his gaze as Jack whispered something to Emily and patted her hand. Where had they been, and why was Emily looking so distressed? Richard put his cup down on the table and went to rise. Before he could complete the motion, Emily reached him and took his hand.

"I need to speak to you quite urgently."

"What is it?" Richard glared at Jack, who had followed Emily over. "Has Mr. Lennox been annoying you?"

"No, he has been very helpful. Can you come with me right now?"

Richard glanced at Violet, who was looking over at him, a question in her eyes.

"I need to escort Mr. Vincent Lennox and his mother home, and then I can meet you at Knowles House."

"Richard, this is rather important," Emily insisted. "Can't Vincent drive his own mother home?"

"He is still too weak to manage the horses."

"Can't Jack take them?"

Richard sighed. "Emily, I can't explain why, but I have to be the one to get Vincent Lennox home safely. I swear I'll be as quick as I can."

She met his gaze and he stared steadily back into her troubled eyes. "I promise I'll be there."

Her smile was tremulous. "All right. Can you bring our mother's letters with you, please?"

"Is that what this is about?"

She squeezed his fingers hard. "Please, Richard. If I can trust you, can you do the same for me?"

"Of course. Now let me fetch Mrs. Lennox's coat."

As he turned toward the door, the butler appeared with another couple behind him.

"Lady Mary Kendrick and Mr. Ambrose, my lady."

Beside him, Emily went still. He wasn't quite sure what he expected her to do, but he reached out and put his hand firmly on her shoulder.

Lady Fisher was smiling. "Mary, what a pleasure to see you, my dear! I thought you intended to return to the country." She turned to greet Ambrose. "Mary was telling me about you the other day. What an interesting life you have led, Mr. Ambrose. Please do sit down. I shall have to get you to come and speak of your experiences to the children who attend my charity school."

Lady Fisher gestured at the Lennox twins, and Richard and Emily. "Have you met Mr. Ambrose before? He used to be a page boy in Lady Mary's family!"

Richard met Ambrose's resigned gaze. "Indeed, we know him quite well."

"I work for Mr. Ross's half brother, Mr. Delornay." Ambrose sounded his usual calm self. "I am already acquainted with all your guests."

"How wonderful. Would you like some tea, Mary?" Lady Fisher inquired. "Mr. Ambrose? I will ring for a fresh pot. What about you, Mr. Ross?"

"Unfortunately, we must be going. Mr. Vincent Lennox still tires rather easily."

"Indeed, he does." Sylvia pressed her hand to Violet's brow.

"He is a little warm. We must get you back to bed, my dear."
She turned to Lady Fisher. "Thank you so much for the tea."

"You are welcome, Mrs. Lennox." Lady Fisher looked inquiringly at Jack and Emily. "You will stay for a few minutes longer and take some refreshments, won't you?"

Richard tried to get Emily's attention, but she was ignoring him, her gaze fixed on the rather beautiful Lady Mary, who had all her attention on Ambrose. He suspected trying to prise Emily away at this moment would be impossible. But at least it gave him time to escort Sylvia home and then take Violet back to his lodgings.

He walked over to Jack, who was sitting down with all the anticipation of a man about to watch a bloody boxing match.

"Keep an eye on Emily for me, will you? And please bring her home to Knowles House within the next half an hour."

"Naturally, Mr. Ross." Jack replied without tearing his gaze from Emily and Lady Mary. "I'd be delighted to oblige you."

Richard departed with Violet and Sylvia, and could only hope that Emily kept both her temper and her wits about her.

As she gazed at the lovely Lady Mary, Emily wondered if she had done something to offend every deity in the universe. Ambrose seemed quite at ease, his conversation relaxed, his smile easy, while Emily sat there vibrating like a tightly strung violin. Jack patted her hand.

"Relax, Miss Ross," he murmured. "You look as if you are about to leap over the table and devour someone."

"Perhaps I am." Emily smiled sweetly at Jack. "You'd probably enjoy it."

"I suspect I would, but I doubt you really wish to add something as trivial as a teatime brawl to your family's already impressive legend."

"That's true. Perhaps I'll wait and murder Ambrose later."

"An excellent idea." Jack brought her hand to his lips and

kissed her fingers. "And by the way, he doesn't like me touching you at all. He's far more interested in watching us than paying attention to Lady Mary's hand on his knee."

"Good." Emily smiled longingly into Jack's blue eyes. "She has her hand on his inner thigh, not his knee. I'm going to kill him very slowly indeed."

"That's the spirit." Jack bit down on her gloved thumb and she shivered. "After you've exercised your sharp wit at Lady Mary's expense, we'll take our leave. I'll try and make sure Ambrose sees me kissing you in the hallway."

"You are going to let me spar a little with her? I thought Richard would have ordered you to take me away directly."

"He did, but you're not my sister." Jack sat back and winked. "Have at her, my dear."

Emily smiled at Lady Mary as she sipped her tea. "It must have been such a surprise for you to meet Ambrose again after all these years."

"It was a most welcome surprise." Lady Mary smiled into Ambrose's eyes. "I adored him when I was a child."

Emily raised her eyebrows. "Yet you did not think to seek him out before?"

"My mother told us he had run away from our country estate, and that he obviously wanted nothing more to do with our family. I cried for days when I realized he had gone for good."

"Hardly for *good*, Lady Mary. What did your mother think he had run away to? A servant with no references and no money hardly has many options, does he?" Emily ignored the warning in Ambrose's gaze. "In truth, if any of my servants disappeared in such circumstances, I would be extremely worried for them."

"As would I," Jack added, and Emily turned to smile her approval at him.

Lady Mary looked uneasy. "I must admit, I hadn't thought of that, but I was quite young at the time. Now, of course, I would wonder more . . ." Her voice tailed off and she stared at Ambrose. "I must speak to my mother about this matter."

"Please don't," Ambrose said lightly. "There is no point in raking up the past." He patted Lady Mary's hand. "There is no need for Lady Kendrick to know that we have even met again."

Lady Mary bit her lip. "I've already told her. I couldn't help myself. In fact, she wants me to bring you to meet her."

Emily held her breath and waited to see what Ambrose would do next. Even from where she was sitting, she could see the indecision in his eyes. Part of her wanted to run over and take him in her arms and tell Lady Mary to go to the devil. But she could do nothing. Her pleasure at baiting Lady Mary suddenly seemed petty compared to the enormity of Ambrose's experiences. He had to deal with this himself. It was his life, and he'd made it clear that she was not his to protect.

Emily stood up. "I do apologize, Lady Fisher, but I have to go and meet my brother at home." She forced a smile. "After telling him he must not dally with his errands, I can hardly be late myself, can I?"

Jack rose, too, and held out his arm to her. "Thank you, Lady Fisher. I should imagine we shall see you next week at the Hoxtons' ball?"

"Indeed." Lady Fisher shook hands with him and kissed Emily on the cheek. "I hope your brother is feeling much better soon, Mr. Lennox."

Jack looked suitably grave. "So do I, my lady. The weakness of his constitution is a severe worry for me."

Emily allowed Jack to escort her along the busy streets to Knowles House. He didn't attempt to kiss her, and for that small mercy, she was very grateful.

12

Richard waited impatiently for Emily to finish saying good-bye to Jack Lennox. For a woman who claimed to be in love with another man, she seemed to be taking a remarkably long time over it. He sat in the library, which was currently unoccupied, as Philip and Helene were out visiting the pleasure house, hopefully annoying Christian.

He'd taken Sylvia Lennox home and then taken Violet back to his lodgings, hoping to give the impression that she was still living with her mother. In truth, she had argued that it would be quite safe for her to do so, but he wasn't convinced.

Emily finally came in, closed the door behind her, and slowly removed her bonnet and gloves. Her expression was bleak enough to make Richard deeply uneasy.

"I brought the letters back, Emily."

"Have you had a chance to read them yet?"

"No, I've been avoiding it. I don't want to know that my mother had a lover. I don't want to give my father any additional justification for his behavior toward her."

Emily took the seat opposite him. "She did have a lover, and I know exactly who it is."

"What have you been doing? Is this why Jack Lennox was by your side today?"

"If you hadn't been so preoccupied with *Vincent* Lennox, you could have accompanied me to visit Mr. Smith." She shivered. "Although after what happened today, you would probably have tried to kill him."

"What happened?"

"This isn't going to make any sense if you haven't read Mother's letters and diary."

"Tell me."

"The letters are all from her to her lover. There are none from him. It is obvious that their affair began before Mother's marriage and didn't end until quite near her death."

Richard struggled to absorb the extent of his mother's deception. "Are you quite sure?"

"Richard, do you think this gives me pleasure—hurting you? I can assure you it does not."

"Why did you go back to see Mr. Smith? Why couldn't you let this thing lie where it belongs? In the past?"

Emily sat forward. "Because you need to see the truth about our mother, so that you can stop blaming our father for everything that went wrong in your life."

"I don't blame him for everything."

"You . . ." Emily shook her head. "There is more. Shall I continue?"

He managed to nod.

"I went back to see Mr. Smith because I had some more questions for him. I suspected he hadn't given me all of Mother's journals."

"And why does it matter? Haven't you accumulated enough evidence against her?"

"That's not fair." She took a deep breath. "Mr. Smith also admitted that he was Mother's lover."

"The *gardener?*"

"It makes a terrible kind of sense. From the age of eleven, she was brought up with Father's family, and Mr. Smith was employed on the estate. She must have known him for almost as long as she knew Father."

"I still find this whole story rather suspicious. Why would this man present himself to you now? What does he hope to gain?"

"I was just coming to that." Emily took a deep breath. "He claims to have another journal that belonged to Mother."

"So?"

She met his gaze. "He wants money for it."

Richard felt as if someone had punched him in the stomach. "*What?* Why would he think we would pay to get it back?"

"Mr. Smith says that Father would not want the contents of the diary to get out. That the scandal would be immense."

Richard shot to his feet and paced the library floor. "Father's whole damned life is a scandal. What would one more matter?" He swung around to face Emily. "Or is it more serious than that? Perhaps Mother was right all along, and Father did eventually manage to kill her. Perhaps her journal incriminates him."

"No!" Emily rose, too, her complexion pale, one hand gripping the arm of her chair. "That is ridiculous!"

Richard glared right back at her. "We'll see about that. As soon as Philip gets back, we'll ask him." He sat down and pulled the box of letters toward him. "And in the meantime, I'll read these letters so that I can face him fully armed."

Ambrose held the door open for Lady Mary and waited until she walked past him and out onto the street. The skies had clouded over again and he could smell the scent of oncoming rain in the air.

"Do you wish me to accompany you home, Lady Mary?" He glanced up at the leaden sky. "I think it is about to rain. Perhaps we should hurry, or I can call you a hackney."

"I'd rather walk. Are you angry with me, Ambrose?"

"Not at all, my lady." He kept moving, one hand on the small of her back as he guided her across the busy road.

She sighed. "You asked me not to tell my mother that I had discovered your existence and I disobeyed you."

"It was hardly an order, my lady."

"But you didn't want her to know about you, did you?" She hesitated. "Was Miss Ross correct? Did you really choose to abandon such a comfortable life with our family, or is there more to it?"

He met her gaze as a series of totally unacceptable emotions boiled and seethed like a gathering storm within his chest. "It is in the past. I have no need to speak of it."

"I don't believe you." She stared at him. "What happened, Ambrose? Why won't you tell me?"

He started walking and she hurried to keep up with him. At the corner of Portland Place, he stopped again and bowed low.

"I believe you will be safe from here, my lady. Good afternoon." Her hand shot out and grabbed for his sleeve, but he stepped back. "Good-bye, my lady."

"If there is nothing to forgive, why are you acting so strangely?" she asked.

"Go home, my lady, and please think no more of me."

"But . . ."

He turned and left her, even though he had no idea where to go next. He simply had to get away from her and the totally unacceptable emotions she aroused in his heart. Soon, he was in an unfamiliar part of town where the color of his skin coupled with the expensive nature of his clothing drew far too much unwanted attention. He glared at each passing person, willing them to fight him, to touch him, to translate their comments about the blackness of his skin into action. But this wasn't the sort of neighborhood where the residents willingly picked fights.

Eventually he recognized the name of a street and realized it was growing dark. Without pausing to think further, he made his way to a familiar address at the end of one of the dark passageways and banged on the door. It took but a moment for his knock to be answered and the door to be flung wide.

"Ambrose!" Jethro Perkins exclaimed. He grabbed Ambrose by the shoulders and drew him over the threshold into an exuberant embrace. "How are you, friend?"

"I'm . . ." Ambrose allowed himself to be held but didn't reciprocate. Part of him wanted to lay his head on the older man's shoulder and weep.

Jethro drew back and studied Ambrose's face. "What is wrong? How can we help you?" He gestured down the hallway. "Come into the kitchen. Cissy is there; she will want to see you."

Ambrose followed Jethro into the warm kitchen and braced himself as Jethro's wife, Cissy, launched herself at him.

"Ambrose, where on earth have you been? Jethro and I were worried about you."

Ambrose bent to kiss Cissy's brown cheek. Her accent held the same lilt as his own and spoke of a shared island home long departed. He remembered his first sight of her and how in his delirium, he'd both feared he was back on the slave ship or that he had finally come home.

"I wrote to you last month."

She grabbed his hand and made him sit at the table. "But writing is not the same as visiting, is it? Why haven't you come to our meetings? We miss you greatly. The children have been asking for you as well."

Jethro cleared his throat. "Cissy, can't you see that the man is not himself? How about getting him something hot to drink and keeping your questions until later?"

"It's all right, Cissy." Ambrose clasped her hand. "I regret my absence more than you know." He exhaled. "I just didn't feel right about coming here and bringing my tales of woe when you are all struggling so much harder than I am."

Jethro smiled. "We all have our struggles, Ambrose, but if we offer them up to the Lord, they soon become manageable."

"You know I don't share your great faith, but I do appreciate everything you did for me, and for what you do for the poor and dispossessed children of London."

Jethro sat down. "We do the Lord's work."

"You saved my life."

"The Lord brought you to us, and we did what we could for you." Jethro reached up and took Cissy's hand. "My wife is always especially happy when we find an abandoned child from her birthplace." He paused. "Are you not happy in your new life?"

"As I told you in my letters, Mr. Delornay and his family have been more than good to me. I am employed and earn an excellent salary."

"A salary that you share most generously with us and others less fortunate than yourself."

"A salary that comes from activities that would shock and disgust you."

Jethro chuckled. "We're Methodists, not zealots. We'll accept help from wherever we can. But if you want a change, lad, we'd be more than willing to offer you a job as a teacher at the new school we're building."

"You're building a school?"

"Aye, the Lord has seen fit to hear our prayers and offer us a way to fulfill our dreams. We'd pay you a salary and give you decent accommodation." He hesitated. "It won't be much at first, but we have great hopes that the school will prosper."

"That is very kind of you, but do you think I would be accepted as a teacher?"

"Why not? You went to school, didn't you?" Cissy said.

"Indeed, I did, a good school in the town of Bishops Stortford that Mr. Delornay paid for."

"And you still feel obliged to work for him."

Ambrose sighed. "In truth, it is a very interesting idea, and I'm honored that you think me worthy."

"But you owe a debt to the Delornay family as well as to us." Jethro smiled. "Ah, well, if you are happy in your work, we are glad for you, and that is all there is to it."

"Thank you for your understanding." Ambrose rubbed a hand through his short hair. "I am content there. I am struggling with a more personal matter."

"Then tell us about it, lad," Jethro urged. "You know we'll keep your secrets."

By the time Ambrose explained about his love for Emily and the reappearance of Lady Mary in his life, both Jethro and Cissy were sitting opposite him at the table, listening intently. The small house was quiet around them, although Ambrose knew from experience that by the morning it would be teeming with children who needed feeding and adults readying themselves to go out and search the slums for those in need.

That's how the Perkinses had found him, barely alive after his beating at the hands of Lord Kendrick and his footman. They'd fed him, tended to his wounds, and tried to teach him about their faith until he'd grown stronger and left them to fend for himself again.

Eventually he came back to them and offered them a substantial share of his earnings from the pleasure house. They hadn't condemned him for leaving so abruptly, or for his choice of profession—a stance that had made him question his attitude toward religion yet again.

Jethro shook his head. "Well, you have gotten yourself into a bit of a pickle, haven't you, lad? But I'd say there are two different problems here, wouldn't you, Cissy?"

"Indeed," Cissy said. "You need to meet with Lady Mary's family so that you can forgive them."

"And if I don't want to forgive them?" Ambrose asked.

"You do, lad. It's the only way you'll find peace," Jethro stated so firmly that Ambrose almost believed him. "Now, as to Miss Emily, do you love her?"

"I always have." Ambrose said.

"And she says she loves you?"

"Yes."

"Then what is keeping you apart?"

"I told you. She is the daughter of a peer of the realm, and I work for my living in her half-brother's pleasure house!"

"In God's eyes, we are all the same, Ambrose," Jethro said firmly, then glanced at Cissy. "Did we ever tell you how we met?"

"No." Ambrose looked up.

"Cissy came to work as an abigail for my mother. She'd been freed by her former master in his will and needed a job." Jethro grinned. "I fell in love with her on the spot, but she took some convincing."

"I didn't want to become the mistress of another white man and be at his mercy." Cissy shivered and Jethro patted her shoulder. "And I didn't believe Jethro when he said he wanted to marry me."

Jethro met Ambrose's gaze. "I kept courting her, and eventually she agreed to marry me. When I told my parents of my intentions, they were not amused. My father threatened to cut off my allowance, and my mother cried that my children would be cursed. Luckily, I wasn't the heir to the dratted baronetcy. I decided I'd rather have Cissy. So we eloped, and we've been happily married ever since."

Ambrose regarded them for a long moment. "With all due respect, I don't want to tear Emily away from her family."

"Have you asked her what she wants? Have you even given her the opportunity to make a choice?"

"How can I? She is so impetuous that she'll swear she's ready to give up everything for me."

Cissy reached over and slapped his hand. "And why should you doubt her? You said you know her well. Would she lie to you?"

"Perhaps that isn't the problem after all," Jethro murmured. "Perhaps it is more that Ambrose isn't prepared to change his life to accommodate hers."

Ambrose glared at Jethro. "That is ridiculous. I am simply not worthy of her!"

Jethro stood up. "Then make yourself worthy of her. Stop being such a coward, lad, and find a way to win the woman you love."

"Father? May we speak to you?"

Philip Knowles paused in the act of removing his hat and gloves, and smiled at Emily.

"Certainly, my dear. Come into my study." He opened the door and waited until Emily and Richard went past him. "Shall I call Helene?"

"No," Richard said. "This only concerns our part of this peculiar family."

"That sounds rather ominous." Philip gave Richard a sidelong glance before sitting behind his desk.

"It is rather a difficult subject to broach, Father, but I hope you will find it in your heart to listen," Emily said.

"That bad, eh?" Philip sat back. "What have I done now?"

"There is no need to be so flippant," Richard snapped. "This concerns our mother."

"Your mother. Of course." Philip turned to Emily. "Are you sure you wish to discuss this with me? I've always found that Richard is quite unable to be rational on the subject."

"As if you are any better. You avoid the topic like the plague!" Richard replied.

"Only because you become so upset when I mention her."

Emily glared at her brother. "If I may speak, Richard? This matter demands all of our attention. Can I at least tell Father what has happened without you interrupting me?"

Richard sank into a chair. "Go ahead. I apologize."

Emily turned back to Philip. "In short, I was recently approached by a man who claimed to have known our mother. He had a box full of her letters and journals."

Philip went still. "Describe him to me."

"He told me his name was Thomas Smith and that he was once a gardener at your family estate. He is a big man with gray curly hair and brown eyes. Despite the passing years, I think I recognized him."

"Damnation," Philip swore so softly that Emily barely heard him. "What did he want?"

"He said our mother wanted me to have her letters and journals."

"Out of the goodness of his heart, no doubt. What else?"

"At first I wasn't sure, but when I met him again he revealed that he hadn't given me everything."

Philip's smile was sardonic. "Let me guess. He gave you just enough evidence to prove that I am the villain of the piece, and your mother, the poor victim."

Richard sat forward. "Wait, did you know about this man, Father?"

"Of course, I did. I also hoped he had died the excruciating death he deserved."

There was a harsh note in her father's voice Emily had never heard before.

"With all due respect, Father, if you knew about this 'relationship,' why didn't you dismiss the man and send him on his way?"

"Because your mother threatened to kill herself if I interfered. And after her first attempt to slash her wrists, I believed her." All the color leached from Philip's face and his hands gripped together tightly on his desk. "I could not allow her to deprive you both of a mother."

"And you were in love with Helene anyway," Richard said. "Were you still seeing her? Is that why you allowed Mother to carry on with her paramour?"

Philip raised his gaze to Richard's. "Helene left me before I married your mother and deliberately dashed all hope that my love for her would ever be reciprocated. I didn't see her again for eighteen years." His expression was wry. "Your mother wouldn't have allowed me to keep a mistress anyway. She complained to my parents if any rumors of my infidelity reached her, and they always took her side."

Emily bit her lip at Richard's appalled expression. It must be very difficult for him to hear such things said about his adored mother.

Philip turned back to her. "So what did Mr. Smith really want?"

"He said he had another of Mother's journals. The last of them. He said you would pay dearly to recover it."

"Did he say why?"

Emily shook her head and glanced across at Richard, who cleared his throat.

"I wondered about that, too, Father. Did I ever tell you that Mother insisted you were trying to kill her?"

"*What?*"

There was a long silence punctuated only by the ticking of

the clock on the mantelpiece. Emily watched as her father's expression changed from incredulity to a quiet stillness that worried her even more.

"Do you truly believe I murdered your mother, Richard?"

"That's hardly the point, is it?" Richard returned. "The thing is, did she write down her fears in her journal? Will you be under suspicion for her murder?"

Philip opened his mouth as if to refute the allegation and then shook his head. "How much does he want?"

"Aren't you even going to defend yourself?" Richard asked.

Philip ignored him and focused on Emily. "How much does Smith want for the journal?"

"He hasn't told me yet, and Richard is right, why aren't you defending yourself?"

Richard got to his feet. "I'm not prepared to pay a blackmailer, even if you are. I'll find this man myself and take the journal from him."

Philip stared at Richard. "Don't do that. Trust me, it will be better if you let me pay the price of my own folly. That's what Thomas Smith really wants, you know, to humiliate me."

"I can't believe this! You are willing to be bled dry to stop yourself being accused of murder?"

Philip stood too. "No, I'm trying to safeguard our family's reputation. Can we just leave it at that?"

"*No*, we damn well cannot." Richard inclined his head an inch. "Good day, sir."

He left the study, slamming the door behind him. Philip sank down into his chair and covered his eyes with his hand.

Emily studied her father for a long moment. "I don't believe you murdered my mother. Unlike Richard, I lived with her all the time. Even as a child I realized her dislike of you was irrational."

Philip sighed and rubbed a hand through his hair. "Thank you for that at least."

"The question remains as to why you are prepared to be bled dry to retrieve that journal? If it doesn't contain accusations of murder, what does it contain that worries you so much?"

Philip met her gaze. "Nothing that concerns you or Richard. I appreciate your faith in me, but my reasons are my own, and I regret that I cannot share them with you."

Emily became aware that she was shaking. "Then I cannot help you."

"You can help me by dissuading Richard from doing anything foolhardy."

"Unfortunately, he is as stubborn as you are, and unlikely to listen to anything I say." She walked toward the door, her gaze fixed on her escape.

"Emily." Her father sounded as wretched as she felt. "Let me deal with Smith. When he contacts you again, tell me, and I'll make sure he never bothers you or Richard again."

She didn't reply. She couldn't even speak. The hallways of Knowles House suddenly seemed endless and unfamiliar. Darting into the drawing room, she retrieved the box of letters Richard had abandoned and took them up to her room. If her father was willing to sacrifice his precious relationship with Richard over Thomas Smith, there had to be a better reason than the accusations of a dead woman. Perhaps if she reread the earlier letters she would understand exactly what it was.

Ambrose walked back to the pleasure house, his thoughts preoccupied by his discussion with Jethro and Cissy. Their great faith made everything seem so simple. He needed to forgive the Kendrick family and to let Emily love him. Yet, did he want to forgive the Kendricks? He hadn't even acknowledged that he was still angry with them until he'd seen Lady Mary. He was afraid that if he let it out, his anger might consume him like one of those volcanoes he had read about in the scientific journals.

He went down the steps to the basement and let himself in through the scullery door. One of the maids wished him a cheerful good evening, and he replied in kind. At least the Perkinses had restored his ability to function normally. No one at the pleasure house would realize how close he'd come to running away from this safe new life he'd created.

He paused, his palm flat to the kitchen door. But had he made himself too safe? Had he become a coward, afraid to express his true opinions for fear of losing everything?

"Ah, there you are, Ambrose." Christian hailed him. His employer was sitting at the table drinking coffee and perusing the daily newspaper.

"I'm sorry I'm late."

Christian raised an eyebrow. "Are you? I didn't notice."

Ambrose took the seat opposite him. "Mr. Delornay, the fact that you are having to sit in the kitchen directing the staff means that I wasn't at my post."

"You put in more hours than anyone except me. You are entitled to break free occasionally."

Ambrose stared down at his joined hands. "And what if I wanted to leave here permanently?"

Christian put down his cup. "Why would you want to do that?"

"What if I had no choice?"

"There are always choices. Some of them are simply more difficult than others. But I wouldn't stop you leaving."

"I am very grateful for everything that you have done for me."

Christian reached across and took Ambrose's hand. "I don't want you to work for me out of gratitude. I hoped we had gone beyond that. I value you for yourself and the times we have shared together." He hesitated. "I am not known for sharing my emotions, and perhaps you have suffered for that, but you are my best friend."

Ambrose turned his hand over and fitted it against Christian's. "Thank you."

"Don't thank me. My reasons for helping you were entirely selfish." Christian stood and smiled down at Ambrose. "If you want to work tonight, be my guest. If not, I'll stay here and manage."

"I want to work."

"Then go ahead." Christian cupped Ambrose's chin. "Whatever you choose to do, you will always be welcome here and in my bed."

Ambrose could only nod as Christian kissed him lightly on the lips and then turned to leave.

13

―――――――――――

"I am quite well enough to return home, Richard. You can't keep me here forever."

Violet scowled at Richard, who sat in a chair by the fire watching her pace the carpet. There was a grim set to his mouth that made her uneasy, and he seemed rather distracted.

"Until I talk to Lord Keyes, or my other government contact, I want you to stay here."

"But then I put you in danger as well."

He raised his eyebrows. "I thought that would appeal to you. And there is something else I want to know. Why were you attacked while Jack was left alone?"

Violet stopped walking. "Probably because they consider me the weaker twin."

"Or because you are the one who holds the secrets that could destroy Mr. Brown."

"No one has tried to kill me again. Perhaps it was a mistake, and they were really after Jack."

Richard sighed. "Violet, you are far too intelligent to believe that. The only reason you haven't been assaulted again is because you have been sequestered here with me. And that brings me back to my original point. You are *not* going back to Harcourt House."

"You can't stop me."

His expression hardened. "I'll tie you to that damned bed before I let you go."

"Naked and spread for your pleasure?"

"Don't tempt me, Violet."

She sauntered over to him and watched his whole body tense. "But I don't tempt you, do I? I suspect I have been replaced in your affections. You see me as a poor substitute for my brother."

He slowly raised his gaze to meet hers. "I'm not in the best of humors. Don't play games with me."

She bent forward and put her hands on the arms of his chair, trapping him in. "I'm not playing. I'm so bored I'll be begging March to bed me soon."

She kissed him and reveled in his sharp intake of breath. Dropping to her knees, she nuzzled his groin and felt his cock kick against her touch. She unfastened his trousers and wrapped a hand around the base of his now-erect cock. His familiar musky scent engulfed her. She breathed it in like a favorite wine before licking the crown of his cock and drawing him deep into her mouth.

His groan emboldened her further, and she started to suck— long, lascivious pulls on his throbbing length that drew him deep and then out again to the very tip before taking him back. His hand cradled the back of her head, holding her close, his fingers digging into her scalp. She shuddered as he leaned forward, and his other hand slid down over her bottom, hiking up the shirt she wore, to expose her sex.

She moaned her appreciation around his cock as he swirled his thumb in her waiting wetness and then eased it inexorably into her arse before plunging his remaining fingers into her cunt. She kept sucking him, bringing him close, and then retreating until he was slamming himself back into her mouth and throat with an urgency that made her grind herself down on his embedded fingers.

"God . . ." Richard gasped and started to come, his fingers painful in her hair, his cock jammed so far down her throat that she could do nothing but swallow the thick heat of his seed.

She wanted to come, too, wanted him to move his fingers to rub her clit, to . . .

"Help me," she moaned. "I want to come."

He pulled out of her and she moaned a protest, but he only picked her up and put her on the bed, his shoulders wide between her outstretched legs, his mouth latching on to her clit and sucking it hard. She screamed her pleasure, and he gave it to her again until she was unable to think, just feel.

Eventually he crawled up the bed and lay beside her, his breathing as labored as her own. She rolled over until she lay half across him, and his arm curved around her waist.

"I still want to go home."

He groaned. "Not now, Violet."

She pressed her lips to the side of his throat. "I don't want you to get hurt protecting me. I couldn't bear it if that happened again."

"You'd rather they hurt Jack or your stepmother?"

"They've already been harmed by Mr. Brown. After my father was murdered, Jack almost died trying to protect Sylvia. He doesn't make the same mistake twice, and he is on his guard now."

"And I am not? I was in France, too, remember? I learned how to survive just as you and Jack did."

She sighed. "But it wasn't the same for you, was it? I was fighting for my King and my country."

"And I thought it was rather an amusing lark."

She touched his cheek. "That's not what I meant, I . . ."

He took her hand and brought it to his lips. "But it is true. Before your death I didn't take it seriously at all. I suppose I always knew that I could go home if I wanted to. I never thought that for you, if you failed, you would have no home to return to at all."

She closed her eyes and allowed her head to drop back onto his shoulder. "I don't want you hurt."

"Then don't lie to me. If you have to leave, have the guts to tell me to my face. I'd rather that than you just disappear again. Now go to sleep."

"You'll stay with me?"

"Until you are asleep, yes."

She allowed a silence to develop between them and was almost at the point of falling asleep when she realized he was still wide-awake, his muscles tense, his breathing ragged.

"What's wrong, Richard?" she whispered.

"Nothing that need concern you. Just old family history."

"Enough to stop you from sleeping."

His faint laugh sounded forced. "I wasn't intending to sleep with you."

"You aren't. What is wrong?"

He was silent for so long she resigned herself to be ignored.

"My mother and father didn't have a very happy marriage. In truth, I blamed my father for it until my sister, Emily, pointed out that it was hardly all his fault. I just knew my mother was unhappy, and that my father was the cause."

"Did she confide in you?"

"When I was home from school, my mother often came to find me in tears with yet another story of my father's perfidy. Even then, I wondered how he could affect her so deeply when he was hardly ever there, but I believed her nonetheless."

Violet held her breath as his grip on her hand tightened.

"But it seems that my father had a good reason to be absent, after all. My mother had a lover from before she was married, almost to the end of her life."

"That does put things in a different perspective."

"Indeed, but it is still hard for me to believe it."

"But it doesn't change the fact that she still loved you, and that you were her son."

"That's true, but it does make me wonder how much she manipulated me to keep me from loving my father. As I said, I ran away to France to get away from him and his scandalous relationship with Madame Helene. I was disgusted by his behavior, and I told him so." He sighed. "I suppose for me it represented yet another slight against my mother. I suspected he'd kept Helene as a mistress for all the years of his marriage, and that was why my mother had been so unhappy."

"And now?" Violet whispered.

"And now, in light of my mother's infidelity, you would think I'd be prostrating myself at my father's feet asking him to forgive me."

"I can't quite see you doing that exactly, but I understand what you mean. What is stopping you?"

He rose up on one elbow and looked down at her. "My mother often claimed my father wanted her dead."

"Did you think it was true?"

"Yes, and now my mother's lover has turned up like a bad penny and is trying to blackmail our family to return my mother's last journal. When Emily and I brought the matter to our father's attention, he insisted he would pay whatever was necessary to retrieve the journal, and that we need not concern ourselves with it any longer."

"Perhaps he wanted to protect you?"

His mouth thinned. "Or protect himself from a charge of murder."

Violet stared up into his bleak face. "Surely not. Your mother is dead and no one would be interested in pursuing the claims of a dead woman and her lover against a peer of the realm." She put her hand on Richard's forearm. "Do you really believe he killed her?"

He stared at her for a long moment and then exhaled. "No, I don't anymore, but what other reason would he have for wanting the journal?"

"Perhaps your mother had other secrets, and he truly does not wish for you and Emily to know about them."

"But what could they be? I read my mother's letters to her lover, and there was nothing particularly striking about them apart from her fear of being discovered and her discussions with her lover as to when she should admit my father to her bed."

"Why did she need to discuss that?"

"Perhaps her lover was a very controlling man. Anyway, I intend to ignore my father and take the journal back myself."

"Are you sure that is wise?" Violet asked. "Perhaps it would be better to let your father deal with the matter in his own way."

"If my father pays this man a single penny, do you think it will end there? The lover will never go away because he'll always have the journal to hold over us."

Violet pulled him down until she could kiss his mouth. "Then do what you think is best. May I suggest you take Jack with you? He is an excellent man in a fight and completely amoral."

He kissed her and then drew back, his gaze both intense and so vulnerable that she couldn't look away.

"Thank you for listening to me."

"You are welcome."

He levered himself off her and sat on the side of the bed. "I'll see you in the morning, then."

"If that is your wish." She longed to ask him to stay with her so that she could hold him close and offer him the comfort he so badly needed but refused to accept.

"It is. Good night, Violet."

He rose slowly and went to the door without looking back.

March was waiting for him in the sitting room, an expectant look on his face. He held out a sealed letter.

"This just arrived for you, sir."

Richard took the note and broke open the seal. "Thank you." He spread out the single sheet and read the contents. "I have to go out again. Would you be so kind as to fetch my hat and gloves?"

"Yes, sir."

In truth, he didn't want to go out into the cold night and meet with Lord Denley. He wanted to go back to Violet and make love to her all night. His stupid rule that he wouldn't make love to her as a woman was beginning to feel as false as his denial that he still had feelings for her. She was such a com- plex package—brave, intelligent, trustworthy, and devious at the same time. She challenged him like no other woman.

The past no longer mattered. He didn't want her to leave him again. He wanted her to stay with him forever.

With a muttered curse, he jammed his hat on his head and made his way out of the front door into the street beyond. As he walked, a fine drizzle of rain blew into his face, making it difficult to see clearly. Luckily, he knew his way to Denley's house without having to think.

Daniels opened the door to him and again demanded to know who Richard was and exactly what he wanted. Richard obliged the old man by raising his voice and shouting out his name so that everyone on the street who was still awake would now know who was visiting and disturbing their rest.

Denley was in his usual place by the fire, a rug tucked

around his useless legs. He wasn't reading or enjoying a glass of port this time. He was staring into the fire, his expression pensive.

"Lord Denley." Richard bowed and then took the seat opposite his mentor. "You said you had news for me."

"I do." Denley nodded. "I still can't tell you Mr. Brown's real name, but I can tell you that there are several accusations against him."

"And are these accusations correct?"

"It seems that those who come forward to complain about Mr. Brown have an inconvenient habit of dying shortly afterward." He shrugged. "It is hard to proceed on a dead man's word."

"Then what is to be done?"

"I understand that a couple has arrived from France who might be key witnesses against Mr. Brown. Do you know of them?"

"Yes, I assume you mean the Lennox twins."

"And this is where things get very complicated, indeed. It appears that Jack Lennox holds vital information against Mr. Brown, and that his twin, Vincent, or should I say, Violet Lennox, has colluded with Mr. Brown. Despite all appearances, Violet is quite prepared to kill her twin to save her accomplice."

Richard struggled to keep his voice neutral. "Why would she do that? Blood is generally considered to be thicker than water."

He realized that Denley was watching him very carefully, a wealth of sympathy in his gaze.

"If I remember correctly, you were deceived by a Violet once—Violet LeNy."

"That is correct."

"And is this the same woman?"

"Yes."

"Then it is possible that you have been doubly betrayed. Did she seek you out?"

"Lord Keyes introduced the Lennox twins to me and asked for my help."

"Did he? How interesting." Lord Denley paused. "You should proceed very carefully, Richard. If she thinks she has regained her place in your affections, she might ask you to help her murder her brother."

"I still don't understand why she would do that."

Denley sighed. "Because she and Mr. Brown are lovers and intend to split the proceeds of their misbegotten gains once they have eliminated all suspicion."

Richard stared at Denley and couldn't speak. Eventually he shook his head. "I can't believe that. Someone has already tried to kill her."

"I suspect that was staged to deliberately draw attention away from her. If she is the one who is being threatened, who would believe she is the assassin?"

"She isn't that devious."

"How do you know? She pretended to die right in front of you once before. Why wouldn't she try and deceive you again?"

Richard got to his feet. "I need to think about this."

"Indeed, and I shall try and find out exactly where Keyes is, and anything else that might help you." Denley held out his hand. "Please be careful. I would hate for harm to befall you."

Richard made his way down the stairs and back out into the quiet street. There was a hollow feeling in his gut as Lord Denley's damning words continued to reverberate in his head. Was Violet simply using him again? Could she truly kill her own brother?

Richard stopped walking, his breathing labored, and realized he had reached the corner of his own street. Could he go back to his lodgings and not wake Violet up and demand answers? He had a terrible suspicion that if he went to her full of anger and mistrust, she would refuse to tell him anything and run off.

He turned on his heel and started back toward the pleasure house. He'd bed down there for the night, wait until his emotions settled, and for once in his dealings with Violet, use his head rather than his heart to decide what he truly believed her capable of.

Emily put the last of the letters down and stared blindly at the wall, her mother's words echoing in her head.

"I have to let him back into my bed, you know why. I cannot avoid him. I cannot abide the thought of letting him win."

A vague memory surfaced of going into her mother's bedchamber seeking comfort from a nightmare and finding someone who was not her father rising up from the bed. She remembered screaming and her mother hushing her, pressing her face into her breasts, and telling her she had seen nothing, that she was having another nightmare, that she was to forget everything. . . .

Emily brought her hand to her mouth and fought the urge to retch. Was that why seeing Mr. Smith in the present had revolted her so much? Had she instinctively feared him? She contemplated the letters again. If what she suspected was true, it wasn't surprising that Philip was so desperate to retrieve the journal and keep its contents a secret.

And if she was right, there was no reason why she shouldn't behave exactly as she wanted. Perhaps she had more of her mother's blood in her than she realized. Maybe this explained why Philip had always refused her requests to visit the pleasure house. He probably feared she would turn out like her mother. She wrapped her arms around herself, suddenly cold. She'd always felt as if she didn't quite belong in the colorful Delornay-Ross family and had tried to pretend that she didn't care.

Tonight, she cared. Tomorrow, she would ask Jack Lennox to accompany her to the pleasure house, and this time she would behave exactly as she wished. She was almost certain that her father would approve.

14

"Mr. Lennox, you're . . ."

"Dressed as a woman, yes." Violet smiled at Ambrose and pirouetted in front of him, making her simple muslin gown cling to her uncorseted figure. "I understand that on Tuesday nights the second floor is dedicated to those who enjoy dressing up as the opposite sex."

"That is correct, Mr. Lennox, although I'm not quite sure if you qualify."

Violet winked at him. "As far as London society knows, I am a man, and tonight I wish to dress as a woman. You may call me Miss Violet." She glanced down at her skirt. "And I intend to enjoy myself. Will you tell Mr. Ross that I am in the smaller of the two salons?"

"If that is what you wish, Miss Violet."

"Don't tell him I'm dressed as a woman. I want it to be a surprise."

Privately, Ambrose wondered if Violet would really want to see Richard, who appeared to be in a foul temper since he'd unexpectedly arrived to sleep at the pleasure house the night before. However, it was not Ambrose's business to pry into the lives of the guests, only to ascertain their needs and act on them.

"I'll tell Mr. Ross when I next see him."

"Thank you, Ambrose." Violet hesitated. "Have you seen my brother this evening?"

"Not yet, miss. Do you wish me to give him a message as well?"

"I wish him to stay as far away from me as possible. In fact, I'd rather he didn't know I was here."

"I understand." Ambrose bowed. "I'll certainly not mention that I've seen you."

"Thank you, Ambrose." Violet blew him a kiss and headed for the second floor.

Ambrose watched her climb the stairs and appreciated her newly revealed womanly form. She certainly wasn't a voluptuous woman, a fact that had enabled her to play the man quite well, but she was tall, slender, and deliciously feminine. Ambrose could understand why Richard found her fascinating, although he guessed that her ability to shift character so well would not sit easily with him.

Ambrose turned toward the kitchen, only to find Lady Mary smiling rather anxiously at him. She wore a blue satin dress with lace flounces that exposed rather a lot of her magnificent bosom.

"Ambrose, good evening."

"Good evening, my lady."

"Have you forgiven me?"

"For what, my lady?"

She moved closer and lowered her voice. "For telling my mother about you. You might not believe it, but she is very anxious to meet you."

"I'm not sure if that is a good idea."

Lady Mary gripped his sleeve. "Will you at least think about it? She can no longer harm you. You can walk out if she says anything offensive."

He remembered Jethro and Cissy's advice, and bit off his instinctive denial. "I'll think about it."

Her face lit up. "Oh, thank you, Ambrose." She stood on tiptoe and kissed him right on the mouth. "Thank you."

Even though she leaned invitingly close, he resisted the urge to draw her into his arms and she stepped back.

"You don't want me, do you? Are you still in love with my mother?"

"Not your mother, no." He took her hand and kissed it. "You will always feel more like a sister to me than a potential lover. I am sorry if that causes you pain."

It was ironic that he'd always claimed that Emily felt like part of his family, but it wasn't true at all. He felt completely differently about her and Lady Mary.

"It's all right, Ambrose. You can't pretend to feel something that isn't there." Lady Mary managed a brave smile. "You will still consider coming and visiting my mother, though, won't you?"

"You were always a persistent child, and I see nothing has changed." He squeezed her fingers. "I swear to you that I will think about it very carefully and let you know my decision as soon as possible."

"Then I must be content with that." She took a deep breath. "And I must go and find my carriage and be off to the ball I'm supposed to be attending."

"I'll take care of that for you, my lady." Ambrose bowed, glad to be on familiar ground again. "If you wait in one of the receiving rooms off the entrance hall, I'll send one of the footmen to tell you when your carriage is at the door."

He left her then to speak to one of the footmen and then descended to the kitchen, deep in thought. To his surprise, Richard was sitting at the table with a bottle of wine in front of him that was almost empty.

"Mr. Ross."

Richard looked up and nodded. "Ambrose, do you want a glass of this excellent red wine?"

"That would be most welcome, Mr. Ross." He took the proffered glass and downed the contents in one gulp.

"Do you want more?" Richard inquired. "I can fetch another bottle."

"I'd better not, or I won't be able to carry out my duties on the second floor." Ambrose sighed. "It has already been a difficult evening, and I suspect it could get worse."

Richard clinked his glass against Ambrose's. "I'm teetering on the brink of despair myself. I'm in two minds as to whether I should simply take myself back to bed and drink until I'm oblivious."

"Before you do that, you might want to hear the message I've been given for you."

"What message is that?"

"Mr. Vincent Lennox wants you to meet him in the small salon on the second floor."

"Vincent Lennox?" Richard's scowl was ferocious. "What in the devil is he doing here when he's supposed to be in hiding?"

"I have no idea, Mr. Ross. I just agreed to pass on his message."

Richard slammed his glass down on the table and shot to his feet. "The little baggage. Excuse me, Ambrose, while I go and find Mr. Lennox and tan his damned backside."

Ambrose said nothing as Richard stormed out of the kitchen. He could only hope that Violet Lennox was capable of dealing with the storm she had quite deliberately aroused. Reaching across, he drew the wine bottle closer and tipped the remaining wine into his glass.

* * *

Richard halted at the entrance to the smaller of the two salons and had time to really observe what was going on around
him for the first time. The usual guests appeared to be absent,
and in their place were a variety of people in costume. Several
of the women possessed rather hairy chins and chests, and
some of the men were shorter and definitely more curved.

He'd forgotten that on Tuesday nights, the pleasure house
dedicated its second floor to those who liked to dress up and
those who liked to fornicate with their own sex.

"Evening, Ross."

He started as a deep voice reverberated beside him, and
turned to find a short man complete with a curled wig, a
plumped-up bosom, and a pink silk ball gown observing him.

"Carlisle?" he ventured. "Is that you?"

The man swept him a curtsy. "It is." Carlisle's blue gaze
swept over him. "I haven't seen you here before. I didn't know
that you enjoyed these 'occasions,' but I have heard rumors
you have a man sequestered in your lodgings." He winked. "So
perhaps you are finally facing the truth about yourself."

"I haven't attended one of these evenings before, no,"
Richard agreed, his gaze scanning the crowd.

Carlisle leaned closer and Richard inhaled his rather sickly
perfume. "Well, if you don't find what you are looking for, I'm
available. I'll fuck anything."

Richard spared Carlisle a grateful smile. "That's very generous of you, but I've already arranged to meet someone here."

"Oh, well." Carlisle pursed his lips and snapped open his
fan. "Off to pastures new, then. Good evening, Ross."

Richard bowed in return and stepped into the swirling
melee. On the loveseat to his left sat two men, their arms locked
around each other, their mouths fused in an endless kiss. Where
the devil was Violet? He glanced around once more and then

turned slowly back to the fire and to the occupant of the other couch.

A woman with short dark hair and very blue eyes sat there watching him. Her thin muslin gown did nothing to conceal the long length of her legs or the swell of her breasts. Richard stared at Violet as myriad conflicting emotions shuddered through him. Friend or foe? Lover or destroyer? What exactly was she to him, and how could he find out?

He took the seat next to her on the couch and turned to face her.

"You shouldn't be here."

She shrugged and the sleeve of her dress slid off her bare shoulder and down her arm. "I was bored. No one here knows Violet. I'm quite safe."

"That's not quite true, is it?"

"What do you mean?"

"Mr. Brown knows who you are, as do his minions."

She held his gaze. "And you expect that to make me cower inside? I have no idea who Mr. Brown is. I refuse to spend my whole life avoiding what I cannot control."

"So why did you come here tonight?"

Her cheeks flushed and she bit down on her lip. "Don't you know?"

"I'm not a mind reader. Tell me." His gaze drifted down to her breasts and her already hard nipples. Despite his suspicions, his cock twitched and began to swell.

"I wanted to seduce you, to make you fuck me as a woman."

He ran his fingers along the edge of her bodice until he reached her taut nipple and pinched it hard. Her breathing hitched and she briefly closed her eyes. At least he knew her desire for him was true. Despite everything, at least he knew that. Doubt stirred like a serpent in the Garden of Eden.

"Why do you want me?"

"I wish I knew." Her smile was unsteady. "In truth, it would be a lot easier if I didn't."

"In truth," he echoed her words. "And what if I asked for proof of this devotion? If I asked you to give yourself to me in every way I demanded?"

She met his gaze, her blue eyes serious. "Then I would offer myself completely."

With his other hand, he unbuttoned his trousers and released his aching shaft from the confines of his underclothes.

"Sit on my cock, then."

"Here?"

"Why not? It is as good a place as any to fuck."

He waited until she straddled his lap, holding his cock away from his stomach to aid her descent.

"You're wet for me, aren't you?" he murmured. "You always are."

He groaned as the crown of his cock brushed her sex and instinctively pushed upward. She gasped his name as he thrust inside her. Ah, God, yes, tight and wet and . . .

Her hand settled on his shoulder and he looked down as the head of his cock slowly disappeared inside her.

"Richard," she whispered, "you're so big. I'm not used to—"

He held still, all too aware of the scant inch of his flesh throbbing inside her. "What are you used to, Vincent? Does your other lover have a smaller cock than mine?"

Her fingernails dug into his shoulder and she glared at him. "That's not what I meant. I'm just not used to having you like this."

"But this is how I want it, hard and fast, me inside you before you're quite ready, me stretching your cunt and making you work for your pleasure." He caught her around the hips. "Take it all. Take me hard and deep."

As she rocked over him, he thrust upward, felt her resistance give way to the tight welcome of her sheath, and kept fucking her hard. She grew wet around him, making him able to go even deeper. He forgot everything as he fucked her, forgot his doubts, his fears, and just concentrated on pleasing himself and her.

He also forgot about the people around them who were watching, and kissed her mouth, bit her lip, her throat, leaving his mark on her as surely as she had left her invisible mark on him. He grabbed her hand and placed it over her clit.

"Make yourself come. Do it."

He watched her touch herself and his cock grew even bigger, or was it that she was tightening around him so hard that it just felt like that? He couldn't tell, didn't care, and just held on as she exploded into a climax and he fought not to join her. His fingers linked with hers over her clit and he rubbed her now-swollen nub, pinching it between his finger and thumb until she came again. This time he couldn't stop himself from climaxing. He just managed to pull out and came against her belly in thick, hot spurts that made him shudder and curse.

Even before he opened his eyes, he was aware of the chatter around them, the comments about his technique and the speculation as to exactly which of the disguised Lennox twins he was fucking.

Ignoring the other guests, he wrapped his arms around Violet, stood up, and started walking toward the smaller, more private rooms that lined the corridor between the two salons. Looking down, he realized that Violet was still plastered to his front; her muslin gown now transparent, soaked with his seed; her breasts completely visible.

With a groan, he backed her up against the nearest wall and bent his head to her breasts, sucking them into his mouth— hard nipple, muslin, and all. She moaned his name and he slid his thigh between her legs until she rode him, until her wet sex was slick against his hard thigh and she climaxed again.

"*Monsieur?*"

He looked up to see Marie-Claude beckoning him to an open door behind her. Picking Violet up again, he strode toward Marie-Claude.

"Thank you."

She shut the door behind him, and Richard walked over to the bed and placed Violet in the center of it. He waited until she opened her eyes and looked at him.

"You offered yourself to me tonight, and by God, I'm going to take everything I've ever dreamed of from you."

He left her there and turned to the chest of drawers against the wall to retrieve the items he required. When he came back to the bed, she hadn't moved, only her quick breathing betrayed the fact that she was as aroused and agitated as he was.

Her eyes widened as she saw the riding crop in his hand. He tapped it against his thigh and she swallowed hard.

"I told Ambrose I was going to beat you for disobeying my instructions and leaving my lodgings. And you know I am a man of my word."

She tried to scramble away from him, but he caught her easily and pulled her over his lap.

"You disobeyed me. You must have expected to be punished."

"I expected nothing of the sort, I—" She gasped as he smacked her buttock.

He waited, but she said nothing else. "Have I finally rendered you speechless, my dear?" He rucked up her damp, filmy gown to expose her buttocks and smoothed a hand over her nicely rounded flanks. "Don't worry, you'll be yelling again quite soon."

Violet couldn't believe she'd allowed herself to be placed in such an undignified position, her flesh laid bare, her person stretched out over Richard's lap. But he had warned her not to disobey him. Why had she doubted he'd make her pay for her transgressions? Was she so blinded by lust for the man that she'd forgotten he had a harder edge to him, an edge that had allowed him to survive in war-torn France?

Her thoughts were abruptly disrupted as the leather of the crop tapped against her buttocks and then again until she was squirming with the red heat of discomfort. He held her steady, one hand flat against her lower back as he wielded the crop. Eventually she stopped fighting him and lay still, breathing through the pain, allowing it to flow through her body. Her world narrowed to the smack of the leather, to his breathing, and to the press of his cock against her side.

She moaned as his fingers delved between her thighs, plucking at her clit, plunging into her soaking wet sex, making her arch helplessly upward into the beat of the crop.

"That's better. I like you like this: compliant and wet."

He pushed her off his lap onto her stomach and she could do nothing but lie there and breathe. The tang of tansy oil assailed her nostrils as she felt him slide a sponge up inside her.

"I want my come in you tonight. I want you to take it all."

Still aware of the heat radiating through her buttocks, Violet could only nod and wait to see what he would do with her next. She didn't have long to wonder because he returned with more oil and sat beside her on the bed.

"I know how much you like being fucked in the arse, so I'll fill you there too." He showed her a thick leather dildo. "You'll take this, get on your knees."

She obeyed him, her body shaking as he caressed her buttocks and slid two oiled fingers deep in her arse. She whimpered, but he didn't stop plunging them in and out of her, each movement amplified by the tenderness and sensitivity of her skin. She tensed when the dildo first pressed against her tight bud.

"Don't fight me." He rested his hand on her tingling buttock. "You said you'll give me everything. Now do it."

There was a peculiar note in his voice, a combination of a

command and a plea she found irresistible. She wanted to give him all of her, to make him see that at least in this, she was his and his alone. She closed her eyes and forced herself to breathe out, felt the dildo slide deep and gave herself to the intensity of the pleasure.

"Violet."

He was holding her around the waist, urging her upright and onto her knees. He turned her to face him. She let him do what he wanted, aware of the thick pulse of the dildo in her arse and the answering throb of her clit.

"Hold still."

He wrapped a long silk scarf around her wrists and then brought them over her head and tied them to the high headboard behind her, making her back arch. She watched him through lowered eyes as he stripped out of his clothes, enjoying the play of muscle, of taut flesh and bone, of his thick cock jutting out from his groin.

He crouched in front of her and pushed her knees wide until her sex was open to him. Holding her gaze, he pumped one finger inside her in a steady rhythm. God, she wanted more, wanted that big cock filling her.

"Please," she whispered.

But he didn't seem to listen, his attention now on his moving finger. He pulled out and she held her breath, but he only started to play with her clit, tugging at her swollen labia, swirling his fingertip through her wetness until she felt everything start to throb and ache like her arse. He knelt back and simply stared at her sex, and she'd never felt quite so exposed or so vulnerable.

Did he like her displayed like this for him? Her desire evident, her blatant need on display? He moved closer again and she tensed as his hands closed on her small breasts. He thumbed her nipples, pinched them, played with them, and finally took one in his mouth, biting and nibbling until she writhed against him; then he did the same to the other one.

She was panting now, her body focused on his hands and mouth, waiting for the next sensual assault, balanced on the point of a new kind of pleasure, but not yet allowed to fall into it. He got off the bed, walked over to a set of drawers, and opened the top one. She waited, hardly breathing until he strolled back to her, one hand cupping something that looked like jewelry.

"I know you are enjoying this, Violet. You always liked it when I played a little roughly with you, didn't you?" She simply nodded, her attention on the glittering gold pins he was laying on the counterpane. "These things will enhance your pleasure, make you more desperate, make you wild."

He showed her a narrow gold bar that looked rather like a double-sided hairpin. "Let's start with your breasts."

His fingers closed around her already sensitive nipple and he drew it out even farther until she was leaning into him. He slid the clamp over her nipple and she hissed at the sudden coldness and pinch of the metal. For a moment, pain radiated from her flesh and she set her teeth against it.

He caught her chin in his hand and made her look at him. "Don't fight it. Relax and breathe through it."

She bit her lip and tried to relax as he approached her with the second clamp, but it was difficult when her mind was already anticipating the sudden ache, the constriction, and the corresponding throb in her clit.

"That's it," he murmured, and licked the distended tip of her nipple and then around the clamp, his wet tongue exploring every angle of the adornment before trailing across to sample and taste her other breast.

She shivered as his mouth moved lower down over her stomach and his tongue swirled around her clit.

"Here too," he whispered against her most intimate flesh. She held still while he attached heavy gold clamps to her labia and then pinched her clit between two fingers and clamped her there too. She moaned his name and came hard, the hot pulse of her need somehow amplified by the heavy constriction of the metal.

"You should see yourself." He manhandled a large mirror toward the bed, and she found herself staring at a woman she didn't know. A woman who was displaying herself wantonly for her man. "I'm going to fuck you hard now."

He climbed back on the bed and crawled toward her, his hazel gaze intent. He didn't bother to untie her hands; he just grabbed her around the hips and brought her down in one smooth motion over his cock. She screamed as he filled her and started to come. Screamed even more as he didn't stop thrusting and just kept making her climax.

His hand squeezed her still-tender buttocks, reminding her of both her beating and the thick dildo filling her. She didn't fight him, just let him take her in the most basic of ways until she couldn't stop coming in an endless stream of arousal. His kisses were no less powerful than the demands of his body, engulfing her, taking her, owning her—as if he wanted to imprint himself on her forever.

He lost his smooth motion and started to speed up, each thrust more shallow until he finally shoved deep and held himself there, and the heat of his come pulsed inside her. His head fell forward onto her shoulder and she heard his sharp intake of breath as she tightened around his cock, as if forcing out the last precious drops of his seed.

"Violet." He groaned her name and then bit the taut skin over her collarbone. When he reached up and untied her hands, she fell against him in a boneless heap and he lowered her down to the rumpled sheets. She moaned as he spread her legs wide and carefully removed the clamps from her now throbbing and sensitive flesh. He eased the dildo out from her arse and she immediately missed the thick pressure.

He crawled closer, his gaze now on her chest, his hands cupping and molding her breasts. Her breath hissed out as he thumbed the gold clamps on her nipples.

"God, I love seeing you like this, Violet, licking and sucking you until you scream my name. Do you like it, too?"

She licked her lips. "Yes, you know I do."

He reared back, one hand on his newly erect cock as he made it harder. "Do you remember in France, the way I'd fuck you even when we were surrounded by others? How I'd put my hand over your mouth to stop you screaming your pleasure to them all?"

"Yes." She watched his hand fist his cock, until his fingers were coated in pre-come and moving fast. "I always wanted you."

He came down over her, slid his cock deep, and began plunging into her. When she tried to bend her knees and wrap her legs around his hips, he held her flat on the bed, his body controlling her response, his weight pressing her into the mattress. Her body shook as she absorbed his thrusts, and pleasure began to build in a different way, so fierce and low that she wanted to growl and bare her teeth at him, draw blood.

Her climax took her by surprise, pulsing through her like a series of stabbing jolts edged with a dark pleasure she had never experienced before. Without thinking, she buried her face in his shoulder and bit down hard, heard him growl in response and climax long and slow inside her. He remained slumped over her, his breathing labored, his heart racing as fast as hers. At some point she knew she would have to listen to her complaining body, but not now, not yet, not while he was still inside her and over her.

Eventually he rolled away and lay on his back, his forearm shielding his eyes.

"I spoke to my government contact yesterday."

Violet went still as she struggled to focus on his quite unexpected words.

"He says that the English government believes you are in league with Mr. Brown."

Blindly, Violet turned away from him and crawled toward the edge of the bed. It seemed to take all her effort to move and forever to reach her intended destination.

"He says that you intend to kill your brother."

Tears crowded the back of Violet's throat and she desperately wished for a dagger. Before she could slide off the bed, Richard caught her, placed her flat on her back again, and covered her with his bigger body.

"Let me go, you imbecile . . . *va chez le diable!*"

She tried to slap his face, scratch his eyes out, *hurt him* as much as he had hurt her. He grabbed her wrists and hauled them over her head, his hazel gaze resolute and fixed on her.

"I didn't say I believed him, did I?"

Violet glared up at him, aware that she was crying but unable to do anything other than lie there and shake with a combination of rage and disbelief.

"I don't think you could murder Jack, and I don't believe you are in league with Mr. Brown." His grip on her wrists loosened slightly. "It seems to me that you are playing an extremely dangerous game, my love. What exactly *are* you planning to do with Mr. Brown, Violet? Double-cross him?"

15

Emily straightened her back and marched into the larger of the two salons on the second floor of the pleasure house. Despite being dressed in men's clothing *and* being masked, she still felt rather conspicuous and expected Christian or Ambrose to spot her immediately and order her home.

The scenes of debauchery around her were quite startling, and she'd barely penetrated the depths of the pleasure house's famed activities. She studied the groups of men and women around her and realized for the first time that finding someone to relieve her of her virginity might not be as easy as she had thought.

After a sleepless night and a day spent rereading her mother's letters, she had decided that action was called for. At three in the morning, it had seemed obvious that she had nothing to lose except her reputation and her maidenhood. And if what she feared was true, her respectability was based on a lie. If Ambrose objected to her solely because she was innocent, he could hardly continue to object if she followed in her mother's footsteps and bedded a man. Then, unlike her mother, she would not marry some poor unsuspecting fool, but offer to live in sin with Ambrose instead.

She glanced around the room again and considered the men. She had no doubt that presented with the opportunity to copulate, most of the guests would happily oblige her. But would they expect to encounter an inexperienced virgin at the pleasure house? She grabbed a large glass of wine from a passing waiter and drank it down.

"Good evening, sir."

She jumped as a tall young man addressed her, and almost dropped her glass.

"Good evening."

"Are you new here?" He considered her masked face. "I don't believe we have met before."

"I'm new."

The man's smile deepened. "How delightful. And what takes your fancy tonight?"

Emily attempted to look bored. "I'm not sure."

"Man, woman, or both?"

"Just one man, I think. I don't want to overdo it on my first night."

"An excellent plan. Then consider me at your service." He bowed. "My name is Michael."

Emily paused to study him. He was tall, handsome, and seemed rather interested in her, but there was nothing about him that sparked her interest. But did that matter? As long as he was a man, surely he would do?

She sighed. "I'm Ross." She extended her hand and he shook it firmly.

"It is a pleasure." He glanced around the salon. "Do you like an audience, or would you prefer to retire to one of the private rooms?"

Emily wasn't sure if she appreciated his lack of embarrassment or was appalled by it.

"In private, please." She glanced up at him. "You do realize I'm a woman, don't you?"

He smiled. "Yes, I had noticed that." He gestured at the doorway. "Would you like to follow me?"

With all the anticipation of a condemned criminal stepping out onto the gallows, Emily followed Michael from the salon. He waited for her at the door and cupped her cheek.

"You are very beautiful."

"Thank you."

He brushed his mouth over hers, and she felt nothing. But perhaps that was for the best. She suspected she'd need to keep all her emotions tightly locked away if she was to get through this horrible night.

"Mr. Ross?"

A familiar voice intruded on her ears, and she turned to see Jack Lennox bearing down on her. His quick glance took in her attentive companion and he captured her hand in his.

"I'm so sorry I'm late, Ross. I had to run an errand for my poor, sick brother." He smiled at Michael. "Thank you for entertaining my guest. I was worried he'd be too shy to talk to anyone."

Jack casually bent to kiss Emily's cheek, wrapped his arm around her waist, and pinched her hard. "Perhaps you might thank your companion for his company, and then we can move on to other, more interesting entertainment."

Emily knew when she was beaten and held out her hand to Michael. "I apologize, sir. Perhaps next time?"

"Absolutely." He paused. "Unless you'd both care to join me?"

As if he feared she might bolt, Jack tightened his grip on Emily's waist and drew her even closer. "Mr. Ross is not quite ready for such delights, but when he is, we will be sure to seek your company."

Jack maneuvered Emily firmly toward the staircase and out onto the landing.

"What on earth were you doing, Miss Ross?"

"Going to bed with a complete stranger. What were you doing?"

He stared her down. "Why didn't you wait for me as we planned?"

"Because I wasn't certain you would turn up. I wasn't even sure if I wanted you to be involved."

"You'd rather be mauled around by a stranger?"

"Yes!"

He opened his mouth to answer her and then shoved her behind the draped curtains at the window.

"Ambrose is coming!"

She shrank back against the wall and watched as Jack sprinted halfway down the stairs and concealed himself there.

After a few tense moments, she waved at him. "It's all right. Ambrose has gone back down to the kitchen."

Emily didn't mention that she'd witnessed Ambrose fawning over Lady Mary again, the kiss she'd given him, the smile that had promised *so* much more. Unfortunately, Emily had been too far away to hear what they were saying to each other. For all she knew, they were arranging an assignation, although Lady Mary hadn't looked too happy as she walked past a hastily concealed Emily. The sight only convinced her that she was doing the right thing.

She turned to Jack. "Are you still willing to help me?"

"Are you still sure about this, Miss Ross?"

"Don't call me that here," Emily hissed. "Call me Ross as you did before. I thought we'd already discussed this."

"We didn't discuss anything. You told me to meet you here so that you could make Ambrose jealous, and I agreed to go along with it."

"Exactly, you *agreed.*" She stared at him. "Have you changed your mind about helping me?"

"Of course not. I'm always delighted to help the course of true love. Although . . ." He hesitated. "I'm not quite certain how you intend to accomplish your goal with me rather than Ambrose."

"I explained this. I need to make Ambrose realize I'm a grown woman who is perfectly capable of understanding all his needs."

"By offering yourself to that man you just met?"

"Yes!" For a moment, Emily wanted to stamp her foot, turn tail, and run back to the comfort of her bedchamber.

Jack's skeptical expression faded and he drew her close. "Are you all right, Miss Ross? You seem rather distraught this evening. Are you certain you wish to go through with your plan?"

Damn him for being so perceptive and not the selfish rake he pretended to be. She'd forgotten he had a sibling. Perhaps she had chosen the wrong man after all.

She managed a smile. "If you don't wish to help me, I can go back and find Michael. I'll quite understand."

"So I noticed." His smile was wry. "You might understand, but your brother and Ambrose will never forgive me if I abandon you now. I'll play my part. I suspect I'll even enjoy it. You are a very beautiful and courageous woman, Miss Ross."

She made a face at him but allowed him to escort her into the larger of the second-floor salons, where she stopped dead. There were even more couples in the room than there had been before. Some of the guests were now naked or busy removing their clothes. She spotted Michael with his arm around a rather feminine-looking man. Emily had never seen so much unabashed depravity in her life. She gripped Jack's arm.

"We don't have to do anything here, do we?"

Jack glanced around as if nothing he saw was out of the ordinary. "We can take a private room and lock the door if you prefer it."

"And Ambrose will still be able to find us?"

"If I make sure someone sees me about to seduce you." Jack smiled wickedly down at Emily. "Perhaps we should begin."

"I . . ." Emily's words were cut off as Jack's mouth descended over hers and he began to kiss her with an expertise that both enthralled and repelled her. Within a few seconds, she'd forgotten how to think, as his tongue met hers in a teasing, gentle duel that made her lean into his strength, hers all gone.

When he finally raised his head, she was wrapped around him, one hand slid into the back of his hair, the other pressed against his heart.

"Oh."

"Oh, indeed." His lowered gaze traveled down over her body. "Did you like that?"

Emily could only nod, and his smile widened. "Good. Now let's go and find a room. I made sure that Marie-Claude got a good look at us, so she'll probably be running to tell Ambrose right now." He took Emily's hand. "In fact, let's make sure of it."

He walked with her across the room to where a small, dark-haired woman was directing the servants at the buffet.

"Good evening, Marie-Claude. Are any of the rooms vacant?" He smiled down at Emily. "My companion is a little shy. It is her first time here."

Marie-Claude stared hard at Emily. "Indeed. The third room on the right is free. You may take that one."

"*Merci.*" Jack bowed. As Marie-Claude turned away, he leaned down to whisper loudly in Emily's ear. "See, Miss Ross? I told you that it would be easy."

Even as Marie-Claude's head whipped round, Jack was pushing Emily into their allotted room and locking the door behind her.

"That should do the trick." His smile died to be replaced by a far more speculative look. "If you truly wish Ambrose to think I have debauched you, you will need to remove a few of your clothes."

"I know that." Emily struggled out of the coat and waistcoat Jack had borrowed from his brother, Vincent, and started on her neck cloth. "How much should I take off?"

"All of it?"

"Surely not."

Emily licked her lips as Jack strolled toward her, suddenly aware of being on her own with a devastatingly attractive man who appeared to have no morals. She went still as he cupped her chin and took possession of her mouth again. His kiss was even more visceral than the first, and it made her ache in quite unaccustomed places.

"Let me help you out of those clothes," he murmured, his hand shaping her buttock, smoothing her in slow, sultry circles. Even though she knew she should say no, the feel of his hands was having a devastating effect on her senses. For the first time she could understand how an experienced man might lead a young lady astray.

She gasped as his palm slid inside her trousers, brushing her buttock as he pushed the fabric down her legs and helped her step out of them. Her shirttails fell almost to her knees, but she still felt naked.

He kissed her again, drawing her against the muscular planes of his body, one hand in her hair, the other on her hip. Her breasts seemed to be aching, and she rubbed herself against the hardness of his chest, seeking relief but only making it worse. She'd felt like this when Ambrose kissed her. Had she been wrong? Perhaps she just craved the touch of any man.

"Lovely," Jack murmured, now kissing her ear, her throat, her collarbone. She gasped as he bent her back over his arm and kissed her breast through her shirt, his mouth dampening the fabric until the tight bud of her nipple was clearly visible.

She didn't stop him when he licked her there, too, and then sucked on her. By the time he'd worked his hand under her shirt and was caressing her hip and her buttocks, she was no longer quite sure where she was, or who she was, only of a need growing within her for something only the male body pleasuring her could provide.

"Jack . . ." she gasped.

"Mmm?" he asked, his fingers cupping her mound, his mouth raining kisses on her face.

"You are going to stop, aren't you?"

He held her away from him, and she wanted to moan her displeasure.

"Do you want me to?" He paused. "I intended to make you come without taking your virginity."

"Make me what?"

He moved the fingers that were still lodged between her legs because she had trapped his hand there. "Climax, come, take your pleasure from me." His thumb circled something sensitive and she shuddered and instinctively pushed down on his fingers. "That's right. If you want me like that, I can also use my mouth and my fingers on you."

But did she want him? Didn't she want Ambrose more? Did she have to make a choice? In her pursuit of sexual pleasure, her mother hadn't cared who she hurt or what the consequences of her actions were. A fresh wave of pain swamped Emily and she could only gaze helplessly up at Jack.

He immediately sat in the nearest chair and pulled her onto his lap.

"It's all right, Miss Ross. Please don't cry. You don't have to do anything at all."

She cupped his chin. "No, I want to do this, I—"

The click of the lock turning in the door stopped her speaking. Ambrose now stood against the closed door, his expression unreadable, his mouth set in a hard line.

"Good evening, Miss Ross, Mr. Lennox."

Jack opened his mouth, but Emily glared at him.

"Good evening, Ambrose." She smiled and made no effort to remove herself from Jack's lap. "Is there something you want?"

"You are not supposed to be here, Miss Ross. You know that."

She turned more fully to face him, watched his gaze fall to the swell of her half-uncovered bosom and the length of her bare legs. "But I want to be here." She kissed Jack lightly on the cheek. "And Jack offered to bring me as his guest."

"I suspect Mr. Lennox will have to answer to your brothers for that piece of foolishness."

"Oh, I don't mind." Jack smiled into Emily's eyes. "She is definitely worth the risk."

"I beg to disagree, Mr. Lennox." Ambrose held out his hand. "Will you come down to the kitchen with me, Miss Ross, and we'll forget this ever happened?"

Emily slowly stood up and made her way over to Ambrose. She ignored his proffered hand and instead got as close to him as she could. She put her hand on his chest.

"Don't blame Jack. I decided that as you weren't interested in me, I should look for an alternative source of sexual enlightenment."

Ambrose tried to shift away from her, but she refused to allow it. "That isn't fair, Miss Ross. I have explained my reasons for my behavior toward you many times."

"Then you should just run along and leave me to Jack. He doesn't love me, but he is quite willing to help me learn."

His hand closed around her upper arm, making her jump. "You have let him bed you?"

"Not quite, but if you leave, I'm sure we'll get around to it at some point."

"I can't leave you here with him. Your brothers would never forgive me."

"My brothers?" She opened her eyes wide at him—anger, fear, and something else she refused to acknowledge driving her on. "Are you afraid you might lose your position? Is *that* what dictates your behavior toward me?"

His grip tightened. "You have never known what it is to have nothing, so do not even jest about being deprived of your livelihood. And I am no coward."

"I'm not so sure."

He yanked her close until she was pressed against him from knee to chest. "What do you want from me, Miss Ross?"

"Isn't it obvious?" She licked her lips. "I want your hands on me, your mouth on me, your body buried in mine."

"Miss Ross, I . . ."

She pushed hard at his chest until he had to let her go. "If you don't want me like that, go away and leave me with Jack. He at least has promised to give me pleasure even if he doesn't bed me."

Jack stood up and bowed as Emily walked toward him. "I'm more than willing to do that."

Ambrose glared at Jack Lennox, who had the audacity to wink at him. Miss Ross seemed determined to put him into an impossible position. He was so tired of being called a coward, tired of denying what he really wanted. But was this the right way to show his love for Emily? He didn't want Jack Lennox touching her, but what was the alternative? Could he perhaps offer her this, and resist the temptation to take her completely?

"I can give you pleasure," he blurted out.

Emily went still, her back turned, and slowly looked over her shoulder. "You would do that for me?"

He gestured at Jack. "I'd rather it was me than him."

Jack shrugged. "It's up to you, Miss Ross."

Ambrose held his breath while Emily considered him. There was a strange air of desperation about her that made him want to take her in his arms and just hold her. It also made him certain that if anyone was going to introduce Miss Emily Ross to the pleasures of the flesh, it was going to be him, and not some unscrupulous rake who would simply count her as yet another conquest to be discarded the next morning.

He held out his hand again. "Please, Miss Ross? Emily?"

She came toward him, and he took her hand and kissed it. "I'll give you more pleasure than you can imagine."

She looked up into his eyes and his whole world narrowed so that he could see only her, breathe her beloved scent in, and feel her quivering flesh against his. She went up on tiptoes, wrapped her arms around his neck, and kissed him.

With a groan, he sucked her tongue into his mouth. He struggled to keep the kiss gentle and respectful, but she would have none of it, her mouth eager, her body writhing against his until his cock threatened to explode just with the feel of her rubbing against him.

He picked her up and laid her on the bed, pulling her shirt up to display her pert breasts and the glorious thatch of hair on her mound. He returned to kissing her mouth, used his hands to learn her shape, to fondle her breasts until she was moaning his name.

With a groan, he kissed his way down to her taut nipple and drew it deep into his mouth, sucking and licking it until she was panting. His hand covered her mound, his middle finger sliding easily into the thick wetness to find the swell of her bud. He circled her there until she met every demand with a roll of her hips, until she was clutching at his shoulders, demanding her due, seeking her pleasure from his fingers.

"Ambrose, I . . ."

"It's all right, Emily. I have you."

He shrugged off the pain of her nails digging into him and bent lower to tongue her clit and suck it into his mouth. She screamed his name, and he felt the tremors of her climax against his thrusting tongue. He barely resisted the urge to shove his finger deep in her cunt and claim her properly.

Instead, he crawled up her body and kissed her mouth, letting her taste herself on his lips. She opened her brown eyes and studied him. He let her stare, praying that she wouldn't turn away in disgust, that she would be pleased with him.

"That was . . . remarkable," she whispered.

"Good." He kissed her again, aware of a tremendous sense of relief mixed with sexual satisfaction.

Her gaze dropped to his trousers. "I want to see you."

His cock kicked against the constriction of his underclothes. "Are you sure?"

"Yes."

He knelt up on the bed and slowly stripped off his clothes until there was nothing left to hide behind, just his gleaming black skin in stark contrast to her fairness. She touched his scarred hip and he went still.

"Turn around."

"You don't need to see—"

She shoved at his hip. "Turn around."

He reluctantly complied and heard her indrawn breath, shuddered when her fingers traced the intricate scars.

"You were only a child when you were brought here. Did they whip *children?*"

"If they cried too much for their mothers." He swallowed hard. "And Lord Kendrick wasn't averse to beating me either."

He tensed as she leaned in and kissed her way down his spine. "I'm so sorry, Ambrose."

He turned back to face her. "I don't need your pity. It was a long time ago."

She didn't back down. "I know, but perhaps I can be angry

on your behalf?" Her gaze dropped to his cock. "May I touch you there as well?"

"If you wish."

She reached forward and wrapped her hand around the base of his shaft. "Oh, it is warm and hard and soft all at the same time."

He closed his hand over hers. "Like this, Miss Ross." And showed her how to move her fingers up and down him. It didn't take long for his pre-come to start to flow, soaking their entwined fingers and making the experience so pleasurable he wanted to moan with joy. How many times had he been touched like this? Far too many to mention, and yet this woman's touch meant more to him than any others.

"I'm going to come, Miss Ross, Emily." He cupped his other hand over the tip of his straining cock and let himself climax. "Ah, Emily, I . . ." He buried his face in the soft spot between her head and shoulder and closed his eyes until he'd finished trembling. She wrapped her arms around him and held him close to her heart, and he wanted to stay there forever.

"That was very entertaining."

Disoriented, Ambrose opened his eyes and turned toward the chair by the fire where Jack Lennox had remained seated. He'd completely forgotten the man was even there.

"Mr. Lennox, have you no decency?" Emily was already scrambling to pull down her long shirt. "Why didn't you leave?"

"Because I wanted to see if Ambrose would pleasure you as well as I would?" He nodded. "And I must confess that he did such an excellent job, I am now aroused myself."

Ambrose couldn't help but look at the man's groin and see he was correct.

Jack winced and stroked himself. "That's the second time I've been hard tonight."

"Then why don't you go and find someone to relieve you?" Ambrose asked.

Jack fixed him with a cordial stare. "Because I am waiting to see if Miss Ross requires anything more of me."

"I'll take care of Miss Ross." Ambrose almost growled.

"I don't think so." Jack rose and sauntered toward the bed, making Ambrose tense up. "Are you completely satisfied, Miss Ross?"

Emily swallowed hard and avoided Ambrose's gaze. "Not quite."

"What?" Ambrose tore his wary gaze away from Jack to stare at Emily. "I gave you exactly what you asked for, what you said Mr. Lennox was going to give you."

She raised her chin at him. "It is true that you gave me great pleasure, I cannot dispute that. But I want more. I want to be bedded completely."

For one second, Jack's and Ambrose's gazes collided, and Ambrose was no longer sure if Jack was playing a game or not.

"Miss Ross . . ."

Emily's lip trembled. "Stop calling me that! Stop retreating from me." She started to scramble toward the edge of the bed. "If neither of you want me, I'll simply go out into the main salon and offer myself to the first man I see!"

Ambrose caught her by the shoulders and stopped her retreat. "You don't mean that. You are worth far too much to want to give yourself to any man." She tried to pull out of his grasp and he looked desperately at Jack, who raised his eyebrows.

"She's already tried to bed one complete stranger tonight, Ambrose, so I suspect she's serious. Miss Ross, what if I offered to fuck Ambrose? Would that interest you enough to make you stay here and rethink your decision?"

"Why in God's name would she want to see that?" Ambrose demanded. "Are you mad?"

Jack leaned up against the four-poster bed and ignored Ambrose, his attention fixed on Emily, who appeared to be listening to him. "I'm not mad. Perhaps Miss Ross would like to watch me with you as much as I enjoyed watching her." His eyes held another message, warning Ambrose not to interfere. "It would add to her sexual experience without taking her virginity. She could even help me out if she wished."

For the first time, Ambrose wasn't sure whose side Jack was on. Or was he simply playing with them both? It seemed the most likely explanation.

"Mr. Lennox, with all due respect, why are you still here? This is a matter between me and Miss Ross."

"I promised Miss Ross I would stay with her this evening, and I always keep my word." He bowed to Emily. "Make your choice, Miss Ross. You can stay with me or with Ambrose, or you can stay and watch me fuck him instead of being fucked yourself."

Ambrose winced at Jack Lennox's crude choice of words and forced himself to look at Emily. "*Or* I can escort you down to the kitchen and get Seamus Kelly to take you home."

Emily stared at him for so long that he feared she was never going to speak again.

"I don't want to go home," she whispered. "I want to stay here with you."

Ambrose let out a breath he was unaware he'd been holding. "Then stay." He tried to clear his throat. "I'll let Mr. Lennox fuck me, and you can watch."

It was hardly ideal, but at least it might help Emily remember exactly who he was and how he earned at least part of his wages. If he was even luckier, it might also stop her giving away her maidenhead.

Jack started to remove his clothes and Emily's eyes widened. He wasn't quite as tall as Ambrose, but he was well muscled and slender. He climbed up onto the bed and smiled at Ambrose.

"I've been looking forward to this." His hot gaze roved over Ambrose's body. "Where should Miss Ross sit in order to appreciate us both?"

Ambrose nodded and indicated the chair Jack had just vacated. "Miss Ross?"

Emily obligingly sat down, a look of intense concentration on her face as Jack lightly ran his hands over Ambrose's flanks. It didn't take long for Ambrose's cock to respond to the caress and to the thought that Emily was watching him. He sighed as Jack knelt behind him and wrapped his arm low around Ambrose's hips, his fingers curling around the thick base of Ambrose's shaft.

"Wet already?" He bit Ambrose's shoulder, making him jerk. "Me too." He raised his voice. "Do you like this, Miss Ross? I'm going to oil my fingers and slide them deep in Ambrose's arse to prepare him for my cock."

Ambrose locked his gaze on Emily's as Jack followed through on his words. Would she be shocked to see him on his knees like this, bent forward as Jack eased the first thick inch of his cock deep in his arse?

He groaned as Jack rocked against him, surprised at the size of Jack's cock and his instant response to it. His own shaft was wet now with pre-come. As if in a dream, he saw Emily lick her lips and stare at him. God, if only she would taste him . . . could he ask that of her, did he dare?

Jack slid deeper, one hand braced on Ambrose's hip until he was fully sheathed inside. His other hand played with Ambrose's pierced nipple, tugging on it and then lowering his fingers to circle the crown of Ambrose's dripping cock. He found the slit and penetrated it with his finger until Ambrose moaned and bucked his hips.

"Would you like to taste him, Miss Ross?" Jack invited, and

Ambrose shuddered. "Take him in your mouth while I fuck him?"

As if in his most erotic dream, Ambrose watched Emily nod and slowly walk toward the bed, her tongue wetting her lips.

Jack gripped Ambrose's cock firmly around the base and drew it away from his belly. "Here, Miss Ross." He squeezed hard and bit Ambrose's ear. "I won't let you come too soon. I want us all to enjoy this."

And then he started thrusting and Ambrose forgot everything but the dual sensation of Emily's tentative mouth on him and Jack's far more vigorous penetration. It was as if he was caught between heaven and hell, held captive by the two opposing forces of his need forever.

Jack's grip on his cock tightened, and his stroke became shallow. "Miss Ross, you might want to step back."

Ambrose hated the loss of her mouth, but Jack gave him no time to think of it because they were both coming hard, he all over Jack's fingers, and Jack deep inside him.

When he came to his senses, Jack kissed him full on the mouth and then climbed off the bed and started to get dressed.

"I'll wait for you in the kitchen, Miss Ross."

Ambrose nodded at him. "Thank you."

Jack sauntered toward the door. "You have no idea how much you have to thank me for, Ambrose, but I'll be sure to remind you at a later date."

When Jack closed the door behind him, Ambrose turned his attention back to Emily, who was twisting her hands together and staring at the floor. He put his breeches back on, took the seat Jack had vacated by the fire, and held out his hand.

"Did I disgust you?"

She shook her head and he was aware of a great sense of relief. "You were . . . beautiful."

"Come here."

She came toward him, and he reached out and put her on his lap, drawing her close against his bare chest.

"What's wrong, love?"

"Why should anything be wrong?" Her voice was a little muffled against his skin, but clear enough to hear. "Perhaps I'm just tired of being the only member of the Delornay-Ross family who isn't allowed to join in the fun of the pleasure house."

"That's not it," he said quietly. "I know you, Emily. Why this urgent need to rid yourself of your virginity?"

She shuddered and moved even closer to him. He bent his head and breathed in her warmth, content just to hold her if that was what she needed, and he suspected it was.

After a long while, she kissed his collarbone. "You are always so restful. I've always envied you for that."

"I learned patience the hard way. It is not something I'm proud of. I've often wished I could be more like you."

She raised her head to look at him. "Like me?" She bit down on her lip. "Sometimes I feel as if I don't belong in the Delornay-Ross family at all."

"I believe in families the youngest child is often over-protected." He smoothed her disordered brown hair away from her face. "They love you very much."

She pressed her face against his chest and he felt the heat of her tears against his skin.

"What is it, love?"

She shook her head, so he just continued to hold her, aware that his body was responding to her nearness in a predictable fashion, and equally determined that she shouldn't be bothered by it. For some reason he felt like he had failed her. Eventually she stopped crying and looked up at him again.

"I thought anyone would do. But when it came down to it, I realized I didn't want just *anyone* to bed me for the sake of it. I wanted you."

It was pointless to ask her to explain her earlier antics when he knew that at last she was speaking the truth. The least he could do was be honest back.

"I've always loved you, you know that," he said. "But I've always been aware that the gulf between us was too wide. I owe your family so much. Taking their daughter from them would have seemed like the final insult."

She sighed. "Why would you be taking me away from them? I suspect they all know how I feel about you, and no one has told me to stop loving you, only that you do not love me."

"I love you too much to risk placing you in harm's way. If your family chose to disown you, I would have no money, no home, and nothing to offer you."

She sat up so that she could look at him properly. "I don't care about those things."

"That's because you have never had to do without them." He shuddered. "I can never forget how it feels to be at the mercy of the weather, of foraging for food in the gutter, or fighting for my life. I find myself unable to imagine going back there, and I could never allow you to join me."

"Do you really think my family would disown me if you asked to marry me?"

He met her despairing gaze. "I don't know."

"Because you are too afraid to ask?" She climbed off his lap and found her trousers. "Perhaps I shouldn't be so hard on you. I haven't asked my father directly either."

"What are you doing?"

"I'm getting dressed so that you can take me home."

A curious sensation of loss made him struggle to form a sentence. "You no longer want me?"

She clutched her coat to her chest. "Oh, God, I want you, but not if you aren't prepared to fight for me." She put on her coat and headed for the door. "On second thoughts, you don't even need to take me home. Jack Lennox is waiting for me in the kitchen."

16

Emily made her way down the backstairs to the kitchen, stumbling down the wooden stairs in her haste to leave Ambrose behind. She knew he'd follow her, and she was terrified that if he caught her and held her, she wouldn't be able to stop herself responding to him. Her body still throbbed from his attention and she wanted more, wanted so much more it frightened her.

When she burst into the kitchen, Jack immediately stood up, his expression alert.

"Are you all right, Miss Ross?"

Behind her, she could hear Ambrose coming down the stairs. "Can you take me home?"

Jack's gaze swept her disheveled appearance and her bare feet. "Don't you want to change first?"

"I don't have time."

But it was already too late; Ambrose came through the kitchen door still wearing only his trousers, his bare chest heaving.

"Don't leave like this, Emily."

Emily hastily buttoned up her trousers and straightened her shirt. She couldn't look at him. She just couldn't.

"*Emily.*"

Keeping her gaze lowered, she moved to stand by Jack's side. "Please, take me home."

"Of course," Jack murmured. He stripped off his coat and draped it around her shoulders.

The kitchen door opened again, and Emily closed her eyes as Christian appeared. His gaze took in their frozen tableau.

"What in God's name is going on here?"

He didn't shout, but Emily still shivered at the cold fury in his tone. Jack put a comforting arm around her shoulders, and Ambrose took a hasty step toward her.

Christian held up his hand. "Stay where you are, Ambrose. Mr. Lennox, why did you take my sister up to the main floors of the pleasure house?"

Emily raised her chin. She refused to be discussed as if she wasn't present. "Because I asked him to. He didn't know that you had decided I wasn't allowed up there."

"I didn't decide that. Your father did, and it is he you will have to answer to for your conduct."

Anger flourished deep in Emily's chest. "If that is true, what right do you have to berate me?"

Christian raised his eyebrows. "The right of the person who owns this business."

"There are plenty of women of my class up there. I saw them."

"But they aren't related to me, and you are."

"Would it make it different if we were strangers?"

"That's irrelevant. Philip would have my head if he knew you'd been up there viewing the rooms with Jack Lennox."

"Oh, it is far worse than that."

"Indeed." Christian's chilly gaze flicked to Jack. "Have you ruined my sister?"

Jack shrugged. "It depends how you define ruined."

Christian moved so suddenly that Emily gasped. In an instant, he had one hand wrapped around Jack's throat.

"Do not speak disrespectfully of my sister in my presence ever again. Do you understand me?"

Ambrose touched Christian's shoulder. "He didn't ruin her. I swear it."

Emily stormed across to Christian and punched him as hard as she could in the arm. "Do not talk about me as if I am not here! And perhaps I *wanted* to be ruined. Have you thought of that?"

Christian released Jack and looked down at her, rubbing his arm. "I'm sorry. Perhaps ruined is the wrong word. A woman shouldn't be judged by her virginity, or lack of it. I of all men know that."

"Thank you." Emily took a deep breath. "Then may I go home now?"

"Not quite yet." Christian turned to Ambrose. "I assume you interrupted them?"

"I did, but . . ."

"Thank you for that, at least," Christian said. "I'm glad that *one* member of my staff kept his wits about him."

Emily tensed as Ambrose stepped forward, his intention to confess quite obvious. She couldn't let him risk everything for her at this point, when she was no longer sure where she stood with him. What if Christian lost his temper and ordered Ambrose from the house? She might never see him again and she refused to be held responsible for him losing his home again.

"Mr. Delornay, it wasn't quite like that, I—"

Emily interrupted him. "You *did* intrude upon us and Mr. Lennox came down to the kitchen to wait for me to get dressed. There is nothing else to say about the matter." She glared at

Christian. "I'm still a virgin, Ambrose is still the perfect employee, and Mr. Lennox is, despite all appearances, a gentleman."

Jack studied her for a long moment. "And as a gentleman, I am quite happy to present myself to your father tomorrow and ask for your hand in marriage."

Emily couldn't help but gape at him. "You don't need to do that."

All at once she regretted interrupting Ambrose. If she'd let him confess his part in her evening, would Jack have dared to say such a thing? Or was Jack simply trying to provoke Ambrose into declaring his feelings?

In desperation, she finally looked at Ambrose, who seemed as dumbstruck as she was. He met her gaze and she saw it then, his anger and his ridiculous desire to be noble and set her free.

"Perhaps that would be for the best, Miss Ross."

The bitter sting of betrayal shook through her. She turned to Jack and took his hand.

"Thank you, Mr. Lennox. I'm sure my father would be *delighted* to see you."

Ambrose turned on his heel and left the kitchen, slamming the door behind him.

Christian let out a soft whistle. "I do believe you have upset my manager, Emily."

"If he is upset, he knows what he needs to do. Good night, Christian."

Emily tucked her hand into Jack's and headed for the outside door. A hackney carriage already awaited them and she allowed Jack to hand her into it. As soon as they pulled away, she shrieked at him.

"What on earth made you say that?"

He shrugged. "I thought it might persuade Ambrose to declare his feelings for you. Why did you keep interrupting him anyway?"

"Because I want him to ask my *father* for my hand in marriage, not my half brother! Christian never reacts quite as one wishes him to. He might have dismissed Ambrose on the spot, and I couldn't have that on my conscience." Emily buried her face in her hands. "Oh, my goodness, whatever have I done?"

Richard waited to see what Violet would say to him, his body tense, his mind braced for her denial. And what would he do then? Walk out and leave her? Abandon his newly renovated dreams of having her for his own? He was a fool, but there was nothing he could do about it.

She licked her lips and stared up at him. "Jack knows about Mr. Brown."

"That he is your lover?"

"No, that I am supposed to be in league with him, and that I have agreed to kill my own twin. Jack is quite happy to go along with my plans."

"He would be," muttered Richard.

"Don't be too hard on him. He expressed just as many doubts as you are probably going to do, but in the end, he trusted me to make things right."

Something inside Richard relaxed. "Why did you hatch such a complicated scheme?"

"Isn't it obvious? It was the only way I could think of to bring Mr. Brown to justice."

"At the risk of your own life?"

"When I agreed to the plan, I thought I had nothing to live for." She hesitated. "I thought you were lost to me."

He absorbed that truth with a glad heart. "And now you know differently."

"I know nothing, only that I had to lie to you again and that sickened me. But I had no choice. There are too many lives depending on my keeping up this masquerade."

"Have you met Mr. Brown?"

She bit her lip. "I don't think so, but as he hides behind a false name, I suppose I might have met him at some time."

"As might I." Richard studied her resolute face. "What is even more interesting is why my contact was told you were a traitor. Have you outlived your usefulness to Mr. Brown? Has he decided that you have no intention of killing Jack and turned on you himself?"

"I did wonder about that. He also might have been protecting me in his own convoluted way. I'm no longer sure," Violet confessed. She pushed at Richard's chest. "I expect you'll be ordering me to step out of this game."

He resisted her attempts to move him and felt his cock harden against her stomach. Grabbing her wrists, he drew her hands over her head and slowly entered her. The combination of her slick wetness and the tightness of her well-fucked cunt around his shaft made him groan.

"I wish I could order you to keep away from the man." He thrust deep, heard her catch her breath. "But I suspect the only place you'll allow me to order you around is here in bed." He thrust slowly back and forth. "And even then I'll have to be careful."

"You . . ." She shuddered as a climax shook through her, and he held still to enjoy it. "You won't stop me?"

"If you'll let me help you."

She stared into his eyes and he saw the tangle of her vulnerability, her need for him, and love, surely that was love binding everything together? He didn't dare ask her yet, could only offer his pitiful services to keep her safe and pray that they were enough.

"If you promise to be discreet."

He thrust once more and then spilled himself slowly and deeply inside her. With a groan, he collapsed over her, his larger body pinning her to the mattress. He released her wrists and felt her hands settle on his back. For a moment he just lay there and breathed in the scent of their lovemaking. He rolled over onto his back, bringing her with him.

"Richard?" she whispered.

"Hmm?"

"Do you promise?"

He smoothed her short hair away from her face. "Yes, I'll do whatever you want as long as you let me sleep for a moment. Making love to you is exhausting."

She tried to punch his chest, but he caught her hand in his and fell asleep.

"Richard?" She was talking to him again, and this time he forced his eyes to open, aware that time had passed as the clock struck ten times. "We can't stay here."

"Why not?"

"Because I feel too vulnerable." She shivered and he was instantly awake.

"Let me take you home."

She climbed off the bed and started to dress in her female garb again. It was a delight for him to see her in that, although he'd also come to appreciate the shape of her comely rear in trousers.

When she had replaced her mask, he headed to the locked door and opened it.

"We can go directly down the backstairs to the kitchen and leave from there. No one will see us."

"Thank you."

She glanced up at him as she passed, and he was struck again by the calm resolve in her gaze and her remarkable courage. He directed her to the end of the corridor and led them both into the servants' stairway. She followed him down the steps and toward the welcoming light of the kitchen.

The kitchen door was slightly ajar, and Richard paused to listen to the voices within, smiling when he recognized Christian talking to Ambrose. He beckoned for Violet to join him.

"Ambrose, I ask you again, what is going on?" Christian was standing by the fireplace, and Ambrose looked as if he was about to go out of the back door.

Richard cleared his throat and both men looked at him. "I apologize for interrupting, but we wished to leave quietly."

"By all means." Christian gestured toward the exit, his gaze still fixed on Ambrose.

"Thank you." Richard took Violet's hand and headed to the door. Just as he reached it, Ambrose stepped aside with a bow and Christian spoke again.

"Actually, before you leave, I should wish you and your charming companion happy." He bowed. "Miss Lennox, I believe?"

Violet's grip on his hand tightened. Warily, Richard looked back at Christian. "What of it?"

"I thought you might be interested to hear that you are soon to be related by marriage."

"What?"

Christian's smile was far too sweet. "Just before you came into the kitchen, Jack Lennox asked our dear sister Emily to marry him. I believe she said yes."

"*What?*" This time it was Violet who spoke. "How can that be?"

Christian shrugged and returned his gaze to his manager. "I'm not sure. Perhaps you should ask Ambrose."

Violet tugged on Richard's hand. "I'd rather ask Jack. He is incorrigible. I'm sure it was his idea of a joke."

"I'm not so sure about that," Christian answered. "He said he intended to call on Philip in the morning."

Violet looked up at Richard in mute appeal and he brought her hand to his lips. "I'll make sure Jack doesn't get anywhere near my father, I promise you."

Richard nodded at Christian. "Good night."

"Good night, Miss Lennox, Richard. Thank you for your custom."

Richard had nothing more to say and escorted Violet out into the night.

Ambrose continued to gather up the glasses and cups from the kitchen table, but it seemed that Christian had no intention of leaving. Eventually he had nothing left to do and turned to his employer.

"What do you want, sir?"

Christian sat down on the nearest chair. "To understand something, to understand you." He paused. "I know that there was more to the incident upstairs than you were allowed to let on. Did you kiss Emily, touch her?"

Resolutely, Ambrose faced his employer. "Yes, I did."

"Why?"

"Because she was threatening to find a man, any man, to relieve her of her virginity."

Christian winced. "That must have been difficult for you to deal with."

"It did present some challenges, sir, especially with Jack Lennox spurring her on."

"That man is a menace," Christian commented.

"Miss Ross claimed that she was tired of being excluded from the upper levels of the pleasure house, and that Jack had offered her the opportunity to experience them with him. When I asked her to return to the kitchen, she threatened to bed any willing man in the place. I felt honor bound to intervene."

"I'm not surprised. Emily has always been prepared to go after what she wants," Christian murmured. "I almost admire her for it."

"Indeed. Jack Lennox was quite happy to offer himself as a willing participant."

"And Emily was prepared to fuck him as a thank you?"

"So she said." Ambrose stared down at his tightly clasped hands. "I couldn't allow that. I just couldn't."

Christian picked up a bottle of wine and poured himself and Ambrose a glass. "Now that doesn't sound like Emily at all. She has always resented her exclusion from the pleasure house, but to act in such a fashion? Jack Lennox is obviously a bad influence on her."

"I'm not sure if she would've gone through with it."

"Well, thank God you stopped her." Christian took another gulp of the wine. "Was she angry with you?"

Ambrose sighed and took the seat opposite Christian. "At first she was, and then when I . . . I offered to take Jack's place, she didn't object at all."

Christian slowly lowered his glass and stared at Ambrose. "Ah, I begin to understand her game now. She has always had a *tendre* for you. I can just see her plotting with that devious sod Jack Lennox. She was probably hoping to compromise your position all along."

"Do you think so?" Ambrose considered Emily's behavior anew, hope rising in his chest. "Then you're not angry at me for touching her?"

Christian reached out and patted Ambrose's knee. "If she was determined to experience a woman's pleasure for the first time, I can think of no one who would have treated her better."

Ambrose stared at his employer. "But I'm a dark-skinned ex-slave and a thief who has nothing to offer her but the salary you pay me."

Christian held his gaze. "For God's sake, Ambrose, you are far more than that."

"But Miss Ross is your sister. You were furious with Jack Lennox when he spoke indiscreetly about her."

"You are my best friend." Christian hesitated in a most uncharacteristic manner. "Did you think I would be angry?"

"Yes, I did."

"Is that why you didn't say anything when Jack Lennox offered to marry her?"

"That was part of it, but I gained the distinct impression that Miss Ross didn't want to hear anything I had to say."

"She did rather cut you off, didn't she? I wonder why?"

Ambrose had been pondering that himself. She'd told him that she wanted him to be honest and admit that he cared about her, and then seemed terrified when he had tried to stand up for her against Christian. Had she changed her mind again?

"Mayhap she decided that Jack Lennox would be a more acceptable suitor, after all."

"Don't sound so bitter and don't give up hope." Christian patted his knee. "Women play the damndest games sometimes. My Elizabeth led me a merry dance before I could persuade her to confide in me."

"I remember." Ambrose sighed. "But it would be better for Miss Ross to marry a man like Jack Lennox, wouldn't it?"

"Not if she doesn't love him." Christian stood and looked down at Ambrose. "And I'll wager this pleasure house that the man she is in love with is not Jack Lennox, but you."

17

_____

Lord Philip Knowles put down his coffee cup and glanced down the table at his wife.

"Did you know we were expecting company for breakfast, my dear?"

"No, Philip, I did not." Helene smiled at Richard. "But it is of no matter. Please sit down, Richard, and I will ring for some more tea and buttered toast."

"Thank you." Richard took the seat opposite Helene. "Is Emily up yet?"

"I'm not quite sure," Helene said. "Do you want me to find out? Were you supposed to be accompanying her somewhere?"

"You're not going to attempt to see that Mr. Smith again, are you?" Philip asked, the good humor fading. "I asked you to leave that matter to me."

Richard faced his father. "And I told you that was impossible."

"Do you still believe I'm hoping to clear my name?"

"I'm not sure, Father. Why else would you be so keen to get your hands on that journal?"

Helene delicately cleared her throat. "Philip, why don't you go and find out whether Emily is awake yet while I talk to Richard?"

Philip's troubled gaze settled on Helene; then he sighed. "All right, my dear, if I must. I'll go and see what has become of Emily."

Richard watched him walk out of the sunlit breakfast parlor with a frown. In truth, he'd half forgotten about Thomas Smith, but he certainly didn't intend to leave his father to his own devices.

Helene put down her cup and turned toward him. "Richard, did your father ever tell you about his encounter with Thomas Smith?"

"What encounter?"

Helene glanced briefly at the closed door and then moved to sit beside Richard. "For reasons that will soon become clear, Philip was reluctant to tell you about this matter." She took a deep breath. "He would hate for you and Emily to read your mother's version of that horrible event."

Richard took her hand. "What happened?"

"I feel awful telling you this, but as I told Philip, I think you should know. It will certainly explain why your father is so keen to get his hands on that journal." She sighed. "One night, your father discovered Thomas Smith in your mother's bed, and there was a terrible fight. Smith was an amateur boxer, and despite your father's best efforts, Smith soon overcame him and tied him up."

"So Father doesn't want us to know that he was bested in a fight by my mother's lover."

Helene hesitated. "It wasn't quite that simple. Smith made Philip watch him bed your mother and then—he sodomized him."

Richard forced himself to keep breathing and then looked deeply into Helene's eyes. "Philip told you that?"

"Yes."

"And you believed him?"

"Of course. We have no secrets between us." She held his gaze. "I doubt any father would wish his children, especially his daughter, to know that about him, wouldn't you?"

There was a ring of sincerity in Helene's words that struck home with Richard. He could well imagine his proud and rather reticent father hating being in the power of another man. Of course, the whole scene painted his mother and her lover in an even uglier light. But, apparently, he was becoming used to the shock of realizing his mother hadn't been quite the wronged saint she had made herself out to be.

He exhaled slowly. "What shall I tell Emily?"

Helene squeezed his hand hard. "Why not tell her that you have left everything in your father's capable hands?"

"I'll have to think on it."

"Thank you. That is all I ask." Helene released his hand and moved back to her original place at the table. "Do you still want breakfast? I'm sure it will be here in just a moment."

As if on cue, the butler entered through the door bearing a heavy silver tray, and the scent of bacon, eggs, and toast assailed Richard's nostrils. Despite the shock of Helene's revelation, his appetite remained undaunted, and he made his selection from the feast on the sideboard.

Philip returned with the newspapers and took his seat at the table. He avoided Richard's gaze and disappeared behind his newspaper.

"Emily is already awake and will be down to breakfast very shortly."

Richard nodded. "Thank you, Father."

He crunched his way through another piece of toast and some excellent bacon. Trying to picture Philip at the mercy of another man proved quite difficult, but he had no reason to believe Helene was lying.

"Do you still intend to take Emily out and visit Mr. Smith?" Philip asked.

"No, Father, not today. I didn't come here about that."

Philip finally lowered his paper and glanced at Helene, who smiled sweetly back at him. "Are you suggesting there might be more trouble afoot?"

"Oh, I believe there will be trouble aplenty, sir." Richard looked up expectantly as Emily sailed into the room, her expression firm, her gaze fixed on him. "Good morning, my dear sister."

She stopped to glare at him. "What are you doing here?"

"I'm sure you know." He sipped his tea. "Do you really think he'll go through with it?"

Emily went red and turned her back on him to collect her food.

"Whatever is going on?" Philip asked.

"You'll find out fairly soon, sir," Richard said. If it hadn't have been for Emily's obvious discomfort, he might almost have enjoyed the moment. "This news is for Emily to share."

Emily sat opposite Richard and considered him with obvious disdain. "And who asked for your opinion?"

"In truth, Christian did last night."

"You were at the pleasure house?"

"I was."

"I didn't see you."

"I'm sure you made certain of that." Richard considered her. "Ambrose seemed rather shaken when I saw him. Did you argue?"

"Ambrose . . ." Emily stopped speaking and stared down at the polished surface of the table. "Ambrose has a perfect right to be angry with me."

"I'd say so," Richard murmured.

Emily swallowed hard. "You don't understand, Richard. I thought to protect him from Christian, I . . ."

"Emily," Philip said clearly from the head of the table. "Would you care to explain exactly what is going on?"

Emily rose to her feet, and her brother and father routinely followed her. She stood poised for flight, her gaze flitting between Richard and the door.

"Perhaps you might prefer to speak to me in private?" Philip asked. "If trouble is approaching, it is always better to be prepared."

Emily nodded and headed for the door.

"Do you want Richard or Helene to join us?" Philip inquired as he opened the door for her into his study.

"No, thank you."

She assumed that in her absence, Richard might tell Helene what had happened between her and Jack Lennox. Helene was always very careful not to interfere in Emily's life, but for once, Emily almost wished she would. Whatever the outcome, her father was going to be disappointed in her, that was certain.

She waited until Philip sat behind his desk, clasped his hands together, and regarded her steadily.

"How can I help you, my dear?"

She looked into his familiar hazel eyes and realized anew that she was the only one in her family with dark brown eyes. But did that even matter anymore? A strong desire to weep almost overcame her. Thomas Smith had brown eyes as well. . . .

"A man might come and see you this morning about me."

"Not the obnoxious Mr. Smith, I hope?"

"No, a gentleman, or at least I *think* he is a gentleman. He is trying to prove his rights to certain property and a title here in England."

"And what does this particular gentleman want with me?"

Emily took a deep breath. "To offer for my hand in marriage."

"And how long have you known this man?"

"For a few weeks." She shrugged. "You are already acquainted with him."

"Really." Philip sat back, his gaze watchful. "What is his name?"

"Mr. Jack Lennox."

"One of the twins who came here to ask Helene to write back to their grandmother?"

"Yes."

"And he wants to marry you."

"Apparently."

"It seems rather sudden."

"Why? I understand that you fell in love with Helene the moment you saw her."

Her father's familiar wry smile appeared. "But it took me almost nineteen years to marry her."

"Only because my mother was alive and determined to use you to conceal her affair with her gardener."

"That is rather harsh, Emily."

"But don't you wish she had refused to marry you?"

Philip sighed. "It is true that your mother should not have married me, but you have to understand that she was wholly in my parents' care. She had no one who could help her get out of her arranged marriage." His gaze flicked to the family portrait on the wall. "She wasn't as strong willed as you are."

Emily raised her chin. "Are you defending her now?"

"I'm just trying to say that we all make choices that can lead to unhappiness."

"Your decision to marry her certainly did." He winced and she tried to view him as a stranger and not as the father who had brought her up and always loved her. "I assume you believe marrying Jack Lennox would be another poor choice?"

"You hardly know the man, Emily, and from what I have heard, he is not exactly a catch."

"I thought we'd long given up on the notion that I might *catch* the right man. I *thought* you were quite desperate for me to marry anyone!"

She glared at him, willing him to fight her on this, to *order* her not to marry Jack Lennox, to threaten to disinherit her if she even considered disobeying him. Then perhaps, having broken his heart, she could run back to Ambrose and stay with him forever. . . .

"Emily, my dear . . ." Philip hesitated. "I'm not quite sure why we are fighting over this, or if we are actually fighting about something else. What exactly do you want from me?"

She stared at him. "You're supposed to be my *father.* Don't you know what I want?"

All the color bleached from his face and he briefly closed his eyes, and she knew then, knew that what she had feared from her mother's letters was completely true. She stood up and backed away from him.

"Emily." His voice was remarkably steady. "Have you seen Mr. Smith again? Is this what this is all about? I've been meaning to talk to you about—"

She jumped as the door to the study opened behind her and the butler appeared.

"Excuse me, Miss Ross, my lord, but I have a Mr. Jack Lennox here who would like to speak to you."

Emily stood to one side and saw Jack waiting behind the butler. He winked at her as he walked into the room and bowed to Philip.

"My lord, perhaps Emily has already told you the purpose of my visit?"

Philip glanced distractedly at Emily. "This isn't the best time, Mr. Lennox, perhaps . . ."

Emily grabbed hold of Jack's hand and held it tight. "What my father is trying to say, Jack, is that he is *delighted* that you wish to marry me, and he wishes to bestow his blessing on the match."

"My dear," Philip said.

Emily ignored him as Jack smiled deeply into her eyes.

"I am ecstatic, Miss Ross, there is no happier man in the kingdom than I am today." He brought her hand to his lips and kissed each of her fingers. "Thank you."

Leaving Jack to face Philip, Emily retreated into the hallway and sped up the stairs. She gasped when Richard stepped out of his old room and touched her shoulder.

"Are you mad? Did you let Jack speak to Philip?" His expression was almost comical.

"Why shouldn't I? Jack *wants* to marry me." She shied away from Richard's touch. "Was there something else you wanted? I was hoping to go and see Mr. Smith this afternoon. Would you care to accompany me?"

He regarded her steadily. "On reflection, I think we should leave Mr. Smith to Philip."

Emily struggled to breathe. "What did Philip tell you?"

"He told me nothing. He was far too embarrassed, but I can understand why he wants the journal. Helene told me." He continued to study her. "And, no, I can't tell you what she said. There is no reason why you need to know any of it."

"No reason . . ." Emily shook her head and pushed her way past him. "How wonderfully convenient for everyone. Why on earth would poor little Emily need to know *anything*?"

She ran for her room, ignoring Richard's pleas for her to stop and talk to him. She paused only long enough to lock the door and then flung herself on her bed and cried as if her heart might break.

Eventually she sat up and considered what to do next. There was only one way to prove if she was right, and that was to get the journal from Thomas Smith. She could no longer depend on Richard to help her, and Jack, now being her fiancé, might balk at upsetting her family too. A fierce longing for Ambrose gripped her and she fought another sob. She *needed* him, and this time she was going to insist that he help her, whatever his feelings were.

18

Ambrose opened his eyes and then quickly closed them again as he realized he lay sprawled on the kitchen floor, an empty brandy bottle clutched to his chest. He had no idea what time it was, but the absence of Madame Durand and the kitchen maids fretting over him meant it wasn't yet dawn.

With a groan, he sat up and managed to crawl his way to the table so that he could stand. Pain lanced through his skull, and he clapped one hand to his head. After Christian had left the previous evening, he'd been too agitated to sleep and had ended up drinking steadily until he no longer remembered anything at all.

He put the empty bottle on the table and took a deep breath. Unfortunately, the events were now coming back to haunt him. The joy of finally touching Emily and bringing her pleasure, the agony of her turning away from him and encouraging Jack Lennox to marry her.

He considered making some coffee but decided it would be better to drink some ale to clear his head. The thought of food made him nauseous, so he stoked up the fire and settled down at the table with his tankard of ale.

Emily had insisted that she wanted him to talk to her father. Was he brave enough to risk that? Lord Philip Knowles was a peer of the realm, and socially so far above Ambrose that he might as well have been in heaven. But Philip was also married to Madame Helene. . . .

Ambrose considered this as he sipped at his ale. His salary at the pleasure house was quite substantial, and he had some savings. But he owned no property or land, and had no other income to supplant his wages. And what would he do if he married Emily? It was unlikely that the Ross family would want her to live at the pleasure house. At the very least they'd expect her to have a house of her own.

Did he even want to keep working at the pleasure house? He'd enjoyed his time there, but he wasn't wedded to the place as Christian was. He'd certainly enjoyed the sexual games, but would he miss them if he gained his heart's desire and married Emily?

"Good morning, Ambrose." He looked up to see Christian's wife, Elizabeth, smiling down at him. She wore a thick paisley shawl over her nightgown, and her hair was still braided tightly to her head. "I came down to get some warm milk to help me sleep for a while longer. You look a little fatigued, my friend. Are you all right?"

Ambrose gestured at the empty brandy bottle. "I drank too much and fell asleep on the floor."

"That's not like you." Elizabeth sat opposite him. "Are you worried about Emily?"

He wasn't surprised at her direct approach. He knew Christian told her everything.

"Yes, Jack Lennox is going to ask for her hand in marriage today, and I'm fairly certain she'll take him."

"But she is in love with you."

"So she said, but when it came down to it, she refused to let me stand up for her."

"Why do you think that was?"

He shrugged. "Because she finally realized I was too much of a coward to ever satisfy her?"

"That's ridiculous."

"Of her or me?"

"Of you." Elizabeth sighed. "Really, Ambrose, don't you understand that women don't always say what they mean?"

"I'm quite aware of that," he said stiffly. "Emily *said* that she loved me, and then turned around and accepted Jack Lennox's offer to wait on her father in the morning."

"Probably because she wanted you to defy everyone and claim her for your own."

Ambrose realized he was glaring at his employer's wife. "She was the one who stopped me talking!"

"She was probably afraid for you, then."

Silence fell and Elizabeth continued to study him as though he was a particularly slow pupil. At first, Ambrose couldn't think of anything to say to her. What would Emily have tried to protect him from—his best friend, Christian?

"You speak in riddles." He stood up and bowed. "And I have to go and change."

Elizabeth regarded him calmly. "Think about what I said. Emily is not a fool. Perhaps she understands you better than you think."

By the time Ambrose had bathed, changed into clean clothes, and shaved, it was well past seven o'clock and time for him to start work. He came back down to the kitchen, said a cheerful good morning to Madame Durand, and set about the task of reading the morning newspapers. It was not entirely for plea-sure. He always paid attention both to the latest scandals that might affect the guests and to the fashionable crazes to inspire new ideas for the staff.

He almost checked to see if any notice of an engagement between Emily and Jack Lennox had been announced, but even he realized it would be too soon. While he dressed, he'd decided that despite Elizabeth's hints, there was nothing he could do to stop Jack approaching Emily's father. If she truly wanted to marry Jack, he wasn't going to stop her. For all his faults, Jack was far more socially acceptable as a husband than Ambrose would ever be.

"Here's the morning post, Mr. Ambrose, sir." Seamus Kelly placed a pile of mail on the table beside Ambrose.

"Thank you, Seamus," Ambrose said.

He put down his paper and turned his attention to the mail. Most of it was for Christian, and some that was addressed to Madame Helene would need to be opened and read to see whether it was pleasure house business or not.

His gaze settled on a letter addressed to him in an unfamiliar handwriting. He used his penknife to break the seal and unfold the single sheet.

> *Dear Ambrose,*
> *My mother is rather ill and would like to meet you before she retires to Bath to take the waters. Would it be possible for you to take tea with us today at four?*
> *Yours,*
> *Lady Mary Kendrick*

Ambrose read the letter through three times, noting the Kendrick family address remained the same. Perhaps meeting with Lady Kendrick would keep his mind off the other, more pressing matters currently circling frantically through his mind. Not that he cared if Emily agreed to marry Jack at all. . . .

He screwed the note up and threw it in the fire. Jethro, at least, would be delighted if Ambrose made the effort to see Lady Kendrick. Whether Ambrose would be able to follow his advice and forgive the woman was another matter.

Ambrose returned to sorting the mail but realized his usual peace was disturbed. He'd hoped that by returning to the safety of his allotted tasks at the pleasure house, he'd regain his sense of calm and security, but it seemed as if he was no longer safe anywhere anymore.

He wondered how Emily was faring, and whether Lord Philip Knowles had met with Jack yet. Perhaps Christian had been wrong, and Jack was playing a deeper game than anyone could possibly have imagined. If he married Emily, his claims to his English title would have to be taken seriously, and with Emily's money at his disposal, he would have the power to pursue those claims to the end.

"Ambrose?"

He looked up to see Christian waving at him from the door.

"Yes, Mr. Delornay?"

"Will you come into my office for a moment? I wish to review the staffing numbers for the month."

"Certainly, sir." Ambrose got to his feet and folded up the newspaper. An hour in Christian's bracing presence would concentrate his mind wonderfully and allow no further useless speculation about Emily, Jack Lennox, or his future.

Violet waited until Jack had greeted Richard and taken a seat opposite her by the fire. Before he could speak again, she fixed him with her hardest stare.

"Why on earth did you offer to marry Emily Ross?"

Jack glanced at Richard, who nodded at him to go on.

"I thought she needed my help." Jack sighed. "I *thought* Ambrose would leap to defend her and everything would be out in the open."

"What do you mean?" Violet asked.

Richard came to sit on the arm of her chair and took her hand in his. "Emily insists that she is in love with Ambrose."

"The African manager at the pleasure house?"

"Indeed. They have known each other for quite a few years. I suspect the attraction is mutual."

"Then why has Jack gotten involved?"

"Because Miss Ross asked me to help her make Ambrose jealous," Jack said.

"Oh, Jack," Violet scolded her twin. "When will you learn to stop meddling?"

He shrugged. "Never, I expect."

"Do you *want* to marry Miss Ross?"

Jack sat back and contemplated her and Richard. "She is a remarkable woman. If she wasn't already in love with another man, I might consider it."

"Not if I have anything to do with it," Richard growled. "I assumed my father would send you about your business. How the devil did you persuade him to agree to the match?"

"I didn't. Miss Ross simply declared that her father was delighted with the idea and promptly left. Lord Knowles asked me if I could come and see him at a more convenient time, and I agreed."

"So there is nothing official yet." Violet nodded. "At least we are spared that."

Beside her, Richard stirred. "I'm worried about Emily. She is hiding something from me."

"I agree that she seems quite unlike herself," Jack said. "Her behavior at the pleasure house was quite unexpected. She—"

"Unlike you, Jack, I don't wish to hear the details of what my sibling got up to at the pleasure house," Richard interrupted Violet's twin quite mercilessly. "Which brings me to the other reason we asked you to meet us here this afternoon."

Violet nodded. "I've told Richard about Mr. Brown and how I am supposed to assassinate you."

Jack exhaled. "Well, I'm glad to hear that he knows." He considered Richard. "How on earth did you manage that?"

Violet felt herself blush as she remembered Richard's most unorthodox methods of obtaining information. "Richard believes Mr. Brown must have realized by now that I have no intention of killing you and is now after me himself."

"Have we any idea who he is yet?"

"Apparently not," Richard said. "Although the continued disappearance of Lord Keyes makes me wonder if he is Mr. Brown himself."

"Or has been done away with by Mr. Brown," Violet said.

"I suppose that is possible." Jack crossed his booted feet. "If Keyes is of no further help, how are we going to protect Violet? I had hoped that once Keyes had heard all her evidence, he would pass it on to the relevant people, and Violet and I would be free."

Richard grimaced. "That gives me even more reason to suspect that Lord Keyes was disposed of." He brought Violet's hand to his lips. "Don't worry, my love. I'll keep you safe."

Jack eyed Violet and then smiled. "You really have brought him around, haven't you? Well done."

Violet tensed. "Don't make it sound as if I did it for material gain."

To her surprise, Richard chuckled and kissed her hand again. "It is all right, Violet. I know my own worth. This time I'm going to continue to trust you."

"Right up until the moment when she plunges her dagger into your heart and twists it until you are dead," Jack added, then held up his hands. "I was only joking, twin."

"Then perhaps you might stop?" Violet hesitated. "I thought it might be best to draw Mr. Brown out into the open."

"Did you?" That was Richard, and he didn't sound very pleased with her at all.

"I know you won't approve." Violet looked from Jack's skeptical expression to Richard's furious one. "I just want to catch this man, and the only way I can think of is to offer myself up as bait."

"And you *think* Jack and I will allow that?"

Violet rose from her seat and walked away from the two men, presenting them with her back. "It is not a question of what you will allow. I am quite capable of making my own decisions."

"Violet, you asked for my help! Why ask if you have no intention of accepting it?"

She spun around. "Richard . . ."

"I think there might be a better solution," Jack said. Violet and Richard turned to look at him.

"What?"

Jack met her gaze, his blue eyes sparkling. "You assassinate me. I wager that will bring Mr. Brown out of hiding *and* get me out of my engagement."

Just before four, Ambrose dressed in his best coat and waistcoat, and decided to walk to the Kendrick mansion, which wasn't far from the pleasure house. His early-morning headache hadn't quite gone away, so the fresh air would be most beneficial. And he needed to think because, despite all his best efforts, he had been unable to distance himself from the idea of Jack Lennox marrying Emily. He'd tried to convince himself that he was better off worshipping her from afar, but it wasn't true. He wanted her in his bed, in his life, and with him forever.

He nodded to Christian, let himself out of the kitchen door, and climbed the steps up to the street level. At the corner of the square, he allowed himself to look back at the imposing row of buildings that accommodated the pleasure house. Could he leave it behind? If he accepted Jethro's offer of a job at the new school, would Emily be happy as the wife of a schoolmaster?

Ambrose started walking again. After he had met Lady Kendrick and made it clear that he didn't intend to have any contact with her or her family again, he would reconsider his options. Pleased that he had at least made one decision, he approached the steps leading up to the Kendrick front door with far more confidence.

The door was opened by a man in livery who stared at Ambrose for a long moment and then smiled.

"Ambrose, is it really you? I thought you had disappeared for good!"

"Mr. Trayton, it's a pleasure." Ambrose barely recognized the man who had once been the first footman. "I see you have risen to great heights."

Mr. Trayton smoothed the lapel of his coat. "Indeed, I have. When Lady Mary said to expect you for tea, the whole staff was aflutter."

"If it is permissible, perhaps I might venture below stairs afterward and reacquaint myself with everyone."

"That would be wonderful. I'm sure her ladyship won't mind." Trayton took Ambrose's hat and gloves. "Now let me take you up to her."

Ambrose was surprised to see that very little had changed in the house since his ignominious dismissal all those years ago. He touched the polished oak banister and remembered sliding down it accompanied by the Kendrick children, the potted plant they had destroyed in the hall below . . .

There was a gentle cough behind him. "We need to keep going up the stairs. Lady Kendrick is in her dressing room. Unfortunately, she doesn't have the strength to come down very often."

Ambrose realized he had inevitably headed for the drawing room and returned to the landing where Mr. Trayton was still standing.

"I apologize." Ambrose smiled. "Force of habit."

"I understand. It is hard for me to remember not to take her ladyship's tea into the drawing room as well." Mr. Trayton sighed. "She is most unwell, the poor lady. I hope your visit will cheer her up."

Ambrose didn't comment on that. He climbed the second flight of stairs behind Trayton and concentrated on looking calm despite the fierce beating of his heart.

Trayton knocked on a familiar door and then opened it, stepping aside for Ambrose to go past him. He slowly inhaled. Nothing had changed since his last visit; even Lady Kendrick's perfume remained the same.

"Mr. Ambrose, my lady. I'll bring up some tea." Ambrose's gaze was drawn to the chaise lounge, where Lady Kendrick lay on her side. She was wrapped in several shawls and a thick fur cover. Even through all her wrappings, Ambrose could see that she was as frail as a budding willow tree and just as pale. She raised her hand and just as he had when he was her page, he went down on one knee to kiss it.

"Ambrose, is it really you?"

Her voice was as insubstantial as the rest of her. When Ambrose managed to raise his head and look into her ravaged face, he saw the signs of the wasting disease that was slowly draining her of life, the bright red cheeks and feverish eyes, the difficulty she had breathing. . . .

"Good afternoon, Lady Kendrick."

That was all he could manage. She kept hold of his hand, her fingers so cold and brittle he feared they might snap.

"I was so glad when Mary told me she had seen you again."

He forced a smile. "Our encounter was quite unexpected."

"For a long time I believed you were dead." Her breathing hitched. "My husband told me he had beaten you so severely that you would never survive."

Did he question her now? Her life was ending, and it would be his only opportunity to find out the truth.

She released his hand and motioned for him to sit opposite her, next to Lady Mary. Although his childhood friend smiled at him, the warning in her gaze was clear, and her tension so obvious that he almost felt sorry for her.

"I was very lucky to survive, my lady."

"Mama," Lady Mary said. "You told me that Ambrose had been sent to our country estate, and that he had then run off."

Lady Kendrick raised her handkerchief to her lips and dabbed at them. "At first I thought that was the truth. It wasn't until we arrived at Kendrick Hall that your father told me exactly what he and his ruffians had done." She looked at Ambrose. "He knew that if he'd told me in London, I would have defied him and gone looking for you."

Ambrose held her gaze and saw only her pain and her desire to be truthful. She hadn't known. Something inside him, something hard at his core, finally broke.

"Lord Kendrick told me that you had grown tired of me, my lady, and that the order to dispose of me came from you."

Lady Mary gasped. "How could he have been so horrible? He knew how much we all cared for you, particularly you, Mama."

"Which is why he wanted Ambrose gone." Lady Kendrick sighed. "Your father was a very possessive man, Mary, and I betrayed him by falling into bed with a servant, a *boy* he insisted was more like a son to us. I think that is what appalled him most, that I'd taken an innocent to my bed, a child who was almost part of our family."

Ambrose almost couldn't speak as the terrible memories overwhelmed him. "I didn't object, my lady, so the fault is also mine."

"You were too young to know any better. Despite his deplorable methods, Lord Kendrick was right about one thing. I betrayed both of you." She started to cough, and Lady Mary rose and offered her some water.

Ambrose sat quietly until the paroxysm of coughing eased and Lady Kendrick lay back on her pillows again. She seemed to have shrunk even farther into her cocoon of blankets, as if she was fading away in front of him. Eventually she fixed her gaze on him again.

"I'm not going to recover from this illness, Ambrose."

"That might not be true, my lady. With time and rest and—"

She waved away his inadequate attempt to console her. "No, I'm dying, which is why I'm so glad fate led you across my path again." She glanced up at Mary. "Go and fetch the latest letter from my solicitor. It is by my bed."

While Mary was searching for the letter, there was a tap on the door, and Mr. Trayton brought in some tea. In Mary's absence, Ambrose poured the tea and placed a cup at Lady Kendrick's elbow.

"Thank you, Ambrose," she whispered.

"You are welcome, my lady." He took his seat again, but his fingers were shaking so hard that he struggled to hold the dainty porcelain cup.

Lady Mary returned with the letter and held it out to her mother. "Do you want me to read it to Ambrose?"

"Yes, please, my dear."

> "In reply to your latest request, my dear Lady Kendrick, yes, we can include the bequest as written as a codicil to your will, and we will make every effort to inform the beneficiary, Ambrose, of his good fortune when the sad time arises.
>
> Yours faithfully,
> Arthur Pentland, Esquire"

* * *

Lady Mary looked inquiringly at her mother. "Do you want me to go on, or do you want to tell him the rest yourself?"

"I'll tell him," Lady Kendrick said, and took a quivering breath. "I know that you will find it hard to forgive me, Ambrose, but I wanted you to have something from me after my death."

"But I don't need anything, my lady. I am gainfully employed and quite happy in my life."

"Ambrose, Mary told me where she found you—in a *brothel*—and that is my fault."

"No, my lady, it wasn't like that at all. I chose . . ."

She started speaking over him and he went quiet, afraid that her desire to make him feel better would be the death of her.

"I want you to have the long gold chain with the jewels you used to wear when you were my page boy."

"But, my lady, that piece is part of the Kendrick family heritage. I believe you told me that it came down the family from the time of King Henry VIII."

"It did. But I have spoken to all my children, and they all want you to have it."

Ambrose could only stare at her and then at Lady Mary, who nodded in quiet agreement.

"There is also the matter of your future employment. My son would like to speak to you about that. I believe he wishes to offer you a job on one of our estates."

"I—" Ambrose shook his head. "That is very kind of him, my lady, but—"

Lady Kendrick held up her hand. "I don't want your gratitude; I don't deserve it. I also realize that all the money in England won't make things right for you." She lay back on her pillows. "All money can give you is more choices, choices I took away from you when you were hardly grown." She started to cough again, and this time it seemed as if she would never be able to stop.

Ambrose got to his feet, but Lady Mary was quicker. She rushed to her mother's aid and glanced at Ambrose over her shoulder.

"Ring the bell, will you? Mother needs to go to bed now. She has exhausted her strength."

"It's all right. I can carry her." Ambrose picked up Lady Kendrick and held her close to his chest. She was as insubstantial as one of Elizabeth's children. Her cheek came to rest on his shoulder and she sighed.

"Dearest Ambrose."

He laid her gently on her bed and helped Mary tuck her in. She watched him carefully as if his face was precious, as if she was trying to imprint him on her memory.

He took her hand and kissed her fingertips. "Good-bye, my lady."

"Good-bye, Ambrose," she whispered. "Pray for me."

He nodded and walked out of the all-too-familiar bedchamber without another word. Lady Mary didn't try and detain him, so he just kept going, forgetting his agreement to visit below stairs and finding his way back to the house of pleasure by instinct rather than design.

For once, there was no one in the kitchen, so he was able to escape upstairs to his bedchamber and lock the door behind him. With a groan, he sat down on the edge of his bed and held his head in his hands. He waited for the tears that clogged his throat, his *heart,* to fall, but nothing happened, so he continued to sit and not think. It seemed the only way of keeping himself whole.

19

Emily stole into the kitchen of the pleasure house and looked for Ambrose's familiar face, but he wasn't sitting at his usual place at the table. In the servants' dining room, she could hear Christian giving instructions to the staff for the early evening shift, but there was no hint of Ambrose's gentler tone.

"He's upstairs in his room."

Emily jumped at the sound of Elizabeth's quiet voice and turned to the kitchen door. Christian's wife was already dressed for the evening in a fine gown of blue silk that made her look quite ethereal. She came toward Emily and held out a key.

"You'll need this. I think he locked himself in."

"Why are you helping me?"

Elizabeth smiled. "Because they all treat you like a little girl who needs protecting, and I don't think you are one. If you want Ambrose, you are going to have to be brave and claim him as your own."

"Like you did with Christian?"

Elizabeth smiled. "I was far too scared to do that. But Ambrose is nothing like Christian. He needs to be loved, and you are just the right person to give him that."

"I do love him."

"I know, and he obviously loves you too."

"But my family . . ."

Elizabeth touched her cheek. "They will come around. After all, they accepted me, didn't they?" Her expression changed. "Now go and make that man happy, and worry about the Delornay-Ross clan afterward."

Emily took the key and headed for the stairs. She'd never been in Ambrose's bedchamber before, but she knew it was situated in the private part of the house near where Richard had his room. It was already getting dark and the corridors were gloomy. She wished she had brought a candle with her.

There was no light shining from under Ambrose's door, but she knocked anyway. There was no response, so she knocked again. She glanced down at the key in her hand and carefully fitted it to the lock. Her heart was thumping so loudly that she thought he'd probably hear it through the panels.

The key turned without a sound, and with a quick prayer, Emily pressed down on the latch and entered the room. It was so dark that she almost didn't see the figure sitting on the side of the bed. She leaned against the door and studied his slumped position.

"Ambrose?"

"Go away, Miss Ross."

She was almost tempted, but something stopped her. She walked over to the fireplace and struck a spark to light the kindling in the grate. When that caught, she found a candle by the bed and lit that too.

Ambrose remained on the bed, his gaze on the floor, his hands clasped together between his knees. He'd discarded his coat and was dressed only in his shirt and buckskin breeches. She went across to him and sank down on the floor at his feet.

"What's wrong?"

She still couldn't see his face properly, but she didn't need to see him to sense his anguish.

"Nothing that concerns you, Miss Ross."

He sounded most unlike himself, but she didn't mind. She had no idea who she was anymore either.

"What happened?"

He reached down and grabbed her by the elbows, bringing her up on her knees until her face was level with his.

"Go away, Miss Ross. I don't need you. I don't need anyone."

She met his gaze. "I'm not going anywhere until you tell me what is troubling you."

"Why is it important to you? Shouldn't you be out celebrating your engagement to Jack Lennox?"

She swallowed hard. "I'd much rather be here with you."

"You have no idea who I am, or what I've done." His grip tightened. "I'm not worthy to kiss your feet."

"You're the man I love!"

For a second, he held her immobilized, his ragged breath matching hers, and then gave her a gentle shake. "Don't be such a fool. Have you any idea of my life before Mr. Delornay found me?"

"I know that you were on the streets through no fault of your own, that the Kendrick family brutally abandoned you, that—"

"Lord Kendrick had me beaten because I was fucking his wife. Most men would say his actions were completely justified."

"Do you think so?"

He held her gaze. "Yes."

"Stop lying to me! *Tell* me."

He let go of her and stood up, presenting her with his back.

"I met Lady Kendrick today for the first time in almost twenty years. She tried to tell me she was sorry for what had happened, that the responsibility was hers and hers alone, but I fucked her, didn't I? I went along with her desires."

Emily shook her head. "But she was right. She was an adult and you were, how old were you when she seduced you?"

"Old enough to fuck, obviously."

"Ambrose, you are not quite thirty now. If this happened almost twenty years ago, you could barely have been ten, twelve? Good Lord, you were a *child,* and she was right, she should not have touched you! You thought of the Kendricks as your *family.*"

He moved sharply away from her and slammed his fist into the wall. "I tried to forgive her like my friend Jethro told me to, but I couldn't. As soon as I saw her I realized I was still so very angry with her."

"Did she expect you to forgive her?"

He turned slowly back to face her. "No, she didn't even ask." He grimaced. "She decided to try and buy her forgiveness instead."

"What do you mean?"

"She has left me something in her will. Did I mention that she is dying?" Emily shook her head. "Aye, and I still couldn't bring myself to say the words she wanted to hear."

"Why should you?" Emily fought to keep her voice level. "She didn't ask you to forgive her; she must know that what she did damaged you."

He leaned against the wall and regarded her. "I went willingly to her bed."

"Did you?"

"I wanted to please her."

"But not like that."

He looked away from her. "No." He sighed. "Not like that. It changed everything."

Emily got to her feet and walked across to him. With great care, she wrapped her arms around his neck and rose on her tiptoes to kiss his mouth.

"I still love you."

"You don't know me."

She kissed him again. "Then *let* me know you."

He smiled without humor. "After I fucked Lady Kendrick, Lord Kendrick and his henchmen beat me half to death. I was lucky enough to be found by a Methodist couple who work in the East End slums and help starving children. They saved my life, and what did I do to repay them? When I was well again, I rejected their God and ran away to fend for myself on the streets again. That's where your brother found me, trying to pick his pocket.

"Lady Kendrick thought I'd ended up working in a sordid brothel because of what she'd done to me. I didn't have the heart to tell her that the pleasure house is an exclusive club, and that I enjoyed my work immensely."

"It's all right, Ambrose." Emily kissed him again, trying to erase the pain and shame in his voice, to make him see that nothing mattered but how they felt about each other now. "I understand."

He wrenched his mouth away from hers. "Then leave me be."

"I can't." She cupped his chin. "I don't care about what you were, or what you did. I *know* you. Perhaps that is why you fear me."

"What do you mean?"

"Do you think that if we are lovers, it will destroy our friendship? Make it something tawdry and cheap? Something to be ashamed of?" She held her breath as he inhaled sharply. "Or is it that if things go wrong, you cannot bear to be cast out of another family you have grown to love?"

The silence between them seemed to go on forever.

"That isn't true."

"Are you sure about that?"

He pulled out of her embrace and took a stumbling step back. "Absolutely, Miss Ross. In truth, you are using me to escape your reality."

"And what reality is that?"

"You're afraid to love a man of your own class, so you hide behind your supposed feelings for me."

"That is ridiculous and totally unfair!"

"Is it? You're terrified that you'll turn out like your mother."

She started to tremble. "And what's wrong with being like her? She loved one man for her entire life. Just because he wasn't the right social class wasn't her fault."

"So is that why you've chosen to love me?"

Tears slid slowly down her cheeks and she raised her hand and slapped him hard on the cheek. His head snapped back, and she turned and marched toward the door.

His hand closed over hers on the door latch.

"Don't cry, do not *ever* cry for me."

He turned her around and began to rain kisses over her mouth and cheeks. She didn't stop him and started to kiss him back until their mouths clung together, until his hands roamed freely over her body. She moaned into his mouth and he kissed her even harder, fusing their bodies together from head to toe.

Her knees gave way and she slid to the floor, the wall the only solid thing at her back. Ambrose followed her down, his hips against hers, and she felt his cock, hard and hot against her covered mound. She wrapped herself around him, desperately seeking his skin, pulling at his shirt to release it from his breeches.

"Wait . . ." Ambrose murmured.

But she was beyond waiting, and continued to tug at his shirt, her fingers searching out the buttons of his breeches and unfastening them. With a sigh, she slid her hands over his lower back, the muscled curve of his buttocks, and heard him gasp her name.

Ambrose knew he should stop her, but he didn't want to. The feel of her hands on him was too exquisite to deny.

"Take it off," she commanded. "Your shirt, take it off."

She was already pulling at it, and he took over the task, pulling it over his head, leaving his chest bare to her questing and teasing hands. His cock throbbed against his unfastened breeches, wanting her there too. And as if she'd heard his unspoken plea, her fingers closed around the base of his shaft and his breath hissed out.

She hadn't forgotten the lessons he'd already taught her, and his cock was soon wet and slick in her hand. He pushed into her palm, his tongue echoing the thrust and withdrawal, his own hand under her skirts seeking out the warmth and welcome of her sex.

"Emily," he breathed, as his fingers encountered her wet and wanting cunt. He played with her bud, her folds, and finally thrust his finger in and out of her in a shallow rhythm that had her moaning and moving with him. Each roll of her hips drove him a little deeper and widened her narrow entrance for his eventual possession. And he would possess her. He was too far gone now to do anything else.

Reluctantly, he took his hand away and knelt back to gather Emily in his arms. Her face was flushed, her eyes hazy with need. She reached for him.

"Don't stop now, don't you *dare* stop."

Ah, that was more like his imperious Emily. He picked her up and laid her on his bed, pausing long enough to expertly remove her clothing and the rest of his own before stretching out naked over her. She trembled beneath him, her nipples hard points against his chest, his throbbing cock pressed between their bellies.

He kissed her mouth and then her throat, and settled to suck on her nipples. One hand toyed with her breast, while the other was between her thighs circling and playing with her clit. He felt her pleasure build, concentrated on her flesh to the exclusion of his own, and finally felt her tighten around his barely embedded finger.

"Ambrose, I . . ."

He silenced her with a deep kiss and pressed his thumb hard against her bud until she arched her back and climaxed, allowing him to push his finger even deeper and continue giving her pleasure. With all the skill he possessed, he made her come again, this time managing to slide two fingers inside her.

He pulled back to watch her face as she climaxed, the way she thrashed against the sheets, her expression so full of mingled joy and surprise that he knew he'd always remember it.

She gripped his arm so hard that he winced.

"I want you inside me. I *need* you there, I can't . . ."

He lowered himself between her thighs and guided the head of his cock inside her, easing his way, allowing her willing flesh to part for him and make him welcome. With a small sound, she wrapped her legs high around his hips, drawing him even deeper until he was embedded to the hilt.

He took as much of his weight as he could onto his forearms and began to thrust steadily in and out of her. She watched his face, her eyes betraying every fleeting emotion, the rise of her pleasure, the reflection of his. . . .

He'd made love to more bodies than he could count, but this was different. This was Emily, and whatever happened he would never forget her and how she'd made him feel. She climaxed around his shaft and he stayed still, enjoying the sensation, readying himself to push her even higher.

She came again, her fingernails digging into his shoulders, and he felt his own climax gather at the base of his spine, and just managed to pull out before he spent his seed deep within her welcoming warmth.

He lay over her and waited until her frantic breathing slowed and his own heart resumed its steady thump. She sighed and he rolled onto his back and arranged her over him. Her head fitted neatly under his chin as if she had been made for him.

He had no idea what he should say to her, or how she wanted him to proceed. All he knew was that making love to her was like coming home. . . .

"Ambrose," she whispered. "Will you ever forgive me?"

"For what?"

"For forcing myself on you like that."

He smoothed her disordered hair away from her face. "You didn't force me."

She raised herself up a little so that she could look at him. "I *ordered* you to—"

He placed his finger on her lips. "I wasn't listening. I was already too busy kissing you and wanting to be inside you."

She blushed and sank back down onto his chest.

"Still, you mustn't feel as if you are obliged to do anything about me; we can still remain friends."

"Friends? Don't tell me that you still intend to marry Jack Lennox."

"Of course not!"

"Then why did you stop me defending you in the kitchen to Christian?"

She sighed, her breath warm against his skin. "I feared that Christian would cast you out."

"*Christian?*"

"Yes, my half brother, the tyrant who runs the pleasure house to his own impossibly high standards."

"Christian would never do that to me."

She shivered. "He is quite terrifying when he is in a rage."

"That is true, but you forget that I know him very well.

After you stormed out of the kitchen with Jack, he gave me his blessing."

She reared up over him, one elbow planted firmly in his chest. "He did what?"

He fought a smile. "Christian told me that he quite understood your desire to be bedded by a man who knew what he was doing, and that I was an excellent choice."

She stared at him for so long that he almost forgot to breathe. "But when Jack Lennox spoke disparagingly of me, Christian was ready to strangle him."

"But Christian *knows* me."

"He loves you."

He hesitated. "Does that offend you?"

"No, why should it?"

He held her gaze. "We have been physically intimate."

"I know that, which is one of the reasons why I thought he would be angry."

"Which is why you interrupted me. You were trying to *protect* me."

She nodded and the remaining pins in her hair gave up the struggle and her hair fell down around her shoulders. Ambrose caught his breath and wrapped an errant curl around his finger.

"Is that what brought you here today? The desire to straighten things out between us? I hoped you would come back."

She sighed. "I did come to see you. I didn't quite expect this."

"*This* was as unexpected as it was glorious." He touched her cheek. "I have been selfish, sharing my worries with you. What did you want from me?"

She turned her mouth into his hand and kissed his palm. His cock jerked and he fought the urge to pull her beneath him again.

Her smile went awry and her eyes filled with tears. "I wanted you to help me."

"Emily, love, I'll always help you."

She seemed unaware that she was crying, her tears pooling on his chest like clear crystals. "I need to get my mother's last journal back from Thomas Smith."

He hesitated. "Are you sure you don't want to leave that to your father or Richard?"

"If they retrieve the journal, I will never know if what I fear is true."

"Emily." Seriously disturbed now, Ambrose sat up and held her in his lap. "What do you fear, and why would your family conceal anything from you?"

"Because they wouldn't want me to worry my little head about something that happened long ago."

"What do you think happened?"

She wiped at the tears on her cheeks. "From the letters I have already read, I think my mother was pregnant with me before she allowed my father back in her bed."

Ambrose enfolded her carefully in his arms. "Are you quite sure about that?"

"Almost certain, and what is worse, Richard knows and doesn't want to tell me."

"That sounds most unlike him." Ambrose considered her. "He doesn't usually go out of his way to protect your father."

"But this time he probably thinks he is protecting *me.*" She put her hand on his chest. "Will you help me?"

"Of course, I will."

She gazed at him through her tears, and he thought of how badly her family had misjudged her courage and her maturity. If she wasn't Philip's child, she should at least be told the truth to her face.

"We'll go and find Mr. Smith tomorrow."

"Thank you." She hesitated. "I just need to know where I stand."

"What do you mean?"

Her smile wobbled in the middle. "If I'm not a member of the Delornay-Ross family and merely a gardener's bastard, they can't tell me whom to marry or what to do anymore, can they?"

"It doesn't stop them loving you, Emily, or wanting to keep you safe."

She leaned against him and buried her face against his chest as if she didn't want to hear his words. "Will you let me stay a little while?"

"Yes." He laid her carefully down on the sheets and went to lock the door. He climbed back into bed, drawing the blankets over them both.

With a small sigh, she cuddled against him and he drew her even closer. The scent of their lovemaking surrounded him, and he realized he was more content than he had ever been in his life. They hadn't discussed the future, and maybe that was just as well. Both of them had to find their own paths. For the first time in years, Ambrose found himself praying that Emily would find peace, and that their chosen paths would interlock and keep them together for as long as they both drew breath.

Aghast at his thoughts, he dropped a kiss on the top of her head. Hadn't he learned never to hope, never to pray, never to expect anything but the worst? How did he even dare dream of a future with the woman sleeping beside him? He drew in a deep, steadying breath. He dared to dream because he loved her and would lay down his life for her. If that wasn't worth dreaming about, he might as well kill himself and be done with it.

20

Richard glanced down at Violet as they waited for Helene and Philip to appear in the drawing room of Knowles House. It was almost the dinner hour, but Richard had decided that the matter was too important to wait until the next day.

"You realize that this plan is bound to fail, don't you?"

Violet patted his arm. "Stop being such a pessimist. I see no reason why anything should go wrong."

"She's right, Richard," Jack added as he strolled across from the window. "Where has your spirit of adventure gone?"

"Up in smoke," Richard muttered. It was all very well to make daring plans, but when they involved the woman he loved, he found he was reluctant to put them into action.

Helene and Philip entered the room, and Richard waited until everyone was seated and the butler had withdrawn before gesturing at Jack.

"Mr. Lennox has some additional information about his family's decision to come to England that you should both hear."

He waited as patiently as he could for Jack to explain about his grandmother's continued connection to the Royalist party in France, and the twins' own disastrous involvement with Mr. Brown, which had led them to escape to England.

Finally, Jack was drawing to a conclusion. "We had hoped that once Violet gave the necessary information about Mr. Brown to Lord Keyes that the threat would be nullified and that we could stay here safely."

"But Lord Keyes has disappeared, and Mr. Brown seems to be trying to kill Violet," Richard added.

"Wait one moment," Philip said. "Who is Violet?"

"Vincent is Violet," Helene said serenely. She smiled at the quieter of the twins. "I wondered when you would feel safe enough to reveal your true identity."

Violet rose and bowed to Helene and Philip. "I never wished to deceive you, or your family, madame. I fear I had little choice in the matter."

"So it seems," Philip commented. "Now, how do you think we can help you sort out this muddle?"

Jack cast a wary glance at Richard, who decided it was time to take charge of the conversation.

"There are two ways you can help. Firstly, we need to find out exactly who Mr. Brown is."

"You don't know?" Helene asked.

"We're not certain, but with your contacts within the government, we hope you can find out—discreetly."

"I am always discreet." Helene nodded emphatically. "And I am more than willing to expose the identity of this pig who has helped murder so many of my countrymen."

"Thank you, madame," Jack said.

"And what else, Richard?" Philip asked.

"I'm hoping that we won't need to do this, but do you remember that horse you rescued from the traveling folk last year?"

"I didn't rescue him, Richard. I offered to keep him until he recovered from his injuries. He was in no state to be traveling the length and breadth of the country. The family will be returning soon, and I intend to give the horse back to them."

"That is very generous of you."

"Not really." Philip shrugged. "The Costello family has saved more than one of my horses with their potions and charms. I was delighted to be able to offer them something in return. I'm still not sure what this horse has to do with the business in hand, though."

From the baffled expressions on everyone's faces, neither did anyone else. Richard hastened to explain. "The horse can do tricks."

"What do you mean?" Violet asked.

"He was regularly sold at small horse fairs, and then within a day or so, he would become 'lame' or fall with a rider on his back. While his new owners considered what to do with him, he would make his way back to the Romany camp."

"By himself?"

"With a little help." Philip fought to conceal a smile. "Of course, as soon as the enraged owner came to find the camp, they would be nowhere in sight, leaving him with no horse and out of pocket."

"Clever horse," said Jack with a grin. "But how does that help us?"

"Don't you see? We'll borrow the horse and stage a dramatic accident with you on its back in the park at the height of the social hour." Richard glanced at his father. "I'm sure you know the right commands to make the horse perform, don't you?"

"I do," Philip said. "And I'm quite willing to lend you the horse, if you explain exactly why Mr. Lennox needs to have a very public accident."

Jack sat forward. "That's the easy part, my lord. Mr. Brown wants Violet to kill me."

Philip focused on Violet. "And you intend to honor that promise?"

"Well, yes and no." Jack grinned at his sister. "We want to make it look as if I've died, but I'd rather it was just a hoax."

Philip raised his eyebrows. "Especially as my daughter has just decided to become engaged to you."

"There is that to consider as well," Jack agreed. "But having a horse than can perform on demand would be a great asset to our plan."

"What exactly do you expect to achieve with this daring plot?" Helene asked. "Are you hoping that Mr. Brown will finally reveal himself to Violet, and accept that she is on his side?"

"That's what we hope."

"And what then?"

"If I finally meet Mr. Brown, I will bring him to justice," Violet said quietly. "No matter what the cost."

Richard studied Violet's resolute face. Would he ever get used to the notion that the woman he loved had no intention of allowing him to protect her? It was a frightening concept, and one he still struggled with. All he could do was involve himself with her plans, and try and make sure that they were as perfect as possible.

Philip was speaking again. "I'll send down to Knowles Hall for the horse. He should be with us tomorrow. Will that suit?"

"Thank you, Father." Richard nodded at Philip, who took the opportunity to walk across to him when Helene turned to speak to the twins.

"You seem surprisingly at ease with all this talk of spies and espionage, Richard." Philip hesitated. "I fear that Helene was right when she suggested that your years in Europe had not been spent entirely in the pursuit of pleasure."

"I can't talk about that, sir."

Philip nodded. "I understand, but might I say that I regret

not taking the time to ask you about your experiences? I self-ishly assumed that you were solely intent on avoiding me."

Richard sighed. "At first I was, but I soon realized there were far bigger issues at stake than mine."

"Did you meet Violet when you were there?"

"Why do you ask?"

"Because when you look at her, I see myself when I met Helene."

"I met her several years ago in France. I thought she was dead." Richard raised his eyes to meet his father's. "I love her and intend to marry her, sir."

"I'm pleased to hear it." Philip nodded. "She will make you an excellent wife."

"Even with her checkered past?"

"As if that would matter to me."

Richard turned to look at Violet, who was smiling at something Helene had said to her. "I'll marry her if she survives the current mess."

"She'll survive. I'm sure you'll guarantee it." Philip patted his shoulder.

"It is not quite that simple. If she'd only let me protect her, I'd feel much more certain."

Philip chuckled. "Good lord, there is no chance of her allowing that. She is just like Helene." His expression sobered. "And she will come to you on her own terms. The tighter you try to hold on to her, the more easily she will slip through your fingers."

"I'm beginning to realize that, sir." Richard nodded to his father. "I'm hoping Helene will find out who Mr. Brown is before we have to execute this ridiculous assassination plan, but I fear it will take too long. As soon as Violet's enemies find out that she is out in public again, I suspect they will come after her."

Philip patted him lightly on the shoulder. "Then perhaps

you should complete your plans as quickly as possible, and be ready for anything." He started to walk back to Helene. "Now, will you all be so obliging as to join us for dinner? Emily pleaded a headache, so it will just be us."

Richard hesitated. "Is she all right? She seemed rather upset when I saw her last."

"She's upset with me." Philip sighed. "When she has calmed down a little, I'll attempt to explain exactly why I didn't want her to read her mother's last journal. In truth, I've been avoiding the subject. I hoped she would never have to know."

"There is no need to be concerned, sir," Richard said quickly. "I told Emily not to worry about pursuing the matter and that there was nothing she needed to know."

"And how did she react?"

"She was very upset. But Helene and I thought it better if she didn't know about what happened between you and Smith. . . ."

Philip stopped walking. "Good God, no wonder Emily was dismayed when you told her not to worry. That wasn't the reason why I didn't want her to read the journal at all."

Richard paused beside his father at the door to the dining room. "I don't understand."

Philip shook his head. "It's not your fault." He drew in an unsteady breath. "As I said, I should have talked to her about this matter when she reached adulthood. But I never imagined Smith would reappear like some malignant monster to stir the pot."

"Sir, what exactly are you talking about?"

Philip turned on his heel and walked back into the hall where he met the butler coming toward him. "Burton, is Miss Emily upstairs?"

"I don't think so, my lord. I believe she went out earlier and has not yet returned."

"Ah, will you ask her to come and see me in my study when she does return?"

The butler glanced down at the letter on the silver tray he was carrying. "If I'm not mistaken, sir, this note is in Miss Emily's handwriting."

"Thank you, Burton." Philip took the note and opened it. "She's at the pleasure house and isn't feeling well, so Christian has offered her a bed for the night in the family quarters." Philip let out his breath. "It isn't ideal, but at least I know where she is."

Richard took the proffered note and read it through. "If she truly is unwell, perhaps you might wait until the morning to talk to her."

"I'll do that." Philip glanced at Richard as he folded the note and put it in his pocket. "I ask for your patience on this matter. I need to speak to Emily first, and then it is up to her if she wishes to share the information with you. All I will tell you is that it changes nothing about how I feel about either of you."

For the first time in his life, Richard felt as if he and his father were equals, his father neither plaster saint nor sinner, but a complex man who had done his best to play the hand he had been dealt.

"Of course, I'll wait, Father. Now, shall we join the others for dinner, and I can tell you more about our outrageous plan?"

Ambrose waited until he was certain Emily was asleep and got quietly out of bed. He pulled on his breeches and shirt, and made his way down to the kitchen. To his surprise, it wasn't that late, and the staff was still busy coming in and out of the kitchen replenishing the buffet and opening new bottles of wine.

He spied Seamus sitting at the table eating a big plate of chicken and took the seat next to him.

"Would you mind running some errands for me tonight?"

Seamus put down the chicken leg he'd just finished picking clean. "Always willing to oblige you, sir."

"There's no hurry, so please finish your dinner. When you're done, I'd like you to take a note to Mr. Smith at the Angel Inn, Islington."

"The rascal who upset Miss Emily?"

"That's the one. He still has one of her mother's journals in his possession."

Seamus scowled. "Is he staying there, sir? If he is, perhaps I can persuade him to give the journal up."

"I doubt he is still in residence, and I don't want you to confront him. After you deliver the note, wait and see if someone takes the note on to Mr. Smith and follow him. I'll make sure to give you a lot of coin so they'll deliver the letter fast."

"I can do that, sir. Anything else?"

"That depends on what happens tomorrow. I'm assuming Mr. Smith won't bring the journal with him to a meeting with Miss Ross."

"You're probably right about that. He'll want to see his money first."

"If we ascertain that he doesn't have the journal, I'll signal to you, and you can take yourself off to his new lodgings and see if you can find it there."

Seamus wiped his mouth on his sleeve. "And what if it isn't there, sir?"

Ambrose knew his smile wasn't pleasant. "Then we'll pay him something to keep him sweet while we work on a new plan to retrieve it."

"Aye, sir."

"I'll go and write a note for Mr. Smith." Ambrose stood and tried to sound nonchalant. "And while you are out, you might care to call into Knowles House and tell them that Miss Ross is not feeling well and has decided to stay the night in the family quarters here."

Seamus looked up. "Oh, no need for that, sir. Mrs. Delornay gave me a note that Miss Ross left with her. I delivered it earlier."

"Ah, well, that relieves you of one commission." Ambrose nodded. "Now I must write this letter and send you on your way."

Violet allowed Richard to help her out of the hackney and keep hold of her arm as they walked up the steps to his lodgings.

"I really should go home, you know."

Richard glanced down at her. "Why?"

"Because I understand from Jack that your reputation is in shreds."

"Mine?"

"Because you are concealing a man in your apartment—an apartment that has only one bedroom."

"Ah, well, that is true." He smiled as he shut the front door behind him. "And perhaps it was time that my reputation for being such a boring individual received a boost."

"You seem remarkably happy for a man who is now rumored a sodomite."

He drew her into his arms and held her close. "I certainly like having your arse, my dear."

His mouth descended over hers and he kissed her hard, the thick ridge of his cock already rubbing against her belly.

"I'm happy because even though you make me act like a fool, I don't regret meeting you again." He hesitated. "I feel alive for the first time in years."

She stared into his hazel eyes. "Are you saying you've forgiven me for the past?"

"How could I not forgive you? Knowing you, loving you, made me the man I am."

Her heart seemed to stutter. "But I'm not good for you."

"If I wanted a quiet existence, then, no, but it seems as if I'm to be dragged into your ridiculous schemes whether I want to be or not."

"You don't have to be." She managed a competent smile. "Jack and I are used to working together."

He slid his hand around the nape of her neck. "God forbid, you are suggesting I leave you to Jack's tender mercies. Someone needs to retain an element of control over this plan."

"That is usually my job," Violet admitted. She met his gaze. "Are you sure you want to get involved with this?"

"Quite sure." He kissed her nose. "Now, will you come to bed?"

"If you want me."

"Why so shy tonight?" His fingers tightened in her hair. "You know I do. That has never been an issue with us, has it? The wanting, the needing."

She let him lead her by the hand into his bedchamber. He hadn't mentioned the future at all. Did he still think she might not survive, or was she simply a passing physical amusement, a project to keep him entertained until something better turned up? All he'd actually said was that they were compatible in bed, not out of it.

Her spirits plummeted. She had no right to ask him anything. The mere fact that she was with him now and that he was *helping* her was amazing enough. Surely she should be content with that?

But as he slowly started to undress her beside the fire, she found herself wishing for more, for everything, for the happy ending that had long been denied her. She would not speak of it. But she would take what he offered her and enjoy every second. That would have to be enough.

21

When Emily came down into the kitchen of the pleasure house, Ambrose was already up and directing the servants cleaning the house. She didn't interrupt his duties but sat at the table and forced herself to drink some hot chocolate and toy with a warm croissant. He'd turned to her again in the night, and they'd made love while she was far more relaxed and able to enjoy it.

Her cheeks heated at the thought of how his skin felt under her hands, the powerful surge of his muscles as he thrust inside her, the immense pleasure that threatened to make her scream. . . . How could she have ever thought that another man would be able to rouse the same feelings in her as Ambrose did?

"Good morning, Miss Ross." She turned to see Seamus Kelly smiling at her. "Is Mr. Ambrose here?"

She pointed at the door. "I think he's supervising the cleaning in the main salon."

"Thank you, miss."

She continued to sip at her hot chocolate and tried to ignore the misery seeping through her joy. How could a person be so happy and yet so frightened at the same time? Whatever happened with Mr. Smith, her next conversation with Philip was going to be very difficult indeed.

Ambrose and Seamus came back into the kitchen together, and Emily tried to look as calm and normal as Ambrose did. When he saw her, a smile broke out on his face.

"Miss Ross, I was hoping that you were awake. Seamus has a message from Mr. Smith. He will meet us in the park at the same place as before at ten." He glanced at the kitchen clock. "We should probably set out fairly soon. Did you bring your warm coat?"

"I—yes—I did. It should be around here somewhere." Was that her breathy little voice? She sounded like a simpering debutante.

"Here it is, miss." Seamus rescued her coat from the back of a chair by the fire. "Let me help you on with it."

"Thank you."

Her bonnet was sitting on the table, so she put it on and tied the ribbons under her chin. Ambrose took a moment to look down at her and she saw it then, the love he couldn't quite conceal, enfolding her, supporting her. Over the past years, she'd come to rely on him to the exclusion of all others. It was only now that she realized what a gift he'd given her.

"Are you all right, Emily?" he murmured.

She smiled back at him. "I feel wonderful. In truth, if we could just sort out this little matter with Mr. Smith, I would feel even better."

"Don't try and be brave. It's not a little matter."

She sighed. "Would you rather I cried all the way there? Because I'm sure that could be arranged."

He touched her cheek. "Emily, Seamus and I will keep you safe, I swear it." He paused. "If you'd rather not go, I could—"

She stopped him speaking. "I have to. This is far too important to delegate to someone else, even you."

He kissed her gloved hand. "Then I can only stand in awe of your courage and respect your decision."

"You went to see Lady Kendrick."

"I had no choice."

"Yes, you did, and even though it was painful for you, you chose to do the right thing and not blame her for your fate. I can only hope to emulate your example."

He offered her his arm. "Then shall we go?"

Emily placed her hand on his sleeve, aware that everyone in the kitchen had stopped work to stare at them and smile. Had she betrayed herself somehow? Did everyone know?

Seamus grinned at her as he held open the door and then winked. "Glad to see you and Mr. Ambrose are talking to each other again, miss. We were all getting worried about you both."

Emily knew she should disapprove of his frankness, but she found it rather sweet that the entire staff of the pleasure house seemed to be willing her and Ambrose to make a match of it. If only she could convince her father of the same thing—*if* he was her father.

That thought plunged her back into gloom, and she barely managed to utter another word before they entered the park gates and headed down toward the lake. The sun was hidden behind a bank of gray clouds, and the lake was as still as a flat iron. Ambrose stopped just before they came into Mr. Smith's view and spoke to Seamus.

"He doesn't appear to have anything bulky on his person. Off you go, and do your best."

"I will, sir." Seamus touched the brim of his cap and disappeared back the way they had come.

"Where is he going?" Emily asked.

"To retrieve something for me." Ambrose patted her gloved hand. "Don't worry about Seamus. Let's concentrate on outwitting Mr. Smith."

Emily gathered her courage, and they set off down the slope

toward the figure sitting on the bench. As her heart threatened to burst out of her chest, Emily was extremely glad that Ambrose was with her.

Mr. Smith turned at their approach and smiled. "Miss Ross, a pleasure to see you again."

Emily managed to return his smile before sitting on the bench. She found herself scrutinizing Mr. Smith's face for signs of likeness to hers. Ambrose came to stand behind her, his hand warm on her spine where Mr. Smith couldn't see it.

"Did you bring the journal with you, sir?" Emily asked.

"Of course not, Miss Ross." His smile was meant to be engaging, but faltered when it reached his cold, assessing eyes. "Why would I do that when we haven't settled on a price?"

"Are you quite certain that you wouldn't just prefer to give the journal to me? If you truly loved my mother, can't you see that she would not have wanted you to hurt her children?"

"Ah, well, that's where you are wrong, lass." Mr. Smith crossed his booted feet. "It was your mother who told me to extract as much money as possible from your father. I'm only following her dying wishes."

"My *mother* wanted this?"

"Aye, she loved me, you see, and she hated your father for marrying her and keeping us apart." Regret shone clearly on Mr. Smith's face and, for a moment, Emily almost felt sorry for him.

"It was hardly all my father's fault, was it? If she wanted to marry you so badly, why didn't she run away with you before he came back from India?"

He sighed. "Because she was too afraid of the scandal, and she was very young."

"But she made herself and everyone around her pay for that choice for the rest of her life."

Emily almost didn't recognize the bitterness in her own voice. Her anger at Mr. Smith abated slightly as she considered her mother's part anew.

"Before I can even consider negotiating for the book, there is something I must ask you." Emily took a deep breath. "Does my mother name you as my father in the journal?"

Mr. Smith sat back and regarded her closely. "I wondered if you would work that out. She doesn't exactly *name* me, but it is obvious from the dates she gives that Philip was only allowed back into her bed after she realized she was breeding. She had no choice in the matter if she wished to avoid a scandal."

His casual use of the name Philip rather than her father's title made Emily clench her hands into fists. But Philip wasn't her father, was he? This despicable individual in front of her was almost certainly her true sire.

"Do you not care that if you make this journal public that I, your *daughter*, will be branded a bastard?"

He held her gaze. "Why should it matter to me? I've never been allowed to care for you or acknowledge you."

"So I mean nothing to you?" Anger rose to replace her fear. "And what if I don't care if you proclaim that truth to the world? What is your journal worth then?"

Mr. Smith smiled. "I'm glad to see you have some of my fighting spirit, lass, but remember, this isn't just about you. There are other secrets in the journal that reflect just as badly on Philip."

"I don't believe he murdered my mother."

He had the audacity to smile. "Do you not? Well, you'll have to read the journal to make up your mind about that one."

She fixed him with her best glare. "Even if my mother makes such a claim, surely you know that no jury would convict him now?"

He shrugged. "All I can say is that if her suspicions are made public, who knows what will happen to the reputation of the already suspect Knowles family?"

Emily struggled to retain her temper. "What you are saying

is that you have no intention of allowing me to buy the journal from you. You simply wish to damage the family reputation."

"Not quite." He considered her for a long moment. "Mayhap Philip could be persuaded to offer me a monthly allowance to keep my secrets to myself."

"But what about your promise to my mother?"

"I think she'd be happy to see Philip paying my bills for the rest of his natural life. She'd probably see it as justice."

"I wouldn't," Emily said. "How much money do you want for the journal right now, along with your promise to never speak of this to another soul?"

Mr. Smith pursed his lips and whistled. "You are a feisty piece, and quite unlike your mother. What a shame that you weren't a boy. I might have been tempted to steal you away and bring you up myself."

"How much, Mr. Smith? I'm sure you already have a figure in mind."

"How about five thousand guineas?"

Emily just stared at him. "That is ridiculous!"

He shrugged. "Your father's annual income is four times that."

"But . . ."

Ambrose touched her shoulder.

"If you might allow me, Miss Ross."

She nodded for him to proceed as she tried to work out how on earth she could afford such an enormous sum.

"With all due respect, Mr. Smith," Ambrose said. "Such a large sum of money would take a while to gather. I expect you'd want it all in gold."

"Aye." Mr. Smith nodded. "I need to be away from this place within the week, so you need to make your minds up fast."

Ambrose withdrew a small leather bag from his pocket,

which clinked. "I am willing to offer you fifty guineas on account."

Mr. Smith stretched out his hand. "I'll take it, but I want the rest sent to the inn by Friday."

"We'll do our best," Ambrose murmured. "Is there anything else you wish to say to Mr. Smith, Miss Ross?"

Emily stared at the man who had so casually admitted he was probably her father and shook her head.

Mr. Smith stood and bowed to her. "I said it before and I say it again, your mother would be proud of you."

She had nothing to say to that either, and she watched as he strode along the path, up the hill, and out of her sight.

"Emily." Ambrose sat beside her and took her hand in his. "Are you all right?"

"He's my father, Ambrose, and yet I feel nothing for him and he feels nothing for me."

"That's because he is a fool."

She squeezed his fingers. "Perhaps I should be glad I wasn't born a boy."

"For all intents and purposes, Lord Knowles is still your father. He has done everything in his power to bring you up as a cherished and beloved daughter."

"But maybe he doesn't know!" Emily whispered. "What will he do if he discovers I'm not really his child?"

"I suspect he knows, Emily. Why else would he have been so keen to get that journal back?"

Emily inhaled sharply. "Mr. Smith said there was more than one secret in the journal. Perhaps beside the accusations of murder, there are hints that Richard is illegitimate, too, or . . ." She paused as she reconsidered her last conversation with Richard. "Or something else that Philip doesn't want me to know."

"You don't have enough money to pay off Mr. Smith." Ambrose met her gaze, his brown eyes steady. "Talk to Lord Knowles. Tell him the truth."

"But if I sold my jewelry or borrowed against my inheritance . . ."

"Emily, do you really think Smith is going to stop at five thousand guineas? Despite what he said, I believe he still wants to get revenge for your mother on her terms, which means he intends to bleed your father and the rest of you dry. You *have* to talk to Lord Knowles. Between his influence and Madame Helene's contacts, Mr. Smith must be stopped."

She stared at him until his beloved features blurred beneath the onslaught of her tears. With a soft exclamation, he gave her his handkerchief, and eventually she occupied herself blowing her nose and wiping away her tears. When she managed to look at Ambrose again, he smiled.

"That's better. Would you care to discuss something else before we have to leave? This is probably not the time or the place for it, but I feel as if I have to speak."

"What is it?"

He squared his shoulders. "As a senior employee at the pleasure house, I earn a considerable salary. Despite giving a percentage of my money to charity, I have managed to save a goodly sum."

"That is all very admirable, but I fail to see what it has to do with my present predicament." She stiffened. "You can't imagine I'd take your money?"

"No, that's not what I meant, I . . ." The sight of Ambrose at a loss for words fascinated Emily. "I have been offered a job as a schoolteacher in a new charity school that will be opening next year, and although the salary is far less than I am earning now, it would at least be a respectable position that comes with accommodation."

"Are you considering leaving the pleasure house?"

He swallowed hard. "Yes, if it meant that I had a home of my own to offer you."

She stared at him as his words sank in. "As your wife?"

"As my wife. Although I can quite understand that such a lowly position would not reflect your present accommodation and rank."

"Ambrose, I have just discovered that I am illegitimate. I hardly think I have a right to look down on anyone who earns his or her own way in life."

He reached for her hand and she realized his fingers were shaking. "Then you would consider it?"

She covered his hand with her own. "I would consider it an honor."

He leaned forward and gently kissed her on the lips. "May I suggest that you sort out your problems with Mr. Smith before we discuss this with Lord Knowles?"

"That seems like excellent advice."

"Don't think that I am afraid anymore. You've taught me how to value myself. I am perfectly willing to approach Lord Knowles to ask for your hand in marriage right now, but I'm trying to be sensible."

She disengaged her hands. "And I understand that." She smiled into his eyes. "Thank you."

"For what?"

"For always being there for me. You are truly my best friend."

He kissed her again, and then stood up and held out his hand. "Let me escort you back to Knowles House, Miss Ross. I suspect you have a lot to discuss with your family."

"I believe I have." She curtsied to him and put her hand on his arm. She wasn't looking forward to the discussion with Philip at all. But despite everything, the thought of Ambrose waiting for her, *wanting* her, regardless of her social status made everything else seem quite unimportant.

22

"Emily still hasn't returned?" Richard asked as his father strode into the entrance hall of Knowles House to greet him. Like him, Philip was dressed for riding, which emphasized the already considerable likeness between them.

"No, although I wasn't expecting her to arrive before breakfast. She has never been an early riser."

"That's true."

Philip ushered Richard into his study. "Helene has already started her inquiries as to Mr. Brown's identity, but she expects it to be a while before she hears anything interesting. She advises us to seize the moment and go ahead with the assassination plan."

"Does she?" Richard groaned. "I fear that she is right, but I still don't like it."

"You'll be pleased to hear that the horse arrived very early this morning, and he is in extremely good health. I suggest you contact Jack Lennox and bring him down to the mews to meet his co-conspirator and get acquainted with his tricks."

"I'll send him a note right now." Richard took a seat at

Philip's desk. "If it would not trouble you, I'd like to ask Violet to bring Mrs. Lennox here as well. The twins are worried that she will be vulnerable if she is left alone."

"Certainly she may come here." Philip warmed his hands at the fire. "I understand that she was present at her husband's murder by that mob and barely escaped with her life."

"Yes, thank God, Jack was able to get to her in time. Mr. Brown seems to have a penchant for disposing of anyone who might have even the slightest bit of knowledge of him. I wouldn't put it past him to have men who are trained to take advantage of anything instantly on the scene in the park."

"So you will have to be careful too."

Richard finished the first note and looked up at his father. "Devil take it, I hadn't thought of that. But if I am in danger, I suspect I'm still fairly low on his list."

"Let's hope so," Philip said with a faint smile. "Although you seem remarkably unfazed by thoughts of your imminent death. In fact, you seem quite energized."

Richard shrugged. "Perhaps I'm not quite as dull as you might think."

"I never thought you dull." Philip hesitated. "It was more as if you had lost something precious in France, and that life no longer seemed as enjoyable."

"Why did you think that?"

"Because I know all about losing someone."

Richard cleared his throat. "I thought Violet was dead and that it was my fault. I believed my life was over."

"I never believed Helene was dead, but when I married your mother, Helene was certainly lost to me." Philip busied himself rearranging the books on his desk. "We have both been blessed to rediscover what we thought lost."

For the first time Richard imagined what it would have been like if he'd had to let Violet go and watch her marry someone else. Would he ever have been truly happy? Perhaps Violet's decision to end their relationship in such a final way had been a blessing in disguise.

He stared down at the sheet of paper and made himself write a note to Violet as well as Jack. Patrick Kelly, Seamus's brother, was guarding her and he would accompany her to Knowles House.

"I'll ask Violet and Patrick Kelly to meet us at the mews. It will give us time to go over our plans and make sure that this damned masquerade works perfectly."

Emily handed her cloak to the butler and smiled at him. It was almost time for the midday meal and appetizing smells were beginning to rise from the kitchen in the basement.

"Good morning, Mr. Blake, is my father in his study?"

"I regret to inform you that his lordship has gone out with Mr. Ross and the Lennox gentlemen."

"Do you know when they will return?"

"I'm not certain, miss, but Madame Helene and Mrs. Lennox are upstairs. Perhaps her ladyship might know his lordship's intentions."

Emily glanced at Ambrose, who nodded. "We'll go up to her. Thank you, Mr. Blake."

"I'll bring you some refreshments, miss."

Emily picked up her trailing skirt and headed up the stairs, with Ambrose behind her. She paused at the door to the drawing room and heard her stepmother's low voice within. After taking a deep breath, she went in.

"Good morning, Helene, Mrs. Lennox."

Helene smiled at her. She wore a plain yellow muslin day dress and delicate lace cap that complemented her fair complexion. Emily had always secretly admired Helene's style but never managed to emulate it.

"Ah, Emily and Ambrose. How nice to see you both. Have you met Mrs. Lennox, Ambrose?"

"Yes, I have. How nice to see you again, ma'am." Ambrose bowed to Mrs. Lennox, took a seat next to her, and they started to speak about the weather.

Emily sat next to Helene on the loveseat. "I was hoping to see Father, but I understand that he is out."

"He is." Helene took Emily's hand. "Have you come to tell him that your engagement to Jack Lennox was a sham and that you are in love with Ambrose?"

Emily narrowed her eyes at her smiling stepmother. "What makes you think that?"

"I hardly think you'd go to bed with a man you didn't love, my dear."

"How do you know what . . ." Emily glared at Helene. "I suppose Christian was right all along. You *do* know everything. I can see where he gets it from now."

Helene laughed. "I know about men and women, that's all, and I've been expecting this to happen for years. Ambrose has always been in love with you."

"And I, him," Emily sighed. "Now I have to tell Philip."

"You can hardly think your father will object?"

"My father . . ." Emily stared across at Ambrose, who was smiling at something Mrs. Lennox had said. "That's the other reason I want to speak to him. When do you think he will be back?"

Helene sighed. "I have no idea. He has been hatching some ridiculous plan with Richard and the Lennox twins."

Despite her own worries, Emily immediately leaned closer. "What kind of plan?"

Helene looked over at Mrs. Lennox and Ambrose, and then lowered her voice. "I'm not sure how much you know about the Lennox family, but they are in danger, particularly Vincent Lennox."

"The man who is currently reported to be occupying Richard's bed?" Emily added.

"Vincent isn't a man. Her real name is Violet, and she is going to make Richard an excellent wife one day." The certainty of Helene's tone made Emily gape at her. "Anyway, that isn't the main reason why they are plotting. Violet is supposed to kill Jack, and obviously she has no wish to do so."

"He really is her twin?"

"Apparently. Richard and Jack have concocted a plan that will make it *look* as if Jack has been killed; but, of course, it will all be staged."

"And what do they hope to gain from this ridiculous piece of melodrama?"

"I *believe* they are hoping to lure their prey into the open so that they can apprehend him."

"And no one bothered to tell me about this? I'm supposed to be betrothed to Jack!"

Alerted by Emily's rising voice, Ambrose and Mrs. Lennox looked across at them.

"That is just typical of Richard to avoid including me in his plans," Emily said.

"Would you want to be included?" Helene asked. "It might be dangerous."

"Ha! Richard has always been the one who avoided danger, not me." Emily stood up. "Where is this attempt to kill Jack Lennox supposed to take place?"

Helene glanced at the clock. "At three o'clock in Hyde Park when the *ton* are on display." She patted the seat beside her. "Why don't you and Ambrose stay and have some luncheon with us, and then we'll all go to the park in my carriage?"

Emily sank back down into her seat. Cowardly as it might seem, it was a relief to be distracted from her own concerns and to speculate about Richard and his new love instead.

"Are you ready, then?" Richard asked Jack and Violet, who both nodded. Violet looked far paler than her brother, which was not necessarily a bad thing, but caused Richard more anxiety. According to the stable yard clock, it was a quarter to three, and the sun had peeked through the clouds, offering a faint hint of warmth to the windy afternoon.

"Shall we proceed to the park?"

Philip mounted his showy chestnut gelding and clicked his tongue to get the horse in motion and out toward the entrance to the mews. Richard mounted, too, and waited for Violet to come up alongside him.

"Do you think it will work?" she asked him, her blue eyes anxious beneath the brim of her tall hat.

"I damn well hope so." He held her gaze. "Even if it doesn't, I'm still going to keep you safe."

Her mouth quirked up at the corner. "If I don't end up dead myself."

"I won't allow that to happen." He spoke with more confidence than he felt. They both knew that.

Behind them, Jack loudly cleared his throat while his horse sidled sideways as if eager to be off.

Richard reined back. "We'd better move out of the way and let Jack join Philip for their entrance into the park. We're not supposed to be anywhere near them at first." He nodded at Jack. "Good luck."

Jack grinned at them both as he moved smartly past. "See you in hell."

Violet shivered, and Richard brought his horse as close to hers as he could, and said quietly, "It won't come to that. If anyone can pull this off, it is Jack."

She regained her composure and smiled. "Indeed. I believe he was born for this moment."

At her display of courage, he wanted to drag her off her horse, take her back to bed, and keep her there forever. No wonder he'd never looked at another woman. No one could compare to Violet. She was everything a man could ever want.

"What is it?"

He realized he must have been staring at her, and quickly gathered his reins in his gloved hand.

"Nothing, my love. Shall we proceed to the park?"

As they approached the fashionable throng, Richard realized that he and Violet were drawing far more attention that he had expected. He cast her a quizzical look.

"It seems that you were right about the gossip."

She studied the curious faces turned toward them. "Do you want me to find someone else to talk to?"

"Let them stare. Perhaps it will distract them from seeing exactly what happens to your twin."

"And direct suspicion more quickly onto me."

"Whatever happens, I'll keep you safe, Vincent." He nodded to an old acquaintance, who drew back as if Richard had blown him a kiss. "I think I see Helene's carriage over by the railings to your left. I knew she wouldn't be able to keep away."

"Perhaps she has news for us. Do you want to approach her?"

Richard checked his pocket watch. "We have time before Jack appears, and time to stop him if my stepmother has miraculously come up with a name."

"But you doubt that, don't you?"

"Unfortunately, yes." He leaned down to knock on the closed window of the carriage. "Good afternoon, Helene, Mrs. Lennox. Have you any news for us?"

Helene leaned out of the carriage and the peacock feathers in her bonnet fluttered in the breeze. "Nothing that will change your plans, although you might wish to know that Emily and Ambrose accompanied us here and are out mingling with the crowds. Emily is most displeased with you."

Richard groaned. "Emily would never forgive me for not involving her in this scheme."

"I believe on this occasion she wishes to help, not hinder you," Helene said.

"That remains to be seen. My sister has always been contrary." He tipped his hat at Helene. "Onward, then."

He waited until Violet spoke a few words to her stepmother and then shaded his eyes to watch the riders trotting up and down Rotten Row. He soon recognized Philip, who was an excellent rider, alongside Jack, who sat easily on his borrowed horse.

"We should get into position," he murmured to Violet. "They are about to make the turn and come back down this way."

Violet nodded and turned her horse toward the thickest part of the crowd, aware of Richard following her, their backs deliberately to the oncoming riders. She could hear the pounding hooves and the murmur of the crowd as one of the riders appeared to lose control of his horse.

Reluctantly, she turned back as the noise grew louder and saw Jack careening toward the mass of walkers, fighting the reins, already halfway off the side of the horse, who was running at a full gallop.

A young lady screamed and started to run, her action caused a ripple among the spectators, spreading them in all directions. Violet was caught between a cross tide of people who were trying to escape the oncoming horse and those who were rushing forward either to help or to gawk at the unfolding disaster. She heard Lord Knowles above the crowd still shouting instructions to Jack and then a peculiar high-pitched whistle.

As if in a nightmare, she watched the horse pitch forward onto its knees, taking Jack down with it in a cloud of earth and clods of grass. Lord Knowles reached the fallen horse first and dismounted, throwing his reins at his groom. He ran straight to Jack, who lay at an awkward angle on the ground, half under the horse.

"Is there a doctor here?" Lord Knowles bellowed.

"Yes, sir!"

Violet looked around and saw the familiar figure of Dr. Bailey shouldering his way through the crowd of onlookers. He knelt beside Jack, obscuring him from view. Involuntarily, Violet urged her horse forward, only to have her horse's bridle held in an iron grip.

"No, leave them be," Richard ordered. "You must not appear too eager to go over to him."

"But—"

"Leave him. Let this play out as we planned it."

Violet jumped as a scream sounded behind her and she saw Emily Ross rushing toward Jack, one hand clasped to her bosom.

"Oh, Jack, no, my *darling!*"

"That wasn't part of the plan, was it?"

"No, but there's not a lot I can do about it now. She does seem to be adding to the authenticity of the moment rather than detracting from it." Richard sighed as Emily flung herself down in a swirl of petticoats next to poor Dr. Bailey, who noticeably flinched.

Violet held her breath as the doctor beckoned to his groom and spoke briefly to him before the man hurried away. Philip took the fallen horse's bridle and gently brought him back to his feet. He spent a moment checking the horse's bleeding front legs and then ordered his groom to bind them.

"Let's start to edge a little closer," Richard murmured. "Philip has his eye on Emily. He won't let her ruin anything."

Violet nodded and followed Richard's lead, the crowd parting at the gentle insistence of the horse's bulky presence. From her high perch, she could see Jack more clearly now. A trickle of blood marred the whiteness of his face and his eyes were closed. Was he truly all right? He didn't look well at all. Dr.

Bailey was conferring in a quiet voice with Philip and shaking his head.

The groom reappeared with three other men bearing a stretcher between them. Philip, who had relinquished the horse to Ambrose, put his arm around Emily as Jack was carefully lifted onto the stretcher and completely covered with a blanket.

Emily gave a convulsive shudder and buried her face against her father's shoulder.

"He can't be dead. He *can't* be!"

A murmur of sympathy ran through the crowd. As Emily started to cry, Philip's hand came to rest on her shoulder and he held her close. Dr. Bailey stopped to close his bag, his expression somber, and then stood up. Most of the crowd had now drifted away; only a group of gentlemen discussing the horse still remained.

Philip's groom, who had turned his attention to assessing Jack's injured mount, began gesticulating at Philip. His voice grew louder until it could be heard clearly over everyone else. "There's something not right here, my lord. I was behind Mr. Lennox when the horse bolted, and nothing scared him, I swear it!"

"Maybe the horse was stung by something." Lord Knowles turned to greet Helene and Mrs. Lennox, who had also arrived on the scene. Mrs. Lennox was crying uncontrollably. He passed Emily over to the women, who held her close.

"I asked them to take Jack to Knowles House, Mrs. Lennox. Dr. Bailey is fairly certain that there is nothing more to be done for him, but . . ."

His words caused fresh tears from Emily and Mrs. Lennox, who clung to each other, sobbing. It was left to a white-faced Helene to guide them into the carriage and take them to Knowles House.

The groom started to examine the reins and the saddle of the shivering horse, who was still bearing no weight on his right foreleg. Violet could only marvel at the horse's acting ability—if it was indeed acting.

"Look, my lord!" The groom held up the left rein. "Someone cut the leather nearly through."

"*What?*" Lord Knowles said. He turned from watching Helene's carriage leave and examined the horse's bridle, his expression thunderous.

"And see this, sir," the groom continued. "The girth has been almost cut through as well."

"That still wouldn't be enough to make the horse bolt, though, would it?" Lord Knowles asked.

"Not necessarily, my lord, but it would make it harder for a rider to stay on the horse's back."

At this point, as arranged, Richard dismounted and pushed his way through to the front of the crowd.

"Father? What's going on?"

Philip ran a hand down the horse's lathered neck. "Did you not see? The horse bolted and fell on Mr. Jack Lennox. My groom seems to be suggesting there was foul play."

The groom meanwhile had continued to feel the horse and made a sound of triumph when the animal reared onto his back legs and shook his head.

"My lord, come and see this."

Philip crouched down beside his groom, who was pointing at something sticking out of the horse's belly. "It looks like a dart of some kind. That would certainly frighten the poor bugger and make him bolt."

Philip waited until the groom 'removed' the small dart and handed it to him.

"But who would want to kill Mr. Lennox?" he asked loudly.

"Perhaps someone just wanted to frighten him?" Richard addressed his father. "He was riding with you. Did one of your grooms have a falling out with him?"

"Excuse me, Mr. Richard," Philip's head groom interrupted them. "None of my lads touched that damned 'orse."

"That seems a little strange." Richard turned back to Philip. "That is one of your horses, isn't it?"

"He's not actually mine." Philip's gaze flicked over to where Violet still remained sitting on her horse. "I . . . offered to keep him in my stables."

That was the truth. Now came the lie. Richard could only hope Violet was ready.

"Then whose damned horse is it?"

Philip sighed. "Mr. Vincent Lennox asked me to stable the horse for him as a gift to his twin brother."

Richard's gaze flew to where Violet sat apparently frozen in place on her horse.

"Is that true, Vincent?"

With a convulsive shudder, Violet kicked at her horse and fled the scene.

Richard made as if to go after her, but Philip held him back.

"Shouldn't we catch him, sir?" the groom asked. "He looked bloody guilty to me."

A chorus of agreement blossomed around them, but Richard shook his head.

"No, I can't believe Vincent would—that he would—no. He's not like that. He loves his brother." He stared at his father. "There must be some mistake."

"Strange how he didn't come forward to help out or even shed a tear," muttered one of the other men.

"He's such a weakling, perhaps he feared he might swoon," someone else said, rather unkindly.

Richard glared at the man. "Vincent Lennox is a good man! He's probably at his brother's bedside right now."

"Stealing the pennies from his eyes," one of the grooms mumbled.

Richard spun around to face Philip. "Father, you cannot believe this. It was an accident! A horrible accident."

Philip had resumed his examination of the horse with his groom but straightened when Richard came toward him, his expression full of compassion.

"I understand that you care about Vincent Lennox, Richard, but the evidence . . ."

Richard went still and glared at his father as if he was oblivious to the avid stares of the remaining crowd.

"You believe Vincent is a *murderer?*"

"That will be for the law to decide, Richard, not us." Philip inclined his head an inch. "Now, if you will excuse me, I need to attend to the horses. May I suggest you repair to Knowles House and provide some comfort to your sister?"

"I'll do that, sir." Richard bowed. "And then I'll seek out Vincent Lennox and listen to his side of the story too!"

Richard marched back to his horse, vaulted onto its back, and was away with a spray of gravel before anyone could accost him further. He didn't allow himself to relax until he was stabling his horse behind Knowles House. So far so good. Now all it needed was for the inevitable gossip to start and Violet's life would be changed forever, hopefully for the better.

23

"How can I possibly speak to my father about Thomas Smith when I am supposed to be hysterical with grief for Jack?" Emily murmured to Ambrose between patting daintily at her eyes with her handkerchief.

Jack lay under the sheets in the best guest bedchamber; apart from a few cuts and bruises, his face was as white as the linen. His hands were folded neatly together in front of him as if he were at prayer. Even though Emily knew the effect was deliberate, it was a curiously disturbing sight, as Jack was very rarely still.

"I'm sure there will be a quiet moment later when you can speak to Lord Knowles." Ambrose hesitated. "Do you want me to stay with you?"

"No, let's not complicate matters too much." Emily patted his sleeve. "I'd rather you went and found out more about this teaching position you were promised, so that when I confront Philip about my plans for the future, we have something positive to tell him."

"I understand." Ambrose glanced around the candlelit room

where several visitors had been allowed in to view the body. Many of them were young and female, and were already sobbing. "But I hate to leave you."

"And that is why you must go. If you stay, I'll be incapable of playing the part of Jack's grieving fiancée."

Ambrose nodded and bent to kiss her hand. "I know you are more than equal to the task."

She smiled into his eyes. "I'm glad you see that. Even if I marry you, I won't become some milk and water miss."

"Thank God for that. I'll go and speak to Jethro about the teaching position." Ambrose took one last longing look at her and then turned toward the door. "If you need me, just send a note to the pleasure house and I'll come at once."

She nodded and watched him walk away, noticed his graceful carriage and the way he exuded such quiet competence. He was everything that she was not, but perhaps that was why they complemented each other so well.

"Are you all right, Emily?"

Helene appeared at her elbow, her expression grave.

Emily gave a convulsive sob and deliberately raised her voice for the benefit of the onlookers. "No, I'm not all right. My fiancé is dead and his brother is to blame!"

"We don't know that, dear," Helene murmured soothingly.

"Then why isn't he here mourning his twin? Why did he flee?" Emily demanded.

Helene drew her to sit down on the nearest couch and Emily took the opportunity to whisper in her ear. "How is it that Jack looks as if he is really dead?"

"I believe Dr. Bailey gave him some kind of potion that mimics the effect of death."

Emily shuddered. "How very Shakespearean of him. How long will it take before Jack regains consciousness?"

"I'm not sure. Dr. Bailey has an antidote that he will administer when it becomes necessary."

"Let's hope that happens before they bury him. Has a date been set for the funeral?"

"Not yet. The local magistrate and the coroner have visited, but everyone is too busy trying to locate Vincent Lennox. There is much suspicion, but very little evidence, which suits our plans perfectly." Helene sighed. "I know that the plan is for Mr. Brown to find Vincent, but I hope Richard finds him first." She crossed herself. "Although then they are both in danger. I'm still trying to find out exactly who Mr. Brown is through the more usual means. We can only hope that everything will work out for the best."

"Indeed."

Emily looked up as Philip came into the room accompanied by Dr. Bailey. They both looked suitably serious as they studied Jack's inert form and then came over to where Helene and Emily were sitting.

Philip kissed Helene's hand and sat beside her. "Dr. Bailey has just given Mrs. Lennox a sleeping draught and she has gone to bed."

"The poor woman," Helene said. "One stepson taken from her so tragically and the other disappeared."

"I'm sure Richard will find Vincent and discover the truth. I don't really believe he meant his brother harm, do you?" Philip asked.

Emily fought a smile. There was just enough uncertainty in his tone to convey his suspicions of Vincent without actually condemning him.

"Indeed." Dr. Bailey's voice was loud enough to cause a lull in the muttered conversations around them. "I'm not quite certain why Mr. Vincent Lennox would wish to dispose of his brother, but the evidence is certainly damning. He was the last person to touch that horse before his twin mounted it and set out for the park."

"Hush now," Helene said. "Let's wait and see what happens.

Vincent might have been felled by grief and needed time to compose his feelings."

Emily took the opportunity to glance at the other occupants of the room through the lace of her handkerchief and noticed that everyone was listening avidly. She would guarantee that the society gossips of London would soon be awash with all the details from Jack's deathbed. There was nothing like a little family rivalry to titillate the jaded senses of the *ton*.

Her thoughts turned to Richard and the elusive Vincent Lennox. She could only pray that both of them would survive their encounter with the unpleasant Mr. Brown and return safely home.

Violet pressed her back against the wall as the door to Richard's bedchamber was kicked in, then turned to hurl herself through the already open window. She hadn't expected Mr. Brown to act so quickly. There was no sign of Patrick Kelly, who was supposed to be guarding her. Had he gone to find Richard? She certainly hoped at least one of the men would track her. She also hoped that Richard's poor manservant was still tied up where she had left him to make her entrance to Richard's lodgings look suspicious and had not been killed by Mr. Brown's men.

As she scrambled to regain her footing on the wet cobblestones, a large hand descended on her shoulder and spun her around. She didn't recognize the man, but she knew his kind. He was built like a prizefighter. Even though she knew she stood no chance against him, she still put up a fight, which was swiftly ended when her attacker punched her in the gut, making her double over. She hardly registered the second blow to her head as the world dissolved into white agony.

When she regained her senses, she tried to open her eyes to see if she recognized where she was. Unfortunately, everything was still black. It took her a panicked moment to realize she'd been blindfolded. She breathed in deeply through her mouth and then exhaled. Her other senses caught the smell of a coal fire, brandy, and a hint of wet dog. In truth, she could be in any gentleman of her acquaintance's study.

Already aware that she wasn't alone, she concentrated on maintaining her even breathing. She was tied to a chair, her arms bound tightly behind her. Someone had removed her cravat, coat, and waistcoat to make sure she couldn't wriggle free of them. As carefully as she could, she flexed her wrists and tested her bounds, and found them immovable.

"You won't escape, Violet."

The quiet amusement in her captor's voice did nothing to reassure her. She tried to think if she knew him, if he was at all familiar, but her knowledge of English accents was far less acute than her French. At least now she was certain it wasn't Lord Keyes.

His chair creaked as he leaned forward, and she inhaled the strangely familiar fragrance of bergamot and lemon underscored with peppercorns.

"What do you want, Mr. Brown?"

She was pleased she sounded so calm.

"To congratulate you."

"For what?"

"For disposing of your brother as we planned."

She pictured Jack as she had last seen him, lying on the ground, and had no difficulty shivering.

"You are regretting what you did?"

"He was my twin." She allowed her anguish to show. "I should *never* have agreed to help you."

"It is too late for regrets now, my dear." His chair scraped on the wooden floor and she tensed. "And think how rich we shall be."

"I don't want anything from you anymore," she whispered.

"You are feeling guilty. It reminds me of when you pretended to die for that stupid Englishman Richard Ross."

"That was not the same at all." Her voice was shaking now. "God forgive me, I gave up Richard for the cause of France. I gave up Jack for *money.*"

"And you now believe it isn't worth it?"

She shook her head, then gasped when he grabbed her chin and pushed her head up.

"I've wanted you for a long time, Violet Lennox. I've always admired your intelligence and resourcefulness. Don't tell me that you have chosen to become a coward now that the end is in sight?"

His mouth descended over hers and she could do nothing but endure the bruising pressure of his lips against hers. His fingers clenched harder on her jaw, forcing her to open her mouth for the invasion of his tongue. While he kissed her, his hands roamed over her body, shaping and pinching her breasts until she thought she would either gag or scream.

"No!"

When he drew back, he was panting as hard as she was.

"What's wrong, Violet? Do you think I care whether you want me or not?"

"I'll fight you until my last breath."

"I'll enjoy that even more." His soft laughter chilled her. "Perhaps I've been a little too hasty. Once you get over your guilt, I'm sure you'll be eager to be fucked."

"Never."

Her head snapped back as he slapped her hard on the cheek. "Guilt drives you, doesn't it? You bed that fool Richard Ross because you feel guilty about deceiving him all those years ago."

She didn't speak as she tried to master the pain. She wouldn't speak to him about Richard. She would *not.*

"Of course, despite your considerable amoral skills, you are still a woman who has to deny her base instincts and cover up her guilt with the lie of love."

He cupped the cheek he'd slapped, his fingers caressing her jaw.

"Let me make it quite simple for you. If you wish Richard Ross to live, you will follow through with our plan and come and whore for me instead of him."

"I don't want either of you. Don't you understand? I'll never forgive myself for killing my twin," she whispered.

"Oh, you'll forgive yourself. A few months with me and you'll forget all about him, and that coward Richard Ross." His fingers drifted closer to her mouth and she sank her teeth into them.

With a startled curse, he wrenched his hand free and struck her again. She couldn't help but scream this time. Before she recovered, she felt the cold press of steel at her throat and the sting of the blade nicking her skin and then slicing through her shirt to expose her breasts.

He wrapped his hand around her throat. "I can see that taming you will be an adventure."

She heard the familiar sound of buttons sliding through doeskin breeches and the pungent scent of his cock just before he pushed it against her closed mouth.

"You'll suck my cock now, and if you bite me, I'll let my men have you until you're the one begging me to slit your throat."

His grip tightened around her throat, making it impossible for her to breathe through just her nose.

"Suck my cock, Violet, and then you'll only have to attend your brother's funeral and not your lover's."

She obediently opened her mouth and prepared to endure.

* * *

"Emily?"

Emily paused on the stairs and looked back at her father.

"What is it?"

"Do you have a moment to talk to me?"

She hesitated, her hand clenched on the banister. Philip had dealt with Jack's laying out and the steady stream of visitors all evening, and he looked exhausted. Helene had insisted that she would sit with the body while Philip rested. Dr. Bailey had also been given a room for the night at the house so that he was close at hand. They had no intention of leaving Jack unattended for a second.

"Please, Emily."

She sighed. She might as well face him now. His day could hardly get any worse. She came back down the stairs, and he ushered her into his study and closed the door behind them.

"Will you sit by the fire?"

He gestured to a chair and then knelt to build up the blaze, adding wood and coal from the basket on the hearth. Emily sat down and waited until he took the seat opposite her.

"What is it you want?"

He stared down at his riding boots. "I've been wanting to talk to you all day. We didn't finish our discussion about what is to be done with Mr. Smith."

Emily regarded him steadily. She wasn't used to him being so tentative. "It has already been a difficult day. Are you sure you wish to discuss this now?"

"We'll have to discuss it at some point. I suspect Smith won't wait forever."

"He will not. I saw him this morning."

Philip looked up. "Alone?"

"Certainly not. I took Ambrose with me."

"Ah." Philip returned his gaze to his boots. "And what further revelations did Mr. Smith offer you?"

Emily took a deep breath. "He merely confirmed my suspicions about something I suspected from reading my mother's letters."

"That I am a murderer?"

"No, that you are not my father." There was silence and Emily became aware of the crackle of the fire and the deep ticking of the clock on the mantelpiece. "He also asked for an extortionate sum of money, money I do not have."

"You were willing to pay him off yourself?"

"Naturally, but Ambrose said it wouldn't do, and that a man like Thomas Smith would never go away and would attempt to bleed our family dry. Smith told us it was more a matter of revenge than a matter of money, and I believed him. In his own twisted way, he loved my mother."

"Emily." Philip hesitated. "Could we set the issue of the money aside for a moment and talk about what Smith told you about your parentage?"

She met his anxious gaze. "He said that I was conceived accidentally, and that my mother had no choice but to take you into her bed again to pretend I was legitimate. Did you know?"

Philip nodded. "Yes, I even went along with it because it meant I had something to use against her." He shuddered. "That sounds harsh, but once I saw you, I was determined to keep you safe from . . . from him."

"Thomas Smith is my father, then?"

"He planted his seed, yes, but your father?" Philip hesitated, his gaze finally meeting hers. "I consider that honor to be mine."

Emily studied him for a long while. "You never made me feel anything less than loved, but this is still a shock."

"I understand that. I was a coward. I should have told you the truth. But after your mother died, I prayed that Smith would never come near our family again. I thought you were safe."

"Because you were afraid he would expose your secret?"

"Emily, for all intents and purposes, you *are* my child. Legally I am responsible for you, and you are legitimate because I was married to your mother. You have nothing to worry about."

"That is all well and good, but it doesn't answer my question."

"From the moment I held you in my arms I resolved to forget about your true parentage and just love you as my own."

"And you did." She swallowed hard. "I have never felt anything but loved."

"I'm glad of that at least, although I wish I'd had the courage to tell you the truth. I was too afraid to spoil things between us."

"Is Richard illegitimate as well?"

"No, for the first year of our marriage, Mr. Smith kept away from your mother."

"Did you tell Richard that I was not your child?"

"No, I told him that if there was anything you wanted to share with him, you would do so."

"Then why was Richard so keen to stop me going after the journal?"

Philip dropped his gaze to his desk and began to rearrange the papers. "Because Helene shared something else that might be mentioned in there. Something that doesn't reflect well on me at all."

"If this is about you murdering my mother, I would think Richard would want to retrieve that journal even more, not suggest we leave it to you."

Philip clasped his hands together and stared down at them. "No, although I'm fairly sure she writes about that as well. This is a little more personal, something I hoped to avoid you hearing about."

"Even though you told Richard."

Philip took an audible breath. "Helene thought Richard

needed a good reason to stop chasing the journal, so she told him about my unfortunate encounter with Mr. Smith."

"You *met* him?"

"I found him in your mother's bed. We fought."

"And?"

"He beat me, and then he buggered me."

Emily simply stared at Philip's bowed head as she struggled to imagine such a scene.

"And my mother did nothing?"

"She was in love with him."

"But still . . ." Emily found herself shaking her head. "I can understand why you didn't wish me to know about this."

"Thank you."

"He is a very large man."

A faint shudder ran through her father. "Yes."

"He wants five thousand guineas for the journal, or a monthly payment for the rest of his life."

"Indeed."

"I don't have that much money, and I am loathe to give it to him anyway. Ambrose said I should tell you."

"Ambrose is a very wise young man." Philip stood up and began to pace the room. "Did Smith say when and where he wished to have the money delivered to him?"

"He wanted the gold left at the Angel Inn, Islington, by Friday of this week. But I believe Seamus Kelly might already know where he is actually living. You might care to consult with him."

Philip turned to face her. "Will you trust me to take care of this matter?"

Emily held his gaze. "Only if you tell me that you won't give in to all his demands."

A smile flickered across Philip's face. "You have the heart of a warrior, my dear." He took a step toward her and held out his hand. "Do you forgive me?"

Emily studied his familiar features for a long time. "For being my true father and never holding my parentage against me?"

His smile was so tender it made her want to cry. "I could never do that. You were always mine in my heart."

Emily took his hand and he drew her close. She closed her eyes and allowed him to hold her.

"Mr. Ross, sir!"

Richard spun around and saw Patrick Kelly framed in the doorway to his lodgings. His apartment was in chaos; the bedroom door smashed off its hinges and his manservant badly shaken after being tied up. Even worse, there was no sign of Violet. They hadn't expected Mr. Brown to act quite so fast. He was still cursing himself for his stupidity.

"I have her, sir."

Richard could only nod as a wave of unexpected relief threatened to overwhelm him.

Patrick surveyed the apartment and then looked at Richard. "I took her to the pleasure house, sir. It was closest to where I found her."

Richard paused only to pat his poor servant on the shoulder before following Patrick out the door.

"She's alive?"

"Aye, sir."

"Damn it all to hell!" Richard growled. "I wasn't there to protect her."

Patrick grimaced and touched his forehead where a large purple bruise marred his pale, freckled skin. "I'm more to blame. You set me to watch her, and those bastards overwhelmed me. By the time I'd regained my senses, they'd taken her. I had to follow their carriage on foot."

They were nearing the pleasure house now, and Richard took a moment to look around him before he changed course into Barrington Square. Not many people knew the private areas of the pleasure house backed onto the house behind, and he had a suspicion that they were being followed. He would make sure that everyone at the pleasure house took special note of who was allowed into the private quarters.

"Where exactly did you find her?" Richard asked.

"It was more like she found me, sir. I was tracking the carriage and then suddenly it appeared again, the door opened, and Miss Violet was tossed out into the gutter." Patrick paused as Richard unlocked the front door. "For a moment, I feared she was dead, but when I picked her up, I saw she was breathing, so I brought her here."

"Thank you, Patrick."

Richard made his way down to the connecting basement area between the two houses, emerging into the main kitchen. Christian was sitting with Elizabeth at the table eating, but both of them looked up as Richard entered.

"I put her in your bedchamber," Christian said. "She wouldn't let me or Elizabeth help her."

"Why does she need help? Has she been injured?" Richard asked sharply.

"She's not badly hurt." Christian patted his shoulder. "She'll probably require a bath, though. Go and see for yourself."

Richard pounded up the backstairs until he reached the second level and headed for his bedchamber. He could see light under the door, but there was no sound or movement. He knocked but didn't wait for an answer before turning the latch and letting himself inside.

Violet was sitting in a chair by the fire, arms wrapped around herself, knees drawn up to her chin. Richard knelt at her feet, looked up at her, and went still.

"Who hurt you? I'll kill him."

Her face was bloodied and bruised, and her shirt was ripped beyond repair. He put his hand on her knee and she flinched.

"Don't touch me."

"Did Mr. Brown do this to you?" She wouldn't look at him, and his heart clenched with fear. "Violet . . ."

"You have to go."

She didn't sound like herself, her voice so cold and distant that it chilled him.

"I'm not leaving you."

"You don't understand. You must." She swallowed with some difficulty. "He'll kill you if you interfere with his plans."

"Does he think me so weak that I'll walk away from you at the first sign of a threat?"

"I'm not asking you to walk away from me, I'm telling you to leave." She bit her already bloodied lip. "I don't want you anymore."

"And I don't believe you." He rose to his feet and went to pull the servant's bell. "You need to bathe and then we'll talk about this properly."

"I don't *want* to talk to you."

He stared down at her. "I'm not giving you a choice. You forced me away from you once before, and I've regretted it ever since. I'm not going to let you ruin both our lives again."

While they waited for the bath to be filled, Richard helped himself to a large brandy and silently observed his shivering companion. She was covered in mud and other unpleasant substances from her fall in the gutter, her shirt had been deliberately sliced open, and someone had hit her. That last made him want to find Mr. Brown and slowly strangle him.

After the servants had left, he walked toward her. "Let me help you out of your boots."

She stared at him and shook her head. "I can do it myself, and I would appreciate you leaving while I bathe."

He returned her stare with interest. "I'm not leaving you alone." He crouched in front of her and grabbed the heel of her muddy boot. "Brace yourself."

He put the boots outside the door to be cleaned and turned

back to Violet. The expression on her face as she attempted to remove her coat made him furious all over again.

"He didn't just slap your face, did he? Where else are you hurt?" He eased her out of her coat and waistcoat, and realized her cravat had already disappeared. Her shirt almost fell off it was so badly ripped.

"Damnation. Where else are you in pain?"

She wrapped her arms around her chest and allowed him to help her out of her riding breeches and underthings.

"One of his men punched me in the stomach."

She sounded as if she might swoon, and he steadied her against his side. "What else?"

"Nothing."

She shuddered convulsively as he helped her into the bath. He didn't believe her, but he'd let her bathe first before he demanded anything else. Her clothes lay in a pile on the carpet and he gathered them in his arms.

"This lot is only fit for the rubbish heap. I'll put them outside."

She nodded, her eyes closed, her head against the back of the metal bath. He could see fingermarks encircling the slim column of her throat. Knowing she was safe, at least for the moment, but worried that she might faint, Richard took the pile of clothing to the door. The scent of blood stung at his nostrils along with something else, something musky and male.

He paused at the door and touched her ripped shirt, which was stiff with blood and other substances. With another curse, he dumped the clothes on the floor and returned to the bath. For a moment, he panicked as he saw her dark head disappear under the bath water. Just as he was about to yank her up again, she surfaced and rubbed the washcloth over her face and then over her mouth again and again and again.

Richard sat on the nearest chair and carefully studied what he could see of her body. There were rope marks on her wrists and upper arms where she'd been tied up. He could also see her breasts now, bruises and broken skin where someone had touched her. The heat of his anger was replaced by a cold rage that made his hands shake.

"Did he rape you?"

The cloth stilled and she didn't look at him.

"Did he?"

She sighed. "No." She wiped her face again.

"Are you sure? I smell his seed on your clothing."

"That's because he made me—" She swallowed convulsively.

"Made you what?"

"Suck his cock."

Richard stared at her bowed head. "I'm going to kill him very slowly and *feed* him his own bloody cock for that." He took a calming breath. "Is it Lord Keyes?"

"No, I think I would have recognized his voice."

"You were blindfolded?"

"Yes."

Richard nodded and went to retrieve the large drying sheet he had left to warm by the fire.

"Are you ready to come out of the bath?"

She shivered. "I don't think I'll ever be ready, or I'll ever be clean."

Richard reached over the bath and picked her up. She clung to him, soaking his coat and shirt. He wrapped her in the bath sheet and sat her on his knee in front of the fire.

After a long while, she nudged him with her nose. "You should not be here."

"Don't start that again." He kissed the top of her head.

"He said that if I didn't leave you and come to him, he would kill you. I can't let him do that."

"Did he threaten you before or after he forced you to suck his cock?"

She sighed and nestled closer. "I couldn't stop him."

"Of course, you couldn't."

"It was . . . horrible."

He smoothed her still-damp hair. "I'm sure it was."

She licked her lips. "But I can't seem to get rid of his taste."

Mindful of her swollen lip, he kissed her very gently. "When you feel better, I'll kiss you until you taste of nothing but me. I'll fuck you so much that you'll smell just like me, dripping wet, full of my come." He kissed her again. "I'll hold your breasts in my hands and slide my cock between them and come all over you. I'll come in your mouth as many times as you'll have me, or in your arse, or your cunt, whatever you need so that you'll not think of him ever again. You'll only taste of me, of us."

He felt her relax against him and smiled against her hair. "And now I'm going to put you to bed so that you can sleep for a while."

She opened her mouth. "You won't . . . ?"

"I won't do anything until you are feeling better, I promise." He held her wary gaze. "We are in this together."

"Thank you."

He lifted her into his arms, took her over to his bed, and tucked her in.

"Sleep for a while. I'll make sure that everything is well at Knowles House and that Jack is safe."

He left a candle burning by the side of the bed and made his way down the back stairs toward the kitchen. Without saying a word to the staff assembled in the warm, cozy space, he kept walking and descended into the cellar until he could go no farther. He picked up the nearest wine bottle and smashed it hard against the wall, then reached for another.

"Could you choose something a little less expensive next time, brother?"

He looked up to see Christian on the last step and slowly lowered the bottle he had clenched in his hand.

"What do you recommend?"

"Anything to the left of you." Christian sat down on the bottom step. "Might I ask why you feel the need to destroy perfectly good wine?"

Richard smashed another bottle and then stared at the reddish pool of wine that was now trickling down onto the stone floor. "I can't get my hands on the man I really want to destroy, so this will have to suffice." He inhaled the heady bouquet of the rich wine. "He touched her, Christian. That bastard *fondled* and hurt her." His harsh breathing echoed around the stone vault.

"Then he deserves to die," Christian said. "Do you feel better now?"

"A little."

"Then might I suggest we return to the kitchen? There is a note for you from our father."

Violet waited until she was certain that Richard had left and then cautiously opened her eyes. She didn't have time to wait to see if Jack was still presumed dead. If Mr. Brown believed it was true, that was all she needed to know. She eased herself out of the warm covers and considered what to do next. Richard had taken all her clothes and, in truth, she had no wish to wear any of them again. But there had to be some garments either in Richard's room or one of the others. Thank goodness he hadn't thought to lock her in.

It took her longer than she wanted, but eventually she assembled the basic necessities for a gentleman to wear and put them on. God, she hurt in so many places it was hard to stay on her feet, but she had no choice. She couldn't allow Richard to suffer again. And, in truth, she wanted the pleasure of killing Mr. Brown herself. If she survived that, perhaps she could come back to Richard on her own terms with nothing between them but love.

With a last longing look back at the bed, she let herself out of the room and crept down the servants' stairs until she emerged into the blackness of the night on Barrington Square.

"So Jack Lennox is 'dead,' his twin is under suspicion of murdering him, but there is no hard evidence to support this, and you hope there never will be." Christian studied Richard across the table.

"Yes."

"And Vincent Lennox is currently under my roof after being beaten by a spymaster who wants everyone connected with his despicable crimes dead. Do I have this right?"

"Yes."

"And why didn't anyone tell me about this before?" Christian demanded.

"Because you didn't need to know," Richard replied. He shoved a hand through his already disordered hair. "Now we just have to wait for Mr. Brown to try and contact Violet after Jack's funeral."

"You think you'll be able to stop him kidnapping her this time, do you?"

Richard glared at his half brother. "Don't remind me. I already have Patrick Kelly watching her every move."

Christian took a sip of his brandy. "What I don't understand is why you don't just wait for Helene to discover the identity of this gentleman for you."

"Because Violet and Jack had already been threatened and I was afraid that if we waited too long, one of them would really be killed." Richard groaned and buried his face in his hands. "And Violet threatened to take on Mr. Brown by herself."

Christian consulted Philip's note. "Father says that Jack's death seems to have been accepted by the majority of the *ton*, and that he is going to arrange for the burial on Friday. In the meantime, how do you intend to clear Vincent's name?"

"I don't need to. If we get our hands on Mr. Brown, we can blame him for everything and reinstate the Lennoxes' reputation and hopefully their father's estate to them."

"And if you don't?"

"I can't even contemplate that." Richard rose from the table. "I need to go and see if Violet is awake, and tell her how things are progressing. You'll make sure that none of the staff gossip about her presence here?"

"Naturally." Christian inclined his head. "Might I suggest that she dresses as a woman while she is here? That will definitely confuse matters."

"I'll suggest it to her." Richard hesitated before he turned to the door. "Thank you, Christian."

"You are welcome. I only wish someone had thought to include me in all the excitement." He smiled at Richard. "I also think Violet Lennox will make you a fine wife."

Richard grimaced. "If she'll have me."

"She's in love with you. She'll have you."

"If only it were that simple."

Christian sat forward. "It is, Richard. Just don't let anything else get in your way."

"I'll do my best. By the way, when Ambrose comes back, will you tell him that Philip wishes to see him?"

"I will."

Richard left Christian drinking his wine in the kitchen and walked slowly back up the stairs to his bedchamber. As soon as he opened the door his gaze went to the bed and his heart seemed to jolt in his chest. Violet wasn't there. He checked the whole room, but there was no sign of her. With a curse, he turned on his heel and ran back down to the basement.

As he burst into the kitchen, Seamus Kelly came in through the back door.

"It's all right, Mr. Ross. Patrick followed her. She's gone back to Harcourt House."

Richard sank down onto the nearest solid surface and struggled to breathe. At least she was safe—at least he knew that. But it wasn't enough.

"Why in damnation did she run?"

"Because she is a woman and she loves you."

"What?" He slowly raised his head to stare at Christian, who was still sitting calmly at the table.

"She wants to protect you."

"Then she is a fool! I'm the one who should be protecting her!"

"If she is anything like the other women in our family, she probably doesn't see it like that."

Richard looked down at his trembling hands and imagined them around Violet's throat. "When I find her, I'm going to . . ."

"May I give you some brotherly advice?" Christian turned fully to look at him. "At the moment, Violet is safe and well protected at Harcourt House. I'll send more men to make sure of that. Why not leave her there until your temper settles down and she realizes she needs your help?"

Richard glared at Christian for a long moment. "You're right. Do you think she'll realize she needs me?"

"I'm always right." Christian smiled. "Hopefully she'll realize it *before* she puts herself into any more danger."

"That isn't very reassuring," Richard muttered.

"I know."

24

"Ah, Ambrose. It is so good of you to assist me in this matter."

Ambrose waited until Lord Knowles sat behind his desk before taking the seat in front of him. When Christian had told him that Lord Knowles wished to speak to him, Ambrose had briefly considered not going. Emily had told him to wait until she had spoken to her father about their decision to marry, and she hadn't told him anything to contradict that.

He straightened his spine anyway. If Lord Knowles wished to discuss his relationship with Emily, he was more than willing to do so. After speaking to a delighted Jethro the evening before, he now knew he had a secure job to move on to and a place for Emily to call home that wasn't associated with the pleasure house.

He realized Lord Knowles was speaking and refocused his attention.

"As I was saying, Emily told me about her conversations with Thomas Smith and the excellent advice you gave her to seek my help anew."

Ambrose shrugged. "I thought it best, my lord."

"And I'm glad you did. Emily can be rather stubborn. From what I understand from my wife, you are one of the few people she listens to."

"You know that Miss Ross and I are friends?"

"How could I not?" Lord Knowles's smile was warm. "The minx has spent more time chatting to you in the kitchens of the pleasure house than she has dancing at any ball."

"I hope that hasn't given any offense, my lord."

"Why should it? You are an exceptional man and a good friend of Christian's. Who better to trust my daughter with?"

"As to that, sir . . ."

"I wanted to talk to you about Seamus Kelly." Philip talked over him and Ambrose subsided. "I understand from Emily that on your instructions, he followed Mr. Smith to a different address. Did Seamus locate the journal?"

"Unfortunately, Seamus didn't have time to get into Mr. Smith's rooms, but he did find out where he was lodging."

"Excellent. Do you think he could show me where it is?"

"You intend to confront him, my lord?"

"I do." Philip's expression hardened. "I intend to retrieve that journal and make certain that Mr. Smith never troubles a member of my family again."

"Might I accompany you, my lord?"

Lord Knowles studied Ambrose for a long moment. "You may. I intend to surprise him tonight."

"Before Mr. Jack Lennox's funeral." Ambrose cleared his throat. "Will Miss Ross be attending the funeral?"

Philip sat back and folded his hands together on the desk. "I can hardly keep her away when she considered herself affianced to the man, can I?"

"And if she wasn't engaged to him?"

"Emily will make her own mind up as to exactly where her feelings lie."

Ambrose took a deep breath. "I think she already has, my lord."

"And why might you think that?"

"Because I would like to ask for her hand in marriage."

Philip considered him. "Does she return your regard?"

"I believe so. I will no longer be working at the pleasure house. I have savings and I have secured a position as a schoolteacher at a new Methodist school in east London." Ambrose remembered to breathe. "I will be able to support her quite well, if not to the style to which she is accustomed."

"I don't think Emily will care about that if she loves you."

Ambrose met Lord Knowles's calm gaze. "I think she does, and I love her more than anything." He shifted his feet. "Unless you feel that a man of my color should not marry someone of hers?"

"Why should I care about that? It is for Emily to decide, and having turned down several very eligible gentlemen of the *ton*, I suspect she knew what she wanted all along."

"I have no knowledge of my parents or my family, my lord. If Mr. Delornay hadn't rescued me from the streets, I'd probably be dead by now."

"But he did rescue you, and you have grown into an estimable young man of good character. A man I would be proud to include in my family—officially. You have always been part of the pleasure house family."

Ambrose struggled to speak. "Thank you, my lord."

"Thank me after we have dealt with Mr. Smith and gotten through the funeral tomorrow. *Then* we will have time to discuss your plans with Emily." Philip stood and held out his hand. "I'll tell my wife, if that is acceptable to you. She has long been your champion and suspected which way the wind was blowing."

"She has?" Ambrose shook Philip's proffered hand.

"Helene is a remarkable woman in many ways. Now, do

you wish to stay and dine with us, or do you need to get back to the pleasure house?"

"I need to speak to Seamus and bring him back here with me for tonight."

"That's true. Perhaps you could both meet me here at nine?"

"Certainly, my lord." Ambrose turned to leave. "And thank you."

It wasn't until he was out on the street that he managed to breathe again and promptly startled an elderly couple by letting out a whoop of pure joy. Lord Knowles hadn't ordered him from his sight for daring to fall in love with his daughter. In truth, he had made Ambrose feel as if he would be a welcome addition to the family.

Family.

Ambrose stopped walking and his vision blurred. Emily loved him and her family seemed ready to accept him. As Jethro had been telling him for years. He was, indeed, truly blessed.

Violet studied Jack carefully, but he looked remarkably well for a man who was to be buried the next morning. The Delornay family had managed to find a suitable corpse to substitute for Jack in the elaborate coffin that now sat in state at the local chapel. Jack had been secreted in the attics of Knowles House and was apparently unaffected by all the uproar.

"You seem well," Violet said.

"What did you expect?" Jack stood up and stretched. "I've a few bruises from when the horse came down on me, but other than that I'm fine." He studied her carefully. "In fact, I look a lot better than you do. What happened?"

"I finally met Mr. Brown."

"And?"

"It wasn't a pleasant experience. He gave me time to attend

your funeral, and after that he expects me to leave Richard and come to him."

"I assume you told him to go to the devil."

"I did. Richard and I had already agreed that there was no point in me pretending I could kill you and not suffer for it. When I refused to go to him, Mr. Brown grew angry." She drew an unsteady breath. "He said he would have Richard killed if I didn't obey him."

Jack sat down on the side of his bed. "So you decided to be noble and run away from Richard again." At her look of surprise, he shrugged. "I might be dead, but I've been listening to all the gossip from the staff."

Violet winced. "Don't say it like that." She sat next to Jack on the bed. "I can't let Richard be killed. I love him. I have to stop Mr. Brown by myself."

"Violet, if Richard had ordered you to keep out of the way while he saved you from Mr. Brown, how would you have felt?"

"He *did* try, but when I refused, he understood it was important for me to be involved."

"Then why can't you see that he needs to be involved in this too? Whether he has mentioned it or not, the man loves you, Violet. You need to give him the opportunity to feel like you are in this fix together."

Violet sighed. "I just want this to end. I want to live out the rest of my life in a sea of quiet tranquility. Is that too much to ask? I want a home and a family, but it is so hard to trust anyone, isn't it?"

Jack squeezed her hand. "After our past, indeed it is, but I think Richard would die for you if you let him."

"But that's the whole point. I don't want him to die."

"Then work with him and save each other." Jack kissed her cheek. "I can't wait to attend my own funeral tomorrow. You are going to be there, aren't you?"

"Yes, I am. Even though I am under suspicion, no one has been able to prove I did anything to your horse. I doubt I'll be welcome, but the Knowles family name will protect me."

Noises floated up from the stairwell below and Violet stiffened. "I should go. I don't want Richard finding me here."

"Still skittish, my love?" Jack walked over to the door and pushed it open a crack. "I don't think they are coming up. You're quite safe."

Violet crossed to the small attic window and pulled back the tattered curtain. She carefully climbed out on the roof and smiled back at her twin.

"I'll see you tomorrow, Jack."

"If you don't slip on those infernal roof tiles."

She blew him a kiss. He had always been far more afraid of heights than she was. "Good night. I'm so glad you aren't really dead."

He waved her off, and she carefully scrambled over the rooftop and shimmied down the drainpipe at the corner. From there it was a matter of minutes back to Harcourt House. She noticed a large shadow detach itself from the row of elm trees. A glimmer of light from the streetlamp illuminated Patrick Kelly's red hair and she relaxed.

Just as she was about to run for the safety of the next alleyway, a hackney pulled up at the front of the Knowles mansion and Violet pressed herself against the wall. She watched two very familiar figures alight from the vehicle and go up the steps to the front door. Why were Ambrose and Seamus Kelly visiting at such a late hour?

A gust of wind with a hint of rain blew around the corner into her face. She decided it was better to find shelter at Harcourt House than stand outside in the dark speculating about the goings-on at the Ross's house. Jack was safe and that was all that concerned her. Tomorrow she would have to deal with both Richard and Mr. Brown. She definitely needed her rest.

* * *

Ambrose glanced back down the steps.

"Is Patrick here? I thought he was guarding Violet Lennox."

"He is, sir," Seamus replied, his gaze following Ambrose's. "Mayhap Miss Lennox decided to visit her brother."

"That wouldn't surprise me at all. She seems to be the adventurous type," Ambrose said. "She'll fit well into the Delornay-Ross clan."

The door opened and they stepped inside out of the cold. Before the butler could even announce their arrival, Lord Knowles came into the hallway, already dressed to leave.

"Good, you are here. Seamus, do you remember how to get to Mr. Smith's lodgings?"

"I do, sir." Seamus nodded. "It's a fair step from here, but not too difficult to find if you know your way."

"Then let's be off."

Violet carefully let herself into her bedroom at Harcourt House and stood for a moment regaining her breath and considering the quality of the silence around her. Something was different. She remained by the window and without turning her head, let her gaze travel around the small room. With a small sigh, she withdrew her dagger and walked over to the curtained bed.

Of course, he'd known where she was, but he'd respected her enough to allow her the time to come to terms with what had happened. A surge of love shook through her.

She placed the tip of the blade against his neck until he flinched. "You should not be here."

"Are you going to slit my throat?"

Richard's quiet tone stirred something within her and she sheathed the dagger. As her eyes became accustomed to the dark, she saw that he was naked—the bed covers drawn up to his hips, the linen raised over the thrust of his already erect cock. She slowly took off her clothes and climbed on top of him, heard his soft groan as his cock brushed her skin.

She smoothed her hands over the planes of his chest, making his nipples harden under her palms and his cock jerk against her belly. She leaned over him, allowing her breasts to drift over his mouth, and let him suckle her hard as she rocked against him.

"Ah, God," he murmured. "I needed you. I couldn't stay away any longer."

She knelt up and grasped his shaft at the base, drawing it away from his flat stomach, and brushed the wet crown against her clit until they were both groaning. Shifting her stance, she started to lower herself down over him, taking him in inch by inch, watching him watch himself being engulfed.

When he was fully inside her, she rose and fell over him again and again until she was gasping his name. His hand slid from her hip to her sex and he played with her clit, bringing her to a peak of pleasure that tightened her internal muscles until she could feel every thick inch of his throbbing cock.

"I love you, Violet. *Je t'aime.*"

She closed her eyes against the pleasure and felt him groan and start to come, the heat of his seed pulsing deep inside her. With a soft sound, she collapsed over him and he held her steady, his arms wrapped around her.

"Violet, please listen to me. I know you don't want Mr. Brown to kill me, but you must let me help you destroy him. If he kills you, what point is there to my existence?" He kissed the top of her head. "I need you. I've been unhappy without you—unhappy for years. Once this is over, we can get married."

She opened her eyes. "You want to marry me?"

"I've had enough of this aimless existence. I want to settle down and be very boring for the rest of my life. Could you stand that?"

She buried her face in his chest to hide both her smile and the sudden onset of tears. "Yes, I believe I could."

"Then it is quite simple. We'll defeat Mr. Brown and live happily ever after."

Violet realized she had nothing to add to that but a fervent prayer that her lover would be proved right.

Ambrose waited for Lord Knowles's nod before he used his old skills to unlock the door to Mr. Smith's rooms. They'd used a series of bribes to placate the landlord of the small tavern and his staff to encourage them to turn a blind eye to any goings-on. A loud snoring sound came from within the bedroom, indicating that their prey was not only present, but sleeping without a thought of being interrupted.

While Lord Knowles and Seamus went into the bedroom, Ambrose paused to light a candle from the embers of the fire in the grate. The sound of cursing quickly muffled brought a savage smile to Ambrose's face as he took the sparse light through to Mr. Smith's bedroom.

Seamus had already gotten the older man in a headlock and was busy tying him to his bed while Philip held a dagger to Smith's throat. Ambrose put the candle down on the bedside table and helped Seamus move Smith into an upright position and bind him tightly.

Philip waited until Smith stopped trying to fight his bonds, and then stepped back into the light.

"Do you remember me, Mr. Smith?"

"I always remember men I've buggered, especially the ones I left bloodied and beaten." Smith spat in Lord Knowles's direction. "How are you, Mr. Ross, your lordship, as you are now?"

"I'd be better if you hadn't tried to extort money from my children."

"I promised your wife I'd get you back for all those years of misery you put her through."

"She chose to marry me, Smith."

"You know she had no bloody choice!"

"I offered her one. It's hardly my fault that she didn't take me up on it."

"She was a child!"

"We were both children." Lord Knowles leaned forward. "And now you seek to make another generation pay for our sins."

"And why not? You and your children have everything and I have nothing."

Lord Knowles nodded to Ambrose. "Search the place for that journal and anything else you can find."

Still keeping an eye on the enraged figure on the bed, Ambrose started to search for the journal.

"You seem to forget that I've already paid you off once before, Mr. Smith."

"Oh, that." Smith scoffed. "That wasn't enough."

"Obviously. And therein lies my problem. What *will* be enough? How do I know that you won't be back in another few years to blackmail my family again?"

"You can afford it."

Lord Knowles sat down at the end of the bed and studied his captive. "I can certainly afford to pay you off once more, but it would be far cheaper to simply dispose of you once and for all." He glanced up at Seamus. "I'm sure you could arrange that for me, Mr. Kelly, couldn't you?"

"Aye, my lord. All we'd have to do would be to knock him out and leave him down by the docks. The whores and thieves would soon pick him clean and dump his body in the drink."

"Sounds like justice to me, Mr. Kelly. What do you think, Smith?"

"You'd never know if I had died, though, would you?"

"True, but there is another way." Lord Knowles drew a folded document out from inside his coat. "If you agree to my terms, you could find yourself leaving for Australia tomorrow morning at high tide with a goodly sum of money."

Smith's eyes narrowed. "How much?"

"Five thousand guineas if you return the journal and anything else my wife gave you to use against me." Lord Knowles unfolded the papers. "When you reach Australia, the captain of your ship will give you a letter to my man of business there to acquire your money."

"But what if I miss England and want to return?"

"That, Smith, is not my concern. If you come back here, I *will* kill you, as will my heir and my daughter's husband. There will be no more chances for you."

Ambrose had no luck finding the journal and turned to tell Lord Knowles so. Smith was still staring at them as if he couldn't decide what to do. Ambrose found himself hoping the man would refuse the deal. He would gain a certain satisfaction at seeing the man who had made Emily cry die a painful death.

"What guarantee do I have that you will give me the money?" Smith asked.

"When you go onboard the ship, the captain will show you the chest full of coins he carries in my name. You can personally escort the chest to my overseer and make sure the money is paid directly to you." Lord Knowles held out the sheaf of documents. "All the arrangements are written down here. Perhaps you would care to look them over."

Smith nodded, and Lord Knowles brought the documents closer to him and angled the candle so that he could see them more clearly. Seamus returned from his search equally empty-handed, and Ambrose stood back and considered where else they might search the cramped rooms.

"All right, I'll do it." Smith's voice sounded loud in the silence.

"Then hand over the journal and anything else my wife gave you."

Smith jerked his head toward the fireplace. "There's a box up the chimney, about an arm's length at the back on a ledge."

Seamus wrapped his arm in a blanket, knelt in front of the still-warm fire, and carefully felt around. "It's here, my lord."

He brought the box over to the bed and Philip opened it. There were two journals, not one, and a piece of jewelry. Lord Knowles took the books and picked up the gold locket. When he snapped open the catch, Ambrose saw a portrait of a dark-haired woman who reminded him of Emily. Lord Knowles shut the locket and tossed it toward Smith.

"You may keep this if you wish."

Smith stared at Lord Knowles and Ambrose held his breath. "You want to kill me, so why not just do it? No one would know or care what happened to a nonentity like me."

Lord Knowles gestured at the locket. "Because of her. Because you truly loved Anne, and it's the last thing I can ever do for her." He abruptly stood up. "Seamus will stay with you until the rest of my men arrive and escort you to the ship. It leaves at high tide on the morrow."

He nodded at Ambrose, who picked up the journals.

"Good bye, Mr. Smith. I hope I never have to clap eyes on you again in this life."

Ambrose followed Lord Knowles out to the carriage and waited until Lord Knowles gave the coachmen his orders.

"Do you want to take the journals, my lord?"

"I suppose I should read them to make sure that if Smith does come back, I am prepared." He sighed. "The thought doesn't appeal to me."

"But better to know than not, sir, surely."

"That's true." There was a long pause while Lord Knowles looked out of the window. "Do you think I did the right thing?"

"By letting him go?"

"Yes."

Ambrose reflected on that last conversation and all that had gone before it, decades of unhappiness, of thwarted love, and sexual indiscretion. It reminded him of his own recent conversation with Lady Kendrick and his decision to let the past go.

"I think you did the best thing for your conscience, my lord, and that is what is important."

"Thank you." Lord Knowles sat back with a sigh. "Now all we have to do is survive Jack Lennox's funeral tomorrow, capture this spymaster, and all will be well in our world—or, at least, I hope it will."

Ambrose could only silently agree.

25

Richard wasn't sure if it was a good or a bad sign that the church service for Jack Lennox was so well attended. They hadn't advertised it, but the small chapel was quite full. Mrs. Lennox looked suitably pale and had to be supported up the aisle to her seat by Philip. Richard performed a similar service for Emily, who had draped herself in long, flowing veils and sobbed constantly into her handkerchief.

As he tenderly assisted her into the front pew, he bent to whisper in her ear. "You missed your true calling, Em. You should have gone on the stage."

Her muffled chuckle was for his ears only. "I must admit I am quite enjoying myself. I almost wish I could fling myself into the grave, but ladies aren't supposed to attend the actual burial service, are they?"

Richard wished he could enjoy the occasion more, but he was too busy scanning the congregation for signs of either Violet or the ubiquitous Mr. Brown. In truth, if Mr. Brown were here, it would be easier to spot him once the mainly female attendees went back to Knowles House for the funeral breakfast.

He sat through the service, allowing Emily to clutch at his sleeve and shudder with sobs.

When it drew to a close, he tenderly handed Emily into a waiting carriage and went to find Philip. The chapel graveyard was almost full, but his father had used his influence to obtain a secluded spot for Jack up against the far wall under a row of weeping willows. Richard shivered as he picked his way through the uneven lines of gravestones, some of them already blackened with decay, the engraved names barely visible.

Standing by an open grave did make a man reflect on his own mortality. What if Jack had really died? He was younger than Richard. What if it had been Violet? Richard found himself crossing himself like a papist at that horrific thought. In truth, it could still be Violet if they didn't manage to apprehend Mr. Brown as quickly as possible. And he wanted her to be his wife, desired that more than anything he had ever wanted in his life before.

A slight movement in the frigid air to his right drew his attention to a slender, black-coated figure. He half-turned to see Violet approaching the funeral party, her face pale, her eyes downcast beneath the brim of her hat. She remained at the back of the crowd. He wasn't even sure if anyone else had seen her. He also noticed Patrick Kelly a discreet step behind her. He prayed it would be enough to keep her safe as Jack's coffin was lowered into the ground and the vicar spoke his final words over the grave.

As the last shovel of earth covered the new mound, Richard let out his breath, which immediately condensed in the coldness of the air. Most of the mourners began to move toward the assembled carriages, their pace quickening, anxious to get out of the cold and away from such morbid surroundings.

Philip went, too, glancing back at Richard with a slight nod as he shepherded the vicar along with him. The wind blew through the dark-set trees as a lone figure finally approached the grave. Richard withdrew back into the shelter of a large mausoleum and watched Violet fall to her knees in front of the mound and bow her head as if in prayer.

He located his pistol and drew it out of his pocket, checked that it was loaded and that the powder wasn't damp. How much time would Mr. Brown give Violet? During their planning, that had been the question that had troubled them most. Mr. Brown had acted so swiftly to capture Violet last time that the consensus was that he would do the same again. Richard forced himself to lean back against the cold stone and wait.

While she knelt on the unforgiving ground, Violet mourned all of those who had died because of Mr. Brown's greed. She had no idea how long she grieved, all she knew was that her body was shaking from the cold and that her knees ached. Mr. Brown had decimated her family, her mother, her father. . . . She tensed as the scent of bergamot and lemon curled around her, but she didn't move. She had yet to pray for God's forgiveness when she deliberately took a man's life.

"Miss Lennox."

She slowly made the sign of the cross and then stood up, turning slowly to face the man behind her. To her surprise, his face was quite unremarkable, almost nondescript, but then that was probably an advantage in his chosen profession. He would blend in anywhere. She judged him to be about twenty years her senior, his hair graying at the temples, and traced faint lines around his eyes and mouth.

Who was it that said the eyes were a window to a person's soul? She couldn't remember, but looking into his pale, dead gaze was like staring into an abyss. She suddenly shivered and he smiled.

"I knew you'd come."

She could only nod her head.

He held out his hand. "It's time for you to complete your part of the bargain and come away with me."

She placed her hand in his and gasped as the barrel of a pistol prodded her ribs. Although she knew that Patrick Kelly and Richard were watching her, she also knew they would be unable to reach her before her captor pulled the trigger. Her brain seemed to come out of its trance, but her feet kept walking.

"Don't think about fighting me, Miss Lennox. I have men stationed all around the perimeter of the graveyard. We'll find a quiet spot by the chapel wall where you will be quite overcome with guilt for murdering your brother and blow your own brains out. I've even written you a suicide note."

"How kind of you. I thought we were going to be together for the rest of our lives."

"I did consider it, my dear, but it seems that in the end you are just too sentimental for your own good. You fell in love, and that is the ultimate weakness."

They were close to the high exterior wall that bordered the rear of the chapel and the shadows were lengthening. A flicker of motion warned Violet that Richard and Patrick were attempting to reach her, but there wasn't enough time. Well, if Mr. Brown insisted she was going to die, the least she could do was make it look like a suicide pact.

She pretended to stumble, and as he recoiled, she was able to release her primed pistol from her pocket and shove it under his chin.

"I hope you wrote a note to cover your own death, Mr. Brown."

He went still and brought his pistol up to her head. Behind him, Richard shouted her name. Mr. Brown turned them both slowly toward him.

The grim determination on Richard's face turned to shock and he lowered his pistol.

"Lord *Denley?*"

"I'm sorry it has to be like this, Richard. After I told you that Violet was a traitor, I was hoping you'd kill her for me. Unfortunately, you decided to forgive her."

"But you're a *cripple!*"

"Obviously not." Lord Denley tightened his grip on Violet's arm. "Now, do put away your gun, dear boy, and accept that Violet wants to come away with me."

Violet stared straight at Richard. "Don't believe him. He intends to kill me."

Richard held her gaze and raised his pistol again, the agony of betrayal ripe on his face. "I trusted you, Denley. I thought of you as a *father.*"

"Which is why I am offering you the chance to walk away."

Richard shook his head. "I can't do that."

Lord Denley laughed. "I'll kill her before you can kill me."

The barrel of Richard's pistol wavered. Behind him, a dark shape materialized on top of the high cemetery wall, making Violet blink.

"Leave me, Richard," she whispered. "Save yourself." She pushed her own pistol against Lord Denley's throat.

"No, I can't let you do that!" Richard protested.

"Are you absolutely sure that you have the right Lennox twin, Mr. Brown?"

Lord Denley's head jerked upward toward the wall. *"What?"*

The instant she heard Jack's voice, Violet relaxed her knees and rolled as far away from Lord Denley as she could. The deafening roar of two pistols firing at close range made her ears ring. The smell of gunpowder mingled with something more visceral made her feel sick. With a shaking hand, she disarmed her own pistol and crawled over to the wall, putting her back to it.

Richard was running toward her, followed by Patrick Kelly, and both of them were shouting. She wrapped her arms around her raised knees and stared at Lord Denley's beautifully polished boots. His arms were flung out, his pistol still smoking, and his face . . . She swallowed hard. She couldn't look at the bloodied remains of his head. Jack had always been a damned fine shot.

"Violet, Violet!" Richard was holding her by the shoulders and shaking her now. "Are you injured? Did he hurt you?"

She could only stare at him and shiver like a newborn foal. Jack crouched down next to her and briefly touched her face. She could only thank God that neither of them had been wounded.

"You didn't have to do that for me," she whispered. "I was quite willing to kill him myself."

"And be killed?" Jack glanced at Richard, who stood up and began shouting for someone to help remove Lord Denley's body. "I didn't want you to have that stain on your soul."

"I've killed before."

"I know, but that is all finished with now." He took her hand, his gaze intense. "You wanted a new beginning, and now you have the chance to have it with Richard at your side."

She brought his hand to her lips and kissed it. "Thank you, my twin. I only wish you didn't have this on your conscience either."

He shrugged. "I'm a dead man. I have no conscience." He looked up as Richard came back toward them and rose to his feet. "Take care of her, Mr. Ross. I'll go and tell Lord Knowles the good news."

She nodded and managed a shaky smile for Richard, who took up Jack's vacated position at her side.

"Do you think you can walk, or shall I carry you?"

Before she could reply, he scooped her up in his arms and was striding toward the nearest carriage. He dumped her on the seat and climbed in after her. The carriage moved off, and he came down on his knees and buried his face in her lap. She stroked his hair and realized he was shaking as much as she was.

"I can't believe Lord Denley was Mr. Brown all along. I'm such a bloody fool. By going to him, I almost sealed your death warrant."

"No, you didn't. You forced him to have to plan to kill all of us and do it quickly. You made him reveal himself to us." She patted his shoulder. "It is all over now."

"When Jack appeared on that wall, I thought . . ."

"I know."

He raised his head to look at her. "Let's get married and live a very safe and unexceptional life in the countryside with our many well-behaved children."

She smiled tremulously at him. "You'll get bored."

"I won't, I swear it." He hoisted himself up to sit beside her. "As long as you are there to keep me happy."

"And we can escape to the pleasure house every once in a while."

He kissed her very gently on the mouth. "Whatever it takes to keep you from losing interest in me, my love."

She cupped his chin. "I'll never do that." She shivered. "I can't believe 'Mr. Brown' is really dead."

"You'll believe it when Jack is raised from the dead and takes control of his inheritance, making all charges against you meaningless." He put his arm around her. "It will probably take some time. I'll suggest to Philip that I take you away to the Continent for a prolonged wedding trip. By the time we return, everyone will have forgotten about poor Vincent Lennox and see only the Honorable Mrs. Richard Ross, my new wife and the love of my life."

"Oh, Richard, you make it sound so easy."

"It is." He smiled at her. "Christian told me that when it came down to it, nothing should be allowed to get in the way of my love for you. And when I thought I had lost you—" He swallowed hard. "I promised myself that if you survived, I would never make that mistake again. That I would take you, and love you, and never ever let you go."

She simply stared at him until he drew her back into his arms and kissed her. "Perhaps you should listen to Christian more often."

He drew back with a mock frown. "One piece of good advice does not make up for everything else he has subjected me to over the years." His smile grew tender. "But I might even thank him for this."

She kissed him again and finally managed to stop shaking.

EPILOGUE

By the *ton's* standards, it wasn't a large wedding, but Helene considered it far superior in many ways. For one, it meant she was able to attend and not have to listen to the members of the *ton* either ignoring her or gossiping about her behind her back. When that inevitably happened, it made Philip angry on her behalf, and she didn't want to spoil a day that was so special for him.

After consulting with the happy couples, they had decided to invite only those people who were intimately connected with the Delornay-Ross family through blood or through their connection with the pleasure house. Helene smoothed down the skirts of her blue satin dress and contemplated the rapidly filling pews.

The pleasure house staff filled the back seats; Seamus and Patrick Kelly's red hair and height made them easy to spot. Marie-Claude sat in between them wearing a new bonnet with cream ostrich feathers curling at the brim. Just in front of the servants sat the plainly dressed couple Ambrose had invited and Lady Mary Kendrick. Helene waved at her daughter Marguerite and her husband, Lord Anthony Sokorvsky, who had chosen to sit in a row that also contained Lord Valentin Sokorvsky and his wife, Sara.

Philip came up behind Helene and touched her shoulder.

"Are you almost ready to take your seat, my love?"

"Yes, I am." She took a deep breath. "This is a magical day, isn't it? All our children will be married."

"Leaving us free to do anything we wish?"

She smiled into his beloved eyes. "Indeed, although I have promised the Lennox twins that I will return to France and meet with their grandmother."

"That is remarkably brave of you." He kissed her hand. "As Christian is too busy keeping an eye on his charges, let me escort you to your seat."

Helene smiled at her various acquaintances as she walked up the aisle and took her seat in the front pew. Philip left her and a gust of air from the opening of the door into the side chapel announced the arrival of the two grooms and their supporters. Ambrose had Christian by his side, and Richard had Adam Fisher, which made the arrangement very cozy.

As expected, both of the bridegrooms looked rather nervous. Ambrose was dressed in a dark blue coat and tan trousers, while Richard had opted for brown and black. Christian had time to wink at his mother before he arranged the wedding party to his liking and beckoned imperiously down the aisle.

Philip stepped forward with Emily on his arm. She wore a deep rose-colored satin dress that suited her complexion admirably. Helene's lips twitched as she noticed how Emily was trying to make Philip speed up so that she could get to her bridegroom in the fastest possible time.

Just behind them came Jack Lennox and his sister, Violet. It was the first time Helene had ever seen the younger Lennox twin dressed as a female. She wasn't surprised to see that Violet was taller than most women and very slender. Her expression was a little more apprehensive than Emily's, but Helene understood that all too well. Violet's life hadn't been easy, and she was probably afraid of her good fortune. But Richard would soothe those fears. He was very much like Philip at his core.

As the vicar read the opening lines to the marriage service, Helene let out a contented breath, said a quiet prayer, and prepared to sob quietly into her handkerchief.